ADELA RIMBON
1228 SHERWOOD MILLS BLVD
MISSISSAUGA ON
L5V 1S7

P9-CRG-999

THE DUCHESS

Books by Jude Deveraux

The Velvet Promise
Highland Velvet
Velvet Song
Velvet Angel
Sweetbriar
Counterfeit Lady
Lost Lady
River Lady
Twin of Ice
Twin of Fire
The Temptress
The Raider
The Princess
The Awakening
The Maiden
The Taming
The Conquest
A Knight in Shining Armor
Wishes
Mountain Laurel
The Duchess

Published by POCKET BOOKS

JUDE DEVERAUX

THE DUCHESS

POCKET BOOKS
New York London Toronto Sydney Tokyo Singapore

This book is a work of fiction. Names, characters, places and incidents are either products of the author's imagination or are used fictitiously. Any resemblance to actual events or locales or persons, living or dead, is entirely coincidental.

POCKET BOOKS, a division of Simon & Schuster Inc.
1230 Avenue of the Americas, New York, N.Y. 10020

ISBN: 0-671-68971-1

First Pocket Books hardcover printing October 1991

10 9 8 7 6 5 4 3 2 1

Printed in the U.S.A.

Chapter One

London

1883

Miss Claire Willoughby fell in love with Harry, the Eleventh Duke of MacArran, the first time she saw him—as did every other woman in the drawing room. But it wasn't just the incredible beauty of the man that made Claire love him. It wasn't his shoulders, which were the width of a garden-hoe handle, or his thick blond hair and brilliant blue eyes. Nor was it his legs, well muscled from years of riding unruly horses, and exposed to their best advantage beneath the brilliant green kilt. No, it wasn't what she saw that made her sway on her feet: it was what she heard.

At the sight of the kilt, with the silver-topped sporran hanging from his waist, the ivory-handled dirk in his heavy sock, the tartan thrown over one shoulder and pinned with the laird's badge, she heard a lone man playing the bagpipes. She heard the wind across the fields of heather and the drone of the pipes. She heard the guns of Culloden and the cries of the widows as they grieved for their fallen men. She heard the shouts of joy at victory; the silence of misery at defeat. She heard the sound of hope at the rise of Bonnie Prince Charlie and heard the despair when he was defeated. She heard the treachery of the Campbells, and she heard the long, long wail of pain of the Scots in their centuries-old battle against the English.

All the sounds echoed in her head as she watched Harry, this man descended from generations of MacArran lairds, walk across the room. The other women saw only an incredibly handsome, dashing young man, but Claire looked beyond that and saw what she heard.

She could imagine this blond giant sitting at the head of a heavy oak table, a silver goblet in his hand, flickering firelight reflected on his face as he called on his men to follow him. Here was a leader of men.

What Harry saw was a short, bosomy young American woman who was pretty, true, but what made her almost beautiful was the expression on her face. She had a look of eagerness, a look of interest in all things and everyone. When she looked at Harry he felt that he was the only one on earth worth listening to. There was curiosity and intelligence in her big brown eyes. Her small, trim body moved quickly, and she walked with a purposefulness that most women didn't possess.

Harry quickly came to like the fact that Claire was a girl of action. She couldn't sit still even for a moment and always wanted to go places and see things. Claire suggested outings and ordered the lunch and all Harry and his friends had to do was show up. She made him laugh and she entertained him. Sometimes she talked too much about Scotland's history, but he found it highly amusing that recounting some battle that had taken place over a hundred years ago could bring tears to her eyes. There seemed to be a hundred dead men whom she considered heroic figures, who she said had led lives of great bravery and importance. When she talked of these men, her eyes turned dreamy and unfocused—so Harry spent that time contemplating her lovely bosom.

It was when she mentioned that Harry's dead brother was one of her heroes that he sucked a cherry pit down his windpipe and nearly choked to death. Miss Claire Willoughby, never at a loss for action, pushed him over a chair so his belly slammed into the back of it, then she hit him between the shoulder blades so hard the pit flew across the drawing room to land with a splash in the punch bowl.

It was that action that made Harry know Claire was right for the job. Bramley House needed a mistress who could think and react quickly. And all of Harry's houses needed a mistress who had Claire's money.

As for Claire, she was stunned at having a Scottish duke pay attention to her. When she was in Harry's presence, she could hardly breathe. She listened to him and looked at him and smiled at him. She said what she hoped he wanted to hear and did what she hoped he wanted her to do. And when she was out of his sight, she thought about him and sighed.

Claire's mother was beside herself with delight when she found out that her daughter was pining for a man who was a duke. "But he's also the laird of Clan MacArran," Claire said, but that meant nothing to her mother.

Arva Willoughby had once been a great beauty and now she didn't seem to notice that her flesh bulged above and below her corset. She wasn't going to allow her daughter, who was much too studious for Arva's taste, to miss an opportunity such as this. Arva did everything in her power to instruct her daughter in the art of winning a man.

For one thing, Arva didn't allow the young people to spend time alone together. Arva said that a man's interest was piqued by absence, not by seeing him every day. She said that a woman saw enough of her husband after they were married, she didn't need to see him *before* the marriage too.

"Mother," Claire said, exasperation in her voice. "The duke has not asked me to marry him and how do I know if I *want* to marry him if I don't get to know him?"

As usual, Arva had an answer for everything. "You may think you know about life because you've spent your few years with your nose in a book, but you know nothing whatever about men and women."

Claire was too happy to allow her mother's pessimism to upset her. She smiled and thought of Harry and his ancestors striding across the Scottish Highlands.

It was only after she'd known Harry for over a month that Claire began to have doubts. "Mother, Harry and I never seem to have anything to talk about. He listens to me and smiles at me, but he never comments on what I say. Sometimes I think His Grace doesn't even know who Bonnie Prince Charlie is."

"My dear child, whatever are you complaining about? That young man is divine looking and he's a duke. What more could you want?"

"Someone to talk—"

"Hah!" Arva snorted. "What does conversation matter in a marriage? After the first year you never so much as say more than pass the butter, and if you have good servants you don't need to say that much. Your father and I haven't spoken to each other in years and we love each other madly."

Claire looked down at her book.

Arva put her hand under her child's chin. "I know what it's like to be young and in love. You have doubts. We all do at your age. But, trust me, there's nothing to worry about. Your young duke is handsome, kind, thoughtful—just look at the flowers he sent to you last week—he is everything a woman could ask for. And if he doesn't talk a great deal, that's to your advantage. And you say he listens to you? My dear, a man who listens to a woman is worth his price in diamonds."

Claire gave her mother a weak smile and Arva took the book from her hands. "You'll ruin your eyes reading so much." She looked at the cover. "And who is Captain Baker?" she asked, naming the author of the book.

"An explorer. The greatest explorer the world has ever known. It's rumored that he's a relative of the duke's."

Arva looked at the light in her daughter's eyes and frowned. "Dear, I know what it's like to dream. I, too, had dreams, but I've learned some things in my life. A woman's entire future depends on her husband. These men you dream about, these . . ." She looked about Claire's bedroom, full of books that were packed and unpacked in trunks wherever the Willoughbys went. "These inventors and artists and writers and this one, this explorer, they aren't men you can live with. There are men you live with and men you—Well, never mind, you'll find out about that part of life after you are married. I won't have to tell you a thing and I daresay young Harry is worldly enough to be understanding."

Claire wasn't sure what her mother was talking about, but she knew she didn't like it. "I want to love my husband."

"Of course you do. And you love Harry, don't you? How could you not?"

Claire thought of Harry, of the way he looked in his kilt, of the way he looked at her with his blue eyes.

Arva smiled at her daughter. "And there are other considerations. Think, Claire, what it will be like to be a duchess. Your every whim taken care of before you know you want it. You'll be able to meet all these wayward creatures you read about. How could they turn down an invitation from a duchess? You will have freedom, Claire, freedom to do whatever you want whenever you want to do it." The smile left her face. "And there is the little matter of your grandfather's will. Your father and I approve of young Harry and if you marry him, you will receive your inheritance. If you do not . . ." She smiled again.

"I'm not threatening you, dear, you do what you must, but there is your little sister to consider."

With that Arva swept from her daughter's room, leaving Claire alone. Sometimes her mother seemed like a silly, frivolous woman, a woman of little education and not much brain power. But sometimes her mother almost frightened Claire.

Claire put Captain Baker's book aside and smoothed her dress. Whatever was she concerned about? Harry, duke of MacArran, was a divine man and, yes, she did love him. As her mother said, how could she not love a man like Harry? There wasn't a thing wrong with him. If a woman were to create the perfect man, she would invent Harry.

Claire laughed aloud. She was being silly. She was in love with Harry and she was probably going to be a duchess. She was the happiest, luckiest young woman in the world.

The next Sunday afternoon Harry took Claire out alone on a lake, rowed her to a pretty little island in the middle, and helped her from the little boat. Claire sat upright on a tartan robe that Harry had brought for her, her hands folded on her lap, while he sprawled in the grass beside her. He wore an old-fashioned linen shirt with huge gathered sleeves. The linen looked as if it had been washed a thousand times and was a soft yellow with age. It was laced at the neck with a drawstring and Harry had left it open so that part of his smooth skin was exposed. He wore his green kilt, not the drawing room kilt, but one that was faded with age and use. He made no concessions in his movements to the fact that what he was wearing was actually a skirt; he sat with his legs apart, mounted horses with his usual quick, strong gestures (it was rumored that one young lady had fainted the first time she saw the kilt-clad young duke mount his horse). Now he sprawled on the grass, his kilt spread about him, a four-inch-wide belt about his waist, and looked at Claire.

"I've grown rather fond of you, you know."

Claire's heart was in her throat, pounding. She didn't know if it was the man himself, or what he represented to her, or, as her brat of a sister said, if it was the sheer beauty of him, but Harry did odd things to her insides. "I . . . like you too," she said.

"I was wondering if you'd like to marry me."

Claire turned to him, her eyes opened in shock. She had been expecting this, hoping for this moment, but it was still a shock. There was nothing she could think of to say.

"I know it's asking a great deal," Harry continued. "I have a few monstrous pieces of property, including a hideous old house called Bramley. It's falling apart, and there are a few other problems in my life as well, but I do rather like you."

Claire began to breathe again, and she tried to swallow the lump in her throat. She wanted to recover herself before she answered. There were times, when she was away from Harry, that she had doubts about their suitability for each other, but not when she was with him. When she was with him, she could only see him and hear the bagpipes in her head.

She hesitated, not wanting to appear too eager to become his wife. Of course, what she was thinking, as she looked at his strong legs, was that she would climb a snow-covered mountain barefoot if she could marry this heavenly man and become a Scottish duchess. "Is your house very old?" she asked, trying not to allow her voice to squeak.

Harry leaned his head back, catching the warmth of the sun on his face. His lashes were quite long and thick. "I don't remember. Bramley was built in twelve hundred, thirteen hundred, something like that."

"It's a castle?"

"It was at one time. Part of it's old and falling down, but some ancestor of mine built around it."

It took her a moment to understand what he meant. "Someone put a facade on it? You mean there's a castle hidden inside your house?"

"Mmmmm," was all he said.

Claire's imagination ran away with her. She imagined one family having lived in the same house for centuries; she imagined all the history that must be in a house like that. "Is Bramley very large?"

He put his head down and grinned at her, making Claire's heart skip a beat. "I haven't seen all of it."

A house so large its owner hadn't seen all of it. It was a difficult concept for her to imagine. "Yes," she whispered. "Yes, I will marry you."

With that Claire could no longer contain herself. She jumped up and began to twirl about, her skirt held to one side. He couldn't help laughing, as she was rather like a puppy in her exuberance. He did so like American girls; they said what they thought and acted on their impulses. "I shall make you the best duchess in the whole world," she said. "You'll see. Oh, heavens, but I think being a duchess will be so very interesting."

He didn't say another word but slowly lifted one of his big hands, put it behind her head, and drew her face down to his for a kiss. Claire had never kissed a man before and she was anxious that she should please him. She tried to follow his lead and do what he wanted her to, but when he pulled her down to him, then pushed her body on top of his, she moved her head away. She had to use some strength to get away from him. When she was at last back on the robe, she was out of breath as she blinked at him. He had a wicked look in his eyes.

"I don't think I'll mind marriage much after all," he said, and leaned back on his arms again.

They sat in silence for a while, Claire trying to calm herself. The very oddest thing had happened: when Harry was kissing her, she could no longer hear the pipes.

"You must come and meet my mother," he said. "It's hunting season and there'll be some shooting. You can stay at Bramley with my family and after a while we'll get married."

"Yes," was all Claire could say.

They didn't say any more for a while—Claire had realized some time ago that Harry didn't like to talk much—but sat in companionable silence until he said it was time to go. As he helped her into the boat, he kissed her again, softly and sweetly on the lips, then rowed her to the far shore. Claire smiled at him and thought of the future that awaited her.

What followed were weeks of preparation. Claire's mother was swooning with happiness over her daughter's announcement and the impending visit to stay at Bramley and meet the duchess. Claire wanted to spend every minute of every day with Harry, but Arva had other plans for her daughter. "After you're married you'll spend more than enough time with him. Believe me, you'll see more than you want to see of a man after he's your husband," her mother repeated yet again.

Claire wasn't about to allow her mother's cynicism to upset her. She saw Harry whenever she could, never alone, but always with other people. They went with four of Harry's friends to choose her engagement ring, a fat blue diamond surrounded by emeralds, and she knew she was going to miss him dreadfully when she went with her parents and sister across the Channel to be fitted for a divine wardrobe by Mr. Worth.

Claire returned from her first fitting at Worth's Paris salon and looked about the suite of rooms of the hotel. It wasn't the Ritz, but her mother said it was where all the really fashionable people stayed. Yet the carpet was frayed, the seat on one of the chairs was torn, and there were spiderwebs hanging from the ceiling. Claire knew it was now necessary to stay in places like this, and it was just as necessary to her mother to believe her little lie that this was actually the most fashionable hotel.

"I'm off, dear," her father, George, said to his plump wife.

Claire knew where her father was going, for she'd seen him sneak a thousand franc note from the little box her mother oversaw. Her father was going to the races—where he'd lose the money, as he always did. Frowning, Claire pulled off her gloves and tossed them on the top of a dusty table.

Her mother instantly picked them up. "You can't have such disregard for fine things. There won't be more of these until after you're married."

"If he marries her," said Claire's fourteen-year-old sister, Sarah Ann, better known as Brat, while she went through Claire's jewelry box again.

Tired and irritable from a day of standing still while she was pinned and repinned, Claire snapped the jewel case shut.

Brat just laughed. "I shall marry a man who adores me. He will do whatever I tell him to do. And he will be very, very rich. I'm not going to marry a man who's poor even if he does have nice legs."

"You'll marry who I tell you to marry," Arva said as she grabbed her younger daughter's ear and pulled her from the room. Claire shrugged when she saw them, for she knew her mother would never actually punish her adored younger daughter no matter what she did. Within minutes the clever child would have her mother feeding her chocolates and promising her some forbidden outing.

Claire walked to the window and looked at the trees in the little park outside the hotel. The leaves were just beginning to turn in the fall air, and she thought of her home in New York. Both Paris and London seemed so different from New York, so much slower. She thought of all her nineteen years in New York and her summers in the coolness of Maine. She had taken her easy life for granted up until now, had thought it would never change. She was used to kissing her father good-bye as he went out the door to go away on his yacht, or off to some week-long hunting trip, or off for months to the wilds of the West after grizzly bear and mountain lions.

She'd grown used to the sound of her mother giving orders to their many, many servants as Arva decorated their big Fifth Avenue house for yet another party. Claire used to stop and admire the thousands of orchids hanging from the walls and mantles and the ceilings as she left on her way to the library or the museum.

For the most part, her parents had ignored their two daughters, thinking they were well cared for in the hands of their governesses. Both Claire and Brat had found it easy to bribe their overseers; for the most part, they'd led their own lives. Brat liked society, just as her mother did, and often wandered down to her mother's parties, where everyone made a great fuss over her prettiness.

But Claire hadn't much taste for society. What she liked were libraries and museums and talking to people who were knowledgeable in their chosen fields. Her mother hated it when Claire brought home for tea ancient professors of obscure branches of history. Arva always made derogatory remarks about how much the skinny little men could eat. "I like intelligence," Claire had said.

But both Arva and George had been too busy to pay much attention to their daughters until their accountant had that horrid talk with them. After that, it seemed to Claire, their lives had changed overnight.

Now the house on Fifth Avenue was gone, the house in Maine was gone, her father's yacht had been sold. All of it, their possessions and their whole way of life, had disappeared.

Now it was up to Claire to do something about it. When she married Harry and became the duchess, everything would be all right again. Her parents would have what they most wanted and her little sister would have a chance to get a rich man who adored her.

As Claire looked out the window, she smiled. She had been

dreading it all, but Harry had made it easy. The old saying that it was as easy to fall in love with a rich man as a poor one was true. It had certainly been easy to fall in love with a duke.

On their third day in Paris, books that Claire had ordered while in London arrived. She began to read them between fittings, and between her mother's constant warnings and questions. ("Will people have to curtsey to you when you're a duchess? Will they have to curtsey to *me* since I'm the mother of a duchess? How will people address me? Is it as Your Honorable?") Claire soon gave up trying to explain the difference between aristocracy and royalty, and she hated breaking the news to her mother that she, as the mother of a duchess, would have no title at all.

The books were about the history of Harry's family, the Montgomerys. She found out how old it was and that this Scottish branch of the family, which was called Clan MacArran, had at least once had a woman as its chief. In the early fifteenth century one of the Montgomery men had married into the MacArrans and had taken the name MacArran, and then more Montgomerys had married more MacArrans until the Montgomerys were almost a separate clan. In 1671 Charles II had given the family a dukedom. There was a great deal of speculation as to why he'd done this. Some said it was for having rendered years of faithful service, but there was also a rumor that the MacArran laird had volunteered to marry a very ugly and very shrewish woman who was rumored to be a half sister of the king.

For whatever reason the clan was awarded a dukedom, at the time there was a great deal of discussion as to what name the family should be called. Should the family name be MacArran and the dukedom called Montgomery or the other way around? There was a legend that a coin was flipped. So, Harry was the duke of MacArran, yet his name was Henry James Charles Albert Montgomery.

During those days in Paris, Claire sometimes thought she was going to break under the fatigue of fittings and preparations and being part of her mother's busy social life, but she kept remembering that Bramley was waiting for her at the end of it.

At night, tired as she was, she often couldn't sleep, so by lamplight she read the books on Harry's family and novels by Sir Walter Scott, read the Scottish author's accounts of the beauty of the Highlands and the courage of the men who lived there. Claire went to sleep dreaming of heather and armies of men who looked just like Harry.

When Claire and her family returned from Paris, Harry was waiting for her. He escorted her to his carriage with the ducal crest on the door. Autocratically, he told her parents and sister that he and Claire were traveling to London alone. Claire could have cried with joy at the prospect of a few minutes away from her mother's admonitions. Once inside the carriage, she saw that Harry had filled it with pink roses. She took the fluted glass of champagne he handed her and smiled at him—and suddenly she wished he'd kiss her. She wished he'd take her in his arms and hold her. She'd like to have him force all doubts from her mind.

But Harry didn't touch her.

"I've missed you," he said, smiling. "Did you think about me?"

"All the time," she answered, looking at the way his broad shoulders practically filled one side of the coach.

"And what were you doing while you were away from me?"

"Buying dresses and reading. What did you do?"

Harry smiled at her over the glass of wine. He wasn't about to tell her what he had done, for it involved mistresses and a few actresses, and some horses that he'd lost too much money on. But he was going to marry a very rich heiress and it didn't matter how much money he lost.

"I thought about you," he said and the way he said it made Claire's heart flutter a bit.

To control herself, she looked out the window. "My mother won't like that I am alone with you."

"I think your mother would allow anything if it resulted in her daughter marrying a duke."

Claire gave him a look of surprise. "I'm marrying you because I love you, not because I want to marry a duke."

"Is that so?" he said, smiling, and when he smiled like that Claire forgot everything in the world except him. "And what about all this history you keep talking about? What about that place? That Cull something or other?"

"Culloden? But that was—"

"Yes, yes, a very great battle." He leaned forward and took her hand in his, playing with her fingers. "When I think of marriage, I think of other things besides war. You're not going to lecture me on history after we're married, are you?"

His fingers were on her forearm. Only lace separated their skin.

"I'm looking forward to getting you into bed," he said very softly.

Claire held her breath as he leaned toward her. She knew she should not allow him such liberties, but, on the other hand, they were going to be married in a short time. Thanks to several books she'd read—books she wasn't supposed to read—she had a general idea of what happened after the marriage ceremony.

As his lips covered hers, Claire didn't do any more thinking. Had it not been for the abrupt halt of the carriage she wasn't sure what would have happened, but as she stepped from the carriage, she was frowning. She wished she loved Harry as much when he was touching her as she did when she was looking at him or thinking about him.

For the next two weeks her mother kept her so busy she had no time alone with Harry or with her thoughts.

At the end of those two weeks, he came to her family's rented town house to tell her he was leaving London to return to his home in Scotland. There were a thousand things Claire wanted to ask Harry about his mother, about the rest of his family, about what was expected of her as his fiancée, but she didn't have a chance to say a word, for Arva chattered throughout the brief meeting. When Harry was ready to leave, he kissed Claire's hand while Arva said good-bye, and then he was gone. Claire blinked back tears as she went back to her room. It would be one whole week before she saw him again, and she was anxious for her life to begin.

Chapter Two

Claire mounted the horse expertly, hooking her right leg over the pommel of the sidesaddle and taking the reins from the groom. She and her family had arrived at Bramley late the previous night after an exhausting journey from London. The three days the trip should have taken had actually turned frustratingly into four. The roads were rutted and frequently they'd had to pause to allow sheep to cross the road. Her mother had complained unceasingly, while her father and little sister had played one card game after another until Claire had wanted to scream. None of them seemed to realize the importance of the fact that they were visiting Scotland for the first time.

George Willoughby had looked up from his cards only long enough to comment on the fact that the country looked a bit barren to him.

"How can you say that?" Claire had gasped. "The heather is in bloom. Don't you know what happened on this very spot in 1735? In that year—"

She broke off as her father began to yawn.

Sarah Ann, her brat of a little sister, gave Claire a look and said, "I'll bet Harry knows all about Bonnie Prince Charlie and everything else that happened in Scotland. Or were you too busy kissing him to do much talking?"

Claire, tired and nervous, made a lunge for her sister, but the child managed to escape her even in the close confines of the hired coach.

"I do wish you two would stop arguing," Arva said. "You're giving me a headache. And, Sarah, I don't think you should call Harry Harry. You're to call him 'my lord.'"

"Your Grace," Claire said in exasperation.

"Beat you again," Sarah said to her father. "Mother, my dear older sister wants you to know that Harry is to be called Your Grace. She wants you to know that she's read many books on the subject and knows all there is to know about everything. You, on the other hand, haven't read anything so you couldn't possibly know about Scotland or anything else." Brat gave her mother a smile of great innocence and sweetness.

"I said no such thing," Claire said. "I merely—"

But Arva wouldn't listen to her oldest child. "Claire, I know you think I'm frivolous. You've never missed an opportunity to let me know what you think of my trying to obtain a position in society, but, Claire, I am your mother and I do believe you owe me some respect. We can't all know what you do. We can't all . . ."

Claire listened to her mother's familiar droning as she turned to glare at Brat. For the millionth time Claire wondered if her sister had been born the way she was or if she had been dropped on her head moments after her birth. Whatever the cause, Sarah Ann got great pleasure from causing her sister misery.

"It's your turn to deal, Brat," George said fondly to his youngest daughter. Whereas Arva seemed to have no idea what her younger daughter was like and could not understand why her husband and Claire called the child Brat, George knew exactly what the child was doing. Sometimes it infuriated Claire that not only did her father know, but he seemed to love, every rotten, underhanded, manipulative thing his daughter did. He found the child as amusing as Claire found her infuriating.

By the time the Willoughby family reached Bramley, it was nearing midnight. There was only a quarter moon and they could see no details of the house that was to become one of Claire's homes, but they could see the size of it. "Vast" did not begin to cover it. The house seemed to stretch for acres across the land. It was a tall house, at least four stories, but the height of it was dwarfed by its width. Just to walk from one end of it to the other would have been a good hike.

Claire looked at her mother, who was practically hanging out of the window of the carriage. The size of the place had done what, as far as

Claire knew, nothing else on earth had been able to do: Arva Willoughby was speechless.

They stopped at the approximate center of the house and the coachman pounded on the door; it seemed an eternity before someone came to open it. The time lapse gave Arva time to recover her voice and state her opinions on the fact that no one was waiting to greet them.

"You'd have thought they would have left someone on duty to meet us," Arva said. "After all, my daughter is going to be a duchess. Do they think we are nobodies seeking shelter? Maybe Harry's mother is mad because she will no longer be a duchess when my daughter becomes the duchess. Maybe she—"

Claire, who thought she couldn't bear much more, turned on her mother. "She will continue to be the duchess," she said through clenched teeth. "She will be the *dowager* duchess, but a duchess all the same."

Arva sniffed. "I'm sure I don't know all that you know, dear. I'm afraid I haven't had your advantages. But then I have given you those advantages, haven't I?"

"Mother, I—" Claire began but stopped when at last the big oak door was opened by a kind-looking, sleepy-eyed older man wearing a dressing gown.

Within minutes, Arva had pushed her way into the entry hall and was ordering the dispersal of their entourage of goods and people. There were two carriages full of trunks and cases, and another carriage that held Arva's maid, George's valet, and Brat's governess, who was a timid little woman thoroughly terrified of her young charge. "And my eldest daughter, my daughter who will be the duchess, needs a maid. Her maid"—there was a sneer in Arva's voice that told what she thought of the ungrateful woman—"ran away and married an Englishman."

The man, who Claire guessed was the butler, stood listening to all Arva's demands without so much as a flicker of interest. "Ah, now, there's no accounting for taste," he said softly in his Scottish accent. Whether Claire was the only one who heard him or not, she was certainly the only one who laughed, and the man turned and gave her a bit of a smile.

In spite of all of Arva's demands and the energy she put behind them, it was an hour before they were shown to their rooms. Claire undressed herself and fell into the huge four-poster bed and was asleep before she could pull the cover up.

But she didn't sleep long. She awoke curled into a ball: she was freezing. There was little cover on the bed and no fire in the fireplace. Her teeth chattering, she made her way out of the bed and began to look for the bathroom. There was none. Nor could she find a switch for the lights.

After staggering about the dark room for a while, she managed to find matches and candles and lit one, holding it above her head to try to see the room. But all she could see was an enormous bed and heavy oak furniture looming against the walls. There was a painting as large as a wardrobe on one wall, and she looked up to see a woman staring down at her. The woman in the painting wore a smile that made Claire think she understood.

Claire opened the door to a vast old wardrobe and smiled to see it full of her clothes. While she had slept, someone must have unpacked for her. On second glance she saw that the clothes in the wardrobe weren't hers. She pulled out a garment. From the look of the dress it was at least fifty years old.

A shudder of cold shook her shoulders. This was no time for sight-seeing; if she didn't get on some clothes other than her cotton nightgown, she was going to perish from the cold.

She opened both doors of the wardrobe and dove into it in a serious search for something warm to wear. There were men's clothes and children's, and clothes for women who must have weighed two hundred and fifty pounds. Way in the back she found a riding habit. A good, long, hard ride might warm her, she thought. The habit was a bit strange, with big sleeves and a high, belted waist, and Claire could see it was going to be too short for her, but it was wool and it came fairly close to fitting her.

She found drawers full of yellow, musty-smelling underwear, and managed to find enough to keep her skin from touching the heavy wool of the habit. There were also several pairs of knit stockings.

"Shoes," she muttered, beginning to like this adventure. She had always loved playing dress-up with her mother's clothes when she was a child, and now she was able to again.

She found shoes, just as she knew she would, and managed to

squeeze her feet into a pair of high button, pointed toe, black leather shoes that were beginning to crack with age.

When she was at last dressed, she looked at herself in an ancient pier glass and giggled at the result. In the dark room, with its high ceilings and walls that looked to be covered in red brocade, she looked like something from out of the past. As she started out the door, she saw another cabinet, opened it, and found gloves and a few hats. She pinned a jaunty little hat that looked like a miniature of a man's top hat at a rakish angle on her head, took a pair of sturdy leather gloves that were much too big for her, and left the room.

She had always had an excellent sense of direction, and she remembered the way down three corridors, and two short flights of stairs to the front door. The door was not locked, and from the rust she could see on the lock, it looked as though it hadn't been locked in a hundred years or more.

Assuming the stables were at the back of the house, she started walking. Ten minutes later she was still walking as she tried to find the end of the house. Even with the gloves, she was rubbing her hands together for warmth, and she was concerned about frostbite of her frozen toes. When at last she came to the edge of the house, she took a left and kept walking. Altogether it took nearly thirty minutes to reach the stables. "I should have looked for a bathroom," she muttered as she reached the stables.

It was barely growing light now and she could see a lantern lit inside the stables; she could hear voices.

A young man coming out of the stables nearly ran into her before he saw her, and when he did see her, he looked as though he'd seen a ghost. With her old-fashioned clothes, Claire imagined that she did look a bit like a ghost.

"Hello," she said to the young man. "May I have a horse? I'd like to go riding."

The man didn't speak but nodded his head and started back toward the stables. A moment later an older man came out and asked her questions about whether she wanted a man's saddle or a sidesaddle and if she could ride or not.

"I can ride whatever you have," Claire said with confidence.

She stood on the cobblestones of the stableyard and waited while the horse was being saddled. One by one all the men who worked in the stables came out to stare at her with undampened curiosity, and Claire began to feel as though she were a circus performer come to town. Twice she turned and gave the men weak smiles, then turned away again.

At last the horse was brought to her and the older man gave her a leg up. He watched her critically until he saw her firmly seated, then stepped back.

"There's a path to the east," he said, and Claire nodded her thanks to him. As she started off she turned back and waved to all the men standing and watching her. They smiled back and some of them waved in return.

Once off the cobblestones, she urged the horse into a faster pace. She didn't dare break into a gallop, for she didn't know the path and was concerned with sharp turns and tree branches. Once in the trees, she dismounted and made use of the bushes, then she stood on a tree stump to remount.

Gradually the sun rose and she could see ahead of her. She broke through the trees and came to a long, open track, actually a carriage road, and she could see that there were no dangers ahead.

"Come on, boy," she said to the big gelding. "Let's get warm." She applied her heels to the animal and it leaped forward, apparently as glad as she to be moving.

Claire put her head down and urged the animal forward into a run that could have won a race. She was feeling wonderful, more free than she'd felt since crossing the ocean, when everything happened at once. From out of the trees to her right, just as she was cresting the little hill, stepped a man. He was walking very quickly and for some reason didn't seem to have heard a horse pounding across the hard-packed earth.

Horse, man and, most of all, woman were startled.

The horse reared and Claire went flying over the top of its head, landing hard on her left arm. The horse went left, toward what looked to be a marshy pond. The man, after putting his arm up to protect himself from flying hooves, started toward the woman.

"Not me," Claire managed to gasp out as she tried to sit up. "Catch the horse before it falls in that swamp."

The man just stood there for a moment, as though he didn't understand the language she spoke.

"Go on," Claire said, waving him toward the horse. She was

cradling her left arm as she tried to sit upright. Rubbing her arm, she watched the man drop the stick he was carrying and begin to run after the horse.

Run in a fashion, she thought as she watched him. The man limped, barely able to move his right leg, and there was a way he held his shoulders that made her think every step he took was painful. She felt a wave of guilt for having sent an old, crippled man after her horse, but then pain shot through her arm and she hugged it to her chest.

She watched as the man caught the reins of the horse and managed to calm it. Painfully, Claire got up, her arm held close to her body, to await the arrival of the man with her horse. She walked toward the field to meet him.

When she got close enough to be able to see him she realized with a start that he was ill. He was looking at the horse and she couldn't see his eyes, but only great illness could cause a person to look as he did: his skin was an unpleasant-looking greenish yellow.

"I am so sorry," she began. "Had I known you were—" She broke off. What could she say? Had she known he was at death's door she would not have ordered him to chase her horse?

The man opened his mouth to speak, but then his face lost its odd color and turned paper white. His eyes rolled back into his head and his knees began to bend.

With horror, Claire realized the man was about to faint. "Sir!" she gasped, but he just kept sinking toward the ground.

She quickly ran forward, putting her right arm out to catch him, but he fell forward onto her. She staggered backward under the weight of him, her left arm, which hurt so much, held out to the side. She spread her feet wide apart, trying to brace herself against his weight. She looked about for help, but all she saw was the horse calmly munching grass.

"Now what do I do?" she asked herself aloud. The man was a dead weight against her, his arms hanging down to the sides of her, his face pressed into her shoulder.

With great difficulty, and very slowly, she managed to lower herself to the ground, going first on one knee, then on the other. She tried to talk to the man, even tried smacking him on one cheek, but when she felt how thin his cheek was, just skin over bone, she didn't tap him again.

For all that there didn't seem to be much meat on him, he was a large man, broad shouldered and tall, so she couldn't lower him with her good arm. At last she managed to extend one leg and then the other. She was now sitting with him lying prone on her, his head on her breast, his body between her legs. She offered a silent prayer that no one would come along and see her like this, then used all of her one-armed strength to roll him off of her and onto his back.

When at last he was lying beside her, Claire found she was panting from the exertion. "Sir," she called to him a few times, but he didn't move. She put her hand to his neck to feel his pulse, praying that she hadn't killed him. He was alive and in fact he seemed to have gone from a faint to being soundly asleep.

Claire, sitting beside him, gave a sigh. Now what did she do? She didn't dare go off and leave him there alone. For all she knew wolves still roamed the Scottish woodlands. As she glanced at the man she saw he was beginning to shiver.

With another sigh, she removed her ancient wool jacket, being careful not to hurt her arm. After she put the jacket over him, she gently smoothed his sweat-dampened hair from off his forehead.

She looked at him then and saw that he was an older man, probably in his late fifties or early sixties, and from his color, he didn't look to have much longer to live. There were two old scars on his cheeks, one on each side, long, dreadful-looking scars, and she wondered what horrid thing had happened to him to cause such scars. She traced the scars with her fingertips.

Despite his age, his hair was thick and dark and a heavy dark moustache almost covered his upper lip. She noticed his lips were still full.

"You must have been quite handsome in your day," she whispered to him, again smoothing his hair from his face. She looked down at the rest of him. He was quite tall, probably taller than Harry, but not built as Harry was. This man didn't have Harry's thick muscle; he wasn't compact as Harry was, but more drawn out, tapering down to slim hips from wide shoulders.

As Claire looked down the length of him, she had to smile, for the man was dressed as oddly as she was. He wore an old shirt, a shirt that was much, much too thin for this cold morning, and she could see that he wore nothing beneath it, for the dreadful color of his skin showed through the thin fabric. His legs were encased in dirty, greasy, worn buckskin trousers that were torn in a few places. They were the type of buckskin trousers a Regency gentleman might have worn to his club. Oddly enough he had on a pair of the most beautiful boots Claire had ever seen. She always recognized quality in clothing when she saw it, and these boots were indeed the best.

Perhaps he was a gentleman fallen on hard times, she thought. He shivered again, but then so did she. She looked up and saw that the sky was covered with gray clouds. It was then she realized that a mist of rain was falling. It wasn't real rain, not rain as she knew it in America, rain that announced itself with thunder and lightning, but a soft, cold rain that was more like a very wet fog. She rubbed the upper part of her injured left arm to try to warm herself, but it was no use. All she could do now was wait for the man to wake up and hope they didn't both die of pneumonia. Feeling rather protective of him, wanting to make sure he was going to be all right, she moved around him, leaned back against a tree and watched the misty rain coming down. Perhaps if she thought about crackling fires and . . . and the house her family sometimes rented in Florida, she would get warm.

Trevelyan opened his eyes slowly and blinked away the mist that covered his lashes. He lay still for a moment while he remembered the events that had led up to his lying on the cold, wet ground. He remembered coming out of the woods, nearly colliding with a rearing horse, then seeing a girl flying through the air. He had started toward her, but then, in an autocratic way, and in a flat accent that could only be American, she had issued an order to him as though he were one of the stable boys.

It had been easy to catch the horse, as the creature associated people with food and shelter, but, even so, the activity had been too much for him. Just as he reached the girl and opened his mouth to tell her what he thought of her, he felt his knees give way under him and there was nothing but blackness before his eyes.

Now he woke to find himself on the ground, and on his chest was a garment that looked as though it belonged to a child. The sound of a sneeze to his left made him turn his head.

Leaning against a tree, shivering from the cold and looking thoroughly wretched, was the girl. As he lay there, blinking against the eternal Scottish rain, watching her sneeze three times in succession, he studied her face. He was sure he'd never seen such wide-eyed innocence in a human being before. She's barely more than a child, he thought. She rubbed her nose with her hand, then turned to look at him.

She was pretty, but he'd seen prettier women—if you could call her a woman. He would have guessed her age to be about fourteen had it not been for a rather splendidly developed bosom that the combination of the rain and the thin blouse was showing off to its advantage.

"You're awake," she said, and looked at his intense, dark eyes. And when Claire looked into those eyes, she thought she might have to revise her first impression that he was a harmless old man. She had never seen eyes like his: dark, compelling, yet frightening at the same time. His eyes showed intelligence, complexity, and knowledge. He was looking at her so intently, with such unblinking fervor, she felt as though he were reading her mind. She frowned and looked away.

As for Trevelyan, he thought she had the most guileless, innocent eyes he had ever seen.

He started to raise himself on his elbows. At his movement, she was instantly at his side, leaning over to assist him. At one point that fine bosom of hers was pressed against his cheek. When she had helped him to her satisfaction she leaned back, and he smiled at her.

Again, Claire frowned at him. There was something about the way he looked at her that she didn't like. He had looked at her . . . her mid-chest with a Machiavellian smile that made her want to smack him. He is capable of all manner of bad deeds, she thought. He is as completely unlike Harry as one human can be from another. This man's dark, dangerous eyes weren't like Harry's innocent blue ones.

She straightened her shoulders. She was not going to let the man frighten her.

"Whatever is a man like you doing out in weather like this?" she asked, sounding like a schoolteacher scolding one of her pupils. "You should be home in bed. Don't you have people to take care of you? A wife? Daughters?"

He blinked away the water accumulating on his face. "I was taking a walk," he said, frowning. "And what do you mean, a man like me?"

"I didn't mean to offend you, it's just that it's cold and wet and from the look of you, you're none too healthy. Will you be all right while I fetch help?"

"Help for what?"

"Why, for you, of course. Perhaps the men can bring a stretcher and they can carry—"

At that Trevelyan got off the ground as quickly as possible—and he would have died before he let her see that he was dizzy from the quick motion. "I can assure you, miss, that I am capable of walking on my own and I don't need a stretcher." To Trevelyan's absolute disgust, in spite of his firmest self-control, he felt himself sway on his feet, but then, to his delight, the girl slipped her right arm about his waist and moved his arm about her shoulders.

"I can see that you need no help at all," she said sarcastically. She felt much better when she wasn't looking at his face. At least she had succeeded in wiping that smug look off his face, that look that seemed to insinuate that he knew every thought she had before she had it.

He leaned against her. She barely came to his shoulder, but he thought her to be the perfect height. Of course had she been six feet tall or four and a half feet he realized he probably would have still found her to be perfect. "Perhaps I do need a bit of help," he said, trying both to sound weak and to keep his amusement out of his voice.

"Let me get my horse so you can ride back to your home."

"And what will you do if I ride?"

"Walk," she said, then, under her breath, added, "Maybe it will get me warm."

Trevelyan smiled down at the top of her head. "Horses terrify me. Vertigo, you know. Perhaps you could walk with me. Just for a while, until I'm feeling a bit stronger."

Claire tried to hide her grimace. She had no desire to spend her morning playing nursemaid to this man. She knew she should have sympathy for him, after all, he was obviously ill and he had fainted, but she had no sympathy for him. She found him unsettling, annoying. He made her feel angry and she didn't know why. Maybe it wasn't the man. Maybe it was that she was wet and cold and hungry. By now, surely, the household would be stirring and there would be food, nice, hot food, and she could find her own clothes and—

Trevelyan saw her expression. "You do not have to go with me," he said, pulling away and bending to pick up her damp jacket from the ground. "Please allow me to assist you to your horse. I'll be fine on my own."

She looked up at him, but not as far as his eyes. She avoided his eyes. She looked at the scars on his cheeks and at the color of his skin and knew she had to help him. As she slipped her arms into the cold jacket, she was tempted to leave him there, but her conscience wouldn't allow her to leave a man who was as sick as he was. If he had another fainting spell and lay in the rain and caught some terminal infection, it would be her fault.

"No," she said with a sigh. "I'll help you get to shelter."

Again she slipped her right arm about his waist and again he leaned heavily on her, making sure that he limped now and then to show her he did indeed need her help. They started walking down the path, the horse docilely following them.

"Who are you?" Trevelyan asked.

"Claire Willoughby," she snapped, then cursed herself for being so ridiculous, but the man's touching her bothered her. He made her feel strange: angry and restless in a way that she didn't like.

"And what, Claire Willoughby, were you doing out before it is full dawn, riding a horse at a neck-breaking speed and wearing clothes that don't fit you? Have you escaped your governess?"

Claire was too wet, too cold, too hungry, and in much too much pain from her arm to be polite. And, too, the man was making her more uncomfortable by the minute. "I would like to know why a man of your age and obvious ill health is allowed to roam these woods unattended. Have you escaped your nurse?"

Trevelyan blinked a few times at her words. He was used to women finding him physically attractive and he didn't like that this pretty young thing didn't. He decided to try again. "I take it you're staying at Bramley. Why?"

"Could you put a little less weight on me?"

"Yes, of course." He straightened a bit and for a moment didn't lean on her quite so much, but within seconds he was again pressed against her as they slowly walked down the path. Trevelyan was so much enjoying the feel of her that he thought he might lead her the long way about, taking her through the Wild Wood. There was an old gardener's cottage at the far end of the wood, and it was at least five miles away.

"Are you going to answer me?" he asked.

Claire, for all that he seemed to think she was fresh out of the schoolroom, realized he was enjoying leaning on her. Horrid old man, she thought, and wished with all her might that she had left him back there in the rain while he was lying on the ground asleep. Right now her objective in life was to get away from this man. "Perhaps you should tell me who you are. Is your house very far away?"

"Not far." He moved his cheek down to the top of her head. She'd had on a little hat when he first saw her, but it was gone and now there was only her dark, damp hair.

"Do you mind?" she snapped, then winced when pain shot up her arm.

"You're injured," he said in a firm voice that was different from the helpless tone he'd been using.

"No, I'm not. I merely bruised my arm. What I am is hungry and wet and cold, so I'd very much like to get back to the house."

"You'll be even colder once you're inside."

"I thought so," she murmured.

"You thought what?"

"That you would know about the house. You've lived there, haven't you? Do you know the duke?"

He took a moment before answering. "I know the duke rather well."

She smiled at the mere thought of Harry. "We're to be married," she said softly.

Trevelyan was quiet for a moment. "Ah, little Harry. Has he grown up then? The last time I saw him he was just a boy."

"He has grown into a splendid man," she said, then cleared her throat in embarrassment. "I mean he's . . . he's . . ."

"I understand. True love."

The way the man said it, with so much cynicism in his voice, made Claire stiffen. "You don't have to make fun of something you know nothing about."

"But I know everything about true love. I have been in love hundreds of times."

She gritted her teeth, all the while knowing that she had no reason to be so angry at the man. "A person experiences true love only once in a lifetime. If she is lucky. I don't think most people find it at all. If you have been in love hundreds of times, then I don't believe you've ever been in love, not really, truly in love."

"As you are in love with young Harry?" He could not keep the amusement out of his voice, and when he felt her stiffen he almost laughed out loud. "How very young you are."

"And how very old you are," she snapped.

That made Trevelyan stop laughing. Perhaps he was old. Perhaps all that he had seen and done and heard in his life had made him old before his time. "I beg your pardon, Miss Willoughby," he said. "I am Trevelyan."

She didn't feel like forgiving him. He was a cynical old man and she wished she'd not had the misfortune to run into him. "Trevelyan what?"

For some reason that seemed to make him think. "Just Trevelyan, that's all. Nothing else." He knew he'd hurt her feelings so he tried to tease her. "I was born before people were given two names."

She didn't laugh at his joke. "Are you related to the duke's family?"

"Perhaps I'm the second gardener. What do you think?"

"I think you're probably Harry's uncle or maybe his cousin. Whoever you are, you are *not* anyone's servant."

That pleased him more than he was willing to let her know. "And what makes you think I'm not a servant?" He was hoping to hear her say that in spite of the fact that he was recovering from a serious illness, there was a bearing about him that was almost regal.

"Your boots. No working man would have boots of that quality." Under no circumstances was she going to tell him that he was not anyone's idea of a servant. If he looked at a prospective employer with his dark, questioning eyes, he'd never be hired. Or maybe he would, Claire thought, but he wouldn't be hired to do a servant's work.

"Oh," he said, disappointed with her answer.

They walked in silence for a while, neither of them speaking, Claire wanting only to get away from him. She didn't like him so near her. "I've been away for some time. Perhaps you could tell me the news of my . . . relatives." His tongue fairly tripped over the word.

Claire was silent, struggling along the damp path, supporting him and her painful arm.

"Do you know much of the duke's family? Or are you marrying into the unknown?"

"I know rather a lot, actually," she said, implying that Harry had told her. She wasn't going to tell this man that in between being fitted for dresses and dancing with Harry, she had spent a great deal of time researching the history of her future husband's family.

"I believe there have been some recent deaths," he said.

"Harry's father and the eldest son died less than a year ago in a boating accident. When Harry's father and oldest brother died that made Harry's other brother, the second son, the duke. Up until then he had been the earl of . . ." She paused as she thought, then looked up at him. "The earl of Trevelyan."

He glanced down at her widened eyes. "There's no need to look at me like that. Trevelyan is a common enough name in England and I can assure you I'm no earl."

"Mmmmm," she said thoughtfully. "True enough, I guess. Harry's brother would have been younger than you." She paused. "The second son was killed but two months ago."

"Killed? Surely you mean he died."

Again there was that infuriating amusement in his voice, as though he thought her stupendously stupid. "I don't think you should make jokes. Why don't you know of a man who is in your family?"

"The family and I have never been close. Tell me about this son who was killed. I sense something in your voice, something I don't understand."

She was amazed at his perception. She opened her mouth to speak, then closed it. She shouldn't tell him what she knew, but then she so wanted to tell someone. She had tried once to talk to Harry about his brother, but Harry had not wanted to discuss the subject. She could understand that, could understand his grief at losing three family members in close succession. Twice she'd tried to talk to her father, but he hadn't wanted to hear either.

Trevelyan nudged her with his shoulder. "Out with it. Tell me what you've heard. All lies, I'll wager."

"They are *not* lies," she said emphatically. "I have my information from the best of sources and I plan to do something about it."

"Do something about what, and who told you these lies?"

His hand was slowly moving down her shoulder until it was just at the top of her breast. She pushed it away and gave him a hard look but he ignored her, just kept that little smirk on his face. Curse him, she thought. She didn't want to say a word to him; she wanted to get away from him and that's all, but there was something about him that made her want to talk. And besides that, there was her need to talk to someone, somewhere, about what she thought about. Not since she'd left America had she had anyone who could understand what she read. She had met no one in England who was interested in anything besides the latest party.

"The Prince of Wales told me," she said, and smiled when the smirk vanished.

"The Prince of Wales told you what?"

"Have you ever heard of the explorer Captain Frank Baker?" She had his attention now. He stopped walking and stared at her. It was heady to have someone listen to her with such intensity, with such depth of feeling. It made her feel as though she were more than her money and her pretty face and what she wore to a party.

"I've heard of him," Trevelyan said softly. "But what does an innocent creature like you know of someone like him?"

"How you do presume to know about me," she said with more smugness than she thought possible. It felt wonderful to have wiped that smirk off his face. "For your information I have read every word Captain Baker has written about his travels and what he's seen all over the world."

She had more than wiped the smirk off Trevelyan's face. He gaped at her. He was truly and genuinely shocked at her announcement.

"*All* of his writing?"

"All of it," she said, feeling very pleased with herself.

He didn't speak for a while as they started walking again. "Except for the chapters written in Latin," he said at last. "Not the chapters on . . ."

"On the sexual habits of the people in other countries? The chapters written in Latin? I've read those, too. When I was sixteen—"

"A great long time ago," he said sarcastically.

She acted as though he hadn't spoken. "I told my mother I could not consider myself educated unless I had an in-depth knowledge of Latin, so she hired an old man to be my tutor. Thankfully, he believed that all knowledge was good, so he helped me translate Captain Baker's Latin chapters. There are some very unusual words in those chapters."

"Unusual, yes," he said thoughtfully, then recovered himself. "And what does the Prince of Wales have to do with all of this?"

"The prince told me it was believed that Harry's brother, the second one, the one who was killed, might have been Captain Baker. Of course it's not known for sure, because Captain Baker went to great lengths to keep his identity a secret."

"But I heard his desire for secrecy was because he was wanted for criminal acts, that he would have been hanged if his real identity were known."

"I don't believe that," she said fiercely, turning on him, moving so quickly out from under his arm that he almost fell. "I don't believe that for a second! You couldn't have read a word of his work if you could even repeat that dreadful rumor. It was created and spread by men who weren't half the man he was. He was a great man." This Trevelyan quite simply infuriated her. Perhaps her anger was irrational, but it was there just the same. At the moment she was sure that if he dropped dead in front of her, she'd put her foot on his chest, throw back her head, and laugh in triumph.

"Was he, now?"

"You can stop laughing at me," she hissed. "It's ignorant fools like you who make fun of what you know nothing about. Captain Baker was—" She broke off, for she didn't like the way he was smiling at her, as though he knew everything and she could never possibly know anything. "Oh, come on," she said, not bothering to disguise the disgust in her voice. "I'll take you back to wherever you're staying."

Trevelyan put his arm back around her shoulders and they started walking. "What do you mean, you plan to do something about this information?"

"After Harry and I are married, I plan to write Captain Baker's biography." To Claire's disgust, this seemed to amuse the man a great deal.

"Do you, now? And have you told Harry about this?"

"Yes." She had no intention of telling him any more than that simple yes. It was one thing to tell a stranger of her intention to write a biography of a great man, but quite another to tell him of what went on between her and the man she loved.

"I see. You do not plan to speak more of what goes on between you and young Harry. The privacy of lovers and all that, is that it?" He smiled when she refused to answer him. "All right then, tell me of this Captain Baker. What has he done to make you think so highly of him?"

"He is—was—an explorer. No, he was more than that. He was an observer. He went where no literate men have gone before and he looked and he saw and he wrote of what he saw. He was fearless in his travels. He was a man hungry for knowledge of all the peoples of the earth. He was good and kind and loyal to his friends. When he died, the world lost a great man." Her voice changed, betraying her bitterness. "While he was alive, he was ignored by the world. Ignored and unappreciated. I plan to change that. After I'm married to Harry I plan to write a book about Captain Baker that will let the world see what a great man it has lost." She paused and calmed herself. "I believe that most of the captain's private papers are at Bramley."

Trevelyan was quiet for a while. "You're planning to marry the young duke in order to gain access to these papers?"

Claire laughed. "Do I seem so callous? I'm marrying Harry because I love him. I was already considering marriage to Harry when I learned that his brother was—"

"Might be," he corrected her.

"Yes, might have been Captain Baker. To write of him is a plan I have formed since accepting Harry's proposal."

"And when shall you do this?"

"What do you mean?"

He smiled at her. "How do you plan to discharge all of your duties as duchess and still find time to write this book? Surely it will take a great deal of research?"

She laughed. "That it will. The man never stopped writing. I've read a dozen or so volumes of his and Harry says there are boxes full of his journals and letters moldering away in trunks in the house. Besides writing all those books and hundreds of letters to the people who may or may not have been his family, Captain Baker also wrote to his many, many friends all over the world. At one time he was blind and he *still* managed to write. He fastened two parallel wires down the side of a board, affixed the paper to the board, then put another wire across the paper and used it as a guide for his hand. *Nothing* stopped him from writing."

With each word she spoke Trevelyan stiffened. "I thought you revered the man. I thought you said he was a great man."

"He was."

"Yet you complain that he wrote too much."

"I did no such thing."

"You said that he wrote to everyone, thereby making his letters common. Some biographer you will be if you have such disdain for him."

"Disdain? Common? Are you trying to put words in my mouth? I think the man was magnificent, but I'm a realist about him. I know his strengths as well as his weaknesses."

"And how do you know that? Did you ever meet him?"

"No, of course not, but . . ." She searched for the right words to explain herself. "When you read a book that you love, a book that is close to you, you feel you know the person who wrote it. The writer becomes your friend."

"And you feel you know this man in a personal way?" he asked stiffly.

She was glad of his anger, glad she was getting to him. Men like him hated the idea of a woman doing anything except gracing a drawing room. "Yes I do. He was a man of great humor, of great physical strength, of great—" She stopped.

"Yes, go on. Tell me about this man who is beyond reproach yet who bored his audience with his volumes of writing." When he spoke, there was anger in his voice.

"You have such an ability to twist what I say," she said, pleased at having caused his anger. "He was a man of great personal attraction."

"Ah. Attraction to whom? Paper-eating insects?"

"To women," she said quickly, then could feel her face turning red.

"I guess he attracted them by drowning them in written words."

She grimaced. "No, he knew things. Things about women."

"Such as?"

She didn't say a word.

He recovered his composure and he was once again the smirking man she had met. "I can see you're going to the perfect biographer for a man like Baker. You'll write lovely, sweet, flowery passages to describe what he wrote about the women of foreign lands. Or do you plan to ignore that part of his life altogether and write only about the parts of him that make for acceptable drawing room conversation?"

"I plan to write about all of him, but I don't intend to give you, a man I don't know, vicarious pleasure by telling you the details of Captain Baker's love life." She stopped and pulled away from him. "Now, sir, I think that—" She broke off as she heard a noise to her left, and turned to see Harry approaching. He was still some distance away, but there was no mistaking the way Harry sat a horse.

Trevelyan watched her with interest, saw the way her face changed from anger to a soft, almost melting look when she saw her fiancé.

"It's Harry," she said in a whisper, and there was an altogether different tone to her voice than the one she'd been using. He saw her change from an angry little spitfire to a wide-eyed, adoring simpleton. She didn't so much as notice the sneer of disgust on Trevelyan's face.

"You have not heard my name," Trevelyan said, wondering if she'd heard him, as he stepped into the trees and managed to disappear from sight completely. But he stood in the shadows and watched.

Claire lifted the long edge of her riding habit, the part that was made for riding sidesaddle, and ran a few feet toward Harry, but he'd kicked his horse forward as soon as he saw her. When he dismounted the horse was still moving.

Harry put his strong hands on Claire's shoulders and she leaned toward him. He seemed so fresh and clean, so simple after that other man, she thought, then corrected herself. No, Harry wasn't simple. Harry was just different.

"Where were you?" Harry asked, bending toward her. There was genuine concern on his face and in his voice. "No one knew where you'd gone and I was worried." He held her at arms' length and looked at her. "You're wet through."

She smiled at him and rubbed her cheek against his hand. "I couldn't sleep. I was cold and so I went for a ride. I fell and hurt my arm."

To Claire's surprise, Harry pulled her close to him, against his warm body, as he took her left forearm in his strong hands. She gritted her teeth against the pain as he applied pressure to it.

"It doesn't seem to be broken. I think it's just bruised." He kissed the tip of her nose. "I would have gone with you if I'd known you wanted to ride."

She snuggled against him and he held her tightly. "You're so warm." And so uncomplicated and so good, she thought. You're so different from that other man, that Trevelyan.

He laughed at that. "I'll take you back to the house, we'll get a doctor to look at your arm, then you're to spend the day in bed. I don't want you catching cold."

"May I have a fire in the fireplace?"

"I will see that you have a roaring fire. And we'll put fifty pounds of blankets on the bed if that's what it takes to keep you warm."

"Harry, I do love you."

He bent forward as though to kiss her, but Claire pulled away. As well as she knew anything in the world, she knew they were being watched.

Harry chuckled as he lifted her into the saddle of his horse and mounted behind her.

Neither of them heard Trevelyan walk away through the woods.

Chapter Three

Low moaning woke Harry from a very sound sleep. Reluctantly, he opened his eyes. There was an eerie red light in the room, and standing at the foot of his bed was a monster. The creature was at least eight feet tall, draped in black, and had the most hideous face ever seen.

Groggily, Harry half sat up and moved his head forward a bit to get a better look at the thing that was groaning as though it had been lately killed and had come back to haunt the living. He yawned. "Uncle Cammy, if that's you, you'd better get back to bed. You'll miss breakfast."

At that the monster quit groaning, stepped down from the footstool, walked to the side of the bed, and removed its mask. What the disguise could not do the unveiling did: Harry came awake fully.

"Is that you?" he whispered. "Trevelyan?"

Trevelyan removed the black cloth that covered his body and grinned at his younger brother. "None other."

Harry sat up then and leaned back against the padded head of the bed. "Pour me some whisky, will you? There, on that table."

Trevelyan went to the table and poured out two glasses nearly full of single malt Scotch, handed one to his brother, then sat on a big carved oak chair near the bed. "Is that all I get? An 'Is that you?' No fatted calf? No welcome home parade?"

Harry took a deep drink of the whisky. "Does Mother know you're here?"

Trevelyan drained the glass and poured himself more. "No." He narrowed his eyes at Harry. Several people had written about the intensity of Trevelyan's eyes. Whenever people met him, it was what they remembered the most and remarked upon. His eyes were black and intense and angry.

Harry finished his whisky. He hated scenes, hated controversy, and with the return of his brother from the dead, he knew there was going to be one hell of a fight. "She ought to know," he said as he held out his glass for a refill.

Trevelyan didn't answer, but looked at his half empty glass. "I don't plan to stay long, only long enough to recover my strength, write a bit, then I'm off."

Harry was beginning to fully understand what it meant that his older brother was not dead after all. He looked at Trevelyan in the pale red glow of the lamplight and he may as well have been looking at a stranger. He'd been two years old when Trevelyan was sent from home and he'd seen his brother only a few times in those intervening years. To say that Trevelyan was the family black sheep was an understatement.

"You know, of course," Harry said slowly, "that this makes you the duke."

Trevelyan snorted, telling what he thought of having a title. "You think I plan to settle down now and manage this monster of a place, as well as the others? How many of these places do you own now?"

"Four," Harry said quickly, studying his glass rather than looking at his brother. Trevelyan always had a way of reading a person's innermost thoughts. And if he couldn't read them, he could usually ask so many questions that a person was worn down by him.

"Come on, what's on that English mind of yours?" Trevelyan said amiably.

"You're as English as I am, and, besides, I'm half Scots."

"Is that why you've been running about in that damned kilt? Is your ass freezing?"

"As a matter of fact, it is," Harry said, smiling, then made the mistake of glancing up at his brother.

"It's the girl, isn't it?" Trevelyan said.

"What do you know of her?"

"A bit," Trevelyan said mysteriously.

At that Harry began to laugh. "It was *you. You* were the old man she met. You were the one who caused her horse to throw her. You were the sick old man who fainted on her." Harry sat up straighter in bed. It seemed that all his life his brother had been an adult. One of their uncles had said that Trevelyan had been born full grown, that he hadn't wanted to bother with childhood and so had skipped it. It rather pleased Harry to hear his older brother called an "old man."

"You should have heard her," Harry continued. "She was disgusted, couldn't stop talking about the old man."

Trevelyan got up from his chair and walked to the far side of the room. But she didn't tell you my name, he thought. "Do you know that she wants to write a biography of me?"

Harry was feeling more self-confidence in the presence of his brother than he ever had in his life. "She wants to write about everything. Read about everything. You're about the seventh or eighth man and the third woman I've heard who she wants to write about." Harry paused. "Did you tell her who you were?"

"No. I told her I was related to the family and she told me about the dead brother who may or may not have been—" He paused. "An overzealous letter writer."

"She does give her opinions, doesn't she?"

Trevelyan turned back to his brother, and his eyes were as intense as a snake's. A man had once told Harry that he'd met Captain Baker and he could swear that the man could go for hours without blinking. "You seem to like her well enough."

Harry shrugged. "She's all right, but then she *is* an American."

"And quite lovely," Trevelyan said under his breath.

At that Harry started to come out of the bed. "Now see here, Vellie, you can't mean to try to take her. She's *my* heiress and no one else's."

Trevelyan sat back down on the chair and gave his brother a smile. "An heiress, is she? Is that why you want to marry her?"

"One does have to keep a roof on the house. And Mother—"

"Ah, yes, our dear mother." Trevelyan held his glass up to the light. "How is our mother?"

"As well as she can be."

"Still running everyone from her room, I gather. Has your little heiress met her yet?"

Harry swallowed more of his whisky. "Not yet. Claire just arrived yesterday."

"Do you think she will like your heiress?"

"Does it matter? Claire is suitable."

"For an American."

"At least she's not one of those loud, brash, pushy Americans. Always talking about ways to make money. Always wanting to change things, then calling it progress."

"You can certainly tell that this family is against change. Grandfather's clothes are still hanging in the wardrobe in his room, just as they were when I left here when I was nine. Tell me, is Mother still charging for the newspapers?"

"Economies have to be made. Mother's not bad, not really."

"To you she's not," Trevelyan said softly, and the way he said it made Harry look away.

After a moment of silence, Harry spoke again. "What do we do now? Tell the world the second brother has come back from the grave and is to be the duke? Or perhaps, from the look of you, you're ready to stop all your wanderings and tell the world who you are. Or have been. However you want to say it."

"I told you my plans. I want to rest and write, that's all. You can be the bloody duke for all I care." He fixed Harry with those eyes of his. "I want my expeditions financed. And, by the way, how the hell does the Prince of Wales know that Captain Frank Baker might have once been the earl of Trevelyan?"

"Father told the queen. He thought she should know and should give you a few medals."

Trevelyan laughed at that. "What would I do with them?"

"Hock them and pay for another of your trips?" Harry said, and made his brother laugh. Harry drained his glass and looked at his brother. "Honestly, Vellie, what *do* we do now?"

"Vellie," Trevelyan whispered. "No one's called me that in a long time." He smiled at his brother. "We don't do anything. You keep building that big monument on the hill to your dead brother and I continue being Captain Baker. You marry your heiress and raise a few brats and put a new roof on this building." He paused. "And you send me money for expeditions."

"It'll never work. Too many people in the family know who you are. Mother knows what you do." Harry frowned. "And look at you. You look more dead than alive. No wonder Claire thought you were an old man. You can't continue to go on five-year expeditions into nowhere. You won't live another three years."

"All the better for the family then," Trevelyan said with some bitterness, then he leaned forward to look hard into Harry's eyes. "You know as well as I do I've never been a part of this family. All I need now is a place to hide until I'm steadier on my feet, then I'll be off again. If Captain Baker turns out to be alive after all, then it will dispel all rumors that he was part of your family. The earl of Trevelyan died months ago. Leave it at that."

"But when Mother hears you're alive she'll—"

"Tell her someone else has assumed the identity of Captain Baker. Tell her anything. I couldn't care less what the old harridan thinks—if she does think."

Harry leaned back in the bed. He might not know his brother well, but he knew him well enough to know there was no use trying to reason with him. "Where are you staying?"

"Charlie's room." Trevelyan grinned. "I doubt that anyone will find me there. I can walk early and late so no one sees me, especially since this house is run on Mother's clock."

Harry ignored the dig. "Do you have everything you need? Food?"

"I have a man to take care of me and he brings me food. I'm not fool enough to ask how he obtains it." He paused. "Who's the child?"

Harry smiled at that. "You mean the little beauty?"

"I've only seen her from the window, but she looks to have potential."

"She's Claire's little sister and she's exquisite. She's only fourteen now and I can't imagine what she'll look like when she's eighteen or so. She's an enchanting child but for some reason her father and Claire call her Brat. I cannot imagine anyone less deserving of such a name."

"Yes, but then you always were an excellent judge of character, weren't you?"

Harry ignored the remark. Trevelyan's anger was his own problem.

"I'll leave you to your sleep now," Trevelyan said, starting for the door.

"Stay away from her," Harry said.

Trevelyan paused with his hand on the door. "I don't want your little heiress. There's marriage and eternal fidelity in that young woman's eyes."

"Marriage to *me,*" Harry said.

At that Trevelyan turned to look at his brother and there was a combination of both pity and laughter in his eyes. "Marriage to you and your debts and your mother," Trevelyan said with glittering eyes. "Now go to sleep, little brother." With that, Trevelyan left the room.

By the time Claire climbed into bed at the end of her second day at Bramley, she was shaking with exhaustion. But it wasn't exhaustion from having done anything all day; it was exhaustion from having been *wrong* all day long. For one whole day of her life, everything she had done had been absolutely, completely, and totally wrong.

Yesterday, at Harry's insistence, because of her injured arm, she had spent the day in bed. She had been cosseted and cared for by the servants. Food had been brought to her on silver trays. Nothing in the world had been too much or too good for her. All in all it had been a lovely day, a day such as she had imagined being a duchess would be like.

But then last night Harry had told her that this morning her real life would start, that it would be good for her to start learning how his family really lived. Claire had asked a few questions and found out that this decree had come from his mother. Claire had asked when she was going to get to meet his mother, but Harry had been vague, saying that it would be soon, but his mother was ill a great deal and stayed in her rooms.

So, this morning Claire had awakened feeling happy and jubilant. She was at last going to be part of Harry's family. She was going to take her rightful place at his side.

But it had started to go wrong from the first. Harry's mother had personally chosen a maid for Claire, someone to help her until Claire could find her own maid. At eight A.M. precisely, Claire had been awakened by a thin little woman who could best be described as gray. Her hair was gray, her skin was gray, and the way she held her mouth was gray. She looked as though she had been born with a scowl on her face. She introduced herself as Miss Rogers and asked Claire what she planned to wear today. Claire said she would wear her red wool dress. Miss Rogers sniffed and returned to the bedroom carrying Claire's dark green wool dress.

At first Claire thought the woman had misheard, but, no, she had heard all right, but Miss Rogers thought the green was better suited for the morning. Claire gave in to the woman, thinking that perhaps she knew better.

Claire went down to breakfast at exactly three minutes to nine and there were at least twenty people waiting to go into the dining room. Claire was quite startled at this as she'd not known there were guests other than her own family at Bramley. She made her way through the people to Harry and asked him to introduce her, but Harry was deep in a discussion about some horse that he planned to buy that day and said he didn't know who half of them were. "Relatives, I guess," was all she could get out of him.

Before Claire could introduce herself, the dining room doors opened and all the people went rushing into the room to take their seats. Claire was left standing just inside the door, but a man dressed in livery held out a chair for her. Harry was sitting at the head of the table and Claire's chair was a long, long way from his.

There must be some mistake, she thought, so she got up and went to Harry. "They have placed me far away from you," she said.

She was aware of the profound silence in the room as every one of the strangers as well as the servants turned to look at her. Her mother never rose before noon so she wasn't at the table, but her father was happily seated halfway down the opposite side.

Harry looked up at Claire in puzzlement, as though he didn't understand what her complaint was. "Everyone is seated by rank, and you are an American."

Claire could only look at him.

Harry, not seeming to know what she didn't understand, attempted to explain. "After we're married and you're the duchess, you may sit at the foot of the table."

"Oh," was all Claire could say. She tried to keep her chin up as she made her way to near the end of the table—the end where untitled Americans were seated. Even after they were married, she would still not be allowed to dine next to her husband.

Once she was seated and the first course of fried sausages was served, she decided to make the best of it all. She turned to the man next to her. "Lovely day outside, isn't it?" she said.

All motion at the table stopped. There were no more sounds of eating and everyone paused to stare at her. She leaned forward to look at Harry. He made a little gesture of shaking his head to let her know she wasn't supposed to talk.

She looked down at her food and began to eat in silence. By the second course of more fried food, a liveried footman came by and handed the men newspapers and they began to read. Claire thought that if she weren't allowed to talk, then she too would read. She took a newspaper from the tray when it was offered to the man on her left.

Once again there was that silence. *Now* what have I done wrong? she thought. She looked around her and saw that none of the women were reading newspapers, just the men. While trying to hide her disgust at the absurdity of this, but not really succeeding, she tossed the unread paper back onto the footman's tray.

She looked about at the silent people, all of them concentrating on their food or their papers. But down the long length of the table was one woman who was looking at her. She was a plain-faced woman, but Claire couldn't help thinking that with a more fashionable dress and just a touch of cosmetics, she could be made to look a great deal better than she did. The woman smiled at Claire and Claire smiled back. The woman was sitting near Harry so she must have a very high "rank," Claire thought.

After the long meal Claire practically ran to reach Harry before he disappeared into the bowels of the house. "Could I speak to you?"

He frowned a bit but recovered himself and led the way into a small drawing room. He turned to her, trying to conceal his impatience. By now his horse was saddled and waiting for him.

"Could you explain to me about breakfast?"

"What about it?" he asked, glancing at the clock on the mantle.

"Why does no one talk?"

"Mother believes that the most important meal of the day is breakfast and that people can't digest their food properly if they're talking."

She frowned, for he sounded as though he were chanting something he'd memorized. "Then why not have silence when your mother is present at the table and let people converse when she isn't? It would make for a much more pleasant meal if people could talk."

He smiled indulgently at her. "But Mother is the duchess."

Claire did not say, but *you* are the duke. "I see. And she rules the house even when she isn't there."

"Of course. Now I really must go. Your father and I are going to look at some horses today."

"But what about the newspapers?"

For a moment, Harry looked puzzled. "Oh, I see. Mother doesn't think women ought to read newspapers."

"What *does* Her Grace think women ought to read?" Claire's voice was heavy with sarcasm, but Harry didn't seem to notice.

"Actually, she doesn't think women should read very much at all. She says it makes them discontent. Now, darling, I must go." He gave her a quick kiss on the forehead and started for the door.

"Harry! May I go with you?"

Harry, his back to her, rolled his eyes skyward. When he turned back to her, he was smiling. "Darling, I would love to take you with me, but you'd be bored to death. Besides, we're going on horseback, and the doctor said you're not to use your arm for anything heavy, and that includes pulling on a horse's reins. You just stay here and enjoy yourself."

Claire tried to hide her disappointment. "May I explore the house?"

"Of course you may," he said in a put-upon-male voice. You're free to do whatever you want. But the east wing of the house is full of people's rooms so perhaps you shouldn't disturb them, and the west wing is falling apart. Rotten timbers and all that, so you'd better stay out of there. I really must go now. See you at dinner." With that he left the room before she could ask any more questions or request anything else of him.

"I may do anything I want except talk, read, ride, or look at the house that will be mine someday," she said to herself, but then made herself stop being pessimistic.

At least she was free to explore the core of the house, if not the wings, and she knew the first place she wanted to see: the library. She asked a footman to direct her to the library, and as soon as she approached it, she smiled. She could hear laughter inside and was glad of the sound.

But the moment she opened the door and stepped inside, the laughter stopped. The room was full of men, all of them smoking huge cigars and reading newspapers or talking, and when they saw her, they halted. It didn't take any great detective work to figure out that this was a "no females allowed" room. She backed out and nearly ran into the footman.

"I believe, miss, that you want the gold drawing room."

She smiled at him in gratitude and followed him through three rooms. The house had been done in the Adam style and everywhere was the most exquisite detailing. The walls were covered in silk brocade, brocade so old that in places it was shattered, but it was still lovely. Several of the chairs that were placed here and there were obviously in need of repair.

The gold drawing room was so named because it was practically covered in gold leaf. Mirrors were framed in gold leaf, all molding was picked out in gold, and the furniture dripped gold. There were eight women in the room, all of them huddled by a meager fire, all of them bent over embroidery frames. From the looks of the worn covers on the chairs, their work was needed.

When Claire entered, the women had been talking in low voices, but they halted when they saw her. She had the distinct feeling that they had been discussing her. No one made any effort to include her in the conversation; no one seemed the least curious about her, so Claire smiled at them and walked about the room, hoping they would resume their talking. But they didn't, and after a while she left.

She went back to her bedroom and told Miss Rogers she had decided to take a walk and that she needed her brown walking costume and her sturdiest shoes. Miss Rogers's shock had registered on her gray face.

"Now what?" Claire said tiredly. "Am I not allowed to walk?"

"Her Grace says ladies should not walk in the morning when the dew is still on the ground. You must wait until the afternoon."

"Well, I'm not going to wait until the afternoon. I'm going to walk *now.*"

Miss Rogers sniffed, letting Claire know what she thought of this insolence. As a result Miss Rogers could not find the dress Claire wanted to wear, nor could she find the shoes. Claire ended in finding her own clothes and dressing herself.

It was eleven-thirty in the morning before she was able to get out of the house. She stood outside the door and breathed deeply of the fresh, clean Scottish air, then began walking. Maybe it was her suppressed anger at herself, at all the people in the house, but whatever it was, she spent hours walking.

For all that the house needed a great deal of refurbishing, the gardens were divine. There was a wild garden, so called because it was meant to simulate nature, if nature were perfect, that is. There was a small garden of topiary animals that made her laugh. There were three enclosed flower gardens, an orchard, and there were two lovely buildings where one could sit and look out over the hills in the distance.

When she at last returned to the house at three-thirty, she was tired and hungry and happy. The outdoors and the exercise had renewed her spirits.

When she entered her room, Miss Rogers was waiting for her with her usual sour look. "I am starved," Claire said happily.

"Luncheon is from one until two."

"Yes, I know, and I'm sorry I missed it." To herself she wondered if luncheon was as delightful as breakfast. "Have something brought to me on a tray."

"Her Grace does not allow food taken to the rooms unless one is ill. It makes too much work for the staff."

It was on the tip of Claire's tongue to say that servants were there to work, but she restrained herself. "Then tell the staff I'm ill and have something brought to me. I've been walking for miles and I'm hungry."

"I cannot go against Her Grace's requests," Miss Rogers said.

For a moment the two women looked at each other, and Claire knew that this small, withered little woman was going to win because Claire did not want to cause problems in the household. Claire's intuition warned her that Harry would be told if she broke the rules and he would be displeased by her breaking of them.

"I shall get my own food," Claire said in disgust, and stormed past the woman. At home in New York, in her parents' house, she had often eaten in the kitchen after she'd come in from one of her long walks or from a ride in the southern part of the city.

It took her a while to find the kitchen. Every footman or maid she asked for directions looked as though she'd said something obscene. By the time she did find the kitchens, she was thoroughly frustrated and her head was hurting from hunger.

As soon as she reached the door that separated the staff quarters from the main house she heard laughter, and, smiling, she pushed the door open and went into the first room. The men with their sleeves rolled up, polishing the silver, stared at her in horror. The women washing the dishes gasped. By the time she reached the kitchen and saw the cook sitting on a chair reading, of all things, a newspaper, Claire was feeling as though she were a freak.

"I've been walking," she said as firmly as she could manage, "and I'd like something to eat."

No one seemed able to speak.

"I am hungry," she said in exasperation.

It was at that moment that the butler appeared and very quietly but firmly escorted her from the kitchen.

"Might I suggest, miss, that you remain on this side of that door," he said as though talking to a wayward child. "If you need anything, tell Miss Rogers and she will see that you get it." With that he left her standing alone.

Claire wondered whether a tantrum of rage or tears would be better. She gave in to neither, but very quietly and sedately wandered into the hall and looked for some place to sit down. She couldn't go to her own room or to the gold drawing room or to the library.

She found a pretty little room done in blue silk and sat down heavily on a little chair. She wondered when the next meal was.

"Harry run off with another woman?"

Claire looked up to see her little sister standing in the doorway.

"Why aren't you having lessons?"

"I gave her a headache. What's wrong with you?"

"Nothing that about half a pound of roast beef wouldn't cure."

"That's easily solved. I'll get you a sandwich."

Claire wasn't fooled by the brat's offer to help. "You can't. They won't allow you in the kitchen."

Brat just smiled, then smiled more broadly when Claire's stomach growled loudly.

"How much?" Claire asked. She knew all too well that Brat would never consider doing something for someone without payment.

"Tell Mother I'm too old for lessons."

Claire just looked at her.

"I want my ears pierced and you can give me your pearl and diamond earrings."

Claire continued to look at her sister.

"All right, then. Twenty bucks."

"I don't have any money with me."

Brat smiled. "I know where you have it hidden. I'll have you a meal in no time."

Within minutes, Brat was back with a fat roast beef sandwich slathered with a mild horseradish sauce, a bowlful of sliced tomatoes, and a large glass of milk. All this was carried on a big silver tray by a very handsome young footman.

"Put it there," Brat said to the man.

"But Her Grace doesn't allow eating in this room," the man said with a bit of fear in his voice.

"She does now," Brat said and winked at the man. He turned and left them.

"However did you manage this?" Claire asked, her mouth full. "There are so many rules."

Brat looked astonished. "You don't have to *obey* rules."

After that Claire tried her best to learn all the rules before she broke them. Her brat of a sister might be able to break the rules and get away with it, but she wasn't trying to make a good impression. In fact, Brat's philosophy of life seemed to be that people should try to impress her, not the other way around.

For tea Claire wore what Miss Rogers suggested and she was in the gold drawing room promptly and she sat where she was told to sit. The women around her spoke in hushed tones about people she didn't know; they didn't so much as acknowledge Claire's presence. Claire sat with her hands on her lap and her eyes downcast. Once she looked across the table to see the plain-faced woman of the morning smiling at her, and Claire smiled back.

Claire changed dresses again for dinner. At this meal it seemed that people were allowed to talk—but the talk consisted only of dogs and horses, neither of which interested Claire, so again she was silent.

After dinner the men and women separated and went to different drawing rooms, and from there they went to bed.

Only by accident did she see Harry before she went to bed. He was yawning and looked as though he were already half asleep.

"Don't the men and women ever get together?" she asked between his yawns.

He grinned at her in a way that made her take a step backward. "They make babies, if that's what you mean."

"No, I mean, don't the men and women *talk* to one another? At home—"

"Darling, this isn't America. You're in Scotland now, and things are different." He gave a great yawn.

"Did you buy your horses?"

"Mmmmm." He gave another yawn. "I must get to bed. See you in the morning, darling."

"At breakfast?" she said, but Harry didn't notice the sarcasm in her voice.

"Yes, at breakfast. Good night."

Chapter Four

Claire looked at the watch pinned to her breast and stamped her foot in annoyance. She had done it again. For the second time in four days she had missed luncheon. It was now only ten minutes after one o'clock, but she knew from experience that she wouldn't be seated after the duke was. She had tried to talk to Harry, to ask him why his mother made all the rules when he was the important one in the family, but Harry'd only said, "That's the way it is. That's the way things have always been."

Now she knew she had two choices: she could go back to her room hungry or she could find her sister and pay her twenty-five dollars to fetch her a sandwich. (The brat's fees had gone up.)

But Claire didn't want to do either of those things. She would try to train herself to do without luncheon, and tea if necessary, to get some time to do what she wanted to do. Of course it might help if she had any idea what she wanted to do. She had spent three days exploring the center section of the house, looking at the pictures, mentally figuring out what needed repair and how much it was going to cost after she and Harry were married. She had spent another two days walking about the gardens. She so desperately wanted to get into the library that one night she had slipped downstairs with the intention of sneaking into the room when no one was there. But there was an old man in the room even at that hour. Claire gave a little gasp and fled back up the stairs.

Now, hungry from her long walk and knowing it was going to be hours before her next meal, and, too, knowing how the other women gave her disapproving looks when she ravenously gobbled down sandwiches and cakes at tea, she kicked at the outside wall of the house. When that didn't help, she sat down on a little bench, her head in her hands, and for the thousandth time felt like giving way to tears.

But it was while she had her head down that she saw what looked like an opening in the bushes. Her curiosity overriding her hunger, she got up to examine the space. There was indeed a path through the greenery that surrounded the west wing of the house. She made her way through the shrubbery. Within a few feet she came to a door that was completely hidden by the bushes. She had tried every door both inside and out to this wing and had found all of them to be locked, but she knew before she touched this door that it would be unlocked. It was not only unlocked but the hinges had been recently oiled; the door opened easily.

She stepped into the darkened interior and felt as though she'd stepped back in time. Before her rose a high, two-story stone room that she knew without being told was part of a castle. There were rotten tapestries hanging from the walls, and at one end was a fireplace meant to roast whole head of cattle. Scattered about the room were broken chairs and benches and tables. There was a heap of what looked to be armor and weapons in one corner.

As her eyes adjusted, she walked about the cold room, cold as only stone that hadn't been heated for a century or so could be, and looked at the objects. She ran into several cobwebs, but they didn't bother her since she was much more interested in what she was seeing.

Leading out of the big room were two sets of spiral stone stairs, and she started up one of them. The stones were worn away from thousands of feet traveling up and down the stairs; they were slippery with damp and cold.

On the second floor she explored several rooms. Some of them still contained bits of furniture. She picked up a heavy sword from the floor and carried it to the light of the single window in the room. Several panes of the old semitransparent glass were gone, and there were bats in the room. She examined the sword carefully and once again she heard the bagpipes in her head. What she had experienced so far at Bramley was completely removed from what she had imagined Scotland to be like, but, here, holding this sword, she began to feel some of what she had expected.

Still carrying the sword, she went up another floor and walked into a large room. Light streamed into the room, and as she looked at the tattered shreds of fabric hanging from the walls, she could imagine what this room had once been—and what it could be again.

She hugged her arms about her, rubbing them against the cold, and whirled about. "After I'm married I shall restore this place," she said aloud. "I shall make these apartments ours and they shall be as glorious as they once were. I shall hang tartan cloth on the walls. I'll have the tapestries repaired. I'll—"

She didn't say any more because she stepped on a rotten board and the floor gave way under her, the sword flying across the room. She screamed as she went down, but she had sense enough to throw her arms out wide so she didn't go all the way through and fall to the stones of the floor below. She yelled once for help but then stopped. Who was going to hear her through several feet of stone walls? Who was going to find her? No one seemed to care when she didn't show up for meals. Would it be days before she was missed?

"Well, well."

She looked up to see the man she'd met before, the man who called himself Trevelyan, standing in the doorway. Immediately, all the emotions she'd felt when she first met him came back to her. She didn't like the way he was standing, leaning against the doorway in an insolent way; she didn't like the expression on his scarred face, a face that seemed to be younger than she'd remembered.

"I heard something down here, but I thought it was rats. Looks as though it's just one big rat."

"Do you think you could possibly make nasty comments later and help me out of this *now?"* And when I get out, I shall use the sword on you, she thought.

"You look like you're doing all right. Remember, I'm a decrepit old man. I might have a heart attack if I helped you. Maybe I'd better get your big strong duke."

She was trying to find something to grab on to so she could pull herself up, but there was nothing. "Harry has gone to buy horses."

"Does that rather a lot, doesn't he?"

"He's going to race them." She stopped floundering and looked up at him. "This is becoming painful. Could you *please* help me?"

Trevelyan took a few steps toward her, bent, put his hands under her arms, and easily lifted her out of the hole. For a moment she stood very, very near him, not touching him, but close enough to feel his breath on her face. When he looked down at her, her heart began to pound. Anger was what was causing the pounding, she thought, but the pounding didn't feel exactly like anger. He gave her a little smile, as though he had found out something that he'd wanted to know, then turned and walked away.

Claire began dusting herself off. "Thank you so much. I was becoming concerned that anyone would ever find me and that I'd—"

She stopped, since she was talking to an empty room. He was no longer in the room. She went to the doorway and looked down the stone stairs but saw no sign of the man. She looked up and saw just a bit of motion as he climbed the stairs.

Good, she thought. She didn't want to be around him. His cynicism, his entire attitude toward life, was something she didn't want to be near.

But then she remembered talking to him on the day they first met. It would be nice to talk to someone. Actually, it would be heavenly to talk to someone.

She straightened her shoulders, lifted her skirts, then followed him up the stairs.

At the top of the stairs she entered a room that was small compared to the one below, but still it was a nice-sized room and she could see that all of the best furniture from the old castle had been put here. There was a tapestry along one wall, and against another wall was a more modern settee that was upholstered in torn yellow silk. There were several big chairs with carvings of bearded men on them. In the center of the room, oddly enough, were eleven small tables, a chair at each one, each table covered with stacks of paper, notebooks, fountain pens, and bottles of ink.

Claire forgot how cold she was, how much she detested the man whose room this was, and started toward the nearest table.

"Leave that alone!" Trevelyan commanded from behind her.

Guiltily, she turned toward him. He was standing in the doorway with a cup and saucer in his hands, sipping at something steaming. Claire's hunger pangs and cold returned. On one wall was a fireplace with a small fire burning. She left the table and went to stand with her back to the fireplace. Perhaps he'd offer her something to eat. She tried to remove the look of defiance she knew she was wearing and smiled at him.

He gave her a raised-eyebrow look, as though he knew just what she was thinking, went to the nearest table, sat down and began writing. "I don't remember issuing invitations, so you may leave."

Claire didn't move. For all his hostility, for all that she sincerely disliked this man, oddly enough she didn't feel half as unwelcome here as she'd felt when she tried to enter the library. "Are you staying here?"

"I don't have time to talk to little girls. I have work to do."

"Oh? What are you working on?"

"Nothing you'd understand," he snapped.

She stood where she was, warming her hands, wanting very much to see what was on the tables. They were certainly an odd assortment of tables: two were Jacobean, one a Queen Anne, one that looked as though it had come from the gold drawing room, two tables that had obviously been outside in the rain for quite some time, while the others were from every time period in between. Some were quite valuable, some worth little more than firewood.

As he sat at the far table, his back to her, she leaned as far forward as she could without taking a step that he might hear and tried to see the papers on the nearest table.

He turned abruptly and stared at her. Claire straightened and tried to act as though she hadn't been prying. She tried to cover her nosiness with a little smile, but her red face gave her away.

He picked up his tea cup, sipped at it, then replaced it in its saucer before he spoke. "Why aren't you eating? Isn't a meal being served now?"

"I missed luncheon again."

"Again? Have you missed it often?"

"Unfortunately, yes. I can't seem to calculate my walking so I get back in time to change for luncheon. But I'm sure I'll eventually learn."

He gave a little snort at that, a snort that let her know he had doubts she'd ever learn anything. "In the meantime you starve." He turned back to his writing. "I guess it's one of the fees you'll pay for being a duchess."

Claire made a little face at his back after he turned away. She knew she should leave but she couldn't think what she'd do if she did leave.

She didn't like this man, didn't want to be near him, but the sight of books and papers was too intriguing to her. She *couldn't* leave.

Very slowly, without making a sound, she reached out to pick up a paper off the nearest table. It was covered with writing. She no more than had the paper in her hand when he snapped at her.

"Put that down!"

She dropped the paper so suddenly that it fell to the floor. She stood still for a moment, shaking like a child, but then she smiled at his back. He was acting as though he were ignoring her, but he was aware of every movement she made.

"What are you writing?" she asked.

"If I'd wanted you to know what I was writing I would have invited you to a reading." Still with his back to her, without so much as a glance at her, he got up and moved to another table and instantly began writing again.

Claire started to tell him that he'd left his cup of tea behind but then she seemed to become fascinated with it. It was still steaming and it looked like the best cup of tea she'd ever seen in her life. "I have no intention of disturbing you," she said and found herself walking toward the table with the cup on it. "I was merely out for a stroll and I saw the door open and I went inside. Harry, I mean, His Grace, said I could explore all that I wanted."

At the end of this speech she had reached the table with the teacup on it and she had the cup in her hand before she realized what she was doing. She was aware that as soon as she had put her hand on the cup Trevelyan had spun about in his chair to look at her. Feeling quite defiant, she continued moving the cup toward her lips. She was tired of being hungry and of no one seeming to care. She drained half the cupful, then was sure she was going to die.

"It was whisky," she gasped, her hand to her throat.

"Scotland's finest," Trevelyan said, amused.

Claire staggered backward toward him, clutching tables as she moved.

"If you're planning to collapse, might I suggest that you do it on a chair. The floor is quite hard."

In spite of a throat and a stomach that were on fire, she managed to give him a look that told what she thought of his not coming to her aid. She caught the back of a chair and sat down on it hard.

"I . . . could have been killed," she at last managed to say.

"Stealing a man's whisky is an offense, but hardly punishable by death. At least not in most countries. Of course there are the moral implications of stealing anything."

"Would you please be quiet? Can a person die from that much whisky?"

"Not likely."

He was watching her with his intense eyes, and after a moment she began to relax against the chair. "My goodness," she said. "I do believe this is the first time I've been warm since I came to this country. I feel rather . . ." She trailed off.

"Drunk is what you feel." With that he clapped his hands twice and almost at once there appeared a man in the doorway.

Claire, in spite of her relaxed state, widened her eyes. He was the tallest man she had ever seen, several inches over six feet and dressed in a strange white outfit. He wore a tunic that reached his knees and beneath the tunic were trousers that were tight about his ankles. A wide sash edged in pale gold fringe encircled his waist. His face was dark brown, with black eyes, a thin mouth, and a large nose that looked sharp enough to cut metal. Wound about his head was a round bundle of white cloth and in the middle was pinned an emerald that had to be two inches square.

"Oman," Trevelyan said, making the name sound like Ooomahn. "Food for our drunken guest."

"I'm not—" Claire began but stopped. She certainly did feel as though she were floating. "How very pretty the fire is. How pretty the tables are. Does Harry know you're here?"

Trevelyan turned away from her and went back to his writing. "I have His Royal Highness's permission if that's what you mean."

Claire giggled. "Not His Royal Highness. It's His Grace. Not that my mother can remember."

Trevelyan turned back around. "What does your mother call Harry?" His eyes were intense; he looked as though he were exceedingly interested in her answer.

"Whatever comes to mind." She couldn't help laughing. "Yesterday she called him Your Sereneness." Claire put her hand over her mouth. "Harry thought it was very funny. He's such a good sport."

"Perfection, is he?"

"I rather think he is," Claire said in wonder. "He's kind and considerate." She held up her left arm. "Under here is a bandage.

Harry made sure that I stayed in bed one whole day after I hurt my arm."

"Alone?"

At that Claire started to stand. "I will not remain here to be insulted." But as she stood her head began to spin, and she sat back down.

Trevelyan looked up as Oman reappeared in the doorway. "Food is through there," he said and turned back to his writing.

Unsteadily, Claire stood and walked through the doorway and into a bedroom. It was a beautiful room, the walls hung with gold-colored silk brocade, beautiful Persian carpets on the stone floor, and in the middle of the room was the most astounding bed she had ever seen. It was enormous, with two deeply carved posts at the foot that had to be a foot and a half square. The headboard and the top of the bed were also heavily carved. The big bed itself was draped with plush red silk velvet.

She had an impulse to jump onto the bed, but then she saw that a plate of food had been set on a table against one wall and she went to it. But it wasn't food she had ever seen before. There was a bowl of white creamy stuff, boiled potatoes, thinly sliced meat, and a bit of green stuff in the middle of the plate. There were tomatoes and sliced cucumbers also. It was not the same kind of food that she'd eaten since she came across the ocean, or before that for that matter.

She sat down, picked up the spoon, and dipped it into the bowl. Was it soup or was it, for some reason, a bowl of cream? She smelled it.

"It's called yoghurt," Trevelyan said from the doorway. "Fermented milk."

"It looks delicious."

"It's an acquired taste."

At that Claire put a spoonful in her mouth. It was sour but she rather liked it. She smiled up at him and, for some reason, her liking the yoghurt seemed to please him. He came into the room and sat on a chair that was against the wall, took a pipe and a can of tobacco off the windowsill, packed the pipe, and lit it.

Claire tore into the food ravenously. "What are you doing here?" she asked between bites. "Why do you have eleven tables in there? Whose room was this? Are you the only person who lives in this part of the house? Are you very, very ill?"

He looked at her through the haze of the pipe smoke. "Lonely for company, are you?"

"Why, no, of course not. There must be a hundred people living in this enormous house. How can I be lonely?" She looked down at the empty plate. With the food in her, she was losing the delicious feeling the whisky had given her.

"And there's always Harry."

She put her fork down. "I think I'd better go now." She started to get up.

"This is Charlie's room."

She looked back at him. "I haven't met any Charlie."

"Charlie as in the prince of that name."

Claire stood still a moment. *"Bonnie* Prince Charlie? *That* Prince Charlie?"

"None other. He came this way in . . ."

"1745."

"I think that was the year. He came by here and of course some of my relatives, as well as Harry's, were helping him, so they asked him to spend the night. He did." Trevelyan pointed with the stem of his pipe toward the bed.

Claire looked at the bed with new eyes. "Bonnie Prince Charlie slept in *this* bed?"

"Left some things in a drawer over there."

Slowly, Claire made her way to the small table next to the bed and opened the drawer. Inside was a bit of tartan cloth that she knew to be the prince's sett. She had seen several pieces in museums. There was also an old, yellow, folded piece of paper in the drawer. Tentatively, she opened it, and inside was a curl of light brown hair. She looked at Trevelyan. "His?"

"Yes," he said and smiled a bit.

Carefully, she put the items back into the drawer and closed it. "These things should be in a museum."

Trevelyan shrugged and drew on his pipe.

Claire looked at the bed in reverence for a moment, then she did what she had always wanted to do when she saw wonderful things in museums: she touched it. Gently, she ran her hands along the carving of the post and along the coverlet.

"The bed's not exactly fragile. As I sleep on it every night, I can assure you that it's quite sturdy."

Claire looked at him to see if he were joking but then, with a smile of great joy, she climbed onto the bed and stretched out. She was looking up at the underside of the same bed that Bonnie Prince Charlie had looked at.

"I think I hear bagpipes," she said softly. "This is the *real* Scotland."

Trevelyan watched her intently. "And what is your idea of the real Scotland?"

She sat up on her elbows. "The history of what has gone on in this place. Are you Scots?"

"Half. My mother is English."

"Then your parents must have hated each other." She lay back on the coverlet.

"True enough," he said. "I've never seen a married couple hate each other more than my parents did."

"Of course they did. The English have persecuted the Scots for centuries. Did you know that one of the English kings was called the Hammer of the Scots?" She smiled up at the canopy. "But no one, absolutely no one, could defeat the Scots. Not everything the English could do to them could make them surrender. And in the end they won."

Trevelyan drew on his pipe. "If we Scots are so poor and the English are so rich, how have we won?"

"James the First, of course. Elizabeth the First turned all of England over to a Scotsman. All the rest of the English kings and queens are descended from Scotsmen."

Trevelyan stood and walked toward the bed to look down at her. "What a romantic you are. Do you always tell yourself what you want to believe?"

She lifted herself to her elbows. "I know my history and—"

"Bah!" he said. "James the First spent only the first few months of his life in Scotland. He was as English as your young duke, and our present queen, Victoria, is more German than she is English."

Claire well knew all this, but she much preferred to ignore it. "Just the same—" She broke off when he left the room. She lay back on the bed and smiled. It was rather nice to talk to someone who knew some of the things that she did. Actually, it was just plain nice to talk to anyone at all, about anything. She got off the bed and went into the sitting room. He was already back at one of his tables and writing.

"How—?" she began, but he turned on her.

"If you stay you must be quiet. I can't abide chattering while I'm working."

"If you'd tell me what you're working on, I might be able to help you." Just the thought of having something to do made her feel better than she had in days.

"Can you read Arabic script?"

"No, but I can—"

"Then you are of no use to me. Go and sit there." He nodded toward a cushioned window seat. "Get a book or take some paper and a pen."

Claire went to the window seat, sat on it, and looked out the window. She had to open the ancient iron hinges to be able to see, as the glass was old and too imperfect to be able to see through. She looked across the gardens to the woods and the heather-covered hills beyond.

She sat there for a long while, breathing the sweet, cool Scottish air and looking at the hills. After a while she turned and saw that Trevelyan was staring at her. He seemed able to read her thoughts, but she had no idea what he was thinking.

As usual she was startled by the intensity of his eyes and the greenish cast to his skin. "Are you very ill?" she asked softly.

"I have been," he answered curtly and it was obvious that he didn't want to talk about his health. "Do you read or are you one of those simpering misses who is capable of doing nothing for days on end?"

"Are you always bad-tempered or is it just me?"

He almost smiled at that. "I'm the same for everyone."

"Horrible thought," she said under her breath.

He did smile at that, and she saw that he didn't look so ill or quite so ugly when he smiled. Just as she opened her mouth to speak, he interrupted her. "Don't start asking me questions again." He stood and went to two small oak doors imbedded in the stone walls. When he opened the doors she saw there were books inside. She gasped and came off the seat to stand by him, and, as he had his hand on the top corner of one of the doors, she slipped under his arm to see the titles on the books more clearly. She was unaware of how Trevelyan looked down at the top of her head. He leaned forward to smell her hair. It smelled of sunshine and heather and he had difficulty controlling an urge to put his lips against her neck.

Claire didn't know what was happening to her, but suddenly her body broke out in gooseflesh. As though she'd been scalded, she jumped away from him. "I . . . I think I ought to leave."

He was again wearing that infuriating look on his face, his eyes lazy looking, almost hooded. Under his mustache, his lips curved into a slight smile as he pulled a book from the shelf. "I thought you wanted to read. Ah, here's one. *Tibet Rediscovered.* Oh, no, it's in Italian." He started to replace the book on the shelf but she snatched it from his hand, staying as far from him as possible.

"For your information, I can read Italian, but, as it happens, I've read this book. I've read all of Captain Baker's books. I told you I had."

"So you did. So then I doubt they bear a second reading."

"I have read the parts that I like repeatedly."

"What does that mean, 'the parts you like'?"

"Why do you take criticism personally? The man wrote on every aspect of everything he saw. Some of it was quite boring."

"Such as?"

He had taken a step closer to her, but, frowning, Claire moved back. "His descriptions of wagons, for instance," she said quickly, looking away from him. "He would measure them and tell all the dimensions of the wheels and the seats and the length of the thing. He'd go on and on until a reader could scream."

"You should not have taxed your small brain with his books if you didn't like them," he said softly, teasingly. "You—"

She turned to face him, and there was such passion in her eyes that for a moment Trevelyan was startled. Her eyes were the eyes of one who believed in something. It had been so long since he had believed in anything that at first he didn't recognize the emotion on her pretty face. He looked at the way her eyes lit, at the way anger made her lips fuller. How had he not seen that she was a beauty? How had he not seen the passion just under the surface of her? He took a quarter of a step closer to her.

"What is wonderful about his books are the parts about people," Claire said vehemently. "He was a magnificent observer of people. Most explorers' books make for such dull reading. They write of distances, and when they come to something interesting, they write, 'Saw a very unusual tribe today. Believe they eat ants to stay alive.' That kind of thing can drive a reader crazy. You immediately want to know whether they bake or fry the ants, and do they cultivate them.

There are just lots of questions that spring to one's mind. But Captain Baker would never leave the reader unsatisfied. He tells the reader *everything."*

"Including the dimensions of the wheels of the wagons," Trevelyan said automatically, but he was looking at her more than hearing her.

She shook her head in exasperation, then turned back to the case of books. "I don't think you're capable of understanding."

"But Captain Baker no doubt would understand, and of course young Harry would." Trevelyan shocked himself when he heard what sounded like jealousy in his own voice. He was glad the little American hadn't seemed to hear him.

She bent to look at the titles of the books on the bottom shelf as Trevelyan's eyes ran over her body. He so much wanted to put his hands on her waist that his fingers itched.

"Is it your own advanced age that makes you constantly point out Harry's youth? My father does that with younger men. I believe it makes him feel superior."

She straightened and nearly hit Trevelyan's face with her head. *"All* of these books were written by Captain Baker." She turned to face him, bending backward a bit to look up at his face, as he was standing very close to her. Claire looked up at him and for a moment she stopped breathing. No man had ever looked at her as Trevelyan was now. In fact, she wondered if any man had ever looked at *any* woman as he was looking at her. His eyes, usually full of mocking laughter, were now full of . . . She wasn't sure what was in his eyes, but it wasn't laughter.

She stepped away from him. "I believe you're fascinated with the man, too, aren't you?" she said hastily. "That's why you take such offense when you think I'm criticizing him."

"What's that thing on the back of your skirt?" he asked, his voice low.

Claire gave a nervous little laugh. "It's a bustle. Where have you been that you don't know what a bustle is?"

"I've been out of the country for years."

"You must have been." She turned back to the shelves, took a few deep breaths and calmed her heart. "Here, I'll take this one. I've read it at least ten times."

He took the book from her and read the title, *The Search for Pesha,* then replaced it on the shelf. "If you've read it ten times then you must be bored with it."

"I'm not bored with it, I—"

He put his hand over hers and stopped her from taking the book down again. "I have something of his that you haven't read."

Claire snatched her hand away. "But there's nothing of his that I haven't—"

"It's a manuscript of his. Never been published."

Claire drew in her breath at that, then turned and smiled up at him. "Show me, please."

She has the most readable face in the world, Trevelyan thought. Everything she thought or felt showed on her face. And now her eagerness, her desire to know was infectious. He would like to teach her more than she could learn from books. Reluctantly, he moved away from her, went to a small chest against the wall, withdrew a handwritten manuscript, and handed it to her.

"The Scented Garden," Claire read. "Translated by Captain Frank Baker." She looked up at him and smiled her thanks as she held the thin manuscript to her bosom as though it were a precious and revered object.

Trevelyan frowned. She smiled at him in delight, as a child might smile at its father, and he fought to control himself. This young woman was his brother's. This was no woman of easy virtue who could be his for an afternoon. If he touched her there would be endless complications and repercussions. "Go sit over there and be quiet," he said sharply. "I have my own work to do."

She didn't say another word as she made her way to the window seat and climbed onto it. It took her a few minutes to figure out how to decipher Captain Baker's small, spiky handwriting, but it didn't take her ten minutes to realize what kind of book Trevelyan had given her. It was a translation of a treatise on lovemaking.

There was a chapter on the beauty of women and it included descriptions of *all* parts of a woman. The next chapter described men. There were chapters describing positions one took in lovemaking, and following were funny little stories about adultery and various other forms of promiscuity.

Claire read without so much as blinking. Somewhere around five, the tall dark man in white handed her a tray of fruit and some kind of bread and something in a tall metal goblet. She took the food, murmured, "Thanks," and didn't so much as look up from her reading.

At one point she laughed out loud.

Trevelyan startled her by asking what had made her laugh.

"Here," she said. "This sentence. It says that under all circumstances small women like . . ." She looked up at him. "You know, better than large women. It says small women are better at . . . it, you know, making love, than large women."

He looked at her five-foot-tall frame, her knees up, the manuscript balanced on them, her nose close to the pages, and smiled at her in an inviting way.

Claire locked eyes with him for a moment. There were many images running through her head of couples locked in embrace. She shook her head as though to clear it, then started reading again. She read several stories that told of the treachery of women. Those stories made her frown. She looked through the rest of the small book but could find no corresponding chapters on the treachery of men.

At one point, she gave out a loud "ha!"

Trevelyan looked up at her askance.

"It says that men and women can't be friends, that it's an impossibility. I don't believe that and I don't think Captain Baker did either. He—"

"It's a translation, not his own words. You should have known that by the fact that there's not a dimension in it. Not one wagon wheel."

She ignored him as she continued reading. The tall man handed her a tiny glass full of liquid. She drank of it, then gasped.

"Slowly," Trevelyan said.

"I don't think I should drink whisky."

"Nor should you read what you're reading."

She smiled at him, for he was right. She gave a little shrug, began to sip the whisky, and continued reading. The whisky made her warm and the contents of the book made her even warmer.

At last she finished the book, shut it, and turned to look out the window.

"Well?" Trevelyan asked. "Is it worthy of Captain Baker?"

Slowly, she turned to look at him. Her head was full of what she'd read, things she'd never dreamed of before. She looked at Trevelyan, with his dark eyes, his broad shoulders. She looked at his hands, at his long fingers. "I—" she began, then had to clear her throat. "Of course it should be only privately published," she said in a businesslike way. "But I think it could make money."

Trevelyan smiled at her in a patronizing way. "And what do you know of earning money?"

Claire returned his patronizing smile. Maybe it was the light, but right now he didn't look as old as she'd thought he was. "Unlike the British way of inheriting money, we Americans earn ours. In America a man—or a woman—can start out with nothing and earn millions. It merely takes hard work and foresight."

"Yet you're going to marry money when you marry your young duke."

"You must not know much about the family or you'd know that Harry doesn't have a dime." She turned and put her feet on the floor. "I thank you so much, Mr. Trevelyan, for lending me this manuscript. It was most interesting. But now I must go. It must be getting late and I . . ." She broke off as she looked at her watch. "It's nearly seven o'clock. I'll miss dinner if I don't hurry." She put the manuscript on the nearest table, called, "Thanks," one more time, then ran from the room.

As soon as she left, Oman entered the room and picked up Claire's empty dishes. Trevelyan looked at her empty whisky glass and at the manuscript she'd been reading. "She likes whisky and books about sex," he said softly, smiling to himself.

"She is a beauty," Oman said in his own language, a language that Trevelyan had spent some time learning.

"She belongs to my brother," Trevelyan said as he turned away. "She belongs to his world, not to mine."

Chapter Five

After a long, tedious dinner, Harry asked Claire to walk in the garden with him. She was very pleased, for all through dinner she'd thought about her day—and the man she had spent the day with. He was such an odd man, like no one she'd ever met before—and he caused such a range of emotions in her! One minute she hated him, the next minute she was looking at . . . at his hands.

"You looked particularly fetching this evening," Harry said. "You looked as though you were in a dream world. What gave you that look?"

"Nothing special," she said, lying. "I was thinking about something I read today." She was glad that, in spite of the cold temperatures within the large drafty rooms, she'd worn one of her more daring Worth gowns. It was low on her shoulders and left her arms bare—frozen but bare. If the gown earned her a compliment from Harry it was worth a few chill bumps.

"So they finally allowed you in the library?"

She stopped walking and looked up at him. "How do you know about that?"

He just smiled at her, tucked her hand over his arm, and started walking again.

"Harry, do you think men and women can be friends?" she asked.

"Yes," he said tentatively.

She looked back up at him. "Are *we* friends? I mean, can you and I talk to each other about things?"

"What is it you're trying to say?" he asked cautiously.

She took a deep breath. "When I'm the duchess, may I change the rules? May I allow people to eat in their rooms and visit the kitchens if they want? May I allow talking at meals?"

Harry laughed, but in a guarded way. "Of course. When you're the duchess you may do whatever you like. It will be your house."

"May I rebuild the west wing?"

Harry was silent for a moment. "What do you know of the west wing?" When she lowered her chin and didn't answer, he stopped, put his fingertips under her chin, and lifted her face to look at him. "Have you seen Trevelyan again?"

He smiled at her look of astonishment. "I told you that I know what goes on. You mustn't tell anyone about Trevelyan. No one but the two of us is to know he's here," he said firmly.

"Why?"

"He has his reasons. Did you spend the afternoon with him, is that why you missed both luncheon and tea?"

"I was reading in his room." Her eyes brightened. "In the prince's room."

"Do you like Trevelyan?"

"I don't know," she said honestly. "He's an odd duck, isn't he?"

Harry laughed at that. "More odd than you can imagine. Trevelyan didn't touch you, did he?"

Claire looked horrified. "Not in the way you mean. He was a perfect gentleman. Well, not perfect. He makes me very angry sometimes, but he has some interesting books."

"I imagine he does," Harry said sarcastically, frowning into the darkness. He was in a dilemma. He couldn't very well forbid Claire to see Trevelyan. She'd want to know why, and if Harry didn't give her an answer, Trevelyan might. Harry wouldn't put it past his brother to say, "My little brother is afraid you'll find out he isn't a duke." Harry stopped and turned back toward the house. "We have to go in. I have to leave early tomorrow and I won't be back for a couple of days."

"Oh Harry, couldn't we spend a day together? Couldn't you take even one day off from your work? Maybe I could go with you."

"Not this time. This time I leave very early in the morning, long before you wake up." He touched the tip of his finger to her nose. "But maybe the next time you can go with me. And I promise that after I return we'll spend some time together." As Harry said these words, he frowned. He thought he'd finished with courting, but now, thanks to Trevelyan, he saw he was going to have to do more. He smiled down at her. "How about a kiss?" He leaned forward to press his lips to hers but, instead, Claire exuberantly flung her arms around his neck and pressed her closed lips against his. He found her kiss very unsatisfactory; he didn't like virgins and had no desire to teach one what to do. He liked women who could teach him.

When Harry pulled her away from him, she still had her eyes closed and her lips puckered. He was frowning. "I'm almost afraid to allow you out of my sight. I think I should talk to Mother about setting a wedding date."

Claire smiled at him, but she remembered the book she'd read, and all the stories of never-ending passion. Where was the passion between her and Harry? The bells and sirens? But perhaps one needed to know *how* to kiss before one felt passion.

She lowered her arms from Harry's neck and sedately tucked her hand under his arm as they walked back to the house.

When Claire awoke the next morning, it was four o'clock and she wondered if Harry had already left on his journey. Quietly, so as not to disturb Miss Rogers, who slept in the dressing room, she got out of bed and went to the window. It was still dark outside and she could see little. For a moment, she put her elbows on the sill and looked out toward the lake in the distance. As she looked she thought she saw a shadow moving. Maybe it was a deer, she thought, but then she saw it was a man.

"Trevelyan," she said, knowing that it could only be him. She dressed in her walking clothes as quickly and as quietly as she could. Even as she dressed, she told herself she shouldn't run after the man, any man for that matter, but Trevelyan especially. But then she thought of spending the day alone and her fear of loneliness won over common sense. Besides, it wasn't as though Harry didn't know she was spending time with Trevelyan. He knew and he hadn't objected. Pinning her hat on as she left the room, she fled down the stairs. Once outside, she ran around the house and started her search for Trevelyan.

After twenty minutes she was beginning to despair. He was nowhere to be seen. She couldn't call for him, because someone might hear.

She turned around, intending to go back to the house, then nearly jumped out of her skin when she saw him standing utterly still not eight inches away. "You gave me the fright of my life," she snapped. "What are you doing skulking about in the bushes?"

"I had the idea you were looking for me," he said, one eyebrow lifted. "Excuse my presumption." He started to walk away.

Claire was sure he knew she was looking for him, but she tried to keep up the pretense that she hadn't been. "I was merely out for a stroll. Such a lovely morning," she said, looking at the still-dark sky. "I find the cool air so invigorating."

"Good morning, then," Trevelyan said and turned away from her.

Claire cursed under her breath. The infuriating man wasn't going to invite her inside. "In a way I *was* looking for you."

He turned back to her. "Oh? And what did you want of me? More books? Did you think of a new complaint about Captain Baker?"

"I saw you from my window and I thought perhaps I might walk with you. I thought you might like a companion. I know you're here in secret so I thought you might like some company. I was only trying to do my duty as the future duchess. I mean, it will someday be my responsibility to see that all my guests are taken care of and—"

"If I were to stand here for the next six hours, would you continue to make excuses?"

At that she turned on her heel and started back toward the house.

"All right, come on," he said to her back. "That is, if you can walk. I take no ladylike excursions."

She turned back and looked him up and down, noting his broad-shouldered frame that had no excess fat on it, the cane that he carried and the obvious difficulty he had with his legs. "I can certainly go wherever *you* can go."

"We shall see about that."

An hour later Claire was almost ready to regret her bragging—almost but not quite. Trevelyan led her up steep, heather-covered hills and across streams. The first time they came to a stream, with its cold, rushing water, she stood where she was and waited for him to help her across. He kept going, not so much as looking back at her. "Wait!" she called.

He turned back. "What's wrong?"

"How do I get across this?"

"Walk." He turned away and started up the hill.

Claire had no desire to soak her feet so she looked for some stepping stones or something else she could walk across.

"If you're afraid, try that." He had stopped at the top of the hill and was now pointing toward a log that had fallen from one bank to the other. The log was no more than four inches wide.

"I can't walk that."

Trevelyan shrugged and turned away. "Wait!" she called again. "Let me borrow your cane."

Trevelyan looked from her to his cane, then smiled. Something seemed to amuse him. He walked to the center of the cold stream and held it out to her.

"You could give me a piggyback ride, you know."

"Whatever that is," Trevelyan said.

Claire took the cane, then nearly fell into the water from the unexpected weight of the staff. She hadn't looked at the cane before, assuming it to be wooden, but now she saw that it was iron and weighed about twenty pounds.

She refused to let him see her surprise, but she was also determined that she was going to cross that stream on that very narrow log. She did it. She almost fell twice, and once she cursed him under her breath for not helping her, but she made it to the other side. Smugly, she handed him back his cane.

"A Scots lass wouldn't have worried about getting her feet wet," was all he said.

Claire stuck her tongue out at the back of him.

They walked for another hour, and at the second stream, Claire didn't bother with trying to keep her feet dry: she plowed through the cold stream as though it weren't there.

"Why aren't you walking with your duke?" Trevelyan asked her at one point.

"Harry had to go away on business. He left early this morning."

"And where was he off to?"

"I told you, on business. It takes a lot of work to run this place."

This seemed to amuse Trevelyan to no end. "More likely he's off to visit one of his mistresses."

"I beg your pardon."

"Maybe Harry should beg yours."

She didn't talk to him anymore after that, but she wondered if

Harry did have other women. The women in London had certainly liked him well enough. But that didn't mean he was still seeing them. She gave the back of Trevelyan a hard look and vowed she wasn't going to spend any more time with him. He put bad thoughts into her head.

But thirty minutes later it was nearly full light and they had reached the west wing of the house. Claire thought of the long day before her. There wouldn't even be a possibility of seeing Harry. She could always find her mother and spend the afternoon with her. Or she could introduce herself to the other people in the household and . . . And what? Talk of dogs and horses?

She stood by the door that led into the west wing and looked at her watch.

"Miss breakfast again?" Trevelyan asked, his hand on the door.

"No. I still have plenty of time to dress yet." She made no motion to move toward the front door of the house.

"They still have that no talking rule at breakfast?"

"Yes," Claire said glumly, thinking of the long, boring meal awaiting her.

Trevelyan sighed. "All right then, come upstairs and we'll see what Oman can cook for us."

Claire's smile was radiant. She forgot all about her intention of never seeing this man again. Now all she could think of was his cozy room and his books and the fire and the delicious food.

They entered the old part of the house and had reached the sitting room when Oman came from the bedroom and said something in another language to Trevelyan.

Trevelyan turned to Claire and said in a low voice, "Harry's in there." He nodded toward the bedroom.

Claire smiled as she took a step toward the bedroom, but Trevelyan caught her arm.

"This might be personal," he whispered.

"I—" Claire began, but Trevelyan put his hand over her mouth.

"He may not be alone," Trevelyan said in a mysterious way.

Claire opened her eyes wide in disbelief, and Trevelyan removed his hand. He opened a big medieval chest behind her. "In here until I find out what he wants."

"I will not—" she began, but then Trevelyan picked her up by her arms, dropped her into the chest on top of some things that in other circumstances she'd have liked to examine, shut the lid, and sat on it, just as Harry entered the room.

"Where the devil have you been?" Harry asked. "I've been waiting here for half an hour. And whose voice was that I heard? It sounded like a woman's."

"It must have been your imagination. To what do I owe the honor of your visit?"

"MacTarvit's at it again."

"How many this time?"

"Six."

"And your mother's on a rampage? I doubt that she can bear to part with six cows."

"She wants me to put him off the land."

Trevelyan was silent for a moment. "And you thought I might do your dirty work for you."

"Vellie, you were always so good at talking. I thought you might talk to the old man."

"Nobody can talk to him. No one ever could. What about his sons?"

"They're either dead or emigrated. The old man's the last one left."

"And now she wants him off the land. Why not just give him money and send him off to join his sons?"

"He'd never go, and besides, where would I get the money? Sell another picture?"

"What about your little heiress?"

Until that moment Claire had been silent inside the chest, listening to every word and trying to figure out what they were talking about. The name MacTarvit meant something to her but she couldn't remember what. When she heard Trevelyan begin to ask about her in his snide, insinuating way, she didn't want to hear what Harry had to say. She was a little afraid of what she'd hear, and she realized that it was Trevelyan who had put doubt in her mind. She pushed up on the lid of the chest with her feet.

"What the hell do you have in there?" Harry asked when he saw the chest lid move and almost dislodge Trevelyan.

"I'll show you if you want to see."

"No, thanks. I've seen enough of what you bring back from your trips." He didn't say anything for a few minutes as Oman came into the room and placed two glasses of whisky on a table by Trevelyan. When he was gone, Harry spoke again as Trevelyan handed him a glass. "Aren't you afraid that man will slit your throat at night?"

"Oman? Those people living in your house scare me a lot more than Oman does. Speaking of terror, when's your marriage?"

"Later," Harry answered vaguely.

"And is your little heiress happy living under the old hag's rule?" Trevelyan said with great sarcasm.

"Mother's not so bad. You've never given her a chance. As for Claire, I believe she's adjusting." Harry finished his whisky and stood up. "I have to go."

"Off to visit some exotic creature?"

Again Claire pushed up on the lid, but this time Harry ignored the movement. "Actually, I'm going south to look at a mare for her."

"Her? Your little heiress?"

"Exactly."

"Buying gifts for her, are you? It must be true love," Trevelyan said snidely.

Inside the chest, Claire held her breath.

"I like her well enough. Her head is a bit too full of dates and history and the romance of the world, but she's all right." Harry's voice changed from its usual easygoing tone to one of warning. "Keep your hands off her."

"What would a man my age do with her if I did touch her?" Trevelyan said with great sarcasm.

"You heard me," Harry said. "Hands off."

"Tell me, is it her money or the girl you like?"

Claire, who couldn't see the faces of the men, thought Harry took a very long time before he answered. And when he did respond, all he did was laugh, but Claire couldn't tell what the laugh meant, whether Harry was saying he liked her a great deal or he only wanted her money.

Chapter Six

"Well?" Claire said as she stepped out of the chest. Trevelyan hadn't bothered to open the lid for her or to help her out when she opened it, but that wasn't what was on her mind. She was growing accustomed to his not helping her.

He was already at one of his tables and writing. She went to stand in front of him. "What are you going to do about this man?"

"Would you sit down? You're blocking the light."

She stepped to one side but continued to glare at him. "Harry has asked you for a favor and you must do something about it."

Trevelyan put down his pen and looked up at her. "Because you're willing to give the man your life doesn't mean I am. I have no intention of doing anything except what I'm doing. Do you want some breakfast?"

"Of course."

She followed him into the bedroom, where there were two plates of steaming eggs on a table. She guessed they ate in the bedroom because Oman could not fit so much as one more table into the sitting room. She took a bite of her eggs. "Who is this man MacTarvit?"

"Enjoying your food?"

"I've never had anything like it and it's delicious. Who is MacTarvit?"

"Curried eggs. From India."

She glared at him.

"He's some old man. His family's always lived on this land."

She looked down at her eggs. They really were quite delicious. "Why does the name sound so familiar to me?"

Trevelyan took a drink from his teacup—Claire didn't ask if it was tea or whisky—and mumbled, "Tradition."

"What?"

He narrowed his eyes. "I'd think that with your romantic knowledge of your precious duke's clan you'd know exactly who the MacTarvits are." At that he held up his cup in salute to her.

Claire put down her fork and looked at him in wonder. "The whisky makers," she said breathlessly.

He gave her a little smile to acknowledge that she was right.

Claire stood up and walked to the window. "All the great clans had other clans under them who were responsible for certain things. Some clans had families that were bards, men who wrote poetry for them and memorized the family's history. Other clans had pipers." She turned back to look at him. "But Harry's clan had the MacTarvits who made the whisky."

Again he raised his cup to her. "I congratulate you on your memory."

She sat back down and started on her eggs again. "And now this old man is the last one of his clan left in Scotland. The last of the great whisky makers. The—"

"Certainly not the last whisky maker in Scotland. Harry won't have to do without if MacTarvit goes."

"But what will MacTarvit do?"

"I don't think that concerns Harry's mother, the duchess. I think she cares about her cattle being stolen."

"But what about tradition!" Claire said with passion. "Haven't any of you read Sir Walter Scott?"

At that Trevelyan laughed. But it wasn't a pleasant laugh, it was full of cynicism. The laugh had the tone of a man who knows all, has seen all, and is amused by the ignorance and innocence of another.

"I don't care what you think of Sir Walter Scott, but it *is* tradition that the clans robbed one another. If this man has been making whisky for you for years I imagine he can afford to buy the cattle if he wanted to."

"The duchess doesn't pay him."

Claire could only gape at him.

"Her Grace doesn't believe in Scotch whisky, thinks it's nasty stuff and unhealthy, the peat, you know, so she doesn't pay him. She doesn't order it from him, so what comes into the house she feels deserves no payment. Besides, she has always hated the man and wants him off her land."

"It's Harry's land."

Trevelyan gave her a nasty little smile. "If you think that you don't know anything at all."

Claire had finished her eggs and again got up and walked toward the bed, running her hand over the post at the foot of the bed. Here was a bed that Bonnie Prince Charlie had slept in, and they had been talking about a man of a clan that had been whisky makers to their clan for generations, yet they acted as though whether he stayed or not meant nothing.

She turned back to Trevelyan. "You have to do something."

"Why do *I* have to do something? Why not your precious Harry?"

"This is no time for argument. We have to do something to keep this man on the land. You can't dismiss a man who has been loyal for generations. What would your ancestors say?"

"My ancestors would probably say, 'Good riddance.' For all that you seem to have formed the opinion that this is a sweet old man who is being persecuted by my family, the truth is that the MacTarvits have always been the most cantankerous, stubborn, disagreeable men in the world. They make the whisky but they don't sell it, we have to take it from them. We have to *steal* it."

"Just as he has to steal food from you."

Trevelyan stood. "You can stop looking at me like that. I'm not walking all the way to that old man's house just to be shot at. I have work of my own to do and I don't need MacTarvit's ill temper to deal with."

She followed him into the sitting room. "You invented ill temper! The two of you should get along very well."

"We don't. *No one* gets along with any of the MacTarvits. No one ever has. Heaven help the country the old man's sons went to."

"Probably America. America appreciates *men.*"

Trevelyan threw up his hands in exasperation. "I'm not going to go to MacTarvit, either for you or your dear duke, and that settles it. Now why don't you sit over there and read like a good little girl? Oman will fix you something nice for lunch and I'll give you a big glass of whisky."

"MacTarvit whisky?" she said through clenched teeth.

"As a matter of fact, yes. Shall I show you the wound on my leg where one of his bullets grazed me?"

"You mean you stole *this* whisky from him?"

"Of course I did. It's the only way to get any out of him. It's your bloody tradition, remember?"

"You don't have to shout at me. I can hear you perfectly well. If you won't go to him, then I will."

Trevelyan snorted. "You could never find the place. Only Harry and I know where the old man lives."

"And you won't go to him? You're going to do nothing to stop the duchess from sending him away from here?"

"It is not any of my business. I'm a visitor here, remember? I just want to get well, write a bit, then leave. This place is nothing to me."

She looked at him for a long while. "After all Harry has done for you, allowing you to stay here and not telling anyone you're here. You, sir, are an ingrate." With that she turned toward the stairs.

"Where are you going?"

"To spend the day with other people. If you want your privacy so much you may have it. I won't bother you again." As she started down the stairs, she heard him say, "Now I'll get some work done." Claire kept her head up and went down the stairs and out the door into the garden.

She wandered in the garden for a while but very soon it began to bore her. Yesterday had been so lovely when she'd had something to read and someone to talk to. Now she was alone again.

She sat down on a bench and looked out over the little lake that some ancestor of Harry's had created a hundred or so years ago. So far she didn't feel she was doing a very good job of learning how to be a duchess. She wished she could be more like her mother, gregarious and social, never meeting a stranger, but, unfortunately, she wasn't. She'd far rather know one or two people well than know a hundred people only slightly.

"There you are."

Claire looked up to see her brat of a sister. "Those are my earrings," Claire said without much concern, then looked back at the lake.

"What's wrong with you? Missing your lover man?"

"Where do you pick up these disgusting expressions? And why aren't you having lessons?" Sarah Ann started to open her mouth but

Claire put up her hand. "Please don't tell me what you've done to your poor governess. I wonder, have you learned enough to read and write?"

"As well as Mother can."

Claire gave her sister a hard look, but Brat just smiled at her.

"People are beginning to wonder what you do all day."

"Oh, nothing much," Claire said. "I walk a great deal."

"And don't eat at all. At least not at the table with the others." Brat leaned forward. "You have some food caught between your front teeth."

Claire turned away and cleared her teeth with her nail. "Don't you have something to do besides bother me? Such as putting my earrings back where they belong?"

"I can't take them off until my ears heal."

Claire shook her head. "You are much too young to have your ears pierced, and who in the world pierced them for you?"

At that Sarah Ann looked off into the distance. "A person can have anything in the world done in this house."

"What does that mean?"

Brat looked at her sister and there was wonder in her eyes. "Claire, this is the oddest place in the world and the queerest people live here. You know that skinny little man with the long hair who sits across from you at dinner?"

"How do you know where I sit at dinner?"

"I know a great deal. Anyway, that man lives at the far end of the east wing and he puts on plays. He's the only actor and there's no one in the audience. What's really odd is that he'll deliver a line, then change costumes, deliver another line, change clothes, et cetera, and it takes him at least twenty minutes to change into each different outfit. The plays go on for hours. He said that if I'd applaud his every line he'd let me be in a play, but we had a terrible fight when I wanted to be Elizabeth the First."

"No doubt you won."

"I did. He wanted me to shave my head and wear a red wig, but I refused. And you know those two little old ladies who sit near Father? They're thieves. Honest. They steal from everybody's rooms. At dinner, you watch, and at the end of the meal there won't be a piece of silverware left by their plates. They stick them up their sleeves."

"Must make for messy sleeves."

"The butler has to get the silverware from their rooms once a week, unless there're more people for dinner and they need it sooner."

"What about Mother?"

"She spends every afternoon with two old biddies who know everything about everyone. They tell Mother all the gossip about the dukes and earls and viscounts and—what's the other one?"

"Marquises."

"Right. All of them. You should *hear* what they tell about the Prince of Wales."

"*You* should *not* hear. Have you been listening at doors again?"

"If you're mean I won't tell you what I know about Harry's mother."

Claire tried to pretend to be uninterested. "You mean Her Grace?"

"There's a price."

Claire started to leave.

"All right. I'll tell you. The old woman hates all her kids except Harry. He's her baby and she worships him. I heard she was glad when her two older sons died and Harry became the duke."

"What a dreadful thing to say!"

"I'm repeating it, not saying it. Did you know she has a crushed leg? She can walk but not very well and there's a rumor she was leaving her husband when her carriage overturned and crushed her leg. Harry was born six months later. They say Harry worships his mother, that he'll do *anything* she wants." Brat gave her sister a sly look. "He'll even marry whoever his mother chooses."

Claire smiled coldly at her sister. "What a very interesting household. I should make an effort to meet these people. I don't want them thinking my continued absences are out of the ordinary."

"In this family, you could eat live chickens for dinner and they wouldn't consider you odd." Brat stood up. "I have to go now. This afternoon I get to be someone called Marie Antoinette."

"Be careful. She was beheaded."

Sarah Ann looked serious. "I'll remember that."

As she started running down the path, Claire called out after her, "And stay out of my jewels."

Brat waved as she kept running.

Claire went back to the house, dressed for luncheon, and sat through that long meal, trying not to watch the two old ladies as they slipped silverware up their sleeves. She asked the long-haired man across from her about his plays and he eagerly invited her to participate in one. He said that she could be Anne Boleyn or Catherine Howard—both of whom had been beheaded by Henry VIII. Claire smiled politely and declined.

After luncheon she went to the gold drawing room and took a seat next to her mother. The three other women in the room kept giving her significant looks that she was sure were meant to make her leave the room, but Claire ignored them.

"Claire, dear, could you fetch my shawl? I find I am frightfully cold," her mother said.

With a sigh, Claire went to her mother's room, found a shawl, and took it to her. Later her mother wanted a lap robe, so Claire took the hint and left the ladies to their private talks.

"I'm to be the duchess and no one wants anything to do with me," she said under her breath.

She wandered about the center section of the house aimlessly for an hour or so, then thought that if all the people were in the drawing rooms, the east wing had to be more or less vacant, so she decided to go look at it.

For the most part, it was a long hallway of closed doors. There were many portraits on the walls of men and women who must have been Harry's ancestors, although none of them seemed to have his blond good looks. For the most part they had dark hair and eyes.

At the end of the corridor of the east wing she came to a half-open door. Tentatively, she pushed it open, and saw a delightful room done in blue silk, with a rug of peach and blue on the floor. The light streamed through the windows and fell across—wonder of wonders—books! As though a magnet were pulling her, she went to the shelves and began to read the titles. She pulled down Sir Walter Scott's *Waverley.* When she turned, the book in her hand, she gasped, for sitting silently in a chair, looking at her, was the woman she saw at meals, the one who sometimes smiled at her.

"I'm sorry. I didn't know anyone was in here. I'll leave if I'm disturbing you."

"No," the woman said softly, and Claire guessed that she was quite shy. "Please stay."

Claire took a seat. "This is a lovely room."

"Yes."

"Do you come here often?"

"Most of the time."

Claire realized she wasn't going to get much conversation out of the woman so she opened her book, but a few times she caught the woman staring at her. Claire guessed the woman to be in her thirties, yet she was dressed as though she were a schoolgirl, in a pink dress all of ruffles. The dress made her look older than she really was, and her hair was hanging down her back, just as Brat's was, except that Brat was fourteen years old. Mentally, Claire began to re-dress the woman, to pull her hair back, give her pearl earrings and a plain dress of sleek lines that would show off what looked to be an excellent figure.

Claire moved uncomfortably when the woman caught her staring. "Perhaps we should introduce ourselves. I'm Claire Willoughby and I'm engaged to the duke."

"Yes, I know. We all know who you are."

She said it quite kindly, but the words exasperated Claire. "Everyone seems to know all there is to know about me, but I know nothing about anyone else." She could feel her frustration building. "I've tried to introduce myself but the men won't speak to me and neither will most of the women. My sister knows more about the house than I do and yet the house is to be mine someday. I can't figure out who anyone is and Harry doesn't seem to know either. It's all quite frustrating."

The woman smiled at that and Claire thought she could be quite pretty with a little work. "I'm Harry's sister, Leatrice."

Claire's shock showed. "His sister? I had no idea he had a sister. Oh, forgive me for not introducing myself. I—"

"It's all right. It's easy to overlook someone in this house. I—"

She broke off because at that moment a bell over the door jangled. Immediately, Leatrice's face lost all its pleasure and warmth. "Excuse me, I must go. Mother wants me."

Before Claire could even open her mouth, Leatrice was gone from the room. Claire wasn't sure she should stay in the room she now realized was Leatrice's private sitting room, but the attraction of the books was too strong to resist. She settled in a comfortable chair, her feet tucked under her, and began to reread *Waverley*.

At five a gong sounded downstairs and she went down to tea, the men in one room and the women in another. She managed to get a seat next to Leatrice and tried to engage her in conversation.

"Is your mother very ill?" Claire asked.

At Claire's remark, all conversation stopped and all eyes turned toward Leatrice, whose face turned red. A moment later she picked up her teacup; it clattered against the saucer and, in embarrassment, Leatrice put cup and saucer on the table and fled the room.

Arva looked at her daughter in reproach and Claire wondered what she had done that was so wrong.

After tea Claire went to her bedroom to sit and stare out the window. Brat had said the household was odd, but odd did not begin to describe the place. With longing she thought of her home in New York, where she could walk to the park, where she could visit people and places. She thought of her friends who used to come to her house and how they'd talk together throughout the afternoon. And she thought of her family's servants, servants who were there to do whatever she asked. Up until she came to Bramley she'd not thought much about food. If she were reading and she wanted something to eat, she merely rang a bell and food would be brought to her.

Now she was in this enormous house, surrounded by people, and for the first time in her life she was lonely.

Miss Rogers chose the dress Claire was to wear to dinner and Claire didn't protest. Miss Rogers was still sniffing because Claire had worn the off-the-shoulder dress the night before.

Dinner was long and boring and Claire didn't try to participate in the conversation. She missed Harry and she missed . . . No, she didn't miss anyone else. She didn't miss Trevelyan, who was bad-tempered and contrary and difficult to be around. She thought of Harry and hoped he'd return soon. He'd have the mare he was buying her and her arm would be well by then and they could go riding together. When Harry returned, everything would be all right. And after they were married and she could change the rules of the house, things would improve.

After dinner, instead of going straight to bed, knowing that Miss Rogers would be waiting for her with her usual frowns and complaints, Claire went outside to the gardens. It was cold but she was wearing a wool dress, so she thought that if she walked quickly, she'd keep warm.

It was in the topiary garden, with its hedges trimmed in the shape of animals, that Trevelyan stepped out from behind a bush. She put her hand to her throat for a moment. "Good evening, sir," she said, then stepped around him and started back toward the house.

"Not speaking to me, are you?"

"I have nothing to say to you." She kept walking and he began to walk beside her.

"Did you get all your meals today?"

"Every one."

"And you had an interesting day, lots of intelligent conversation? Did you talk of politics or maybe have some enlightening talks about your Bonnie Prince Charlie?"

"It's cold out here and I'm going inside."

"I see. They ignored you again."

She turned on him. "No one ignored me. I met some very interesting people. I met a playwright who's writing a part in his next play just for me. I had a discussion about the Prince of Wales and I met Harry's sister. We spent some lovely time together."

At that speech Trevelyan began to laugh.

Claire couldn't help herself but she laughed also. How utterly heavenly it felt to laugh! How wonderful to be able to say something and have someone understand. "It's really quite an extraordinary group of people who live in that house. Leatrice has a bell in her sitting room and when her mother rings, she has to run. I wonder if she's allowed to leave the room except for meals."

"She isn't."

"How awful. And she dresses like a child. I wonder how old she is."

"Thirty-one."

"Is that all? She looks older. She—" She stopped as she saw Trevelyan sway on his feet. "You're ill again." She took his arm and led him down a path to a bench. By now she knew the garden rather well.

When he was seated, she sat beside him and he leaned a bit against her.

She wanted to put her arm around him, but she didn't. If she thought the other people in the house were odd, Trevelyan was by far the oddest. One moment he seemed like a scholar, the next he acted like a criminal. He hid from everyone at the top of a tower, acting as though he wanted only to be alone. Yet . . . Yet every time Claire left the main house, he came to her. He covered his seeking her out—for that's what she was beginning to see it as—with snide and cynical remarks, but the facts were still the same: he was as much in need of companionship as she was.

She could feel his body relaxing against hers. She had at times felt . . . well, attracted to him. He had looked at her with eyes that bored into her and made her know she should get away from him. But right now she felt almost motherly toward him. She wanted to pull him into her arms and feel his forehead for fever. She wanted to tuck him into bed and feed him warm soup. Instinctively, she knew he'd hate that, so she sat up straight and pretended she didn't realize how weak he was feeling.

"About this morning," she began slowly. "I had no right to get angry at you. You have to do what you think is right, just as the rest of us do." She sighed. "I do wish this man MacTarvit could stay on the land until Harry and I are married, though. Then I shall see that he comes to no harm."

"You're planning to try to usurp Her Grace?" Trevelyan's voice, usually so strong, so full of confidence, was weaker now.

"Of course. Harry says that when I'm the duchess I shall be able to do whatever I want."

Trevelyan laughed at that. "The old woman would die before she gave up her power."

"That's not what Harry says."

"And Harry knows everything, does he?"

He had an unequaled ability to enrage her. She forgot her motherly feelings and stood up, looking down at him. "I hope, sir, that you recover your strength and can make it back to your quarters on your own. I wish you long life and happiness. Now good night." She turned away and hurried back to the house.

Chapter Seven

"You are disturbed," Oman said as he cleared the dishes from the table.

"Women," Trevelyan muttered.

Oman smiled. "This one is different, is she not?"

Trevelyan drew on his pipe. "This one is different. This one is fire and ice. This one is woman and child. This one knows a great deal, yet is the personification of innocence."

He leaned back in his chair and blew smoke rings into the air. "This one could be trouble," he said aloud. Since he'd met her, he'd been unsettled. One minute he wanted to take her to bed and the next he wanted to read something he'd written to her. Tonight he'd felt her tenderness and he'd been surprised by it. Women who were as full of passion as she was weren't usually the type to pay attention to a man when he was ill. Yet she had. She could be motherly as well as passionate—when he thought of the way she'd looked at his hands that day she'd read his translation, sweat began to form on his forehead. He had very much wanted to show her what he could do with his hands.

MacTarvit, he thought. She wants to meet old MacTarvit, wants *me* to keep the old man from stealing cattle. How is it any of my business? Trevelyan thought. What do I care about her bloody tradition?

He blew more smoke rings and smiled. She'd been quite pretty when she was raging at him about old man MacTarvit. Her hair, her eyes, that splendid bosom of hers. "Harry doesn't appreciate her," he said aloud. Harry doesn't know she has a mind, he thought. Harry didn't even know how easily she could be aroused to that passion that was so close beneath the surface, but Harry wasn't interested enough to try to teach her anything. Harry had never wanted to be a teacher. If she were mine, Trevelyan thought, I would spend the time to teach her all that she could learn, and, if she were mine, I wouldn't leave her alone for days at a time. If she were mine I'd—

He broke off, frowning, then stood up. "I'm going to bed," he said and paid no attention to Oman's look of shock. Trevelyan never went to bed before the wee hours of the morning—he said he had too much to do in his life to lose time sleeping.

Trevelyan rose very early the next morning. Leaving his sitting room, he went up a flight of old stone stairs, opened an overhead door, and made his way up to the lead roof. He walked across the edge of the roof, noting that what Harry had said about the roof being in bad shape was true. When he came to another door in the roof, he opened it and went down a narrow, dirty staircase. It was obvious that no one had used these stairs in many years, for he bent to pick up something and saw that it was a toy soldier. It was either Trevelyan's or his older brother's; Harry had not been allowed to play with his siblings.

Trevelyan went down two flights of stairs until he came to a small door and opened it. Just as he knew it would, it opened behind an enormous tapestry.

He made his way from behind the tapestry and into the darkened room and was startled to see a small, round, gray-haired lady standing there watching him. There was almost no light from either inside or outside the room so he had some difficulty making out who she was.

"Hello, Aunt May," he said, smiling. "Still can't sleep, I see."

She studied him for a moment. "You're Vellie, aren't you? You've grown into a man."

"No, Aunt May. Vellie died, remember?"

"Ah yes. So he did." She continued to study him. "Then who are you?"

"Vellie's ghost," he said and winked at her.

"As a ghost you should have a great deal of company in this house," she said and walked out of the room.

"Nothing's changed at all," Trevelyan muttered as he went out another door of the room and made his way to a small sitting room, then found a door in the paneling.

When the house had been a castle there had been several entrances and exits that were secret—so the family would have a way of escaping should there be danger. As later generations added on to the house they continued to make secret passages and staircases and concealed doors. In the eighteenth century an ancestor of Trevelyan's had enclosed the whole structure in a modern, beautiful shell but he had not bothered to change the interior, or, if Trevelyan knew his family, they hadn't had enough money to do a proper job. As a result, the entire house was riddled with secret tunnels and passageways. Trevelyan and his older brother, and sometimes Leatrice, had explored these passages thoroughly.

He lit a candle and made his way up one stair, opened a door quietly, and entered the room that had once been his father's. It was as he thought: no one was staying in the room. He went to the chest that was against one wall and opened it. His hand trembled a bit as he opened the chest, for he could feel his father's presence all about him. It was as though the man might enter the room at any moment.

What would Trevelyan say to the man if he did enter? Would he be glad to see his father, or would he spit on the ground at his feet? Trevelyan honestly didn't know.

It didn't take Trevelyan long to find what he wanted. He pulled out the tartan that was the laird's plaid. It was a deep, rich blue, with a bit of red and some green in it. He smiled as he thought of Miss Claire Willoughby. Let's see if she can identify this tartan, he thought. Trevelyan didn't think the pattern was in any book, for this was the tartan for the laird of Clan Montgomery, and only the laird had the right to wear it.

He removed his clothes down to his smalls, leaving his shirt on, spread the yards of cloth on the floor, then tried to do what he had so often seen his father do: roll himself in the thing. When his father had done it, it had looked easy, but Trevelyan found it was more difficult than he had imagined it would be. Within minutes he was cursing all things Scottish.

"Never wear the small kilt," Trevelyan could hear his father telling his oldest son as Trevelyan used to stand in the doorway watching. "A laird has a responsibility. If the lairds don't carry on the tradition then no one will."

So now Trevelyan was doing his best to wrap himself into the plaid as he'd seen his father do. If one had to wear a damned skirt then why couldn't it be an easy one like Harry wore? He smiled at the answer: he was trying to impress a girl and he knew she would be much more impressed with the long kilt than the short one.

At last he got the fabric rolled about his waist and belted into place. He slung the end over his shoulder and pinned it with his father's brooch. He hung the sporran about his waist, put on the heavy socks, then the shoes with the holes in them, holes that allowed the water of the eternally wet Scottish land to flow out.

When he was done, he looked at himself in his father's mirror, and for a moment, he could almost see his father standing in front of this mirror wearing this same tartan. His eldest son would be in front of him and Trevelyan would be in the back, watching the two of them.

Now Trevelyan turned away and slipped out the door he'd entered. He went up a flight of stairs, across a landing, then had to crouch as he walked through a short tunnel. He wasn't sure which room was Claire's but he had a good idea. His mother was not a woman of great imagination and would therefore probably put her in the third-best guest room—which is what the old hag would no doubt think an American was: third best.

Slowly, so the unused door wouldn't creak, he opened it, and the big portrait of his great-great-aunt moved with the door.

By now there was a bit of light outside, so he went to the window and drew the curtain back. She was in bed, sleeping on her stomach like a child. He smiled down at her, for the bed was a mess. She had kicked the covers and twisted them until most of them were on the floor.

He looked down at her and marveled at her youth. She wasn't just young in age, but young in what she knew and had seen and what she believed of the world. He wondered if he had ever been as innocent as she was. He doubted it.

He sat down on the side of the bed and smoothed her hair out of her eyes. She stirred in her sleep but didn't awaken. The arm of her gown was pushed up to her elbow and he ran his hand down her smooth skin. For a moment it startled him at how much he wanted to run his hands over every inch of her skin.

Wanting to touch a pretty young thing like Claire wasn't what startled him, but that he wanted *her* did. He wanted her to look at him with her big blue eyes blazing with all the passion he'd seen when she'd talked of Bonnie Prince Charlie.

She moved, lifted her head a bit, and gave him a half smile. "Good morning," she murmured, then turned her head to the other side.

It was a moment before she turned back to gape at him.

"Good morning," he said brightly.

She sat up, pulled what cover she hadn't thrown to the floor to her throat. "What in the world are you doing in my room?" she whispered and glanced toward the open door to the dressing room.

He put his finger to his lips and stood.

Her eyes widened when she saw him standing. "Oh, Trevelyan," she said in a hoarse, sighing whisper. "It's the *philamohr,"* she said, giving the Scottish name to the great kilt.

He paused to smile at her, trying his best to not let her see how very, very pleased he was with her reaction. Getting into the contraption had been worth it if she knew what it was, and if she sighed over his name in that tone. He walked quietly to the dressing room and looked in to see Rogers lying prim and proper on her narrow bed. He gave a snort of derision, then shut the door.

"You didn't tell me you had Rogers for a maid."

Claire had to get control of herself, control over her feelings at the sight of Trevelyan in the ancient form of Scottish dress. To her surprise, his legs were not thin as she would have thought. His legs were muscled, as those of a man who has spent much of his life walking over rugged terrain. And he wore the plaid with the grace and ease of someone born to it, as though he had worn it since he was a child. Once again pipes began to play in her head, but they were the pipes of the ancient songs, not the new, modern music that she heard when she saw Harry. She was sure all this was because Trevelyan was older than Harry.

Claire shook her head to clear it. *"Miss* Rogers."

"Monster, isn't she? When we were kids we used to do all we could to terrorize her."

"You couldn't have succeeded." The skirt made by the draping of the plaid swirled about Trevelyan's legs when he walked.

"Not in the least." He leaned over her and Claire drew back from him, her breath held. He wouldn't try to kiss her, would he? But he didn't try to kiss her. He whispered, "Are you ready to go to MacTarvit's?"

As he moved away from her, she blinked at him for a moment, looked at his lips still so close to hers, then realized what he'd said. "Really? You'll take me?" she asked, sounding about ten years old.

"If you can get dressed in a hurry. I don't like to be kept waiting."

With that she almost knocked him down as she got out of bed and ran behind a screen. "My clothes!" she said in a stage whisper. "You'll have to hand them to me."

"You can come and get them," he said in a mock-seductive voice. "I assure you I won't ravage you."

Claire looked at him from around the screen, and put her hand over her mouth to stifle a giggle. "Of course you won't." He'd sounded like the villain in a melodrama and Claire knew how they ended: with the heroine unmarried yet with a baby she had to give away to strangers, then the heroine dying alone in a snowstorm. The Trevelyan who walked about the room in the ancient form of dress, the man who leaned over her and whispered to her, was a threat, but the man who leered at her from behind the screen was not a threat.

Still amused, wearing her long-sleeved, high-necked, voluminous nightgown, she left the screen to go to the wardrobe to get her wool walking suit and her lowest heeled, sturdiest walking shoes, then returned to behind the screen and dressed faster than she ever had in her life. She came out from behind the screen still fastening buttons down the front of her jacket.

"Ready?" Trevelyan asked, pleased that his teasing had amused her.

"No," she whispered back. "We have to adjust you." With that she set about adjusting the gathers that were made by his belt and settling them into neat little pleats. When she was done, she took her time smoothing the drape of wool over his shoulders. She didn't look into his eyes as she repinned the brooch.

Trevelyan held his breath while she touched him, wanting to touch her in return. He wondered what she'd do if he were to put his hands on her hips and run them down to her thighs. Probably run, he thought, or worse, laugh at him. What is someone your age doing thinking about things like that? he could hear her saying. He thought he might like to take her to bed and show her that even though he looked to be an old man, he was only thirty-three and not at death's door as she seemed to think.

"You're not supposed to wear that brooch, you know," she said softly. She didn't want to move away from him. Touching him, she knew he wasn't thin as she'd first thought. He wasn't thin; he wasn't fat.

"What?" he said, pretending he couldn't hear her so he had to lean closer to her lips.

"That's the laird's brooch and only Harry should wear it. See, it has the crest on it but no garter, or belt, surrounding it. The garter shows that you *belong* to Harry's clan. This brooch is the clan chief's." She put her fingers on the brooch.

"I'll have to remember that," he said, clasping her fingertips in his. He wondered what she'd say if he told her the truth, that he was actually the duke and the laird of his family's clan. Would she fall into his arms and tell him she was in love with him, that she'd thought she loved Harry but now knew that Trevelyan was the man she loved? Trevelyan had never had to resort to a title or anything else to get any woman he wanted, and he didn't plan to now.

"Ready?" he asked again and she pulled her hand from his grasp.

She started for the door, but he went to the floor-length portrait, picked up the candle, and nodded for her to follow him. He saw her face light up at the impending adventure. She certainly didn't seem to be cowardly.

Claire followed him down dirty, unused stairs, through cobweb-hung four-foot-high tunnels, up to the roof, across it, back into the house, and at last outside through a door at the end of the east wing.

"Wonderful," she said. "Just wonderful."

He smiled at her. "Feel like walking? It's a long way to MacTarvit's."

"I would love to walk," she said, breathing of the sweet Scottish air.

Two hours later she almost wished she hadn't been so confident. She had followed Trevelyan up and down ravines, across little streams, up one hill that should have been called a mountain, and over four logs that lay across streams too wide and deep to ford. Trevelyan had handed her a piece of dry, hard bread that he'd had in his sporran, and twice he'd lent her his heavy staff.

"Why do you carry a cane made out of iron? Wouldn't a wooden one do just as well?"

"I need to rebuild my strength," he said over his shoulder.

She wanted to ask him about his illness but she didn't, for she'd already learned that he didn't like any mention of it.

After they'd walked for three hours they sat down on a rock and Trevelyan pulled dates from his sporran, frowning at Claire when she began to hungrily devour hers. She managed to control herself enough to munch the fruit.

"Last night when I got back to my room there was a newspaper hidden under my pillow."

"And who do you suppose did that?" he asked.

"At first I thought it was you, but I didn't think there was any way you could get into my room without being seen." She smiled at him, then laughed at his smug expression. "Do you know who I think it was?" She paused. "Leatrice."

Trevelyan looked off at the hills, at the way the soft purple heather blended with the gray-green of the rocks and the grass. He remembered the laughing girl he'd known and the timid woman who now stayed in her room at the beck and call of her mother. "Lee would do that. There's a bit of a rebel inside her."

"That's hard to believe." She told him about somehow offending Leatrice at tea the day before. "All I did was ask how her mother was."

"It's forbidden to mention the old woman's injury. At least not out loud."

Claire ate the last of the dates he'd handed her and went to the stream to get a drink. "Why is the water brown?"

"It runs through peat," he said impatiently. "That's what makes the whisky taste so good. Good Scotch can't be made anywhere else in the world except Scotland because the peat-filled water is here. Are you ready to go?"

She nodded and began to follow him. "Anyway, I finally got to read a paper last night, and you'll never believe what I read."

"That the Campbells are rising again?"

"Don't be cynical. It doesn't become you, although I do think cynicism is natural to you. Were you born believing the world is a bad place or have you developed this attitude?"

He turned and narrowed his eyes at her.

Claire smiled sweetly at him. She was beginning to love being able to pierce his hard outer shell. "I read that Captain Baker's former partner, Jack Powell, is going to speak to the Royal Geographic Society about having entered Pesha."

"Is he?" Trevelyan said softly. "And do you plan to go hear him speak?"

"You are joking, aren't you? Personally, I don't believe that the man ever entered Pesha."

At that Trevelyan stopped walking and turned to look at her. "And how did you come to that conclusion?"

"Because I know Captain Baker."

He turned away so she couldn't see his smile. "Do you, now?"

"You can stop laughing at me. I'll never believe Captain Baker didn't make it into Pesha."

"We have another hour of walking. Why don't you tell me how you reached this conclusion? It might make the time pass faster and I could use a good laugh."

"I shouldn't tell you anything, not with your attitude, but I will. You have to understand what Pesha meant to Captain Baker. I know that to the rest of the world it's just a name of fable, a name that conjures exotic . . ." She trailed off.

He turned back to her, smiling in a smirking sort of way and started walking backward. "Exotic pleasures where a man's fantasies can come true? A city of riches beyond belief? A place where women are beautiful and plentiful and don't wear corsets and bustles that keep a man from feeling their flesh? A place—"

"Would you *mind?* As I was saying, Captain Baker wanted to see the place. He wanted to be the first man from the outside world to reach it and prove it existed, because there were rumors that it didn't exist, that it was merely a legend. Like Atlantis. He wanted so much to find the place that he spent three years of his life looking for it. I've read how when he returned from that first trip without having found it he was sick and dispirited, but he swore he'd return. He vowed he'd die if he didn't make it."

"He *did* die."

"But he didn't die until he had completed the second trip. He didn't die until he was at the dock ready to return home. *I* believe he made it into Pesha."

"Powell says he didn't. He says Baker was too sick to enter the city. Powell says Baker stayed in camp while he, Powell, went alone into the city."

"Ha!" Claire said. "You don't know Captain Baker as I do."

"Do you, now?"

"Don't laugh at me. Captain Baker was a very vain man."

Trevelyan looked surprised. "What has vanity to do with this?"

She sighed. "It has everything to do with this. Baker had the knowledge. After his first trip he'd learned a great deal. He'd found out that on his first trip he'd been hundreds of miles away from Pesha, so he returned to England to raise funds and write up his notes."

"What does this have to do with his vanity?"

"Think about it! After he had done all that work, do you think he would have turned over all he knew to another man?"

"If he were sick and he couldn't go he might have. Do you think the man had no generosity in his soul? Would he rather that no one go if he couldn't? Was he such a selfish man?"

"Not selfish. He was—"

"Vain. I heard you."

"What is *wrong* with you? I was merely telling you that I don't believe Captain Baker didn't see Pesha. I think this man Powell is a liar." She looked up at him with horror on her face. "You don't think Powell *murdered* Captain Baker and took his notes, do you?"

Trevelyan grimaced and turned back around. "Someday I shall have to visit America to see what atmosphere produces such lurid imagination in its inhabitants."

"It's not such a farfetched idea."

"What would Powell have to gain by stealing Baker's notes and lying to the world?"

She was astonished. "Prestige. Honor. Medals from your queen. A place in history. Possible immortality. Not to mention money."

"Isn't that a little exaggerated? Immortality?"

"It is not an exaggeration. The first man who enters Pesha and returns from it alive will be remembered forever." She clenched her hands into fists at her side. "*How* I wish I could have read Captain Baker's notes. He would tell *all* the story. This man Powell would never be able to tell all of it."

"Why not? If he's seen the place he should be able to tell what he's seen."

"But he *hasn't* seen Pesha. He *couldn't* have. No man alive could have entered that sacred city unless he looked, acted, and spoke like a Peshan. Only Captain Baker could have done that. Who is this man Powell but a mere man?"

"And Baker wasn't?"

"No. Captain Baker was a *great* man, and it would have taken a great man to get into Pesha. From what little I've read of Powell he speaks a mere five or six languages."

"The man is only semiliterate."

"Do you sneer at everything?"

"Yes," he answered honestly. "No doubt your Captain Baker sneered at nothing."

She thought about that a while. "I think Captain Baker was basically a cold man. That's what made him a great observer. He could watch unspeakable cruelty and report it. Most of the rest of us would be too sick or weeping too hard or trying too hard to change the behavior of savages to be able to sit back and observe without feeling. But Baker watched it all and never felt anything."

"I think perhaps he felt," Trevelyan said softly.

"No, Captain Baker was a great man and he deserves to live in history but I doubt very much if he had any heart at all." She put her head up. "Look! There's smoke. Is that MacTarvit's house?"

"Yes," Trevelyan said as though from a distance, "that's it."

"Well, come on."

Trevelyan was so lost in his thoughts about what she'd said he didn't realize what she was doing. The shots rang out before he could grab her.

Chapter Eight

It's amazing that two people can see the same thing, yet think they see two completely different things. When Claire saw Angus MacTarvit, all five foot four of him, built like the bull he resembled, she knew that at last she was seeing a real Scotsman, a man who didn't wear a kilt because it could impress a woman but because it was what he *always* wore, had always worn, and what his ancestors had worn. The MacTarvits had probably worn the kilt throughout the ban, when England, in another attempt to subdue the Scots, had outlawed the wearing of kilts.

What Trevelyan saw was a cantankerous little man who'd never given away or shared anything in his life, a man who could be thirty-five or a hundred and five. You couldn't tell his age by looking at him, for he was smoked brown by the peat he used in distilling the whisky. He used peat for whisky; he didn't drink the water and he'd certainly never bathed in it.

Trevelyan turned to Claire, planning to make excuses for the horrid little man, but what he saw were two people who had fallen instantly in love with each other. Claire, her face alight, walked forward, her hand outstretched. "Lord MacTarvit."

"Lord MacTarvit," Trevelyan said with a snort. No one had called the old man anything but MacTarvit for years. But he was the clan chief, even if he was the last of his clan.

Trevelyan saw the old man's face soften, the leathery wrinkles relax into a ridiculous expression that made him look like a gnome. "Ah, lassie," the old man practically purred, taking Claire's hand in his right and caressing it with his left. "Come into this humble home. Would you like a wee dram?"

"Of *your* whisky?" Claire asked, conveying the impression that she'd tasted every whisky in the world and his was by far the best.

Trevelyan, with a grimace, started to follow the two of them into the low, thatched cottage, but MacTarvit blocked his way.

When he looked at Trevelyan, those gnomish features rearranged themselves back into his normal expression of rage. "And what would you be wantin'?"

"If you think I'm going to let her in there alone with the likes of you, your brains are more pickled than I thought."

This seemed to please the old man and he stepped aside to let Trevelyan by, but then blocked his way again. "I thought you were dead."

Trevelyan gave him a hard look. "*She* thinks I'm dead."

MacTarvit frowned at that and stood for a moment as though considering this, then he nodded and went inside the cottage, Trevelyan following him.

From the moment Trevelyan entered that little cottage, everything in it black from centuries of smoke from peat fires, he became an observer. All his life he'd heard members of his family curse the MacTarvits. His father had complained endlessly about the thievery of the family and their refusal to buy and sell like the rest of the modern world. Trevelyan had grown up thinking that the MacTarvits were something the world would be better off without.

But now he sat on a three-legged stool against one wall and watched this romantic young American with this old man and he saw MacTarvit in a whole different light. Angus MacTarvit was a man out of the past. He was a throwback to another time, a time when the clans were powerful and they warred with each other. MacTarvit was from a time when men were valued for their handiness with a weapon and not with a money ledger. He was a man whose family had served another for generations, and now he was the last of his clan and he was trying desperately to hold on to the old ways.

"What be you lookin' at?" MacTarvit said belligerently to Trevelyan.

"Don't mind him," Claire said. "He looks at everyone that way. It makes him feel that he knows more than they do."

Trevelyan snorted at that. "More than the two of you do."

"And now, lassie, why are you here?"

"I'm to marry the duke," she said brightly.

MacTarvit looked at Trevelyan.

"She's to marry Harry," Trevelyan said softly.

Angus frowned at that, and Trevelyan knew he had no idea what was going on, for MacTarvit had recognized Trevelyan the moment he had seen him. And if he knew who Trevelyan was then he knew he was the oldest living son and therefore the duke. Trevelyan smiled at the old man's puzzlement, having no intention of giving him answers to his unasked questions.

"Then what are ye doin' with this lot?" Angus said, pointing his glass at Trevelyan.

Claire looked at Trevelyan for a moment. "We're friends," she said and smiled. "At least we're becoming friends."

Trevelyan gave Angus a smug little smile, which made the old man grunt, then he turned back to Claire. "So they've sent you to run me off, have they?"

"No one sent me. I've come on my own." She took a breath. "I've come to tell you that when I am the duchess you may stay here all your life and you may try your best to steal my cattle. In return I shall steal all of your whisky, even what you have in stock. I'm sure it will age better in my cellars than wherever you have it hidden."

Trevelyan looked at Claire in disbelief. He had expected her to tell the old man she thought all the stealing was a dreadful thing and why couldn't they all live in peace?

Angus's old face also registered disbelief for a moment, then he made a rumbling sound that was probably meant to be laughter and took Claire's hand in his. For a moment Trevelyan thought he was going to kiss it. "Would you like somethin' to eat, girl?"

At that Trevelyan nearly choked on his whisky. The MacTarvits were known for their stingy ways. In a land that was infamous for its parsimonious ways, the MacTarvits were legendary. There was one story that told how a woman had seen a MacTarvit pour milk the cat had not finished into his tea. Once the MacTarvits had been crossing a toll bridge and had peacefully paid the toll of a shilling, but a penny had dropped between the cracks of the bridge and been lost. The toll master said the MacTarvits owed him a penny. Rather than pay the penny Angus and his sons had blockaded the bridge for two days, allowing no one to pass. Trevelyan's father had at last come, given Angus his penny, and the bridge had reopened.

Now he was offering food to this rich American.

"You may not like it," Angus said. "It is humble food."

"She eats anything at any time," Trevelyan said, then leaned back against the wall and watched as the old man prepared a meal for his guest. Trevelyan was very curious as to what he'd serve. A dish of water, perhaps?

MacTarvit went to his fireplace where a meager, smoky fire burned, reached up into the chimney, and withdrew a piece of cheese. The outside was black with smoke but when Angus cut into it, it was white. He shaved off a few slices, then put them into a skillet near the fire to melt. As they were melting he went outside and returned with three pieces of meat—from the stolen cows no doubt. "I guess you'll be wantin' somethin' too," he said to Trevelyan, and there was no doubt that he begrudged Trevelyan the food.

"I'd be delighted," Trevelyan said. He watched as Angus heated another skillet and began to broil the three steaks. When the cheese was melted, he poured in a little thick, rich cream, and swirled it all together. When it was bubbling, he quickly added a generous splash of whisky, the steam rising from the mixture.

From the top of the hearth he took a chipped and cracked plate. It was dirty, but he rubbed it with the grimy elbow of his old, greasy tweed jacket, put a steak on it, and covered the meat with the cheese-and-whisky sauce. He took a knife and fork from a jar on top of the mantel, rubbed them on his sleeve, and handed them to Claire.

Trevelyan watched her, wondering what this multimillionairess would do, but she just smiled at Angus as though he were the Prince of Wales and cut into her steak. "Heaven," she pronounced it. "This is delicious."

Angus smiled in a doddering way that made him look even sillier than he normally did and took another plate from the mantel. He didn't bother to wipe it off but slapped his steak on it, covered it with sauce, and sat on a stool across from Claire and began to eat.

Trevelyan saw that he was going to have to get his own food. He picked up a dirty plate from the mantel, and when he started to wipe it off Claire gave him a look that stopped him in his tracks. Obviously she thought it would be a breach of etiquette to clean his plate. With a grimace he bent to the two skillets. The piece of meat that Angus had left him was by far the smallest. Trevelyan scraped the skillet for the last of the sauce, then took a dirty knife and fork, went back to his stool, and began to eat. At his first bite, he looked at Angus with new respect. The food was indeed delicious.

"It wouldn't be half as good if it hadn't been stolen," Claire said. "Now, my lord, do you sing, or play, or do you know any poetry?"

Trevelyan laughed at that. Ol' Angus MacTarvit singing. It would sound like a bullfrog.

Angus didn't so much as acknowledge Trevelyan's presence. "I do a bit of Bobbie Burns."

"My favorite," Claire breathed.

For an hour Trevelyan watched and listened as MacTarvit quoted the romantic lines of Scotland's beloved Robert Burns. Trevelyan had read the poems, of course, but only because he'd had to. They had never meant much to him, but now, hearing Angus quote them was altogether different. Within minutes he saw tears in Claire's eyes.

"Are you sure you're American, child?" Angus said.

"I'm as much a Scot as you are, Angus MacTarvit," she said with an accent as heavy as Angus's. "It's just that my family has been visiting America for a bit—a few hundred years or so."

The old man laughed with her. "Now, girl, what do you want to do?"

Trevelyan stood. "We need to get back. I have some work that needs to be done and—" He might as well not have been in the room for all the notice they took of him.

"I want to hear pipers," Claire said. "I haven't heard a pipe since I arrived in Scotland."

Trevelyan rolled his eyes when he saw the two of them exchange looks that said this was the greatest tragedy that could ever have happened to a person.

"I'll see to that," the old man said and left the cottage.

"We have to go back. I have things I must do and—"

"Then go," Claire said. "I'm sure Lord MacTarvit will take me back to the house. Or Harry will be back this evening and someone can tell him where I am and he can send a carriage for me."

What she said made sense, and he knew there was no question of her safety. From the look on MacTarvit's face he'd protect her with his life—not that there was much danger in the Scottish countryside. She might fall into a peat bog or, knowing Claire as he was beginning to, she might eat and drink herself into a stupor, but he didn't really think she was in any danger.

"I'll stay," he said.

She smiled at him and slipped her arm through his. "It might do you good to get out of that tower of yours." She stepped back and looked at him. "Do you know that you're looking better than you were when I first met you? You no longer have that greenish cast to your skin." She put her hand up, cupped his chin, and turned his face to one side, then the other.

The moment she touched him, she knew she shouldn't have. She was warmed by food, whisky, and MacTarvit hospitality, and Trevelyan was much too human-feeling. She had meant to be sisterlike when she touched him; she'd meant to tell him he was growing more handsome with each passing day. But the very second she touched him, he turned those eyes on her, looking at her in a way that made her step away from him.

"I . . . I think we should see what Lord MacTarvit has planned."

Trevelyan smiled at her, knowing what she was feeling. And why not? She was young and healthy and he, for all she referred to him as an old man, was not old. Grinning, he started to leave the cottage, but as a dizzy spell overtook him he held on to the door frame. He stood still a moment, not wanting to leave the warmth of the cottage because he was feeling the chill of the day begin to seep into his bones. Malaria was not something a person ever got rid of.

It was early afternoon when they left the cottage and it was dusk when they started home. During the long afternoon Trevelyan sat on the damp ground, trying to wrap his father's plaid around him as he watched Claire with the growing crowd of Scots men and women. Angus had unearthed one piper, but soon there were two more people playing the pipes. Someone put two rusty old swords on the ground and a young girl began to dance over them. Claire asked if she could learn the dance.

Trevelyan sat on the ground, leaned against the wall, and watched as Claire, feet flying, moved over the swords. She picked up the steps quickly and within a couple of hours was doing quite well. The pipers, all of them flirts, as most Scotsmen were, picked up the pace of their tunes until Claire was moving so quickly one could hardly see her feet.

Trevelyan was used to being an observer. In his many travels he had sat and watched many things. He had seen, as Claire had said of him, savagery beyond compare. Once, in a village in Africa, to celebrate his arrival they had crucified a man. He had seen hundreds of slave caravans. The "civilized" world was so horrified at the indignity of slavery, but Trevelyan could tell them that what went on in the villages of primitive people on a daily basis made slavery look like a seaside holiday.

Someone always kept Trevelyan's whisky glass full. Scotch was the best-known help for the wet cold of Scotland. The men started drinking it in the morning and didn't stop all day. Yet rarely did you see a drunken Scotsman, for the cold took so much energy to fight off that it burned up what was in the whisky.

He sat there for hours, sipping the whisky and watching the people as they laughed and at times sang. It wasn't long before people began to walk in from cottages miles away. It was said that a walk of ten miles was a mere stroll to a Scotsman.

He watched Claire and he began to believe what she'd said about being as much Scots as Angus was. Watching her now, he could see she was more Scots than either he or Harry was, or any of the other people living in the big house were. How long had it been since any of his family had been off the estate grounds? When Harry wanted something, such as new clothes or an adventure, he went to London. The rest of the family moved from one estate to another, not caring which house they were in. It was true that the MacArran title was Scots and in theory the duke was the clan chief, but how long had it been since that meant anything to his family? Trevelyan's father had spoken of tradition but he had talked only to his oldest son, the son who was to inherit. To Trevelyan he had said little about anything—except to reprimand Trevelyan when he got into one scrape after another. The oldest boy had been his father's darling and Harry had been his mother's. Trevelyan had spent his time alone, finding out what he could about life and trying not to get caught.

But in the end he had been caught and he had been sent away, returning over the years for short visits. He had gone from being part of the family to being a guest—an ignored guest.

"You're shivering," Claire said, leaning over him. Her pretty face was pink with exertion and he'd never seen her look lovelier.

Trevelyan didn't want a pretty girl to be a nurse to him. "Perhaps you need spectacles. I've never felt better in my life."

Claire smiled at him, then announced to one and all that she was exhausted and must leave, that it was a long walk back. They were surprised that a lady would walk. "It's merely a wee jaunt. It won't take me but a moment," she said, laughing.

She held out her hand to Trevelyan to help him up, but he got up by himself. MacTarvit took one look at Trevelyan and offered him the use of a wagon.

"It's a cold day in hell when I can't walk on my own two feet," Trevelyan growled and started off through the brambles toward the big house.

After saying good-bye to the crofters, Claire ran after him. "That was certainly rude of you. They were very kind to us."

"Kind to you maybe, but not to me." Already he was beginning to feel his legs weaken. Now he wished he'd accepted the old man's offer of a wagon, but he wasn't going to return and admit his weakness in front of all those people. And, more important, he wasn't going to be made to look a weakling in front of Claire.

Claire walked behind Trevelyan, wondering what he was thinking about so hard. He had his head lowered and his shoulders set forward; he looked as though he were a man with a mission. He stabbed the ground with his iron cane and when he moved he leaned heavily on it. Also, she wondered why he'd said the people's kindness had been extended only to her. At least four times she'd seen men stare at him, then nod in recognition. And three of the older women had seen to it that Trevelyan had always been supplied with food and drink.

As they walked, twice he stumbled. The first time she went to help him, he waved her away. The second time, she wouldn't allow him to push her away. She put her arm around his waist, and it was then she realized he was burning with fever.

She looked up at him, saw the determination on his face. In spite of the fact that he was very ill he had stayed with her because she'd wanted to stay, and when Angus had offered him the use of his wagon, Trevelyan had turned it down. Pride and stubbornness, she thought.

He started to push her away but she held on to his waist. "There's no use pretending with me," she said. "I can see that you're so sick you're staggering. You can keep your silly pride in front of them but you can't keep it with me. Now hold on to me and we'll get you home."

For a moment Trevelyan was indecisive as to what to do, but then he relaxed against her and let her help him. "Friends, are we?" he said and there was amusement in his voice.

"Yes, I think we are."

"Then what are you and Harry?"

"We love each other," she said softly.

"Is there a difference between lovers and friends?" he asked as they crossed a stream.

"A great, great deal of difference."

"And which is more important?"

She thought for a while. "I think a person can live without lovers but no one can live without friends."

Chapter Nine

By the time they reached the hidden door of the west wing of the house, Trevelyan was shaking so hard Claire could barely hold him upright. Once inside the door, she called for Oman to help her. The tall man appeared almost instantly, put his arm under Trevelyan's, and half carried him up the stairs.

Claire stood to one side as she watched Oman put Trevelyan into the bed. She had never seen anyone shake as he was shaking, had never seen anyone quite as ill as he was. Trevelyan curled into a ball and Oman pulled the cover over him.

"Will he be all right?" she asked. "He doesn't look as though he's going to live."

Oman shrugged. "It is the will of Allah." With that he left the room. Claire assumed the man was going for medicine or for something to give Trevelyan comfort, but when the man did not return, she went to the sitting room and there Oman stood, calmly eating a piece of fruit and looking out the window at the moon.

Claire knew she could not leave Trevelyan alone. "I want you to go to my sister," she said as calmly as she could. She was fed up with servants who did not serve. "Do you know who my sister is? The young girl?"

Oman looked at her and nodded once in acknowledgment.

"I want you to go to her and have her tell the family that I am ill. I don't want anyone to know I'm not in my room tonight. Get her to tell Harry I'm too sick to see him and—" She looked away. What should she do about horrid Miss Rogers? Brat could figure out what to do. "Tell my sister that *no one* is to know where I am. I will pay her well."

Oman nodded once before he slipped from the room. Claire went back to Trevelyan. "What can I do?" she asked him.

"I am cold. So very cold."

She didn't hesitate before she climbed in bed with him and held him in her arms to try to get him warm. His shaking was so violent that it shook her too; she couldn't imagine how it felt to him.

Claire held him to her, stroked his damp hair, and murmured soothing words to him as though he were a child. It felt strange and familiar at the same time to have a man's body so near hers. He clung to her, holding her, clutching, almost as though he were afraid she would leave him.

"Sssh, my love," she whispered. "Sleep now. Go to sleep."

She didn't know if he heard her or not but the words seemed to have an effect as he relaxed in her arms as she stroked his broad back.

He buried his face in her neck, his chin on her shoulder, and after a long time, the awful shaking stopped. She caressed his temple, smoothing his hair back, and smiled at him. He didn't seem so large now, so infuriating, with his cynicism and his belief that the world was a bad place. Right now he seemed like a sweet, lonely little boy who needed her. She smiled again and kissed the top of his head as he nestled closer to her.

It was an hour before Oman returned. "It is done," he said.

Claire, holding Trevelyan to her, barely glanced up at him, but when she did, she looked back, startled. There was something different about Oman. Since he'd seen her little sister, she could guess at what had transpired.

"Where is your emerald?" she asked, for the big emerald in his turban was gone.

Oman merely shrugged.

"Did you lend it to her or give it to her?"

"A mere three days have I lent it to her. The lowly jewel will benefit from the wearing by one so young and so beautiful."

"Brat," Claire said under her breath, then looked back at Trevelyan's sleeping form. No matter that her sister charged for her services, Claire knew she'd do a good job. No doubt Brat would delight in the melodrama of whatever lies she had to create to keep people from knowing Claire was not in her room.

Claire thought that it was possible that you never knew a person until you'd nursed him when he was ill. Toward midnight Trevelyan was deep enough asleep that she was able to ease out from under him. For a moment she stood at the side of the bed and looked at him. She was beyond tired. Between the dancing, the two long walks, and the fear she'd felt at being near an illness as strong as Trevelyan's, she wanted to sink into a feather bed and never get out of it.

He was on his back, asleep at last. And those eyes of his were closed. Those black, intense, seen-everything, done-everything, bored-by-it-all eyes of his were at last closed. She bent over him and smoothed his hair off his forehead. His hair was too long but somehow it suited him. Oman had lit candles in the room and as she touched Trevelyan's face she looked at him. Earlier she'd said he'd lost the greenish cast to his skin, and he had. Now his skin was a healthy tan and there was even some fat under his skin so he didn't look skeletal, as he had when she'd first seen him. She put her fingertip on the long scar on his left cheek, then on the scar on his right cheek, and wondered how they had been made. Curious, she sat on the edge of the bed and began to touch his face. High cheekbones. A strong, square jaw covered with bristly black whiskers. His thick, drooping mustache was soft and she could see that it half concealed a very sensuous mouth.

"My goodness, Trevelyan, you're quite a handsome man," she whispered. He didn't have Harry's blond, healthy good looks but he had—the devil's looks, she thought. If there were a play, Trevelyan would make a perfect devil and Harry could play an angel. Perhaps she should suggest it to Brat's friend who staged his one-man plays.

"Is he well again?"

Claire jumped, guilty at being caught touching Trevelyan. She turned to Oman. "I think the worst is over. Does he have these spells often?" Claire wanted to know if Trevelyan's illness was permanent or temporary. But at the same time she didn't want to know. She didn't want to know if these shaking spells would eventually lead to his death.

Oman didn't answer, but merely shrugged in a way that could mean that he didn't know, didn't care, or that it was all up to Allah.

"Would you get me some hot water? I want to wash him."

Within minutes Oman was back with a pitcher of hot water and Claire began to wash Trevelyan's face and neck. She pulled back the cover and removed the belt that held his plaid in place. Carefully and with some reverence, she unpinned the laird's badge that bound the plaid about his shoulders and placed it on the table by the bed.

Trevelyan was sleeping the sleep of the dead and she didn't think anything in the world could wake him. He didn't so much as stir when she pushed him and got the plaid from under him. His linen shirt was soaked with his sweat. She unbuttoned it partway down and ran the clean, hot, wet cloth over his skin, which was covered with dried sweat.

It was when she reached his collarbone that she saw the first scar. She didn't know why this body scar should surprise her, especially when his face was so scarred, but it did. She unbuttoned his shirt farther and there were two more scars. No longer trying to be discreet, she unbuttoned his shirt the rest of the way and looked at him.

His chest was lean but there was a great deal of muscle on him. In spite of his weakness now, he was obviously a man who had spent a lot of time in strenuous exercise. But what interested her were the many, many white scars over his ribs. She ran her fingertips over first one, then another. It was her guess that they were knife wounds. What had been done to him? she wondered. The scars ranged from an inch and a half to three inches long. They didn't look as though they had ever been very deep or life threatening, but that there were so many of the pale scars was what was so unusual.

She stood back for a moment and tried to imagine what could have caused such scars. She'd heard of the dreadful treatment English boys endured in their sadistic all-boys' schools, but she'd never heard of anything like this. Suddenly, she wanted to get that shirt off of him and see what else had been done to him. She called Oman to her. "Help me undress him," she said and didn't meet the man's eyes. Let him think this was common practice among American girls, she thought.

Trevelyan groaned as Oman, with Claire helping, managed to get the shirt from Trevelyan's big body. There were more scars on his back. There were four of them, in rows, curving from his spine up and over his left shoulder. They looked like claw marks, as though some great animal had attacked him and torn into his back. She could understand these marks more than she could the ones on his ribs. Her father loved to hunt and he had often come home from a trip to the wilds of the American West with horrifying stories about men who got too close to a bear or a mountain lion and had been clawed.

But what puzzled her about these marks was that she had seen no evidence that Trevelyan liked to hunt. There were no skins of animals about his room as there were wherever her father went. Her father liked to remember every animal he had slaughtered, liked often to relive the event both in retelling the story and remembering it. But, she reminded herself, Trevelyan was in hiding.

She sent Oman from the room and washed Trevelyan's chest and back, then went to a trunk by the window and found another shirt for him. It was an odd shirt, made of fine cotton but printed with little brown and white figures that were, she assumed, meant to be people. She struggled to get him into the shirt and had only just succeeded when he began shaking again. Without a thought, she climbed into bed with him and held him close to her, stroking his brow and trying to soothe him as he thrashed about.

Trevelyan woke slowly. He had trouble focusing and trouble remembering where he was. For a moment he thought he was again in Pesha and that the canopy overhead was Nyssa's bed.

But as he turned his head and saw the stone walls and the heavy oak of the bed—no gilding—he remembered all. For all that he had trouble remembering where he was, he knew that his head rested upon a firm, female breast. He turned to look up to see Claire holding him against her ample bosom, and he could feel his body between her legs. She was sleeping, but at his movement, she opened her eyes and smiled at him.

And as naturally as day follows night, he put his hand on her breast and kissed her neck.

Claire closed her eyes for a moment, feeling his lips on her neck. Without having any idea what she was doing, she moved her legs and Trevelyan rolled on top of her. She could feel the hard maleness of him on her body. He had changed from a sick child to a hungry man in an instant.

His lips moved up her neck to her ear. He took the lobe between his teeth and Claire arched her neck as his hand caressed and massaged her breast.

His hand moved down her side to her waist, over her hip, to her thigh.

Then suddenly, his hand came up again. He roughly took her chin in his hand and turned her to look at him. It was as though he were demanding that she know who he was, that she see him not as a friend, not as a sick child, but as Trevelyan.

She was not up to the challenge. She was not up to what she saw in his eyes. She turned her head away. "No," she whispered.

Without a word, Trevelyan rolled off of her and Claire got out of bed. Her hands and body were shaking. I have to get out of here, she thought. She started for the door.

"How long have you been here?" he asked.

She stopped at the far corner of the bed. "Two nights and one day," she answered, not yet able to control her shaking.

"And you have taken care of me by yourself?"

"Oman has helped." She took a deep breath to calm herself.

"And what have they said in the house of your absence? Harry must have been upset."

She knew what he was doing: talking of everyday matters to keep her from leaving. "No one knows I haven't been in my room. My sister has told them all that I am very, very sick and can't be disturbed. I think she's told them I have something akin to smallpox and cholera combined, but that whatever I have is very, very contagious." She looked at him for the first time. She'd never noticed what thick eyelashes he had.

He smiled. "What an admirable person you are and what a lovely sister you have."

"She didn't do it for free. She 'borrowed' Oman's emerald for three days and she sent word through him that I was to give her my ruby bracelet."

"And did you?"

"Of course. But the truth of the matter is I didn't mind. I don't like rubies. They look like blood. I much prefer emeralds. They look like green things growing."

He closed his eyes and lay back against the pillows. "Thank you."

She couldn't help herself, but she looked at him. She could still feel his lips on her neck. "I think you'll be all right now. Oman says these spells of yours come and go and that you're all right after them. I must go."

He opened his eyes and she saw pleading in them. "Please do not leave."

For some reason, she was sure he rarely used the word please. "I . . . I must. I cannot stay."

He smiled a know-it-all little smile. "You must leave because I kissed you?"

"It wasn't right," she said softly. "We should not—We must not . . ."

"I was half asleep and dreaming. You can't be angry at me for that, can you?"

"I'm not angry. I'm . . ."

"Oh, I see. It's Harry. You're worried because you liked my kisses better than his. Or does Harry kiss you? I seem to remember that he likes horses more than women, and experienced women more than virgins."

Anger made her straighten. "For your information, I *love* Harry's kisses," she said, walking toward his side of the bed. "I love everything about him. He's certainly better looking than you, with your black eyes and your scarred body. I'll wager Harry doesn't have a scar on his body."

Trevelyan continued smiling. "But you know about my body but not his," he said so softly she could barely hear him.

"You are despicable."

She turned to leave, but he caught her wrist. She pulled, but she didn't look back at him.

"I apologize," he said. "I apologize for trying to make love to a beautiful woman who was in bed with me. It was indeed despicable of me. I apologize for envying Harry, who seems to have everything in life. You are right: it is contemptible of me. In future I will try to control myself."

She glared at him. "That is not a sincere apology."

"But then it can't be, can it, for I'm not at all sincere. Hate me for it if you must, but I'd love to do it all over again. *All* over."

Claire couldn't keep from laughing. "You *are* despicable." She pulled at her hand but he kept holding it.

"Stay with me. Talk to me," he said, and for a brief second there was sincerity in his eyes, sincerity and pleading.

"About what?" The moment she said it, she knew she was lost, for even to her she sounded as though she wanted to stay. "I must—" she began.

"Why do you want to be a duchess?" he asked.

"What a ridiculous question." She gave a hard tug on her hand and pulled away from him. "Perhaps we should ask every woman in the world whether or not she wants to be a duchess and see if *any* woman anywhere answers no."

"Even the queens and the princesses?"

"I imagine queens and princesses *especially* want to be duchesses. Prestige without all the responsibility."

"And you want prestige?"

"I want Harry. Now, I really must go."

"No, please, stay and . . . and tell me a story."

"You mean like Goldilocks and the Three Bears?"

"No, a *real* story. Tell me about . . ." He searched for something. Anything to make her stay, to make her remain close to him. She made him feel as though he really could heal, heal from all the wounds he'd suffered throughout his lifetime, not just from another attack of malaria. "Tell me about your parents."

She was silent for a moment. "I'll tell you a love story—a true love story. At one time my mother was a very beautiful woman."

"As beautiful as that little sister of yours?" His eyes dropped to her bosom and his voice lowered to a quiet, seductive level. "As beautiful as you?"

"Do you want to hear this or not?" she snapped, but turned away, her face red.

He smiled and lay back against the pillow, obviously pleased at having had an effect on her. "Please continue."

"You have to swear on your life you will never reveal what I'm about to tell you. My mother would kill me if she knew I'd told. Actually, she might kill me if she knew I knew."

"I do indeed swear," he said, trying not to smile.

"My mother likes to tell people she's from an old Virginia family, but the truth is, she grew up in a shack in the Smoky Mountains. She grew up without an education and only the minimum of food and clothing."

"But she was beautiful?"

"Very. When she was seventeen she left home and went to New

York. I don't know where she got the money for her travel expenses—Brat says she stole it from her family, that her father had sold some hogs the day before and while the family slept my mother stole the money and went to New York. But I always take the stories my sister tells me with a grain of salt. However she got the money, she showed up in New York wearing an expensive suit and got a good job at the perfume counter of a fancy department store. Then she met my father, fell in love with him, and they were married and have lived happily ever after."

"I see," Trevelyan said after a moment. His face had lost that soft look of seduction. Now he looked interested, as he always did when he had a puzzle to figure out. "And together the two of them used that great American freedom of yours, earned a vast fortune so you could be an heiress and become a duchess."

"Not exactly."

"How exactly?" His eyes were so intense she was sure his look could pierce metal.

"My grandfather, my father's father, was known as the Commander."

Trevelyan looked up at her, eyes ablaze.

"I see you've heard of him," she said, and it was her turn to give a smug smile.

"How convenient that your mother fell in love with the son of such a rich man."

"Yes, it was. You can laugh if you want but Grandfather didn't give the newlyweds any money. Not any *real* money, anyway, only about $10,000 a year."

"Poverty!"

"It is if you've grown up as wealthy as my father did," she said quickly.

"But he and your mother struggled by. After all, they did have love."

She ignored his comment, ignored the cynicism in his voice. "My grandfather died fifteen years ago and left approximately thirty million dollars. He—"

"Give or take a few mill."

"He left ten million to my father, ten million to my mother—he believed women should be independent—and ten in trust for me."

"What about your adorable little sister?"

"She wasn't born yet."

"I imagine there's enough for her."

Claire was silent.

He studied her face for a moment. She was busying herself straightening the items on the table by the bed. "What's the rest of the story?" he asked.

She didn't want to tell him any more. Why couldn't he accept a story the way it was told? Why did he always have to look underneath the surface? "I guess the rest of it is that my parents spent their money."

The expression on Trevelyan's face could only be described as horror.

Claire gave a weak smile. "My father is a lover of fine things: horses, brandy, sea travel on his yacht."

Lazy, Trevelyan thought. "And your mother? How did she manage to spend so much?"

"I think she wanted to be part of a society she'd never had access to as a child. So she built a house and gave parties."

"Ten million dollars' worth of parties?" he asked softly.

"Both my parents also spent a great deal on my education, and I've always had whatever I wanted, and so has Brat."

Trevelyan took a moment to digest this information. "So now all the money your family has left is what you have in trust?"

"Yes."

"And how is the trust administered?"

"Since my grandfather died I have received a quarter of the interest each year."

"So, in essence, you've paid for your own education."

She ignored him. "When I marry I receive the principal."

Trevelyan waited for her to say more. "Out with the rest of it."

"I only get the money if my parents approve of whom I marry. My grandfather put that in his will because he had a younger sister and he gave her a few million dollars, but she immediately married a man who gambled. The man spent every penny my aunt had."

"Then what happened to your aunt?"

"After her money was gone she went back to live with my grandfather."

"And it's my guess your grandfather never gave her another penny."

"Why must you *always* be cynical? When my grandfather died he left her the interest from some money, but he said he wanted to ensure that she wasn't the target for another gigolo."

"Liked to control people, didn't he?"

"He gave my parents their money free and clear," she said fiercely, then was silent.

"So now you have two penniless parents and a sister who has never had any money. Who gets your money if you don't marry a man of whom they approve?"

"My parents get it," she said softly.

"I guess they approve of Harry."

"Oh, yes. My mother says no money on earth could buy society like that of having a daughter who's a duchess. And my father says all Harry's friends know how to live."

"You mean they spend their days killing animals and their evenings eating?"

"Harry also runs this house and three others. It takes a great deal of work to manage these estates."

"My dear industrious little American, Harry doesn't any more manage these estates than I do. He hires people to run them. What managing that's done is done by Harry's mother."

"That's not true! Harry is always going away on business."

"Harry's 'business' is buying things. Have you looked at this place? Pictures, furniture, ornaments, horses and carriages in the stables. In succession each duke has married the woman with the most money and spent his life buying things and enjoying himself. It's what Harry's been trained for."

"You're saying Harry is marrying me only for my money."

"And aren't you marrying him because you want to be a duchess?"

"No. I love Harry. And I love this house and this way of life. I love the people and the country."

"You love the romance. You love what you *think* is real. You so very conveniently love exactly what your parents want so you can become a duchess, get your grandfather's money, and give your parents the kind of life they want."

"I don't like you very much."

"You like Harry better?"

"Much. He's sweet and kind and gentle and—"

"Lovely to look at."

"Yes," she said defiantly, putting her chin in the air.

"Harry's family's good looks have enabled generations of MacArran dukes to marry wealthy women."

Claire was silent for a moment. "After these rich women married the dukes, were they happy?"

"For the most part I believe they were. I've heard that all the MacArran dukes are renowned lovers and, surprisingly, for all their self-indulgences, they are generally faithful to their wives."

"A woman couldn't ask for more, could she?" she asked softly, looking at him.

"Were I a woman I'd ask for a great deal more," he practically shouted at her.

She moved away from him; she didn't like the turn the conversation was taking. "I must return to the house. Harry will be home today and I want to see him." She straightened a cushion on the window seat. "I think you'll be all right now. I'll tell Oman—"

He caught her hand as she walked past him and held it for a moment. "Don't go," he whispered.

For a moment Claire looked into those black eyes of his and for just that one second, she saw inside him. For just that tiny moment she saw beneath his outer coldness and she thought, He's lonely. He's lonely, as I am lonely. And he's an outsider, just as I am.

The moment was gone nearly as quickly as it came and the mocking look returned. It was as though he refused to allow anyone to see beneath his mask. He tossed her hand away, as though he could no longer bear to touch her. "Go on. Go to your duke. Harry will want to show you the horse he's bought you." Trevelyan turned away and looked at the far wall.

Claire stared at the back of his head for a moment and quickly made a decision. She told herself she was going to stay because Trevelyan was ill, because he needed a nurse, because he was lonely. But somewhere deep inside her, she knew the truth: she *wanted* his company, wanted his quick mind that made her think. True, he laughed at her, he was snide and cynical, but he was so very alive and he made her feel alive.

Without saying a word, Claire left the room and went to speak to Oman. She wrote a note to her sister, telling her she wouldn't be back until dinner tonight, and Brat was to stall Harry and everyone else who could be stalled.

When Claire returned to Trevelyan's room and told him she had arranged to spend the day with him, he didn't bother to so much as say thank you. For a moment she thought she might reconsider her stay, but the mere thought of another dreary day spent in that house with all of Harry's relatives made her ready to try most anything else.

"What shall we do?" she asked. "Play cards?"

"I shall write for three hours, then I—"

"You get out of bed and I leave."

He came quite close to smiling at that, but he managed to control himself. "I will beat you at chess," he said.

"Oh? Do you think so?"

Later, Claire was to think of this day as one of the most unusual days of her life. It was one thing to spend the day with Trevelyan when he was otherwise occupied, another to spend the day with him when there were other people about, but it was an utterly unique experience to be the sole and foremost object of Trevelyan's attention.

They played chess—in a manner of speaking. Trevelyan never bothered to look at the board. She told him where she had moved her pieces and he instantly, without the slightest hesitation, without the least amount of time to think about the move, told her where he wanted to move which of his pieces.

While they played the game, they talked. Actually, Trevelyan asked her questions and she answered. What little experience of men Claire had had consisted of men who more than anything else in the world liked to talk about themselves. But Trevelyan wanted to know all about her. He didn't just want to know about her life in New York and what she'd read and where she'd been, he wanted to know what she thought.

He asked her what she thought of Englishmen and how they differed from American men. He asked her opinion of English women. He asked her how the American way of life differed from the British.

Claire thought for a moment. "I don't understand how the English nobleman thinks of money. If an American needs money he earns it. He finds a way to invest or invent something or he gets a job. He does something for which he gets paid."

"And the Englishman is different?"

"I don't know how the common man is—isn't it odd to still have a class system in our modern world?—but the upper-class man doesn't seem to even think of earning money. I heard that the earl of Irley was nearly bankrupt and everyone was talking about how he was selling his land and his houses. I happened to say I'd heard the earl owned some very good farmland and why didn't he do something with it."

She moved her first piece on the chessboard then looked up at him. "Everyone in the room stopped and looked at me as though I'd said something obscene."

Trevelyan kept his eyes on her as he told her which chess piece to move for him. He didn't bother to move his own pieces, as though the whole idea of playing was a great bore to him. "And yet you are going to marry into this upper class, as you call it."

"I am marrying Harry because I love him," she said, and by her tone she let him know she wasn't going to say any more on the subject.

"And what do the English think of you?"

At that Claire laughed. "They seem to look upon me as a cross between a Red Indian and a Gaiety Girl. I shock them rather often."

"I imagine you do. I don't think a prim and proper young miss would spend days in a man's rooms as you have done."

His words didn't bother her in the least. "True enough. But we are chaperoned and you are—" Out of habit, she started to say he was old enough to be her father, but Trevelyan raised one eyebrow at her and she looked away, her face pink. "Do you mind if I ask how old you are?"

She'd learned days ago that although Trevelyan asked questions, he did not answer them. He didn't tell her how old he was. Instead, he asked her more about her family, and how her pretty little sister could be called Brat.

"Sarah Ann's prettiness is a curse to her," Claire said with some feeling. "She was born beautiful and there has not been a day in her life that someone hasn't told her she was lovely. When she was about three she climbed onto the lap of one of Father's rich, fat friends and asked him to give her the diamond off his watch chain. The old man thought it was a great joke, gave her the diamond, and started her on the road to ruin. She's learned she doesn't have to do anything for anyone without getting paid for it."

"That seems to be the American way."

"Don't you *dare* say anything against my country. Compared to America this place is—" She broke off, not saying what she had intended to.

But Trevelyan had a way of making her talk. He fixed her with that look of his and it was obvious he meant to outwait her.

She started to tell him, slowly at first, some of the things she had observed in England and in Scotland. "It is a land of the past."

"But I thought you liked that. You fairly drooled over old MacTarvit. And poor Harry is freezing his backside in a kilt merely to impress you."

At that she gave a pointed look to the tartan draped over the back of a chair. He, too, had worn a plaid. Had he frozen in it merely to impress her?

For the first time Trevelyan looked down at the chessboard with great concentration. "So now you don't like the past?" he asked.

"I do. I love history. But I also know that time cannot stand still. There has to be progress or a country becomes like a stagnant pond. There has to be growth and change or a country cannot survive."

"I can't see how you can reconcile your love of kilts with your American ideas of changing everything for the sake of change. What is wrong with things as they are? You sound like one of those damned missionaries, always wanting to convert people to another religion. The one the poor savages had wasn't good enough for them."

She gave him a confused look. "I'm not talking about religion. I'm not even talking about philosophy. I'm talking about bathrooms."

Claire was pleased to see that shuttered, protective look in his eyes disappear. He looked completely bewildered.

Claire stood up and walked to the window. "Look at this lovely house. Look at all the people living in it. This is the late nineteenth century. It's almost the *twentieth* century, yet this house has seventeenth-century plumbing. That is to say, it has no plumbing at all."

She raised her hands in exasperation. "All the people in the house use chamber pots. The water for tubs is hauled by men up flight after flight of stairs." She looked toward the window then back at him. "Yes, I like history. I love it. If I were in charge of . . . of, I don't know what, Scotland maybe, I'd make sure every man, woman, and child in the country knew the story of their ancestors. It saddens me that so many Scots I meet know nothing about their own history. Many of the children have never heard the old ballads. Few of the adults know of the blood that has been shed in trying to gain independence from the English."

"*What* does all this have to do with bathrooms?"

"Everything. It's all very well to know about the past, but it's not all right to live in it. It seems that the people have lost the traditions and the ancient stories, but they've retained their ancient plumbing—and transportation and all the other things that keep them from entering this century."

"I gathered that you didn't think there was anything bad about Scotland."

"For all that you smirk at me as though I'm a child, I can see what is going on around me. MacTarvit lives in a hut just like the one his ancestors lived in three hundred years ago."

"I thought you liked the black cottage."

"I do, but I didn't like the poverty of the people. Lord MacTarvit steals cows. He risks the wrath of Harry's mother when he takes what he needs and no doubt gives most of it away. He—"

"MacTarvit give anything away? Ha!"

"He stole three cows. Do you think that one little man ate all of those cows before they spoiled?"

"Maybe he killed them one at a time."

She glared at him. "All right then, do you think he could have eaten one whole cow all by himself?"

Trevelyan leaned back on his elbow and looked at her with some interest. "What do you think will take these people out of their poverty? American factories? American railroads running through the hills? Will you dynamite the mountains away? Will you have tourists coming to see the quaint Scotsmen in their national dress?"

Claire sat down hard. "I don't know." She looked at her hands in her lap.

Trevelyan watched her for a long while. "What does it matter to you what happens to the people of Scotland? You'll have your money and you'll have your duke. What more do you want?"

"You still don't understand, do you? Becoming a duchess is a great responsibility. It will be my duty to take care of these people. When they go hungry I will have to see that they're fed."

Trevelyan gave a nasty little laugh. "You are talking feudalism. These people merely rent lands from you. No longer is a duke the one who judges courts and decides the fate of people." He raised an eyebrow at her. "You want to have twentieth-century plumbing and sixteenth-century clans."

"Maybe I do," Claire said softly. "It does all seem so complicated."

She sat pondering the question for a while, then looked up at him and smiled. "I don't know how to do what I want to do because I'm not sure what I want to do, but I mean to try."

He laughed at her, then frowned. "Do you think Harry's mother will allow you to do what you want?"

"Oh, yes, of course. Harry has told me I'll be able to do what I want."

Trevelyan grunted in disbelief.

Claire looked down at the chessboard and realized that while they had been talking he had been playing chess, with himself as an opponent. "Did you win or lose?" she asked.

"I won, of course," he said, eyes sparkling.

She laughed and for a moment they shared a flash of something between them. Friendship, Claire thought. They were beginning to form a genuine friendship. In spite of a few times better not remembered, they were becoming real, true friends.

"I've told you things that I've never told anyone," she said softly. "I've told you about my mother and I've told you opinions I've never shared with anyone else." She paused. "It's not easy being rich. It's not easy having grown up as the Commander's granddaughter. In my life—" She stopped and put up her hand. "I know, I know, you're going to say, In your very short life, and it's true that I'm not very old, but I have lived a great deal. My parents are not . . ." She didn't know what to say that wouldn't sound as though she were complaining about them.

"Not always as adult as you'd like them to be," Trevelyan supplied.

"Yes, exactly. There have been many times when I've felt I was the adult."

Trevelyan's impression of her parents, from what he'd heard of them, was that they had the emotional maturity of six-year-olds. He could imagine the two spoiled, rich parents depending on this young girl for all kinds of things, such as marrying whom they wanted her to marry so they could get what they wanted. They'd had a chance in life, a chance such as very, very few people ever got, yet they'd wasted it. And now they were expecting Claire to give them a second chance.

"You were telling me about your life."

"Yes." She turned to look out the window. "There have been many people in my life who wanted to be near me for what they thought I was rather than for what or who I am."

"People who wanted your money," he said bluntly.

"Yes, exactly."

When she didn't say anything else, he tried to figure out what she was trying to tell him. "Are you asking me if I want your money?"

"Maybe I am," she whispered. "I guess I'm suspicious when people are nice to me."

"Except Harry."

She turned to smile at him at the mention of Harry, but right now she couldn't seem to remember Harry. Trevelyan's dark eyes seemed to fill the room.

She looked down at the watch pinned to her breast. "I must go. It's nearly time for dinner, and I don't want to miss the surprise of my horse or the ladies with the silverware."

"Don't tell me those two old ladies are still alive?"

"Alive and happily thieving."

She walked toward the bed. "You'll be all right, won't you?"

"Yes, of course. I have Oman."

"A great lot of help he is. He was going to let you lie in bed without any nursing whatever."

"I must admit that being in bed with pretty girls *always* makes me heal much faster."

Claire blushed to the roots of her hair. "You are wicked. Now I want you to eat a good dinner and go to sleep."

"Yes, ma'am," he teased.

She started to leave the room, then turned back toward him. "Vellie, thank you for being my friend."

His eyes widened a bit at her use of his nursery name, but he didn't say anything. When you'd nursed someone as she had him, you had a right to call a person anything you wanted. He gave her a little smile, then she was gone.

Claire ran down the old stone stairs but when she got halfway down she remembered she'd meant to ask Trevelyan if she could borrow a book. She thought she'd reread one of Captain Baker's books. She ran back up the stairs and into the sitting room. Oman was nowhere to be seen and when she peeped into the bedroom, she saw that Trevelyan was sleeping.

Claire got the book she wanted from the cabinet mounted in the wall then turned to leave. But at the last moment she turned and looked at the eleven tables, each with writing paraphernalia on it.

Since she'd first seen these tables she had been very curious as to what Trevelyan was doing on them, but now she seemed to be bursting with curiosity. She glanced toward the silent bedroom door and went to the first table.

There were many bits of paper on the table, stacks of the little pieces. Some were only an inch square and some were as big as three inches square. All of them were covered with the tiniest writing she'd ever seen. She picked up one of the larger pieces and looked at it, but could make out nothing.

With another glance at the bedroom door she carried the paper to the window and held it up to the fading light. The writing seemed to tell of the walls of a city. It wasn't easy to read the small writing but what she could understand described the height of the walls and what they were made of. On the back of the paper were dimensions of the stones in the walls and a bit of theory on when the walls were built.

She put the paper back on the table and went to another table. These papers seemed to be a translation of poetry from incomprehensible script. Nothing she had seen so far made any sense, so she went around to all the tables. There were four tables dealing only with translations, each from a different language, and not a modern language. There was a table containing pages that seemed to be about traveling in China. Another table had pages pertaining to the search for gold in Arabia.

It was when she reached the seventh table that the answer began to dawn on her. On the seventh table was work on creating an alphabet for the Peshan language. It wasn't that she recognized the language, but there were extensive notes near the alphabet describing the sounds of the language. The name Pesha was everywhere.

Claire didn't think she was feeling too well as she walked back to the first table and looked again at the little pieces of paper. She had read that Captain Baker often went to places where the act of writing wasn't understood. Had he allowed any of the people in these towns to see him writing he would have forfeited his life. So he often wrote on tiny pieces of paper that could be hidden at a moment's notice. When she used to read Captain Baker's accounts of these secret writings, she would thrill at his daring. If even one of these papers had been seen he would have been killed.

She picked up one scrap of paper after another and read what she could. There were notes on the language of Pesha, on the people.

There were tiny sketches of the people in their long gowns, with all their jewelry about their arms. There were notes on the size of and distance between the walls of the city.

She went to the eighth table and there she had the shock of all her short life, for there were notes about her. Written out in what she was beginning to recognize as Trevelyan's strong, pointed handwriting was every conversation she'd ever had with him. She quickly scanned a page that told of her trying to cope with the inhabitants of Bramley. Trevelyan rather brilliantly made her seem like a well-meaning but very stupid child.

Under the written pages was a stack of cartoons. She had seen hundreds of Captain Baker's illustrations and knew his style well. On top was a cartoon of her pushing Harry over a chair and knocking the cherry pit from his throat. She was depicted as a big, strong, rather horsey-looking woman and Harry as somewhat feeble. There was another cartoon of her curled in Trevelyan's window seat, eating an apple, her nose less than an inch from the pages of a book. The caption read, "American Heiress meets Captain Baker in the original Latin."

There was another cartoon of her on a rearing horse. She was using her whip to command an old, sick man to calm the horse. She saw a cartoon of herself sitting at the head of an enormously long table, wearing a coronet and presiding over Harry's odd relatives, each of them perfectly caricatured.

There were more pages of notes, more pages of cartoons, but she couldn't bear to see any more. Very slowly, she put the notes down on the table and walked to the window.

"Find out what you wanted to know?" Trevelyan asked from behind her.

She wasn't startled to find out he was there and had probably been watching her for some time. When she turned to look at him he was wearing a long robe of some strange design and smiling as though he expected her to congratulate him on having kept his secret.

"You are Captain Baker," she said so softly that the sound was little more than a whisper.

"I am." There was pride in his voice, along with that sound of expectation.

"I must go. Harry will be waiting for me."

The smile left Trevelyan's face. He caught her arm before she reached the door. "You have nothing to say? You've asked so much about Captain Baker before now."

She didn't look at him. "I have nothing to say." As politely as she could, she pulled away and started down the stairs.

"I will see you tomorrow?" he asked.

She stopped on the stair but she didn't look back at him. "No, I will not come tomorrow." She started walking again.

"Come or go, I don't care," he called after her, then turned back into the room. What a very, very odd way for a woman to act, he thought. From the first day he'd met her all he'd heard was how wonderful, how great . . . Yes, that was it, how *great* Captain Baker was, yet now that she'd found out she was in the same room with the man she thought to be great, she acted as though he were poison.

His head came up. Perhaps she was in awe of him. He'd encountered that in people before. They had heard of him and knew of his work and when they spoke to him their voices quivered. He smiled and bounded down the stairs two at a time.

He reached her just as she reached the door to the outside. He caught her arm. "There's no reason to be afraid of me," he said. "You've seen that I'm a man like any other. You've seen that I'm flesh like any other man. You may continue to visit me."

"May I?"

"Yes," he answered, completely missing the irony in her voice.

She stood still for a long while and looked at him. "The scars on your cheeks are from the lance in Africa? It went through one side of your jaw and out the other."

He nodded.

"The scars on your back, they're from a lion, also in Africa?"

He smiled broader. It was quite soul satisfying that *this* woman knew so much about him. Many men knew about what he had done in his life, but not many women were allowed to read what he had written. And, right now, had he been given a choice, he would rather Claire know what he had done in his life than any other person on earth.

"And the knife wounds on your ribs?" she asked.

He didn't answer right away.

"You are a Master Sufi," she said softly.

He was *very* impressed with her knowledge of him.

Claire gave him a humorless smile. "Now I know what others don't.

You wrote that you had become a Master Sufi, but one critic said that was impossible, that to pass the . . . graduation I guess you'd call it, you'd have to go through a ceremony. It is, I believe, a ceremony in which you are put into a trance and you inflict—" She broke off, not liking to think of what he had done, but then he was a scholar as there had never been a scholar. He wasn't content with researching a subject, he wanted to experience what he saw. To become a Master Sufi, a priest of what has been called the Religion of Beauty, he would have had to put himself in a trance and, while singing and dancing, stab himself with a knife. It is said that initiates' wounds would later be healed by the touch of their master.

Trevelyan gave her a bit of a bow to acknowledge that she was right.

Claire looked at him a moment longer, then put her hand on the door.

He covered her hand with his. "It doesn't matter what's gone before. You may still visit me. I will . . ." He smiled. "I will teach you Peshan."

She pulled her hand away from his. "And what will I teach you?"

"I don't know what you mean. I know all the languages you know. I—"

"Perhaps I can teach you more about being an American heiress. Perhaps I can teach you what it feels like to be an American who is about to become a duchess."

"I don't know what you're talking about."

Her anger was beginning to show now. She had hoped she would be able to make it out of the old wing of the house before she exploded, but she wasn't going to make it. "Will you write a book on your observations of me? Will I see your cartoons in every bookstore in the world?"

It took Trevelyan a moment to understand what she was talking about. "As you have said, I write about everything."

"Including your friends." She smiled at that. "Now that I see it I don't know how I didn't know who you were from the beginning. The scars. The cold eyes that look at everything and everyone as though they were biological specimens that should be cataloged and categorized. Will you give me a Latin name for having discovered me? *Americanus bakerus.* I assume you do want the credit for having made the identification. Do I get the great privilege of having a male Latin name? Or is it *Americana bakera?*"

"I have never done anything to make you believe I am as you describe. I—"

"Haven't you? At every opportunity you have asked me questions about myself and my family. You've asked how I feel about people I know." Her mouth tightened. "You have asked me questions about Captain Baker, about—" She looked him up and down. "You have asked me about yourself. It was rather like eavesdropping wasn't it, Captain Baker? Or should I call you Trevelyan? Or maybe I shouldn't call you at all."

Again she reached for the door, but he blocked her way.

"I didn't mean to lie to you," he said. "There are reasons that force me to keep my identity a secret."

"So you can spy on people?"

"I don't spy on people."

"Perhaps the people of Pesha would look at it differently." She could see he had no idea what she meant. "Let me explain something to you, whatever your name is. I am not a savage for you to study." She looked away for a moment, then back again. "When I think of the way you sat and watched me while I was at MacTarvit's. And in here I . . . I helped you while you were ill." She took a step away from him, as though she didn't want to get too close. "I am not one of your savages who you think have quaint and fascinating customs. I am an American, a very rich American, and if you write anything about me, I will sue you."

He blinked at her a few times, then stepped away from the door. "I will not write about you, Miss Willoughby. Good-bye, and I wish you all the luck in the world with your duke."

She didn't acknowledge his remark as she walked out of the room.

Chapter Ten

When Claire reached the house the family was already seated at dinner. She didn't bother to go to her room and change out of her dress, grimy now from having been worn for so many days. Nor did she notice the way the servants looked at her. She walked to the dining room doors, put her hand out to open one, and the footman stopped her.

"Her Grace says that the diners are not to be disturbed," the man said.

Claire looked up at him. "When I am duchess I will remember who you are," she said quietly.

The footman opened the door for her.

She marched straight to Harry, seated at the head of the table. They were just starting on the soup course. "I must see you," she said.

Claire had been in the British Isles long enough to know that no one ever, under any circumstances, interrupted an Englishman at his dinner. It was so much a rule that no one had bothered to think of it as a rule. It was not done, probably had never been done, probably had never been thought of being done.

Harry was so shocked that he just sat there and looked at her. His mouth was a bit open and he had his soupspoon suspended in midair.

"I want to see you now. At once," she said.

She didn't look at the other people at the table, but she was well aware that they were staring at her, shocked at this breach of etiquette. Claire had no doubt that she was probably reinforcing their ideas of Americans as barbarians.

Harry put his spoon down, pushed his chair back, and followed her out of the room. "What has happened?" he asked, for he was convinced that only death could have caused this commotion.

"I must talk to you."

Harry's heart began to pound. He didn't think that her news had to do with his mother. Surely he would have been told first if anything had happened to her. The second thing that came to his mind was that Claire was here to break off their engagement. He dreaded that. If he lost his little American heiress, his mother would be angry, possibly more than angry.

By the time they reached the blue drawing room, Harry was prepared for the worst. If something had happened to make her want to break the engagement, he would do what he could to change her mind. Maybe it was his mother's rules against having trays brought to the rooms. If that was what was wrong, Harry thought he might go against his mother's wishes and allow Claire to have meals in her room if that's what she wanted.

He closed the door behind him and leaned against it. "What is it?"

To his surprise, Claire threw herself at him, wrapping her arms about his chest and holding him to her. It took him a moment to realize that the danger was over. He held her at arms' length. "What has happened?"

She began talking but she was so incoherent that it was a moment before he understood what she was saying. He heard the word Trevelyan, and Harry almost laughed in relief. Was that all that was wrong with her? His brother could enrage a saint. His brother had enraged men—to be fair, it was mostly men—from one end of the world to the other.

"What has Vellie done now?" he asked, dropping his hands from her shoulders.

"I have been with him." She wasn't crying but he could feel her shaking. It was his experience that Trevelyan often made people shake with rage or some other emotion.

"Been with him?" Harry said softly and thought about the words. "Do you mean to marry him?"

Claire pulled away from him. "Marry him? Are you out of your mind?"

Again relief swept over Harry. "We will wait and see what happens. If you find that you are with child then we'll be married sooner than we'd planned. I'll pass the child off as mine and—"

She looked at him in horror. "*What* are you talking about?"

"If you have been with him, then . . ."

Claire began to laugh at that. "Oh, Harry, you are funny. I don't mean that I've *been* with him, I mean that for the last few days I wasn't sick, I was with Trevelyan. He was ill and I was nursing him."

"Oh," was all that Harry could say. He didn't want Claire to know that he hadn't known that she'd been ill. He had come in from his horse-buying trip but hours ago and his main concern had been his dinner. He had noticed that she was not at the dinner table, but with Claire that was not unusual. He didn't understand Americans and he had no inclination to try to understand one. If she didn't want to eat dinner, that was her prerogative.

"He is Captain Baker," she said, and there was anger in her voice.

"Yes."

"I want to know about him. I want to know what he's doing here and why he's hiding."

Harry had never seen her so agitated, her face so flushed, her eyes so bright. "Claire, have you fallen in love with him?"

"No," she said, and he could see the honesty in her eyes. "I have not fallen in love with him."

Harry breathed a sigh of relief at that, but then he frowned. It was his experience that when a woman said she wanted to talk about something, it often meant hours and hours of talk. He thought with longing of his dinner. He opened the door, told the footman to bring his dinner to him in the blue drawing room and that he was not to be disturbed.

"Now, my dear, why don't you tell me what Vellie has done to upset you so much?" He wanted to know how much his brother had told her, how much she knew of the truth of how Trevelyan was related to his family.

She started talking in a flood of words. Harry'd always had the impression that she was a quiet little thing, with few words in her—one of the best things about her to his way of thinking—but now there were as many words as he'd ever heard. She told about days spent with Trevelyan. She told of Vellie's having taken her to visit old man MacTarvit. She told of walks and meals and reading his books.

She stopped talking when the dinner was brought and placed on the big table in the room. When the servants were gone and they were again alone, Harry began to eat, but Claire paced the room and talked to him.

"You don't know what Captain Baker has meant to my life. I have studied his work; I have studied his life. I know a great deal about him."

For the life of him Harry could not figure out what Trevelyan had done that had so upset her. Was it that he had lied to her? Was keeping his identity a secret what was making her so angry?

It was when she started to tell of finding the drawings of herself, some of those dreadful caricatures of Vellie's, that he began to understand. The first time Harry had seen the cartoons Trevelyan had drawn of him he had been insulted as he'd never been before or since. Trevelyan had depicted him as a little boy in ringlets, physically attached to his mother, as though they were one person. Sometimes Trevelyan had shown him as having his mother's face and his mother as having Harry's.

Harry started to tell her that Trevelyan made those cartoons of everyone. Harry had seen some drawings that Vellie had made of himself that were almost vicious. Trevelyan often depicted himself as a fool, a man who trusted all the wrong people and was always betrayed.

But something made Harry hesitate. He hadn't been aware that Claire was spending so much time with his brother. He had assumed that she was doing whatever women did with their days. It was a shock to find out that she had spent days and nights with him, had even traveled through the tunnels with him.

"Trevelyan can be quite unkind," Harry said, his mouth full. He watched her. "But women usually like him."

"I did too. I thought of him as my friend, but he was using me. He was studying me. He wrote about me as though I were one of his savages and he was observing my bizarre customs."

"Won't you have some of this roast beef? It's cooked perfectly."

Claire sat down at the table and Harry put a slice of beef on her plate, but she didn't eat. "Tell me about him. What has made him so cold, so much without feeling?"

That startled Harry. Trevelyan a man without feeling? Trevelyan was the angriest, most emotional man alive.

"Why is he here? Why have you taken him in?"

"What did he tell you about his kindred to my family?" Harry held his breath, waiting for her answer. Trevelyan said that he didn't want the dukedom, but all he had to do was change his mind and Harry would be out in the cold. He would have some money from his mother, but not much else. That is, he would have nothing if he lost his heiress—which he did not mean to do.

"He says he's a cousin of sorts."

"Yes, he is. He is related to me, just as the other people in this house are."

"And you take care of them," she said, looking into Harry's beautiful eyes.

"I do my best," he said modestly.

Claire left the table to start pacing again. "Explain his name to me. Why does he keep his identity a secret?"

Harry took his time in answering. "He was sent away from his home when he was nine years old."

"To school?"

"No. As far as I know, Trevelyan has never been to a formal school."

"Then why was he sent away?"

Harry gave a little shrug. "It was only a couple of years after I was born, so I don't really know. I've been told he was a difficult child. He and his older brother used to get into scrapes, always at the instigation of Trevelyan." Harry smiled. "One time the two boys were in France with their father and there was a disease in the town, a plague or something, I don't know what, and there were men with carts who came and picked up the dead bodies. Trevelyan and his brother bribed the cart driver to let them accompany him on his nightly rounds. I was told that inside the pit where they threw the bodies was a blue flame."

"Yes, that sounds like something he would do. He was sent away by his father for pulling such boyish pranks?"

"His mother sent him away. She sent him off to live with her father." Harry swallowed. "The old man was called the Admiral. He was said to be a stickler for discipline and it was hoped he could teach Trevelyan some discipline."

"But he couldn't."

"No. Trevelyan never would do anything anyone else wanted him to do. I think he and the Admiral fought a great deal. I know they came to hate each other. When Vellie was sixteen he left the Admiral and went into the army on commission."

"As Frank Baker?"

"Yes. The Admiral wanted Trevelyan to go into the navy but Trevelyan didn't like ships or water. In the end Trevelyan bought his own commission in the army. So his grandfather wouldn't find him, he enlisted under another name. I think his disguise started out as just another prank, but later became something important to Vellie. He wanted to make his grandfather eat his words when he'd said that Vellie would never amount to anything, that if he didn't have his attachment to our family name, he would be nothing, that he could never attain anything. I think Vellie wanted to prove his grandfather wrong."

"I think he did that. Captain Baker has proved himself to be a great man."

"To some, maybe." Harry was frowning. This woman was *his. Not* his brother's. He turned in his chair and smiled at her. Harry knew how to use his looks to advantage.

With a smile, Claire went to sit on a chair near him.

"Now tell me, why have you been spending so much time with my . . . cousin? Isn't there enough here in this house to keep you occupied?"

"I guess I have been a bit bored." She looked down at her hands. She didn't want Harry to think she was a complainer; she didn't want to do anything to make him think less of her. "Just a little bored." She looked up at him. "Oh, Harry, when am I going to meet your mother?"

"Anytime you want," he said with confidence. But he didn't feel confident inside. When it came to stubbornness, his mother made Trevelyan seem like a child.

"Harry, I want to spend more time with you. I want us to be as we were in London. I want us to go places together and do things together and to have conversations. I want us to be the couple in love, as we really are."

"Well, of course." Harry thought that he ought to call Trevelyan out over this. To Harry, he had done his courting in London and now he was free to live his own life again. The work was done. He had gone to London because he had heard there was a pretty little American heiress up for grabs and he'd gone and won her. Now, because of the interference of his brother, he was going to have to do more courting.

"And I want to spend some time with your sister."

Harry brightened at that. "Leatrice? Why, of course, spend all the time you want with her. She loves all the things that you like."

She moved to look at him. "What are the things that I like?"

"Books. History. You like the Scots a lot."

She smiled and Harry breathed a sigh of relief. Women and their damned tests of love! Every one of his mistresses was the same. They weren't content with a man's presence, they repeatedly wanted him to prove he loved them.

"I know Leatrice likes books. What else does she like?"

Harry reached for his wineglass. He'd eaten few meals in his life without someone nearby to serve him and one of the worst aspects of it was having to fill one's own glass. "You mean besides James Kincaid?"

Claire sat up on his lap. "Who is James Kincaid?"

Harry could have bitten off his tongue. "No one. I was merely making a joke. Believe me, he's no one. He's probably dead by now. In fact I'm sure he is."

"Who was he then?"

Harry drained the glass and reached for the bottle in the silver bucket on the stand by the table. He couldn't reach it unless he turned his back on Claire, but he thought he'd better not do that at the moment. Women who were in a state of distress sometimes thought the oddest things. If he turned away from Claire to get at the wine bottle she just might think he liked wine better than he liked her.

"Lee fell in love with him when she was a girl. Or maybe she had always been in love with him, I don't know. I was just a kid when it happened and I don't remember very well." He didn't remember what had happened before his sister had for the one and only time defied their mother, but he certainly remembered what happened afterward. He imagined there were rooms in the old house that still echoed with Leatrice's screams.

"What happened?"

"Kincaid was entirely unsuitable. Lee *is* a duke's daughter, you know. Kincaid was—" He didn't say any more, because Claire was getting that look on her face that women got when they thought they smelled romance in the air. "Kincaid really is—was, if he's dead—

the most dreadful person. Very strange. Walked around talking to himself. Always had papers falling out of his pockets. The village children used to follow him and jeer at him. Mother was right in not allowing her daughter to marry the man."

"But Leatrice didn't marry anyone else?"

Harry shook his head. He wasn't about to tell Claire of the war that had gone on between mother and daughter. Lee had said that if she couldn't marry the man she wanted then she wouldn't marry any man. Mother had said that if Lee didn't obey her and marry a man the duchess had chosen for her, then she'd make Leatrice's life a living hell. Lee had said, "Better that than to marry a man I hate, as you did, and live the life you have led." It was the last bit of defiance Leatrice had shown toward anyone. Harry knew his mother had long ago broken Lee's spirit, for, as far as Harry could tell, his mother was stronger than anyone else on earth.

Claire left the chair and Harry immediately reached for the wine bottle. "Harry, I must have something to *do.* In America I was always busy."

It was Harry's opinion that *all* Americans were always busy. They seemed to have no conception of how to sit still and do nothing. They were either doing something or talking about what they were going to do. He'd heard that some horrid American woman bragged that she got her guests through dinner in a mere fifty minutes.

"Of course you want something to do, darling. We all need tasks to keep us busy. A man's life is worth nothing if he does not accomplish something during his time on earth." He had read that somewhere and was pleased with himself for remembering it. "What did you have in mind?"

Claire looked out the window. It was dark outside and the curtains hadn't been drawn. She could see her own reflection and the handsome one of Harry lounging in his chair, drinking his wine. She turned back to him. "I want to see all of the estate. I want you to introduce me to your overseers or foremen or whatever you call them. I want you to show me how this great place of yours works, how you run it."

Harry gave her a weak smile. He wouldn't know a foreman of Bramley if he met the man in the drawing room. He'd have to get Charles to help him. "Of course. It will be my pleasure to show you. Anything else?" Maybe the moon delivered to you, he thought. If anyone ever hinted to him that he hadn't *earned* his wife's millions, he'd shoot the son of a bitch.

She widened her eyes. "Harry, you *do* manage this place and the others you own, don't you?"

Americans and their disgusting work ethic, he thought. They all, every last one of them, believed that a man should work. It was a concept he couldn't begin to understand. "Of course I do. It takes a great deal of my time. Has someone said something to you?"

"Trevelyan said you didn't—" She smiled. "It doesn't matter what he said. That's done with now. Now I'm going to start my new life as a duchess. I have a great deal to learn and I'm looking forward to it. Could we go riding early tomorrow morning? I'd like to begin to see the estate. I mean, see it from a worker's point of view."

"Yes, of course you may. I'll take you riding at first light. Or perhaps you'd like to sleep in the morning," he said hopefully.

"No, I don't need that much sleep. And I'd like to meet your mother, and I'd also like for you to find out whether or not James Kincaid is alive and where he's living."

Harry took a deep drink of wine to keep from groaning aloud. "I'm sure the man is dead. I'm sure I heard he was run over by a farm wagon. Probably wasn't watching where he was going. Now, dear, isn't it time for you to retire?"

"Yes, I think it is. Harry, I feel that everything is going to be all right now. I don't know what I was doing spending so much time with that man when I could have been with you. Tomorrow I'm going to start my new life." She put her arms around his neck, kissed his forehead as he patted her arm, then left the room.

Harry sat where he was until a servant came to clear the table. "Call Charles to me," he said.

"I believe Mr. Sorenson has retired, sir."

"Then get him out of bed!" Harry snapped. "He has to tell me who runs this place. And how it's done." He drank more wine and wondered if his ancestors had had to work this hard for the money they'd married.

When Claire awoke the next morning, she was in a state of excitement. Just thinking of spending the day with Harry was enough to make her happy. She went downstairs but was told that Harry was not yet up this morning due to the fact that he had been awake late the night before tending to estate business. The footman told Claire that Harry was usually up before the birds. Something about this statement seemed to amuse the man as he unsuccessfully tried to keep from smiling.

She waited in the entry hall for Harry and he came down, beautifully dressed and ready for their tour of the estate. He introduced her to Mr. Charles Sorenson, who was the estate agent and who would be riding with them on their tour. Claire was a little disappointed that they wouldn't be alone, but she swallowed her unhappiness and went with Harry to the stables.

It was the first time she had seen the stables in daylight, because when she had spent time with Trevelyan he had always wanted to walk. She blocked that man out of her mind. She was doing everything she could not to think of Trevelyan, or Captain Baker.

She was surprised to see the beauty and the cleanliness of the stables, and she was shocked to see that they had running water. The house didn't have running water but the stables did. When she saw the affectionate way the horses greeted Harry, she almost understood why.

She was properly and pleasantly surprised when Harry presented her with the prettiest little mare she had ever seen. The animal had dainty and delicate feet and she softly nickered at Claire's shoulder. "She is beautiful, Harry, really beautiful."

He smiled, glad to have pleased her. He was also very, very glad that yesterday she had not broken their engagement, for he had charged this horse and four others to an account that was to be paid after their marriage, after he had received her dowry. He had also bought some rather fine pictures, and a few pieces of porcelain, and a rather nice piece of fifteenth-century silver.

He helped her onto her horse and they began the tour of the estate. At first Claire asked Harry all the questions she wanted to know, but Harry, with a lovely sense of humility, always referred the questions to Mr. Sorenson. She admired Harry for not trying to make his servant feel his position was less than his master's.

They rode for hours, going over acres of land, traveling down what must have been miles of road. Claire was introduced to gamekeepers and tenants and comptrollers. They rode through woods and gardens and fields. Everywhere they went, people came out of their houses to look at them and offer them food and, for Claire, bunches of heather and flowers. Claire ate and drank of everything and tied all the flowers onto her horse, so that in a few hours she looked like part of the landscape moving slowly down the roads. The children came out to see them and laughed with Claire when they saw her horse, then they ran to gather more of the soft purple heather to tie to the animal.

Claire enjoyed herself immensely, but there were times when enjoyment wasn't easy. Harry was not in the best mood that he had ever been in. He would not eat or drink anything the crofters offered him. At one point he said, "I prefer my food on a plate." When the children offered him flowers he told them to get the hell away. Claire tried to soothe him. Her father found children a nuisance and she could see that Harry did too. There was nothing wrong with that.

She also did her best not to see some other things about the estate. The stables that housed Harry's horses were monuments of beauty, done in marble and mahogany, with brass nameplates for each of his horses. Yet the crofters' houses—which Harry owned just as much as he did the stables—looked very much the same as they must have when the Normans first invaded England.

There were, of course, a few good houses. Claire had been glad to see these places, houses with slate roofs as opposed to thatch, two-story and heated with nice coal stoves instead of ill-vented peat fires. But as she talked to the owners of these houses she was confused. She asked them about farming, what they were doing with the acres of land they rented from Harry. Claire's grandfather had had some farms and he had made them pay very, very well. But here she saw fields lying fallow, plows rusting in sheds, and no one working the land.

She asked Harry about this and got the perplexing answer that the men who rented the nice houses loved animals. She couldn't understand what this had to do with farming.

She was also confused by the wooded areas. To her, timber was a renewable crop. You cut trees and replanted them; they were harvested just like corn. The only difference was that the trees took longer. She saw woodland that looked as though it had been harvested probably twenty years or so before, but now it was being allowed to be covered with undergrowth. There were blackberry brambles everywhere.

She asked Harry about the trees being left as they were and what was being done to harvest them. Mr. Sorenson told her that the underbrush was a good hiding place for foxes and partridge. Claire said she hadn't understood that the estate did a business in these creatures.

Harry looked at her as though she'd lost her mind. "The foxes are for hunting and we shoot the partridge. We don't sell them."

Claire realized she was being an American again. She had seen a fox hunt and she knew that Englishmen loved to shoot things, whether flying or on foot. She had just never realized that cropland was dedicated to that purpose.

By the time they returned it was midmorning and a grumpy Harry went off to eat and Claire went to her room to change from her riding outfit. She didn't listen as horrid old Miss Rogers complained about everything. Miss Rogers was a firm believer in schedules and Claire had changed the schedule for no reason that she could see.

"Leave me," Claire said, then when the old woman stayed where she was, Claire turned and glared at her until she left the room.

Claire sat in her underwear at her dressing table and looked at herself in the mirror. She didn't seem to understand anything about her husband-to-be's life. She didn't understand the people or the country.

She saw hungry people, but fields that could have been used to raise crops were barren. Timber that could have been harvested was not. Even blackberries that could have been put to commercial use were allowed to rot on the ground. She'd seen horses that were housed better than people.

She put her head in her hands. She wasn't a socialist. She wasn't a person who believed that all people should have the same. She was her grandfather's child. She believed in hard work, and those who worked the hardest and were the most clever made the most money. But money carried a responsibility with it. Her grandfather had always said that the best resource was manpower and he had always taken care of his workers. Because of this he'd never had the trouble with strikes and burn-outs that other employers had. Her grandfather had had a long list of people who wanted to work for him.

She tried to tell herself that this was Scotland, that she was no longer in America, but at the same time, she saw the rags the children were wearing. The word "clan" meant children. These people were by tradition Harry's children, yet he didn't act as though he were their father.

She tried not to think of Harry in a bad light. She *couldn't* think of Harry in any way except a good one. If she was in love with him then she was in love with him as he really was, not as she wanted him to be.

She stood and went to the wardrobe to get an afternoon dress. Perhaps Harry didn't know any other way. Perhaps Trevelyan was right and this was the way Harry had been raised. This was all that he knew.

After lunch she would talk to him. Perhaps he would be willing to allow her to make a few changes after they were married. Maybe not drastic changes but enough to make a difference. There was no reason why Bramley couldn't become a paying enterprise. Perhaps that's what Harry wanted too, except he didn't know how to go about achieving it. Yes, that was it. She was sure of it.

She pulled a dress from the wardrobe and began to smile. Yes, that had to be it.

Chapter Eleven

"I want to know every word she said," Eugenia, duchess of MacArran, said to her youngest son.

"Mother," Harry said. His voice was pleading. "I'm sure Claire didn't mean—"

"Let me be the judge of what she meant."

"She's an American. One has to make allowances."

Eugenia fixed her son with a look.

"All right," Harry said in exasperation. "This morning I took her on a tour of the estate. Charles went with us, or I should say that we went with him." He paused a moment. "I had no idea so much was going on in this place. It was interesting—not that I want to repeat it, but it was interesting. I must say that Americans are an odd lot, though."

"What did she do?"

"She seemed to like the children. The whole filthy lot of them. She drank milk from pails that had cow manure on the bottom of them. I don't know how she stood it."

"Perhaps after you're married you shouldn't allow such things."

Harry shrugged. "I don't think it will matter after we're married, because the filthy beggars will be gone, won't they?"

"You haven't told her that, have you?" Eugenia asked sharply.

"I'm not a complete idiot. I'm not going to tell her that you plan to ship her adored crofters off to America or wherever and tear down those hideous old houses and run sheep over the land."

"I have no idea why you sound as though it were something bad. It is what nearly all the other landowners have already done." Eugenia's voice had a sad tone to it. "After all, Harry, I'm doing this for you."

"I know, Mother, and I appreciate it. I'll be as glad as you to get rid of those houses. Once they're gone I shall be able to lead hunts across the fields."

"And you can profit from the sheep."

"Now you sound like Claire."

"What does that mean?" Eugenia snapped. "Are you saying that *I* am like your interfering little American?"

"No, of course not. I merely meant that Claire talks constantly about ways to make money. She wants to cut down trees; she wants to plant fields with corn; she wants to sell bramble jelly. I don't know what else. It makes my head swim just listening to her."

"She means to run this place," Eugenia said softly. "She means to have me out of here."

"I haven't heard her say any such thing. I don't see why my mother and my wife couldn't work together. If you both want to make this place pay then why not work together?"

Eugenia looked at her son for a long while, saw the way he was lounging in his chair, bored with the whole idea of work. Together! Eugenia thought. What Harry didn't realize was that the two women were about to engage in a power struggle, and Eugenia meant to win.

Eugenia gave a loud moan and put her hand to her ankle. Her left foot was encased in a thick, built-up, black leather boot.

Harry came instantly alert. "Mother, are you in pain? Would you like to lie down?"

"No," Eugenia said softly, weakly. "I'm not in pain, at least not more than usual, not more than I have suffered every day since you were born. It's my heart that hurts me. When you marry you will no longer be my son."

Harry sat on the floor at his mother's side and put his head on her knee as he'd done a thousand times before. "What nonsense do you speak? I could never forget you."

She stroked his fine, blond hair. "It's traditional that when the son marries, the mother retires to the dower house. After you're married, your pretty little wife will send me away to some cold place. I will no longer have my things about me, for they will be hers then. But, most of all, my darling, I won't get to see you every day."

"Of course you will. I shall ride to wherever you are every day of my life."

"Harry, my dearest child, how sweet you are. But it will rain and it will snow, and then there will be things to keep you from seeing your poor old mother."

"Mother, I promise that—"

"You won't allow her to throw me out of my own house? The house where I've lived most of my life?"

"But Mother, Claire will be the duchess and she should—"

"I understand. But of course you will be the duke, and it's such a small thing that I ask of you. Merely to stay in my own home."

"Yes, of course it's a small thing." He squeezed his mother's hand as she smoothed his hair behind his ear. "You may stay. I'm sure Claire won't mind."

Eugenia was quiet for a moment. "Do you love her so very much?"

"I do rather like her. Although . . ."

"Although what?"

"The last few days she has been different."

Eugenia's ears perked up and her caressing voice changed. "How is she different? What has changed her?"

It was on the tip of Harry's tongue to say that Trevelyan had upset Claire, but he didn't. It was one thing to tell a few white lies to the woman he was planning to marry, but it was another to tell his mother that her second son had come back from the dead. Sometimes Trevelyan made Harry angry, but he didn't hate his brother, and that's what he'd have to do in order to justify telling his mother that Trevelyan was not dead and was staying in the old part of the house.

"She has trouble adjusting to this way of life," Harry said. "I gather that in America she had a very different sort of life."

"Such as?"

"Busy. Very, very busy." Harry took his mother's hand and kissed it. "I think you're going to love her. I think the two of you will become great friends. You will be the two women I love most in the world."

Eugenia smiled at her son. "Send her to me for tea tomorrow afternoon."

Chapter Twelve

By five o'clock, when it was time for tea with the duchess, Claire was a nervous wreck. She was dressed in her best lace gown, all the lace handmade in France. She had purchased this dress especially with the idea of meeting Harry's mother.

Miss Rogers escorted Claire to the duchess's door, then, with a little shake of her gray-haired, gray-faced head, as if to tell Claire that she, an American, would never live up to standards, she left her there.

"Thank you for the encouragement," Claire muttered. She checked that her dress was straight, checked for the hundredth time that she had the little notebook and pencil she had been instructed to bring, took a deep breath, and put her hand on the doorknob.

The moment Claire walked into the enormous sitting room, she thought, This is where all the wealth is. It didn't take a scholar of art to see that the paintings on the walls were old and very valuable. She recognized Rubens, Rembrandt, Titian. On carved, gold-leafed tables were objects of great beauty and great value. In the rest of the house the furnishings were dirty and torn, but in this room all was spotless. The silk that draped the walls and the windows was new and, to Claire's experienced eye, astonishingly expensive.

Mother will be green with envy, Claire thought as she looked about the room.

But Claire's eyes were soon drawn from the walls and the Aubusson rug to the woman sitting in the big chair near the silver tea tray. She was a stout woman, with steel gray hair severely pulled back from a handsome face. Claire thought that at one time the woman might have been pretty, but now there was a sternness about her that was . . . well, frightening. She was dressed in an expensive gown of dark blue silk, well cut, but at least ten years out of fashion. Below the dress Claire could see the heavy black boot on her left foot.

"How do you do, Your Grace," Claire said, smiling at the woman.

The duchess did not smile back, nor did she ask Claire to sit down. Claire stood where she was, not sure what to do. She watched as the duchess poured a cup of tea and Claire stepped forward, assuming the woman was going to offer it to her.

She did not. The duchess lifted the cup to her own lips and began to drink.

Claire took a step backward, puzzled and feeling awkward.

"So, you plan to marry my son." The woman looked Claire up and down. "Are you a virgin?"

Claire blinked a couple of times. "Yes, ma'am," she whispered. "I am."

"Good. I will not have my son marrying used goods."

Claire swallowed. This was not how she'd imagined a duchess to talk. She took a step toward a chair across from the duchess, meaning to sit down, but the duchess paused with the cup on the way to her lips and looked at Claire in horror. Claire immediately straightened and did not sit down.

"I assume there is nothing wrong with you, that you can bear children."

"Yes, ma'am," Claire whispered. "I believe that I can."

"The bearing of children is your first responsibility as the eleventh duchess of MacArran. You are to bear my son sons of his own. There should be a son produced within the first year of marriage and another son within the second year. After that it is up to my son as to what he wants."

Claire could feel herself blushing. "I will do my best."

The duchess picked up a saucer, put a small, iced cake on it, and began to eat. "Your second responsibility will be to take care of my son. While I am alive I will take care of him. I will see that he has what he needs and that he gets what he wants. But I will not always be here, therefore you will have to take over some of my responsibilities."

Claire thought that by saying she would not always be here, she meant that after the marriage she would be moving to the dower house, a lovely place Claire had seen yesterday. Claire smiled. "I will never be able to replace you in Harry's life and I'm sure he will visit you often. I'm sure that—"

The duchess gave Claire a look that made her take a step backward. There was sure fury and rage and . . . and, she wasn't sure, but it looked as though there was almost hatred in that look. "Visit me? You are saying that you think my son will toss me from his house?"

"No ma'am," Claire stammered. "I assumed that you would live in the dower house."

The duchess gave Claire a look that was almost a sneer. "You want my rooms, do you? You want my rooms as well as my son? What else do you want?"

At the moment what Claire wanted most in the world was to leave that room and never see it again. "I meant no disrespect," she murmured softly, her head lowered. She did not want to anger Harry's mother, didn't want her telling Harry that the woman he wanted to marry was an aggressive American.

The duchess watched Claire, then gave a sound as though she were mollified. "All right," she said at last. "It's better that you and I get along. This will be difficult enough as it is."

Claire let out her pent-up breath and gave the woman a tentative smile. "I think it would be good for Harry's sake if we became friends. He speaks so highly of you."

"Of course he does," the duchess snapped.

Claire tensed again. Everything she said seemed to offend the woman.

"Shall we get on with it?" the duchess said. "You must learn how to take care of my son."

"Yes," Claire said. "I would like to know about Harry. He—" The duchess cut her off, not allowing her to say another word.

"Open your notebook."

Before Claire could get the little book open, the duchess began speaking very rapidly.

"We will start with peas. My son will eat peas with ham and beef, but he's not to be served peas with chicken. Except chicken in cream sauce. Then peas are *always* to be served. Of course he never eats peas with mutton, but peas with lamb are allowed, but only if the lamb is under six months old. Peas can be served with veal but only in the spring. No peas with veal in the winter and of course no peas with fish of any kind. Nor are peas to be served with game, except squab, of course. Shall we proceed to carrots?"

During this Claire had not had time to get her mouth closed, much less her notebook open. But at the word carrots she moved so she could rest her notebook against the back of a chair and began to write as quickly as possible. But it wasn't nearly fast enough. There were instructions about vegetables, meat, game, how to serve Harry's food, when it was to be served. It was all much, much too complex to understand, much less write down.

Once the duchess had finished with the food, she told of Harry's weak back and how he was to be taken care of should he have back pains. The treatment involved tents full of steam and hot towels and compresses full of aromatic herbs.

Claire was never to raise her voice to Harry, never to argue with him, never to cross him in any way. The duchess told Claire what games Harry could and could not play, and she advised Claire to allow Harry to win any and all card games. "To win gives him such pleasure," the duchess said.

She went on to tell Claire what colors Harry's clothes should be. Harry was never, never to have wool next to his tender skin. With an angry look at Claire she told how she did not approve of Harry's wearing of those disgusting Scots' clothes. Her look let Claire know that it was her fault Harry was running around bare legged and that she was close to killing him with her absurd love of these clothes. Claire heard herself murmuring an apology.

The duchess told of Harry's schedule, of when he could and could not do things. She chastised Claire for being so selfish as to drag Harry from a warm bed to take her on a survey of the estate. "My son is a man who tries to please. He likes to give to people. He will do whatever anyone asks of him, for he is generous beyond belief, but this morning I could tell he was nearly ill from having to spend a cold morning yesterday wearing improper clothes and traipsing about the countryside."

Claire had no idea Harry was of such a delicate constitution, that he caught colds so easily or that he had a weak back, and she felt bad that she had been so unobservant as not to have seen it. "I will be more careful in the future," she murmured.

"Yes, see that you are."

At seven, after the two longest hours of Claire's life, Harry came into the room. Claire was so glad to see him she almost ran to him to throw her arms about him, but then she remembered his bad back.

"Mother," Harry said cheerfully, "the two of you have been in here for ages." He went forward and kissed his mother's cheek, then perched on the edge of her chair.

Claire watched from her place behind the chair and saw the way the woman's face softened when she looked at her son. Her eyes looked younger, almost like those of a girl who looked on the face of her lover. Claire looked at Harry and saw the tenderness between the two of them. And as she saw them together, she knew that she would always, forever, eternally be an outsider.

Harry raised from bending over his mother, took a biscuit from the tea tray, and munched as he looked at Claire. Claire wondered if almond cookies were on her list as a yes, a no, or a maybe. "Why are you standing?" he asked.

Claire looked at the two of them, the old woman sitting on the chair that now she thought resembled a throne and Harry draped over the arm of it, his kilt showing his strong legs, and she plainly and simply wanted to run away. The duchess was looking at her with interest, to see what she would answer to Harry's question.

"I can write better when I'm standing," Claire said.

The duchess lifted one eyebrow in acknowledgment of Claire's quick thinking.

"Mmmm," Harry said, not really interested. "And what are you writing?"

"About you," Claire said, smiling at him and not looking at the duchess.

Harry bent and again kissed his mother's cheek. "You old darling, you haven't been boring Claire with all my childhood ailments, have you?"

"I was just trying to take care of you. That's what a mother does." She gave him a look that was so full of love Claire was embarrassed to have seen it. It was too private, too intimate for another person to see.

Harry smiled at Claire. "You will probably hear dreadful stories about my mother," he said, and he was thinking about Trevelyan, "but I want you to know they aren't true. She is the kindest, sweetest person in the world, and I'm sure that in time you will come to love her as much as I do."

Claire looked at the duchess and saw the sly smile on her face. It was an expression that let Claire know she owned her son and always would.

"I must go," Claire said. "I . . . I promised my mother I'd see her before dinner." Quite suddenly Claire thought that she might explode if she had to stay in that opulent room one more minute of her life.

Harry got off the arm of his mother's chair. "Stay and I'll order fresh tea. You can tell Mother all about the horse I bought you. You haven't even named it yet. The two of you can decide on the horse's name."

"I really must go. Thank you, Your Grace, for . . . for everything."

"Wait," Harry said, "I'll go with you."

"No, please don't," Claire said. "I have to go." She was at the point that she didn't care if she was rude or not. All she knew was that, as she lived and breathed, she *had* to get out of that room.

Once the door closed behind her, she felt as though she could breathe again. She felt as though she'd escaped from something bad and horrible. It was as though she'd waked up from a terrible dream as a child and found out the dream was real.

She wanted to keep her head about her. She had to figure out how to handle this. Lots of women had frightening mothers-in-law. It was a universal joke to have a bad mother-in-law. People made jokes about how mothers were attached to their sons. Her own mother sometimes made sarcastic remarks about how men always loved their mothers the best of any female on earth, that no wife can compete with a man's mother.

Claire went back to her room. It wasn't such an awful thing that had happened. The old woman loved her son and she wanted him to be properly fed and clothed and cared for when he was ill. There wasn't any more to it than that.

In her room she found that Miss Rogers had laid her clothes out for dinner. Claire, with some difficulty, unbuttoned the back of her dress herself because Miss Rogers was nowhere to be found. Miss Rogers had her own schedule and she never deviated from it. She had decided to the minute when Claire should dress for dinner and therefore she did not appear until that time. If the crazy American wanted to do something different, then that was her problem, but it was not to interfere with Miss Rogers's life.

Claire lifted the dinner dress. She would go to dinner and act as though nothing had happened. She would smile at Harry and tell him what a pleasure it was meeting his mother, and she'd suggest that from now on he stop wearing a kilt, as he might catch cold.

Claire put her face in her hands. She didn't want to go to dinner, didn't want to face all those people who stared at her but who made no effort to speak to her. She didn't want to see Harry either and have to lie to him about what a lovely person his mother was.

She knew right away that whom she wanted to talk to was Trevelyan. No, she thought, he wasn't Trevelyan anymore, he was the renowned, the infamous, the notorious Captain Baker. If she did go talk to him, would he draw a cartoon of her that showed her with the crippled duchess? Would he show her cowering before the woman?

No, she couldn't talk to Trevelyan. She could no longer trust him. He had betrayed her. He wanted her to talk to him so he could use what she told him.

Who else could she talk to? Her parents? She almost paled at that thought. Her parents, what few glimpses she'd had of them, had fit into the life in this big house as though they'd been born into it. Brat had said their father was considering participating in the plays in the east wing.

But there was someone to whom she could talk, she thought, someone who would know and understand and could give her advice. She tossed the dinner dress back on the bed and pulled her riding habit from the wardrobe. She would miss dinner again and she was sure Her Grace would be told about it, but Claire didn't care. She had to talk to someone.

MacTarvit's old cottage wasn't easy to find, hidden as it was among the trees and hills, and Claire had a difficult time maneuvering the horse through some of the underbrush. Just as he had been when she'd first gone to him with Trevelyan, he was waiting for her. He must have positioned people as lookouts, children probably, Claire thought, because he seemed to know when anyone was approaching. He was protective of his precious whisky, and she wondered how anyone ever got near enough to steal any.

He was standing on a hill, his ancient gun across his arms, the breeze stirring his worn kilt. The moment she saw him tears welled up in her eyes. This man was the only thing she'd encountered in Scotland that was exactly as she'd expected it to be. Everything else was different and bewildering.

When she was still yards from him she dismounted and started running. Angus had no hesitation in knowing what to do: he leaned his gun against a rock and opened his big strong arms to her. She ran to him, hitting him full force, but it was like running into an oak tree. As soon as she touched him, it was as though a river had been released as floods of tears poured from her eyes.

Angus held her tightly. She cried and cried and he just stood there holding her, as patient as the oak he resembled.

After a long while she started to pull away. "I'm sorry. I didn't mean to—"

He shushed her. "Oh, aye, this ol' plaid could stand a wee washin'."

Claire gave a sound that was part tears, part choking, part laughter.

Angus put his arm around her shoulders and led her into his cottage, where he sat her on the one chair, an old wing chair, and handed her a mug the size of a small barrel. The mug was full of his whisky. Slowly, he filled his pipe, then sat on a stool in front of the ever-burning fire and said, "Now tell me what's wrong, lass."

Claire knew that she should at least make some attempt at coherence but she didn't try to. "No one is as I thought they would be. Everything is different and strange and I'm beginning to think that I don't exist. Except for my money, that is. Everyone seems to be very aware of my money."

Angus was beyond patient. He had no other interest in the world except her. She started telling him about yesterday and seeing the estate with Harry, and while she talked she nervously began to draw. She'd picked up a few ancient pieces of stationery with Bramley House written at the top that Angus had had about the cottage for years and a stub of a pencil and begun to draw. Her movements were angry and with every word she spoke she made another line on the papers.

Angus made her explain how it was in America and how Scotland was different. He made no comment on her answers but smoked his pipe and nodded his head.

She told him how perfect Harry was. "Perfect, is he?" Angus said.

"He is, actually, but his mother . . ." She looked down at her mug of whisky.

"Don't think you can shock me with stories of her." There was anger in Angus's voice.

Claire told of her meeting with the duchess. "She isn't going to turn any power over to me when I marry Harry. She is going to allow *nothing* to change. She will control every meal, every breath that anyone in that house takes. I wouldn't be surprised to discover that she plans to choose my clothes each day."

"And what does this perfect Harry of yours say to this?"

Claire began to fidget in her chair. "What could he say? She's his mother and he can't contradict her."

"Has a braw lass like you ever contradicted *your* mother?"

Claire giggled—she had drunk half of the mug of whisky. "Only about two hundred thousand times."

Angus smiled at her. "Yet he is perfect."

Claire looked down at the mug. "Yesterday my little sister said the oddest thing about Harry." Even as she said this, she knew she must be getting drunk or she'd never tell anyone this. Brat was always saying the most dreadful things about people. Sometimes her family met perfectly nice people, yet Brat would later say a person was evil or some such nonsense. Of course, it was eerie how often she turned out to be right.

"What did your sister say?"

"She said, 'You'll never have any control over Harry or influence over him. Three months after you're married Harry won't even know you're alive. He'll see that you have two children, an heir and a spare, then he'll go his own way. He'll be sweet and good to you, but he'll never interest you. You're much too smart in a stupid sort of way. You have to be smart like me and go after what you want.' "

"How old is this sister of yours?"

"Fourteen, I think. Maybe she's forty."

Angus nodded and poured himself some whisky. "And what of the other one?"

"What other one?" she said, but she knew exactly who he was talking about.

"The other boy. The dark one. The one that brought you here."

"Oh," she said slowly. "Trevelyan."

"Aye, that one." He watched as she seemed to be struggling to figure out what to say. "The explorer one."

"You know?"

"I know that much. Tell me what he's done to anger you."

"I thought he was my friend," she began, then started to talk. Trevelyan had been the one person in the house who would talk to her. "We talked about everything. I could tell him anything. I told him things I've never told anyone and he always understood. He never—" She stopped because, even as mellow as the whisky was making her feel, she didn't want to sound disloyal to Harry. She *loved* Harry.

"He was writing down everything that I said. He was studying me," she said. "He wanted to put me in one of his damned—oh, sorry—books. I'm not a subject for study. I'm just a woman, and Captain Baker can—"

"I thought you called him Trevelyan."

"I did. I mean, I do. That's his family name. But he *is* Captain Baker. Do you know of all the things he's done?"

Angus looked at her. When she'd come in, her face had been distorted with anguish, but now her eyes were gleaming. "Nay, I know nothing. Why don't you tell me what he's done?"

Claire took another sip of the whisky and started telling about one of her favorite subjects in the world: Captain Frank Baker. She told of his trips to Africa, to the world of Arabia. She explained about his being a Master Sufi. She told of the languages he could speak. "He can master any language in two months."

She told how he wrote when he was ill. She told of the chances he had taken in his life and what he had learned from what he had done. "Over the centuries whole civilizations have disappeared, like the . . . like the Babylonians." She was pointing her mug at Angus. "We don't know much about the Babylonians, because there was no Captain Baker then. There was no brilliant, brave man to go into the country and observe it and write about it as he has done."

"Doesn't sound real to me. He sounds more like a myth."

"Maybe he is," she said. "I don't know. I don't think he's a real man." She looked up at Angus. "I can't imagine Captain Baker's mother telling his future wife that he can or cannot eat peas with squab. I doubt that Captain Baker *had* a mother."

"I think he did," Angus said softly.

"I bet she died when he was born and he raised himself." She drained the last of the whisky then looked at the mug. "What in the world am I going to do?" She looked up at Angus and the anguish on her face was back again. "The way I see it I have two choices: I can marry Harry and live under his mother's rule. That means that every aspect of my life will be decided by her. I will end up like her poor daughter, holed up in a room, never allowed out, with a few books chosen by Her Grace. I wonder if she will even allow me to see my own children?"

"And the second choice?"

Claire was silent for a moment. "I could break my engagement to Harry."

"Would that hurt you? Do you love the lad so very much?"

"If I do not marry a man of whom my parents approve I will not receive my grandfather's money." She went on to explain, telling him about her grandfather, her parents having spent ten million dollars each, and about her sister having no money at all.

It took Angus, who had difficulty understanding how much money a hundred pounds was, a while to recover at hearing such numbers. "Ten million dollars. And how many pounds would that be?"

"Probably about two million, I guess."

Angus was glad he was sitting down. "And your parents spent that much?"

She didn't try to defend them as she had to Trevelyan.

Angus sat and nodded his head for a while. "So now you're afeared that if you don't marry who they want, they will take your—" He swallowed. "Your ten million and spend it and you won't get any and your little sister will be left poor too."

Claire started to protest that she wasn't really afraid of that, but she'd had much too much whisky to lie. "Yes, I'm afraid so. Both my parents love it here. My father has been out shooting something or other every day we've been here, and my mother has met two duchesses, four countesses, a viscount, and three marquises. They've all told her that after Harry and I are married she can meet the queen or Princess Alexandra."

"And these things mean a lot to your parents, do they?"

"Yes, they do. My father has never been trained to do anything. I doubt he's ever done a day's work in his life. I know that sounds awful but he's too old to start now. He wouldn't know how to begin to be a banker or whatever. And my mother—"

Angus sat there and looked at her, waiting for her to continue.

"My mother wants to feel important, that she is somebody. I think that in her early life she was too often told she was nobody."

"And what do you want, lass?"

"Love," she said quickly, then smiled. "And maybe something to do. I have difficulty being idle."

Angus looked at her as she leaned back against the chair. He knew she was about to fall asleep. "If you could change what's wrong here, what would you do first? Shall we plow the fields? Would you open an American factory and make carriages or some such?"

Claire smiled. "No. First I'd marry Leatrice to James Kincaid."

Angus gave a derisive snort at that. "And here I thought you were serious. You *are* wantin' love and love alone."

Claire, with her eyes closed, smiled broader. "My grandfather said that the cornerstone of all wealth and power was manpower. I think the cornerstone of the duchess's power is her children. She rules Leatrice and she somewhat rules Harry. If I could take one of those people from her, it would weaken her foundation. Perhaps if her own daughter could escape her, then others could also. Perhaps it could start to become a house where the inhabitants had as much freedom and control over their own lives as the servants do."

Angus stood up and looked down at her with new respect. From what he knew of what went on in the big house, what she said made sense. He saw that she was asleep, so he went to a chest along the wall and took out the MacTarvit laird's plaid and draped it around her. Even when he took the drawings from her lap, she snuggled into the chair and kept sleeping.

He looked at the drawings, gave a grunt of a laugh, tucked the drawings back beside her, then left the cottage and started walking. It would take him a couple of hours to reach the big house.

Chapter Thirteen

When Oman told Trevelyan that the old man was coming up the stairs, Trevelyan dismissed his servant and returned to his writing. When Angus appeared in the doorway, Trevelyan had to admire the man. He wasn't out of breath, but he'd climbed the stairs two at a time.

Trevelyan didn't look up from his writing. "What brings you here? I have no cattle to steal."

Angus went silently to a side table and poured himself a whisky, then sat on the window seat and looked at Trevelyan.

At last Trevelyan put his pen down and stared at the man. His weathered old face was drawn into a frown of concentration. "Out with it," Trevelyan said.

"The girl has met the old woman."

"Ah," Trevelyan said and looked back at his writing. "That shouldn't bother her. Her love for Harry—"

Angus interrupted him with a snort. "She bears no love for the boy. She thinks he's . . . perfect, as she says. Yesterday he took her out to see this place." He waved his hand to indicate all of the estate. "Young Harry pretended he knew all of the tenants. Pretended he ran the place. As far as I know he has never *seen* all that you own."

"That *I* own?"

Angus just stared at Trevelyan.

Trevelyan threw down his pen and went to stand before the fire. "What is it you expect me to do? Tell her Harry isn't what she thinks he is? Tell her my little brother is as lazy as the day is long and that his mother rules him?"

"She knows some about the mother." Angus tried to stifle a smile. "The old hag told her how to feed Harry, told her what food he could eat with carrots and beans, told her how to take care of his delicate health."

Trevelyan laughed at that. "Harry can eat a hogshead of anything and he's healthier than two horses."

Angus was quiet for a while. "You could stop this. You could tell them you're not dead."

"I don't want to do that," Trevelyan said. His mouth tightened. "And you bloody well know why. The old woman would make my life hell. She has what she wants. Her precious Harry is the duke and she'll have the girl's money. She'll have everything she wants. Harry's agreed to fund any expedition I go on, and that's all I want."

"And the girl?"

"She's not my concern!" Trevelyan practically yelled.

Angus looked at him for a while. "I saw you with her. You could'na take your eyes from her. You watched her dance, you listened to her talk. You were . . ." He paused as he seemed to be searching for words. "You were proud of her."

Trevelyan turned, put his hand on the mantel, and looked into the fire. "She has a brain. She's been raised with every advantage and instead of dedicating her life to the next gown to wear, she's chosen to read and study. She learned Latin just so she could read my books."

"Oh, aye, the dirty parts."

"What do you know of the dirty parts?"

"The old priest from the village used to read the Latin parts to me. I paid him in whisky to do so, but I think he would have read them without payment."

"You vulgar little man," Trevelyan said but there was no animosity in his voice.

"So you like this girl, yet you plan to let her marry your brother. You know about her grandfather's will?"

"Yes, I know about it. And it serves her right if she marries a man who isn't actually the duke. She wants to be a duchess so much that she's willing to sell herself to a man she doesn't—"

"Are you about to say she doesn't love Harry? He's a fine-looking young man. Looks better than you do, with your frowning face and your pinched look. He's a mighty fine-lookin' lad. Any lassie'd be proud to have him for her own. I'll wager he'll give her a bairn on their first night together, whenever that will be. I doubt that a fine, strapping lad like Harry will wait 'til the weddin' night."

"Quiet!" Trevelyan roared.

Angus looked at him with a sly, smug expression on his brown face. "She said you betrayed her, that you listened to her so you could write about her. You been drawin' those wee pictures of yours again?"

At first Trevelyan didn't know what he meant. Since Claire had left so abruptly a few days ago, he'd tried his best not to think of her, about her. He'd tried not to miss her. But he hadn't been very successful. Twice he'd almost spoken to her. In a mere few days he had become almost accustomed to having her in the room with him. He'd wanted to read her a passage from what he'd written and ask her what she thought of it. He'd wanted to hear more of what she had to say about his writing, because she'd told him, before she knew who he was, that his writing was sometimes boring. Trevelyan told himself not to be vain, but his book sales weren't what he thought they should have been, and maybe, possibly, she, looking at them as a reader, could help him improve them.

"I believe I made a few drawings, yes," he said at last.

"They made her think you didn't like her."

Trevelyan could only stare at the old man. "Didn't like her? What have a few drawings to do with whether I like her or not? I make drawings of everyone."

"Maybe the girl ain't heard of your abilities. Maybe she don't know that them drawin's of yours and that mouth of yours has made people so mad they've shot at you, beat you, and more than once tried to kill you, but it ain't so much as dented your head a bit. Maybe she thinks it ain't polite for people to laugh at others."

Trevelyan shrugged, for he still didn't understand. It couldn't have been something as small as the drawings that made her so angry that day. Surely it was that she'd just found out he was Captain Baker. He thought that when she got over her fear of him, she'd return. "I shall tell her that the drawings meant nothing and she may return. I meant her no harm."

"The girls always did want you, didn't they?" Angus said. "No one else could see it. Not the men, that is. But the girls liked you better than they liked your older brother. He was a handsome devil and he was to be the duke, but it was always you the girls liked."

"You know nothing of me. I haven't been here since I was a child."

"I know more of you than you think, and I'll wager that that mother of yours knows a great deal too." Angus lifted one eyebrow. "So now you plan to take Harry's little American heiress away from him."

"I have no such intention. I have not so much as touched her."

"But you've spent more time with her than Harry has."

"That's his fault, not mine. If I were engaged to her I'd sure as hell not neglect her."

"Aye, you'd woo her with all the things she likes: with books and words and wearin' the laird's plaid."

"She didn't know it was the laird's plaid. She'd never seen it before."

"But many of the crofters had. Many of them knew who you were that day you sat there and watched them dance. They were dancin' for the new laird and his lady."

"She's not my—" He lowered his voice. "She's not my lady and she was never meant to be. We are . . . friends," he said softly. "There is nothing more between us and there never will be. She is determined to marry my brother and become the duchess."

"You could tell her who you are. Her parents would approve the marriage. From what I hear they wouldn't care if the duke were a hundred years old and missing limbs."

Trevelyan gave a one-sided smile. "She would marry me because I'm a duke, but I don't want to marry anyone. I couldn't travel if I were married, and I don't want the responsibility of this house and the others, and I bloody well don't want a wife who marries me for my title."

Angus gave a sound like a laugh. "T'were a pretty girl to tell me that she wanted to marry me because I was the laird of Clan MacTarvit, I'd run to the kirk with her."

"That's just one more difference between you and me. I don't want to marry, I don't want to be the duke, and I don't want to talk to you anymore. I have work to do."

"She means to marry your sister to James Kincaid."

"What?" Trevelyan was stunned. "How does she know of that? That was years ago."

"Your young brother told her."

"And it suits her sense of romance to bring them together. She wants to make them as happy as she is with Harry."

Angus told him what Claire had said about her children being the cornerstone of the duchess's life. "The girl learned that from her grandfather. I think she means to take the old woman's power away from her."

Trevelyan shook his head. "Stupid American child! She has no idea what she's talking about. She has no idea what the old woman is like. Claire is a child, with the innocence of a child. She has dreams of living an idyllic life with Harry and raising blond children with titles after their names. She doesn't even know that people like the old woman exist." His cynicism turned to bitterness. "That woman would kill anyone who tried to take away either her son Harry or her power."

"But I think the lass means to try," Angus said softly.

"Oh, well, she'll fail. She hasn't the years of experience at treachery that the old woman has."

"What will the old woman do when she learns that the girl has tried to defy her and failed?"

"Lock her away somewhere. How do I know? It's none of my concern."

Angus didn't say a word, but continued to sit on the window seat and stare at Trevelyan.

When Trevelyan spoke again he could barely be heard. "The old woman will find out what is happening because Claire doesn't know how to be secretive. All she thinks and feels shows in her eyes. And she will confide in Harry." He snorted. "Her perfect Harry. She might as well tell the old woman directly. Harry will never see it as the threat that it is. If Claire tries to get him to help her marry Lee and Kincaid, Harry will only see it as work he has to do and he'll complain about it to his mother."

"But the old woman will know what it is."

"Yes," Trevelyan said. "The old woman will know that Claire has tried to take some of her power away. And she'll retaliate."

"As she did to a small boy who was a bother to her," Angus said softly.

Trevelyan gave no indication that he heard. "She will wait until Harry and Claire are married. God, she might set the date for very soon. She would never let Claire get away after such an attempt."

"And what will she do to the girl?"

"I cannot imagine," Trevelyan said softly. "Torture her in ways that even the worst tribes I have seen would not think of. She will break Claire's spirit as she has broken Lee's. Did you know that Lee was once a bit of a devil herself? She was the leader in some of the pranks that we—"

He broke off because Angus had stood and was now walking toward the door.

"Where are you going?" Trevelyan snapped.

"You said you had work to do, and I must go back to the girl. She gets cold easily and I must see to her."

"You left Claire alone in that horrid old place of yours? She could be murdered. She could—"

Angus was smiling at him. "This is Scotland and it's the safest place on earth. It's not the wilds of Africa or that city you looked for and couldn't find."

"I *did* find it."

"Nay, lad, you died." For a moment the two men locked eyes, then Angus looked away. "Now I must go back to her. You stay here and write your books. And when you're well you can go back to your strangers in those faraway lands. Leave this place to the likes of Harry and his wife and his mother. It's no concern of yours. You're not the duke. You're not the laird. You're not marryin' the girl. Stay up here with that man of yours and eat and sleep and write and stay out of it. It's no concern of yours."

With that he turned and started down the stairs.

Trevelyan immediately went back to the third table and picked up his pen. He was working on his book about Pesha. He was going to tell the world what it had been like to visit, in disguise, that secret city. After Jack Powell had told the world he was the one to have visited Pesha, thinking there was no one alive who could contradict him, Trevelyan was going to publish his book and tell the world the truth. Jack thought he had taken all of Trevelyan's notes on Pesha when he'd left him there to die, but Trevelyan had much more in his head that was not written down.

It was hours later when Oman quietly entered the room and handed Trevelyan a flat package.

"What's this?" he asked.

"The American lady gave it to me for you."

It took Trevelyan a moment to realize that Oman was calling Claire a "lady"—high praise indeed. He frowned as he opened the package, but as he pulled out the first drawing, his eyes widened.

The drawings were crude, done by an unpracticed hand, but it was easy to see what they were meant to represent. They were drawings of him. She showed him as a highwayman about to be hanged. She showed him as a little boy standing outside a children's party, sneering, acting as though he didn't want to join the party, but his eyes were lonely. She showed him as a man sitting all alone in a tower.

When Trevelyan first saw them, he was enraged. How dare that nobody American make such drawings of *him!* How dare she represent him in such an unflattering light. How dare she—

He looked at the drawings again, and his anger was replaced by hurt. He had no idea she thought of him in this way. He had thought she . . . well, almost worshiped him. To find that this was what she thought of him, was . . . well, painful.

It was the snicker from Oman that made him turn. Oman, stone-faced, unemotional Oman, was trying not to laugh aloud at the drawing of the highwayman.

"I see nothing humorous in this," Trevelyan snapped.

"It is just like you. See, here and here. This is very like you."

"It is no such thing," Trevelyan said as he snatched the drawing out of Oman's hand. "It is—" He stopped, for he did see just a bit of resemblance between himself and the man in the drawing. In spite of himself, he began to smile. "It could not be me," he said, but Oman had already left the room.

Trevelyan took the drawings to the window and studied them, and as he did so, he smiled more broadly. Didn't she know that he was the great Captain Baker? Didn't that impudent little American know that no one laughed at a man of his accomplishments? He, Trevelyan, was the one who did the laughing, not the other way around.

He put the drawings down and went to the fireplace, poking the logs around. Claire was none of his business and all that Angus had told him made no difference. He believed in not interfering. His refusal to interfere had saved his life many times.

But now he remembered the way Claire had taken care of him when he was ill. Of course there was nothing she could do to help him recover from yet another bout of malaria, but she had stayed with him and she had kept his secret. She had let no one know where he was.

He poked the logs around some more. It really wasn't any of his business if she wanted to take on Harry's mother. Harry's mother, he thought with a grimace. The woman was *his* mother too. Not that he'd ever received anything from her except abuse and criticism.

He knew how formidable the old woman could be. As Angus had said, she was capable of anything. Hadn't she sent her second son away to live with her old bastard of a father? She'd sent her own son away when he was just nine years old, not on a visit, but she'd sent him away forever, never again to live as part of the family, because she thought he was discourteous and disrespectful. It had taken Trevelyan only two weeks with the old man to realize how very much his mother had hated him.

And what would the duchess do to Claire when she found out Claire had attempted to usurp her place? Make her a prisoner as she'd done to Lee, Trevelyan thought. And who would defend Claire? Not Harry. He wouldn't want to be bothered with the turmoil. Harry wouldn't want anything to interfere with his hunting schedule. Would Claire's parents defend her? From what Trevelyan knew of them, he didn't think so. They would have obtained what they wanted—no matter that it was at the expense of their daughter.

So, in the end, nothing would have changed. The duchess would still have complete and absolute control over the household—and his sister and Claire would be the woman's prisoners. Life would go on.

Trevelyan tried to think what Claire would be like under the old woman's rule. There would be no more sitting in Angus MacTarvit's cottage and drinking whisky or dancing with the crofters. In fact, there probably wouldn't *be* any crofters to dance with. Trevelyan hadn't asked Harry, but it was his guess that his mother planned to use part of Claire's dowry to buy sheep, and you couldn't graze sheep where people were living.

Trevelyan looked at the fire. It was not any of his business. He'd come back for the sole purpose of recovering his health and writing his books. When that was done he was going to leave, and if Harry made good on his promise of money for expeditions, Trevelyan planned to go back into Africa by the end of next year. There was much more of Africa he'd like to see.

"It is of no interest to me," he said aloud. Then he looked again at the drawings, and in the next instant he called Oman to him.

Chapter Fourteen

Harry was sleeping so soundly that Trevelyan had to shake him awake. Harry rolled over, looked at his brother in disgust, then turned away and closed his eyes again.

"I want to talk to you," Trevelyan said.

"Do you never sleep?"

"Not if I can avoid it." When Harry didn't bother to open his eyes again and looked as though he were going back to sleep, Trevelyan pushed him on the shoulder again. "I'm not leaving."

Harry grimaced and slowly sat up. "For someone who's supposed to be in hiding you do get around. What's wrong now?"

"What happened between Claire and your mother today?"

At that Harry opened his eyes wide. There was genuine puzzlement on his face. "Nothing unusual. Claire said she wanted to meet Mother and she did. They had tea together."

Trevelyan looked at his brother for a long while. Trevelyan was always amazed when people didn't see what was going on around them. No doubt Harry thought that his mother and his fiancée had had a lovely tea together. Harry had probably not even realized Claire had left the room, as MacTarvit said, in a state of terror.

"What has Claire been telling you?" Harry asked.

"I haven't seen her."

Harry smiled at that. He was glad his little American heiress wasn't spending her time with his older brother. "Then how do you know she has complaints?"

"I have heard things."

Harry yawned. Trevelyan's constant air of mystery might interest the rest of the world but it merely bored him. "If that's all you have to say, then I'd like to go back to sleep."

"After you marry Claire are you going to send . . . *her*"—he said the word with contempt—"to the dower house?"

"I don't know why you persist in believing that our mother is a dragon. She is a simple, sweet woman and always has been. If you'd just make some effort to get to know her, you'd find that out. As for your question, no, Mother is not going to move to the dower house. I think it's better that she stay here where I can be near her. She is crippled, as you well know."

"She means to stay here where she can rule the house and Leatrice."

In spite of himself, Harry was beginning to wake up. His brother could infuriate the devil. "Mother is *not* a monster. She loves her daughter and wants to spend time with her. Is that so wrong? Lee is perfectly happy."

"Is that your opinion or Lee's? How long has it been since you spoke to your sister?"

"A great deal less time than it's been since you spoke to her," Harry shot back. "I'd like to know who you think you are to come in here and try to change everything. You leave when you're a child, then run off from Grandfather and no one sees you for years, and now you come back here and expect to give everyone orders. If you want to do that then you're going to have to step forward and declare yourself."

Trevelyan sat on a tall chair by the bed and didn't say a word.

"I thought so," Harry said. "You want to skulk about and run things but you don't want to step to the forefront."

"Your little American wants to marry Lee to James Kincaid."

Harry laughed. "Well, let her try," he said, moving down into the bed. "Claire's perfectly free to make all the love matches she wants. Women like to do that sort of thing."

"You don't mean to help her?"

"Help her? All she has to do is reintroduce them. I don't think they've seen each other for years."

"And what about your mother?"

Harry turned toward his brother, his face furious. "She's *your* mother too. Why do you persist in acting as though you were hatched from an egg and have no mother? If Leatrice wants to marry someone she may do so. She's not a prisoner." Harry refused to think of the argument his mother and Lee had had over Kincaid years ago. Of course it was years ago, and at that time Lee had a suitor who their mother approved of. Now, Harry believed, the situation was different.

When Trevelyan spoke, his voice was soft. "Lee *is* a prisoner and you don't see it, and if something isn't done soon your little bride is going to be a prisoner too."

"You've spent too much time in the sun," Harry said tiredly. "I'll marry Claire and everything will be fine. Mother said she rather liked Claire and thought she'd make a fine wife for me. I think the two of them are going to be friends. I hope they become as close as Mother and Lee are. Now would you mind leaving my room? I'd like to get some sleep." He snuggled down into the covers and closed his eyes.

Trevelyan sat where he was for a while, trying to think what he could say to his brother to make him understand, but he knew there was nothing that he could say. Harry had never been able to see there was anything wrong with his mother.

Trevelyan had hoped to talk some sense into his younger brother. If he could show Harry that Claire needed his help, then Trevelyan would be free. He could go back to work with his mind clear, knowing he'd repaid Claire for having helped him. It had been such a good idea. Such a good idea that had no hope of success because Harry didn't think anything needed to be done. Harry was content to allow what was going to happen to happen.

Trevelyan thought of Claire. He remembered her dancing and laughing. If she married Harry and came to live in this hellhole of hatred, would she become like Leatrice? A shadow of herself? Would she give in to the duchess and do whatever the old woman wanted whenever she wanted it done? Trevelyan thought of how Claire had told MacTarvit that he could go on stealing cows, but Trevelyan knew that within six months after the marriage MacTarvit would be gone from the Montgomery lands.

Trevelyan leaned back against the chair. He didn't want to become involved in this. He wanted to go back to his room and write. He had so much work to do on the Peshan language. He didn't care about these people who were related to him. He didn't want to get involved in the family or the house or with anything to do with them. He liked the idea of their thinking he was dead. It gave him a great deal of freedom.

But another part of him thought of his sister. He hadn't seen her since he'd returned, not in the house or out of it. According to what Claire had told MacTarvit, Leatrice was about the unhappiest person Claire had ever seen.

He looked at Harry, already asleep. It was obvious that his little brother wasn't going to help Claire replace the duchess. Harry was too comfortable to try to change anything. Why should Harry want to change something that was so perfect for him?

So now what was Trevelyan to do? Go back to his room and stay there? Go back to his writing and stay out of this? Allow Harry to marry his American and let her fight it out with her mother-in-law? Claire was a strong and healthy young woman, and if nothing else, she'd outlive the old hag. Then she could do what she wanted.

Again the images that Claire had drawn of him appeared before his eyes. He wiped his hands over his face. Would he return ten years from now and find that happy young woman carrying trays into her mother-in-law's room? Would her handsome husband even notice that his wife's spirit had been killed?

Trevelyan stood up and walked to the door. Maybe if he talked to Leatrice. He wouldn't do anything, just talk to her. Maybe she wasn't as unhappy as Claire thought she was.

Chapter Fifteen

Leatrice, snuggled deep in the cocoon of her bed, at first didn't know what the creaking sound was. In her sleep-dazed mind she knew that any and all disturbances came from her mother, so she tried to rouse herself. What did the old woman want now? Her feet rubbed? Her hair brushed? Hot water? Tea? Did she want Leatrice to read to her? Sometimes Leatrice thought the old woman sat up late trying to figure out things for her daughter to do. Her uncle James had once said that Eugenia couldn't possibly sleep because no one could be as mean as she was without having a full twenty-four hours a day to work at it.

Leatrice pushed the cover off and, her eyes still closed, began to make her way out of the bed. It was when the light penetrated her lids that her eyes flew open. Standing near the east wall, the old door that was hidden in the wall panel open behind him, holding a candle, was the ghost of her dead brother. Leatrice sat up, put her knuckles to her mouth to keep from screaming, then backed against the headboard of the bed, pulling the coverlet with her.

The ghost smiled at her.

Leatrice tried to move farther away and pulled the cover higher about her. If her life had depended on it, she couldn't have said a word. She just sat there, staring in stark terror.

"Ah, Mutt," said the ghost, "it's just me."

Leatrice sat there, still trembling, staring wide-eyed, then she began to blink. This apparition didn't look like a ghost. He looked like a flesh-and-blood man who had entered her room through the old door. She leaned forward a bit to get a better look at him, and he took a step closer to her.

"I'm real," he said. "As real as I ever was."

She let the cover drop from her throat and kept looking at him. Could it really be her brother? "Vellie?" she whispered.

He nodded once, then he was across the room to her. Leatrice opened her arms and he came to her, burying his face against her neck while she hid her face in his hair.

He *was* real! Oh thank God and all that was holy, he was really and truly alive!

Leatrice began to cry then. The tears began to pour from her eyes softly at first, then, as she ran her hands over his arms and down his back, touching him as though to reassure herself that he was actually there, the tears began to run harder.

"Ssssh, love," he whispered, holding her to him, clutching her.

He wore some odd garment of silk, a robe of sorts, and soft boots. He used the toe of one foot to remove first one boot, then the other, and he crawled in bed with her, stretched full length beside her, and held her, as much like a lover as a brother. And he let her cry. When she didn't stop at his first admonitions, he didn't try again to halt her; he just held her while she cried and cried and cried.

It was a long while before Leatrice could control herself enough to speak. And when she had her tears under control somewhat, all she could think of was how good it was to touch someone. It had been years and years since she had felt human flesh against her own. She and Trevelyan were only a year apart in age, and when they had been children they had been close. Their brother Alex had been too full of himself and too dignified to have much time for a mere girl, but she and Vellie had been friends—or, as some people said, co-conspirators in crime.

She hadn't seen him since he was nine, on that most horrible day in her life when he had been sent away with their horrid grandfather. The vision of Vellie, her most beloved friend, her brother, her . . . her soul mate, turning around in that open carriage and looking back at her would be imprinted on her mind to the day she died. Their father had said Vellie would return in a few months, but Leatrice had looked at her mother's stern face and known her brother would not be allowed to return, at least not to live. He had committed the unforgivable: he had defied their mother. He had stood up to her and laughed at her punishments and her warnings and her threats. But in the end the old woman had won, for, after all, Vellie was just a little boy and she was the duchess and his mother. It was she who had the authority. Their father had had his son Alex to train to become the duke, and Leatrice thought that maybe her father had been just a bit glad to see Vellie taken away, for the second son had been a problem since the day he was born.

"Are you really here?" she whispered, her breath coming in jerks as she tried to control her sobbing.

"Really and truly."

His arms were wrapped about her and her back was to his front as he held her close. This was the way it had always been: the two of them together. Even when he was just a bit of a boy their mother had had him whipped for even the tiniest infraction of her rules. Leatrice thought it probably infuriated the old woman that her second son would never cry. He used to swagger away from the woman's beatings, his little shoulders back, a smirk of a smile on his face as though to say she'd not hurt him. But at night, Leatrice would sneak through the tunnels and go to his room and crawl into bed with her brother and he'd hold her and cry. He'd cry and say, "Why does she hate me so?" Leatrice never had an answer for him.

"The papers said you were dead. They said you died of a fever, that you never reached Pesha and that you were sick and—"

His derisive laugh cut her off. "I'm much harder to kill than that. I was sick for a while, maybe more dead than alive, but I healed. I stayed behind until I could stand getting on a damned boat and I came home."

She held one of his hands to her face and rubbed it against her cheek. She knew it had been months since the man Jack Powell, who had traveled with Trevelyan, had returned to England and announced to the world that he and he alone had entered the secret city of Pesha. He'd told the press that Captain Baker had been too ill to enter the city so the captain stayed behind. The man Powell said that Captain Baker had been so ill that he'd had to be carried all the way back to the coast and then, just as they were to board the ship back to England, Captain Baker had died.

"Where are you staying?" she asked.

He hesitated before answering. "In Charlie's room."

Leatrice didn't say anything for a moment. When she did speak, she tried to sound nonchalant. "Have you been there long?"

"A few weeks."

She understood what he was saying. He had been there for some time, but for some reason he had not come to see her. She wondered if he'd meant to come to her at all. She wondered if this was the first time he'd stayed there. Had there been other times when he'd stayed in that old, uninhabited, unvisited part of the house and not come to her?

"What brings you here now?" she asked, trying to sound easy and carefree, as though her feelings weren't hurt.

But Trevelyan knew exactly what she was thinking—he always had—and he laughed at her. Laughed in a way that made her furious.

She pulled away from him, grabbed a pillow, and began pummeling him. "How could you let me believe you were dead? Do you have any idea what I've suffered? Your letters have been the only thing I have in my life. I have *all* of them, every last one of them."

He was lying on the bed, grinning up at her. She hadn't seen him in years but she would have recognized that grin anywhere. It was that same defiant, devil-may-care grin of the nine-year-old boy. "They must fill a room."

She smiled back at him. "Four trunks." She reached out and touched his cheek. "Oh, Vellie, are you really, truly here? Are you sure you aren't a ghost? Aunt May said she'd seen your ghost."

"I ran into her early one morning as I was slipping through the corridors. Haven't any of those old relics *died?* They were ancient when I was a boy. I can't imagine how old they are now."

"Mother would like for them to die, I'm sure, but they don't seem to. Uncle Cammy has enlisted Harry's fiancée's sister in his plays. I wonder if they fight over the costumes?"

"From what I've heard of the Brat I would imagine she wins."

At that Leatrice narrowed her eyes. She was beginning to get over the shock of his return and beginning to realize what his appearance here meant. "What do you know of the child? Have you met Claire? Have you seen Harry?"

Trevelyan turned on his back, put his hands under his head and looked up at the ceiling. "What do you think of Harry's little American?"

Leatrice hit him smack in the face with a pillow and tried to hit him a few thousand more times, but he grabbed the pillow from her and held her arms to her side.

"What is wrong with you?"

"You've been here weeks and you've seen Harry and probably his fiancée but you've allowed me to believe you were dead. How could you do that to me? I've loved you more than anyone else in the world has. For twenty-two years I wrote you at least once a week, sometimes five and six times a week. I told you everything that happened in my life. I poured out my soul to you. For all those years you were my closest and at times my *only* friend. But then you go off to find your beloved Pesha and I hear nothing from you. Not one letter for over two years, then I read in the newspaper that you're dead. I believed it! Do you know how much I've grieved for you? Do know how much I've cried over you? And now I find that you aren't dead. Not only aren't you dead, but you've been living but a few feet from me and you've been sneaking about the tunnels talking to daffy old Aunt May, talking to Harry who doesn't even really know you, at least not the way *I* do, and now—"

She broke off as he sat up, leaned against the headboard, and pulled her into his arms, for she had begun to cry again.

"I thought it would be better for everyone if they went on believing I was dead."

"What a very stupid thing to say," she said, sniffing against his chest. "How could you think it would be better if we thought you were dead?" Even as she said it, she knew the answer. She hadn't thought of it until this moment, but their elder brother's death made Trevelyan the duke.

She pulled away to stare at him, wide-eyed. "Your Grace," she whispered.

"Exactly."

Leatrice put her head back on his shoulder. This did indeed change things. "She won't like this," Leatrice said softly and they both knew "she" meant their mother. "She won't like that Harry is no longer the duke. But I guess he never was, was he?"

"I don't want it," Trevelyan said softly. "I never did. Harry is a perfect duke. He shoots and he gives parties and he can sit in the House of Lords and snooze with the best of them. I would never fit in. I don't want the responsibility of the title."

"But Vellie—" she began.

He pulled her head back to his chest and stroked her hair. "No, I don't want it and I don't mean to take it. Harry's said he'll fund all my expeditions and that's all I want. I have much more to do in my life and it doesn't include moldering away in one of these houses while married to the richest heiress I can find."

It was the second time he had referred to Claire. "Have you met her? Have you met Claire?"

Trevelyan took so long to answer that Leatrice pulled away to look at him. Always, even as a child, he'd had those eyes. Sometimes she thought that those eyes of Trevelyan's were what so infuriated their mother. They were intense and bright and unreadable. They were unreadable unless you knew him, as Leatrice did. When Trevelyan was twelve their father had allowed his second son to return home. But the return had lasted only two weeks, for Trevelyan had been caught breaking into the church cellar one night. He'd said he was searching for tombs. The next week Trevelyan had climbed a ladder and entered the second floor of a widow's boarding house, a house that was reputed to be one of illicit dealings. Their father did not forgive his son the second time and sent him back to his grandfather. There had been other visits, but on each one Trevelyan had managed to anger his father so that he was quickly sent away again.

She may not have seen him very often while they were growing up, but she'd received thousands of letters from him and he'd sent her hundreds of photographs. She'd watched Vellie grow up, for he rather liked dressing in what he called his disguises and having his photo taken.

Now she looked into his eyes and saw that he was hiding something. "What has made you come to me now? Had you planned to come at all? Or had you planned to leave here without even seeing me?" The answer was in his eyes.

She resisted the urge to call him every vulgar name she knew, and, thanks to him, she knew several in some very unusual languages.

She put her head back down. It was no use screaming at him. He had been screamed at by the best and all the noise had had no effect on him. "Tell me everything from the beginning, and I mean everything. I don't want any of it left out."

"It's late and—"

"I'll tell Mother you're here."

He chuckled, knowing it was an empty threat. She'd never in her life tell. "You have forced me into this," he said, smiling. "I came here to this house to rest. I was very ill and I needed a place to hide and to recover. I didn't plan to tell anyone I was here. Truthfully, I wasn't sure the family was here. I can't keep up with the seasons. I thought the lot of you might be in the south now."

She lay against him and listened as he told her about meeting Claire, about fainting after he caught her horse. "It was a bit . . ."

"Embarrassing?" she said, laughter in her voice. She knew his reputation with women. When he was younger, when he was in his teens, he had written to her of his exploits with women, how he had sneaked over the wall of a girls' school in the middle of the night, how he had hidden in one girl's bed when the Sister had come to see what the giggling was about. As he'd grown older, he had told her less of such exploits, but Leatrice, locked away with a harridan of a mother and an uninterested father and two brothers, and living a life of undescribable loneliness, had begged him to tell her of *all* his adventures.

"Claire is very pretty, isn't she?" Leatrice asked as she watched him closely.

"There are many kinds of beauty. Claire has . . . life."

Leatrice knew what he meant. Claire moved quickly and said things quickly and always seemed to be watching people. She wasn't a person who was content to look only into herself. "And did you seduce her?"

At that Trevelyan stiffened. "She's engaged to Harry."

Leatrice stifled a laugh. "That didn't bother you in Egypt with that pretty little dancer. And what about the time you raided the harem? Aren't those women *married* to someone else?"

"They weren't married to my brother."

Leatrice smiled. For all Trevelyan's travels and his bohemian outlook on life, underneath he was as conventional as other men.

"And besides, she didn't like me."

Leatrice looked at him, aghast.

"She said I was old and sick and weak."

Leatrice put her head back down so he wouldn't see her laughing. But he felt her body shake with her humor.

"Laugh all you want, but she wanted nothing to do with me. She's mad about Harry. Talks about him all the time. She says he's perfect."

"Harry?"

"Harry."

They were silent as they savored this great joke. Then Trevelyan started talking again and told her about his other meetings with Claire. "I knew I should have told her to go away, but she was so lonely. She couldn't understand this house, and Harry completely ignored her."

Leatrice understood the feeling of loneliness all too well. Although the big house was full of people, there was no companionship in it. At least not for her. She didn't want to sit in the drawing rooms with her aunts and gossip about the other people they knew, and she couldn't go outside, for she couldn't hear her mother's summons if she were outside. "I know how she felt."

She listened to Trevelyan talk and as she did so she heard more than his words. She heard something in his tone that told her that he liked Claire a great deal. She heard him tell how Claire had read all of Captain Baker's books. "*All* of them," he said, and there was pride in his voice.

She listened as he told of the extraordinary day he and Claire had spent with Angus MacTarvit. Leatrice hadn't seen any of the MacTarvits since she was a child, when she and Vellie used to go sneaking through the brush to try and steal Angus's whisky. She remembered being caught by the old man once and being terrified. But he'd just threatened her and let her go. She had run back to Vellie in a state of terror and he had laughed at her, said that the old man was all wind and nothing else.

Now Leatrice was hearing that Claire had spent the day with the old man and had danced with the crofters. Leatrice could not have been more surprised if Trevelyan had told her Claire had spent the day with the fairies and drunk nectar for tea.

"What else has she done?" Leatrice whispered, some awe in her voice.

Trevelyan smiled. "Taken to Scotch like a sailor and eaten some very strange food and loved it and bribed her sister into lying about her so she could nurse me through a fever. And she's made Harry take her on a tour of the estate and introduce her to the workers."

Leatrice looked up at Trevelyan in bewilderment. "How could Harry do that? He wouldn't know one of his own employees if he ran over the man. I doubt if Harry knows his own valet's name, and the man's been with Harry for ten years."

"It seems that our clever little brother took Charles with him. Old MacTarvit said Claire thought Harry was a man of great humility because he allowed his employee to do most of the explaining."

At that Leatrice laughed, and as she did so she realized that it had been a long, long time since she had laughed. The only light in her life had been letters from her brother, letters that had allowed her to live his adventures vicariously. He had written little of their grandfather, only mentioning now and then that his back was sore from the old man's latest beating or that he was thin from having had to live on bread and water for days at a time. But for the most part his letters had been full of all that he was seeing and doing.

"What else has she done?"

Trevelyan took a deep breath. "She has met our mother."

"She can be quite charming when she wants to be."

"It seems that she didn't want to be. It's my guess that she knew more about Claire than Claire knew about her. I think the old woman sensed Claire's power."

"Power? Do you think Claire's powerful? She seemed rather ordinary to me. She misses a great many meals and my maid says that Rogers runs her. Rogers brags about it in the servants' hall. I think that Rogers reports on Claire to Mother."

"Yes, I imagine she does." Trevelyan was thoughtful for a moment. "You asked me if Claire's powerful. I think perhaps she is, but she doesn't know it. She's little more than a child. Her power lies in that she cares about people."

"That doesn't sound like any power to me," Leatrice said with great cynicism. It had been her experience that survival was the most important thing in life. One did what one could in order to survive.

"You should have seen her with old MacTarvit," Trevelyan said. "She had the old man eating out of her hand. And the crofters adored her. They looked at her with the respect that none of our family has received in a long time."

Leatrice pulled away and looked at him. "Vellie, you're in love with her."

He pushed her back down to his shoulder. "What an utterly ridiculous thought. She's a child and she's in love with Harry and she wants to be a duchess and—" He cut himself off to laugh. "No, dear little sister, I'm not in love with her. Actually, what I want is a bit of revenge."

"Mother," Leatrice said.

"No one else."

"I'll help," Leatrice said without even asking what he planned. "Murder? Shall we feed her some exotic poison?"

Trevelyan laughed. "No, nothing so quick and relatively painless. When Harry is the duke our mother plans on remaining the duchess. She plans to continue ruling this place and the others until the day she dies."

"Of course. Did anyone think there would be anything else? Don't tell me your American thought *she* would be the duchess?"

"She's not *my* American. She belongs to Harry and, yes, Claire thought that after she was married her mother-in-law would quietly retire to the dower house and Claire would become the duchess. Claire had plans of taking meals off the strict schedules." He paused. "She planned to control the money she would inherit upon her marriage and repair the crofters' houses and plant fields and do other American business things."

"My goodness," Leatrice said. "Did she really? Harry could have told her—"

There was anger in Trevelyan's voice when he spoke. "Harry has lied to her and told her whatever she wanted to hear. He's told her she'll be able to do whatever she wants after they're married."

Leatrice sighed. "But then Harry would think she would be able to do so. He certainly does whatever *he* wants. And he thinks Mother is a darling. He can't understand why other people don't think so too."

"Exactly."

"Poor, poor Claire," Leatrice said with feeling. "I would imagine she's used to doing what she wants. Her mother is an awful woman. Quite common. She calls Harry the oddest names, such as Your Honor and Your Serene Grace. The aunts make fun of her mercilessly. I think they feed her misinformation, then laugh at her behind her back."

Trevelyan frowned. "And her father?"

"Lazier than Harry."

"My God," Trevelyan said in disbelief. "I had the impression she ran the family, but I think it's worse than I thought." He put his hands on Leatrice's shoulders and held her at arms' length. "Mutt, I think it's time we did something about this. We can't just stand back and let this girl be taken over by this household."

Leatrice pulled away from him, fear on her face. It was one thing to joke about revenge on their mother, but now Trevelyan's face was serious. "No, Vellie, we aren't children now. We can't pull stunts any longer. Back then I didn't understand what punishment was, but now I do. If I don't behave myself, the old woman has ways of punishing that can make a person want to die. I'm surviving now and I have my small comforts. I don't want those taken from me." She tried to get out of bed, but he held her fast.

"But this is a chance to *do* something about her. This is the chance we've always wanted."

"You maybe, but not me. You saw what she did when you displeased her. She sent you away and you never came back, and to me—" She broke off and looked away.

"She did worse to you than she did to me. She broke your spirit."

Leatrice knew it was an insult of the highest magnitude and she took it as such. She broke away from him and moved to stand by the bed. "You haven't changed, have you? Always trying to get into trouble. Always doing what you shouldn't. You spent your childhood being beaten and starved and locked away in rooms, yet all of it taught you nothing. You never learned anything, did you?"

"No," he said softly. "I never learned. I always fought them. No matter what they did to me, I always fought back. And now I'm an adult and I go where I want to and I do what I want to and I live. But you're still a frightened little girl being locked away in her room. You are thirty-one years old and you have no family, no home of your own. All you have are the letters of a brother you've rarely seen since you were a child and a bell that rules your life."

She wanted to yell at him, to tell him to get away from her, that she wished he'd never returned to upset her. She wanted to tell him that he didn't understand, that he didn't know how things were. She wanted to tell him that her life was fine, that she had everything she needed and wanted, but she couldn't. She couldn't lie to him because he knew the truth.

But something else kept her from lying to him, and that was that she saw a glimmer of hope. For almost a year after Vellie had been taken away, she had continued to keep up her spirit. But Trevelyan was the fighter, not she. It didn't take her long to realize that she was merely a follower, always had been, always would be. By the time Vellie had been gone a year, Leatrice no longer made any attempt to do anything but what her mother wanted. When she was twenty she had tried to defy her mother, but she'd lost that battle and she'd never tried again.

"What do you plan to do?" She couldn't keep her voice from trembling with fear.

"To marry you to James Kincaid," Trevelyan said.

Leatrice stood there blinking at him. "What?"

Trevelyan smiled at her. "It was the American's idea. *Harry's* American. Not mine. She told MacTarvit that the first thing she wanted to do was marry you to the love of your life. She thinks that if she can remove some of the old bat's underpinnings it will weaken her. I don't know if that means weaken your mother's hold over Harry or the household or over Claire's own lovely little self, but that's what she wants to do. I thought I'd ask you if you'd very much mind marrying Kincaid."

Leatrice opened her mouth to speak but no words came out. She sat down on the edge of the bed, looked at her brother, again started to speak and again closed her mouth. She looked away for a moment. Then, when she looked back at him, she smiled. "Aren't Americans the very oddest creatures?"

Trevelyan's eyes twinkled. "Had I any idea I would have forgone Pesha and explored America."

Leatrice laughed. "To marry James? I haven't seen him in years. Or thought of him. What's he doing now?"

"I don't know, but I imagine he's still working on that one book." He said this with all the contempt and derision that a prolific author has for one who takes years to write a single book. "It was about one of the Tudors, wasn't it? Henry the Eighth and all his wives?"

"It was Henry the Seventh and it had to do with his economic policy," Leatrice snapped. "And you can stop making fun of James. There's a great deal of research to be done when writing a biography. All *you* have to do is travel somewhere, then write about it. He has to spend hours reading medieval manuscripts. He has to *find* the manuscripts first and—" She scowled at him. "Just what is so amusing to you?"

"Haven't thought of him in years, have you? How far along is he in his writing?"

Leatrice looked away and blushed. "The last I heard he was into the sixth year of Henry's reign," she said softly.

"What was that? I'm not sure I heard you correctly. He's working on Henry's sixth wife?"

"You!" she said as she tossed a pillow at him.

Trevelyan caught the pillow. "For years James Kincaid was all I heard about in your letters. I think you wrote me about every breath the man took. I began to think he was a god on earth. I was sure I'd never met a man as wonderful as he. In all my travels I have seen many things and met many people but I have never come close to meeting anyone as miraculous as the great James Kincaid. It was difficult to believe he was the same boy who lived a couple of miles from Bramley and who used to run us out of his gardens, said our noise was scaring the birds away."

Leatrice wouldn't look at Trevelyan.

"Haven't thought of him in years, eh? I always wondered, even as a child, why we were always walking past the Kincaid house. Remember how you used to hide behind trees and throw dirt clumps at him?"

"I never did any such thing."

Trevelyan's face lost its smile and he reached down and took her hand. "Why didn't you marry him? Didn't he ask you?"

"Yes, he asked me. He asked me when I was sixteen and when I was seventeen and when I was eighteen." She sighed. "He stopped asking when I was twenty." Her voice lowered. "And now if I'm in a carriage with Mother and he happens to see me he looks away. He hates me."

"No doubt our dear mother—"

Leatrice stood. "Yes!" she said, her hands clenched at her sides. "Yes, yes, yes. It was the worst scene of my life and I don't want to think about it. Now here you are, Vellie, come back from the dead and you tell me that you want me to marry James."

"Not me. Harry's American."

Leatrice took a deep breath and for a moment she looked at her hands. They were shaking. She knew all too well the harshness of her mother's punishments; this American did not. If Leatrice once again tried and failed to assert herself to her mother, she could not imagine what her mother would do to her to discourage further insurrections.

But if she were to try one more time and this time she succeeded . . . She didn't like to think what this could mean. To get out of this house. To get away from the constant bells. To get away from her mother's eternal demands and complaints.

She looked at Trevelyan. "What should I do?"

Chapter Sixteen

Three nights after Claire met her mother-in-law to be, when she went to her room after dinner, two things happened at once. The butler came to her room carrying an envelope on a silver tray, telling her the message was urgent. At the same time, the enormous portrait in Claire's room swung back on its concealed hinges to show Brat standing there. Her hair had fallen from its usually neat single braid to lie across her forehead; there were cobwebs on her shoulders and she looked greatly surprised.

"Hello," Brat said, great delight in her voice.

Claire started to say something, but she didn't want to in front of the butler. She tried to act as though her sister always entered her room from behind a portrait. Claire took the envelope from the butler's tray and opened it.

> *I am being held prisoner. Please help me. The old summerhouse. Come at once.*
>
> *Leatrice*

Claire read the note three times before she understood what it said. She looked up at the butler but his face was impassive. Claire knew she had to get rid of Miss Rogers, who was now in the dressing room. (Claire was back from dinner four and one-half minutes earlier than Miss Rogers thought she should have been so she had therefore not come in to help Claire.) And she had to get rid of Brat.

"May I be of assistance, miss?" the butler asked.

"Miss Rogers . . ." was all that Claire could get out.

The butler bowed. "I will see that she is busy for the evening," he said, then walked through the bedroom and toward the dressing room.

"Oh!" Claire said, "and . . ." She glanced toward the doorway where Brat still stood.

The butler permitted himself the smallest smile. "In this house one learns not to see a great deal." With that he left the room.

Brat sauntered into Claire's bedroom. "You can't believe this place. I found a map. Actually this old man gave it to me. I hadn't met him before. He's in a wheeled chair and there's a legend that he killed four of his wives until the last one shot him, but now he lives at the far end—"

"I don't have time for your stories now. You have to go back to your room and stay there."

Brat looked at her sister. "What's the letter say?"

Claire pulled her riding habit from the wardrobe and Brat's eyes widened. Brat used the opportunity to grab the note from Claire's hand. "I want to go too."

"Absolutely not. I want you to go back to your room and I don't want you to tell anyone about this. I don't know what this is about but I mean to find out."

"Why did Harry's sister send the note to you? Why not to Harry?"

Claire paused a moment in her dressing. "That's a good question, but I have no answer. Now get out of here. And don't tell anyone about the tunnels."

Brat stood there and looked at her sister, then she took a deep breath. "If you don't let me go with you I'll tell Mother you've been seeing another man besides Harry and I'll tell Father you've been mean to me and I'll tell Harry there are footprints in the dust in the tunnels leading to your room and I'll tell—"

"All right!" Claire said. She had no time to argue with her sister. "You may come with me but you must stay in the background and do what I say. Do you understand?"

"Of course." Brat cut her eyes at her sister. "Do you have any idea where the old summerhouse is?"

Claire didn't have to give an answer because at the next moment there was a quick knock at her door, then Harry entered. "Claire, did you receive one of these?" he asked, waving a note just like the one Claire held. He was frowning, but then he saw Brat and his face changed to a smile. "Hello, Sarah. You get prettier every day."

"I do, don't I?"

Claire groaned. "Harry," she snapped, making him look back at her. "Yes, I received a note just like that one. We have to go to the summerhouse."

Harry didn't seem to think there was any urgency in the message. In fact, he acted as though every day his sister sent him notes saying she was being held prisoner. "I must say that this is a great deal of bother. Who do you think is holding her?"

Claire paused as she pulled her boots from the wardrobe. Sarah Ann gave Claire a look that said Harry wasn't the brightest person on earth, but Claire ignored her. "I have no idea, but it looks as though she wants us both there, or else her captor wants us both. Harry, could you leave the room while I get dressed? I'll meet you downstairs in ten minutes."

"Of course," he said and left the room.

Brat sprawled on Claire's big bed. "I bet the two of you have some real interesting talks. Harry has a mind like a fiery blaze."

"Would you stop talking for a moment? I don't know why the two of you are taking this so lightly. This could be serious."

"I don't think it is. If it were, there would be ransom demands and they'd go to the old hag, wouldn't they?"

Claire paused in unbuttoning her gown. "Who?"

"The old hag. The witch. The most hated woman in all of England, Scotland, and, as far as I know, Ireland. But the Scots don't talk much about Ireland so I can't be sure about that country."

"Help me unfasten this," Claire said, trying to understand what Brat was saying. "And do please stop talking."

Claire was ready to go in a matter of minutes, and she met Harry downstairs. He was sitting half asleep in the hall porter's chair. She had to shake his shoulder to get him going. He'd sent a footman to the stables and their horses were waiting for them—as were three men, already mounted, lanterns in their hands and ready to ride.

Claire made a few furtive attempts to talk to Harry about the need for secrecy. She said that Leatrice might be hurt if they came storming into the summerhouse. Harry just looked at her as though she were daft and told his men to go.

Brat, mounted on an unruly gelding, smiled at Claire in a know-it-all way. "Not exactly dime-novel, old West riding to the rescue, is it?" she said smugly.

"Harry's a Scot," Claire answered. "They do things differently here."

"Harry's English," Brat said as she kicked her horse forward, easily controlling the big animal. Their father had put Sarah Ann on a horse before she could walk, and the child had taken to the animal as though she were a female centaur. Claire was an excellent rider, but she wasn't anything compared to Brat.

The six of them went thundering down the lanes. Claire hoped there was no need for secrecy, for secret they were not. They could have been heard twenty miles away. She hoped Leatrice wasn't in real danger and that it was a hoax.

At one point, when they had to slow down to go single file down a narrow path, Brat turned to Claire and said, "You know, I really love this family."

Claire grimaced and nudged her horse forward.

When they at last reached the summerhouse, Claire wasn't prepared for what she saw. The windows were boarded and there was a bolt locking the door from the outside, yet there was smoke coming from the chimney of the little building.

"Open it," Harry said, not getting down from his horse.

It was at that moment that the vicar appeared. He was a tall man, made to look taller by the fact that he was riding a horse that was too small for him. His clerical clothes billowed out over an enormous stomach and he had whiskers hanging down to his chest. "What's this?" the man bellowed. "I was dragged from a warm fire and a good dinner to this place. What's this, young Harry?"

Harry squinted at the man, trying to remember who he was. "I don't know" was all Harry said, then he nodded at the footman to unbar the door.

Inside the room were two people, both of them stark naked. One, a tall, good-looking man in his early forties, was trying to shield the nude body of Leatrice from the view of the people outside the door. Leatrice cowered behind him.

Claire, once she got her mouth closed from the shock of the spectacle, tried to keep Brat from seeing into the room. She might as well have tried to contain a honeybee with a piece of string. Brat was off her horse in seconds, standing at the doorway and unabashedly staring. Claire was trying not to do the same.

In the next instant the shock was broken by the booming voice of the vicar. He was calling down the wrath of God on the fornicators.

Harry at last got off his horse, went inside the building, and gave his coat to his sister to cover herself. "What do you have to say for yourself, Kincaid?" he demanded of the man who was now trying to cover his private parts.

At the name Kincaid, Claire began to realize what was going on. MacTarvit, she thought, and tried to keep from smiling. He had somehow arranged this.

In the background the vicar was still raging, saying that all hellfire was going to come down on these sinners. Claire was thinking with love of MacTarvit, knowing he was the one who had somehow managed to lock these two into a room and take their clothes from them. And he'd arranged for a vicar to be there when they were found.

"They must be married," Claire heard herself saying loudly. It wasn't easy to be heard over the vicar, who was talking about the eternal damnation of these two people.

Claire looked at Harry. "You're her guardian and you can witness the ceremony. She *must* be married at once."

Harry looked startled. "I'm not sure Mother—"

"Their souls are in jeopardy," the vicar shouted. "They must be made to pay for their sins."

Claire looked at Leatrice. With her long hair down about her shoulders and her legs bare beneath Harry's coat, she looked a great deal better than she did in the ruffled clothes she usually wore. Claire raised her eyebrows in question to Leatrice and Lee gave her a little smile and a nod.

"Harry, they *must* be married at once! Now. This minute. You can't let all these people see something like this and expect to stop the gossip. Your family name will be ruined."

"I'm not sure . . ." Harry said.

Claire could see that even now the hold his mother had over him was formidable. "Harry, I understand," she said softly, but making sure that the wide-eyed servants around them heard. "If you don't have the authority to force a man who has defiled your sister to marry her, I quite understand, and I'm sure everyone else here understands too."

"I think I have—I mean, I do have the authority, but—"

"We'd better go," Claire said. "I just pray that your sister does not bear a child from this." She looked at the men standing by the wall and gawking at the whole scene. "We must swear you all to secrecy. No one must hear of what has gone on here tonight." Her voice told that she didn't believe there was much chance of the secret being kept. "Come with me, Leatrice. You may ride with me."

Harry gave a sigh that was probably audible a half a mile away. "All right," he said, then looked at the vicar. "Marry them."

Claire felt a little thrill of triumph go through her and she tried to think of what she could do to repay MacTarvit for having arranged this. The vicar told one of the grooms to give Kincaid a coat, then he began the ceremony. Claire was so thrilled at what was taking place that at first she didn't listen or pay attention to what was being said. She glanced at her sister and saw that Brat was staring at the vicar with a frown of concentration. Claire looked between Leatrice and Kincaid toward the vicar, and as she did so, he looked straight at her.

He could disguise his shape and his voice and his mannerisms; he could change the way he talked, but he couldn't hide those eyes. Trevelyan looked out at her from under bushy eyebrows and his expression was one of such smugness that she glared back at him.

For the rest of the "wedding" Claire had to clamp her jaws together to keep from speaking out. After the "ceremony" Harry dutifully kissed his sister, then shook hands with James Kincaid and got back on his horse. Claire imagined he was not looking forward to telling his mother what had happened tonight.

Claire dawdled in the summerhouse, even after two of the grooms doubled up and gave a horse to Leatrice and James. Claire watched the "vicar" mount his small horse and ride away. "Go with Harry," Claire said tightly to her sister.

"What are you going to do?"

"Nothing that is any of your business. It's well past your bedtime."

"Yours too. You're going to see that man, aren't you?"

"Why in the world would you think I'm going to visit a man at this time of night? I want to enjoy the night air. Go back with Harry."

"I'll hide all your jewelry and I'll tell Mother about those books you have hidden in the false drawer of your big trunk."

"You really are the most infuriating child. I *can't* take you where I plan to go. It's very important that it's kept secret."

"Does this have to do with the man you visit in the west wing?"

Claire glared at her.

"All I have to do is tell Mother there's another man and she'll—"

"Shut up and get on your horse."

Brat smiled at her beautifully, as she always did when she got what she wanted.

It didn't take Claire long to ride back to the west wing of the house. When she'd dismounted, she looked at Brat and started to try once again to get her sister to go back to the main house, but she didn't waste her breath. Right now she was too angry at Trevelyan to worry about her sister.

She climbed the old stone stairs quickly, taking note that at intervals burning torches had been set in the walls, as though Trevelyan were expecting a guest.

She walked through the room with his writing tables, not wanting to think of the last time she had seen them. Brat was right behind her, her eyes wide as she looked about the place. There were masks and cloths and spears from Trevelyan's travels hanging about the room. Oman stood to one side and smiled at Brat as she walked past. The child grinned back at him.

Trevelyan was in his bedroom, standing by a washbasin and pitcher, looking in a mirror and trying to remove his false beard. He'd already removed his vicar's robe and his padding and now wore snug buckskin knee breeches and a big linen shirt; his legs were bare from the knee down. The eighteenth-century-style knee breeches must have come from the trunk of an ancestor, but they suited him.

He turned and smiled at her when she entered. His look told her that he expected praise for what he'd just done.

"How could you *do* that?" she asked. "You're no more a man of the cloth than I am. They're not married."

He gave a little laugh of dismissal, then looked behind her. "Is this your beautiful little sister?" He walked past Claire and studied Sarah Ann for a moment. "I had been told what an enchanting child you were, but no one told me half of it." He lifted Brat's hand and kissed first the back of it, then the palm.

"Trevelyan!" Claire snapped at him. "Just what do you think you're doing? She's a child."

"She is on the verge of womanhood," he said, still holding Brat's hand and looking at her. Brat was gazing at him with wide eyes and as though she were going to fling herself on him at any moment.

Claire pulled her little sister's hand from Trevelyan's.

Trevelyan winked at Brat, then went back to the basin and mirror and started pulling on his beard again. "Now, you were saying."

"That you acted as though you had the right to marry them and you didn't. They're going to Mr. Kincaid's house tonight thinking they're married and they're not."

"Is that all? Damn!" he cursed when the beard threatened to take some of his skin away with it. "I'm a Master Sufi, remember? Would you like to see my diploma? It's fourteen feet long and quite beautiful."

"Yes," Claire said before she thought. "I mean, no. We have to get them married. Properly married." She couldn't bear another moment of seeing him struggle with the beard. "Sit down and let me do that," she said, pointing to a chair at the foot of the bed.

Trevelyan went to sit on the chair and Brat climbed on the bed, sprawling on her stomach, her chin propped in her hands as she stared at Trevelyan, who was no more than a couple of feet from her. Claire poured hot water into the basin, put a cloth in, wrung it out, then placed the cloth on Trevelyan's face over the false whiskers.

"We have to get them a proper vicar. They have to be married properly."

"Religion is a matter of opinion," he mumbled through the cloth.

"It is not," she said, then continued before he could say another word."There's God and that's it."

"I guess it's how you interpret God that matters."

She took the cloth from his face, then slowly peeled the whiskers away."What did you put this on with?"

"Something Oman made." When the whiskers were off he turned to look at Brat, who was watching him like a snake watching its prey.

"Claire," Brat said, her voice absolutely serious. "I think he is possibly the most handsome man in the world."

"What a delightful, intelligent child," Trevelyan said.

Claire groaned then turned a stern face to her little sister. "Don't say *anything* to him. He isn't what you think he is. He's different from other men. He . . . he goes around the world doing things with women. He hasn't any heart or soul. He isn't involved in life. That's why he can pretend to be a vicar and pretend to marry someone. It's all a joke to him. All of life is a joke to him. He doesn't participate in life; he just observes."

This speech seemed to have no effect on either Trevelyan or Brat. They kept looking at each other.

"You're the explorer," Brat said at last.

"I've seen a few things."

"Yes, I've read—" Sarah began.

"Brat!" Claire said, but her sister didn't jump at the sharp sound. She couldn't seem to take her eyes from Trevelyan's. Claire placed herself between the two of them. "My sister has never read anything in her life. She terrifies her governesses and they don't dare demand anything of her. She—"

"I've read the dirty parts that were written in Latin in the back of your books. Claire translated the chapters and I, ah, found the translations."

At that Claire turned to look at her sister, horror in her eyes.

Brat looked around her to Trevelyan. "What is infibu . . ."

"Infibulation."

"Yes, what is it?"

"Why don't you come and sit on my lap, you pretty child, and I'll tell you anything you want to know."

When Brat started to get off the bed, Claire twisted her arm so she yelped in pain. "Trevelyan, stop it. She's just a little girl."

"Of course she is," Trevelyan said in a sarcastic way, then looked back at Claire. "Did you come here to complain to me? I don't know what made me think so, but I thought you might have come to thank me. MacTarvit said you wanted Lee and Kincaid married and they are."

"They aren't *really* married. They're just living together. Tomorrow you have to go to them and tell them the truth, that it was you who performed the ceremony—if it can be called that—and that they must go to a proper man of God."

Trevelyan's face lost its good humor. "I'll do no such thing. I am as qualified to marry people as anyone is. I daresay more so. I doubt that your average country vicar has been through what I have to earn his certification."

"That's not the point."

"Then you explain it to me. What *is* the point?"

"They have to be married properly. By a man with a proper religion."

Trevelyan was no longer laughing. He got up from the chair and went to the basin to wash his face. "You little prude," he said. "There are many religions and Sufism is just one of them. Leatrice and Kincaid are as married as any two people can be."

"And what does that mean? That they're as married as two people can be?"

"Just what I said. In some places marriage is a very flexible thing. The ways of the Western world would seem absurd to the people in those places. The very idea of staying married to one person forever is ridiculous." He dried his face, walked to the big wardrobe along one wall, and opened it. Claire had never seen inside it. It was filled with boots: soft boots, stiff boots, leather boots, painted boots, embroidered velvet boots.

"Oooooh," Brat said and came off the bed to stand by him.

Trevelyan looked down at her with an adoring smile.

"May I try them on?"

"You may do anything you like," he said in a caressing voice.

"Stop it!" Claire half shouted. "She's a child."

Trevelyan pulled a pair of boots from the wardrobe and sat down to put them on. "In some countries a fourteen-year-old girl is considered too old for marriage. Men like to get them young; then they can raise them to be the way they want them to be. If a man wants a woman who contradicts everything he says and tells him he's wrong at every turn he can raise her to be that way." He lifted one eyebrow at Claire. "I've not heard of a man wanting those traits in a wife, but then I've seen some strange things."

He pulled on a boot. "Could you explain something to me? Before you knew that I was Captain Baker, you couldn't say enough good about him. I heard he was a great man, that the world owed much to him. I heard that you believed that Captain Baker and *only* Baker could get into Pesha, that no other man was man enough to get into the city. But now that you know that *I* am Baker, I can't seem to do anything to please you. My drawings, which you once loved, you now hate. You no longer seem to think my books are enlightened—now they're too dirty for your precocious little sister to read, and you think that being a Master Sufi isn't enough to enable me to perform a simple marriage ceremony."

She looked away from him, for all that he said was true. "Heroes aren't real," she said at last.

He put on the second boot and stamped his foot to the floor. "Oh, I see, now I'm a bloody hero."

"Don't curse in front of my sister."

He moved to stand in front of her, glaring down at her. "I'll bloody well curse any bloody time I want to. *You're* the one who wanted Lee married to Kincaid and I did it for you. I got them there and locked them in together. I even crawled through the attic and pulled up their clothes using a hooked pole. I'm the one who arranged it all, yet you can't even say thank-you to me. All you can do is complain."

When Claire didn't say anything, just stood there with an obstinate look on her face, Trevelyan walked to a chest and threw back the lid. He rummaged inside for a moment, then withdrew a sheaf of papers. "If you'd rather that Leatrice wasn't married by a Master Sufi, what religion would you prefer?"

He pulled a few papers from the portfolio. "An English religion? Here are certificates saying I'm qualified to perform services in four English religions. Or would you prefer an American religion? American certificates are the easiest to obtain. All you do is tell someone that you have the 'call' and you're considered one of them."

He tossed several pieces of paper at her feet, then looked back at the portfolio. "Or would you like a religion from India? Arabia? I have several African religions. Their certificates are rather interesting. One of them is written on bark and two are on animal skin. I don't think you'd like me to tell you what they used for ink."

He tossed the rest of the papers on the floor at her feet and looked at her. "Are those enough religions for you? Do I seem qualified to perform a marriage ceremony now?"

She looked down at the papers, not stooping to touch them, then back at his eyes. "But you don't believe *any* of them," she said softly.

Trevelyan's eyes blazed. "I believe *all* of them."

She could only glare at him. "You made Harry look like a fool," she spat at him. "You knew Harry wouldn't want to go against his mother."

"Is that what's bothering you? It doesn't take much to make Harry look like a fool."

She raised her hand to slap him at that, but he caught her wrist and for a moment he held it as his eyes locked with hers. Her heart was pounding in her throat.

He tossed her arm from him as though he were throwing something away. "Get out of here. I don't know why I thought you were different. You're the same as all of them. You like to read my books, you like to hear of other lands and their strange, quaint customs, but when it comes down to it you're as corseted as all the other *ladies.*" He made the last word sound filthy.

"That's not true," she whispered. "I believe in what Captain Baker has seen and done. I think he—"

"Not *him.* Me. *I* am Captain Baker. He's not a hero. He's a flesh-and-blood man who loves and hates and . . . and likes boots and pretty girls no matter what age they are and—" He cut himself off and looked away from her. When he spoke again, his voice was soft. "Go on, get out of here. I need to do some work. Tell Leatrice to find herself a . . ." He swallowed. "A man with a real, true, sanctioned-by-God religion to marry her, tell her that a marriage performed by an unbeliever isn't any good." When he looked back at her, his eyes were blazing. They were so hot that Claire took a step backward. "Don't come here again. I don't want to see you again."

Claire could only nod. Without a word, she put out her hand to Sarah Ann, who was standing behind her. Sarah took her sister's hand and walked out with her, through Trevelyan's writing room, then down the stairs to the outside.

"He's not like anybody else in the world, is he?" Brat said when they were outside.

"No," Claire whispered, "he's not."

"I think you'd better marry Harry. Harry will be much easier to manage."

Claire gritted her teeth. "Harry has his mother."

Brat looked up toward the windows of Trevelyan's rooms. "Harry and his mother combined aren't like *he* is."

Claire didn't have anything else to say, and they walked together to the main part of the house.

Chapter Seventeen

Claire behaved herself for two whole weeks. She told herself she'd been making a fool of herself with Captain Baker and that she had to start taking her life as the future duchess more seriously. For two weeks she attended every meal. She dressed for breakfast in a lovely, conservative dress and at the table she spoke to no one, just as she was supposed to do. At ten she dressed in her riding habit and went out for a sedate ride, accompanied by a silent groom. She returned from her ride, changed into a dress for luncheon, sat through the long meal and listened to the men and women talk of dogs and horses. After luncheon she read a book that had been personally approved by the duchess, or she tried her best to take up needlepoint, but she couldn't seem to concentrate on the canvas. At four she put on a tea gown and went down to tea with Harry's ancient relatives. She attempted to have a conversation with them but they mostly just looked at her. After tea the ladies went to their rooms to rest. Claire stopped herself from crying, "Rest from *what? For* what?" Obediently, she lay on the bed in her room, closed her eyes, and tried to be still. After the rest, she began the long process of dressing for dinner. She didn't wear any of her low-cut, shocking, fashionable dresses, but only the most conservative, unshocking dresses. After a three-and-a-half hour dinner, she went back to her room to retire for the evening.

By the end of the second week she was sure she was going to go mad. She had visions of herself running about the house screaming and pulling her hair out. She began to understand why the other inhabitants of the house were so eccentric. It was one evening when she was watching the two old ladies slip silverware up their sleeves that Claire wondered what it would feel like to be a thief. She picked up her salad fork and put the handle to her sleeve.

Just as the utensil was disappearing up her sleeve, she felt eyes on her and looked up to see the butler staring at her. Claire gave a start and put the fork back on the table.

The next morning she confronted Harry. "I have to have something to *do.*"

"You may do whatever you like," he said, as he pulled on his riding gloves.

"May I go with you?" For the last several days she had seen Harry only at meals, but she hadn't spoken to him. Every day he had been out hunting with her father and some other young men who had come from London for a visit.

Harry gave a quick frown, then tried to smile. He didn't believe in women on hunts. They tended to be restless. "Of course you may. But you'll have to abide by the rules of the hunt."

Claire agreed. She would have agreed to anything in order to get away from the dull routine of that house. She promised herself and Harry that she'd be quiet and not cause him any distraction while he was hunting.

But the minute she was on the horse and riding beside Harry, it seemed that weeks' worth of words flooded from her. She was so eager to talk to someone. "Harry," she said under her breath so the others wouldn't hear, "I've been dying to know how your mother took the news of Leatrice's marriage. I haven't heard so much as a whisper about it." She looked away so he wouldn't see the way her mouth tightened. She'd heard whispers enough in the last few days, but when she'd approached, the whispers had ceased. Twice she had been tempted to do what Brat did and hide behind doors and eavesdrop.

Harry looked surprised. "Mother wished her daughter all the happiness in the world. She said had she known Lee wanted to be married she would have arranged an elaborate ceremony for her. As it is, with the way Lee disgraced herself, Mother doesn't feel she should reward Lee's misconduct with a settlement."

Again, Claire had to turn away. The duchess had certainly gotten herself out of that one. Claire wondered if Leatrice and her new husband had enough to live on.

"You don't know who the man was who performed the ceremony, do you?" Harry asked.

"Why do you want to know?" Claire tried to keep her voice light.

"Mother asked. I think she's had someone doing some searching." Harry smiled. "I don't think Mother is too happy with the man. I think Mother believes she could have dissuaded Lee if that man hadn't come along and performed the service."

Claire gave Harry a weak smile and turned away. She knew that everything she had felt about the duchess that first day was correct. The horrid old woman wanted Leatrice for her servant and she didn't mean to release her.

Claire's next thought was concern for Trevelyan. What would the duchess do if she found out that Trevelyan had performed the ceremony? Claire had had only that one meeting with the woman, but she didn't think the duchess was the type to forgive easily. What would she do if she found out one of her husband's relatives was hiding in the west tower and had helped to take away what the duchess considered to be hers?

In the next moment, Claire's head came up. What would the duchess do if she found out Claire had been involved in taking Leatrice away?

"Claire?" Harry said. "Are you all right? You look pale. Perhaps you should return to the house."

"No, I'm fine, really," she murmured and smiled at Harry. Above all, she didn't want to return to that house and its boredom.

Eight hours later, she was thinking of the quiet peacefulness of the house with longing. Harry had led her to something called a butt, a little three-sided, roofed shelter, and told her to sit still and not talk. There was nowhere to sit and nothing to sit on, so she'd had to sit on the damp ground. Harry and a man who did nothing but load his shotguns had stood at the other end of the butt and had shot at birds all day long.

Ten minutes after they had arrived it had begun to rain, not a deluge but a steady drizzle that seeped through the roof and sides of the butt and soon had Claire soaked.

Harry asked her if she wanted to return to the house. Claire told him no, that she was having a lovely time and what did a little rain matter? She knew that if she were a coward this first time and gave up, Harry would never again allow her to go with him.

At one they had a cold lunch and Harry kept on shooting. He was wearing tweeds and she could see that he too was soaked, but he didn't seem to mind or even notice. Claire remembered what the duchess had told her about Harry's delicate constitution, but he didn't look delicate now.

Claire sat in the corner, the ground under and around her growing wetter by the minute, and pulled her knees up to hug them. All around her shotguns were going off. She wondered if one day spent in a leaky shelter could leave her permanently deaf.

She sneezed, and Harry turned a furious face toward her. "Claire, if you can't keep quiet you'll have to return. Your noise frightens the birds."

"How can a sneeze frighten them if a thousand shotgun blasts don't?" she said before she thought.

She saw Harry and his loader exchange looks that told what they thought of taking women on a hunt.

It was nearly dusk when Harry finally said they were going to return to the house. Claire would have cried with relief if the thought of adding more water, even tears, to her soaking body hadn't horrified her. She was so cold she had difficulty in standing and her wool dress, soaked as it was, must have weighed fifty pounds. Also, it smelled like a wet dog.

"I didn't think you'd enjoy this," Harry said. "Ladies never—"

"I've had a marvelous time," Claire said, trying not to wiggle her nose as she suppressed a sneeze. "It has truly been an enlightening experience."

Harry put his arm around her shoulders and hugged her companionably. "Some English girls like to hunt, but I've never met an American girl who did. I liked having you here today. You're good company. Tomorrow we're going north after partridge and in a few weeks we'll stalk deer. But you have to be quiet when we go after the deer, not like today." He hugged her shoulders again. "Claire, I think you and I are going to make a perfect couple. I've always wanted a woman who would hunt with me. I've been a little concerned that you were too bookish, but after today I can see I was wrong. After we're married we can spend many days together. Days just like this one."

Claire gave a sneeze and he patted her shoulder. "Let's get you home and into some dry clothes. Tomorrow we go for partridge."

Harry's face suddenly brightened and he put his hands on her shoulders, turning her to face him. "I have a marvelous idea! For a wedding present I'll buy you a pair of shotguns. Your very own. Engraved silver. I'll write to London today and have someone come up and fit you. The stocks will be perfectly sized for you." He smiled happily. "I'm looking forward to marriage more and more."

Claire tried her best to smile back at him but her teeth were chattering too hard.

"Come on," Harry said. "We'll fix you up with a nice, hot pot of tea."

Claire thought with longing of MacTarvit's cozy, warm cottage and his even more warming whisky. "Yes," she said. "Tea would be lovely."

Thirty minutes later Claire was back in her room and Miss Rogers was complaining nonstop about how wet Claire's clothes were.

"I hope you don't expect me to salvage that," the little gray woman sniffed as she looked at Claire's riding habit. "Fine quality it was, even if it was a Frenchified design, but it's ruined now. Of course we English and even these Scots aren't used to having the money to waste that you Americans have. For all I know you Americans can afford to throw away good clothing after one wearing. I can't say. I have my duty and that's all. It's not for me to judge my betters, so to speak. Although it's hard to think of someone from a country that was mostly savages so few years ago as being better than an Englishwoman, but who am I to say? I just—"

"Miss Rogers!" Claire said as firmly as her chattering teeth would allow. "Would you call the footmen and have a bath brought up here?"

"At this time of day?"

"Yes, at this time of day."

Miss Rogers sniffed. "I'm sure that to the likes of someone in your station in life it means nothing for the extra work to the servants. We're nothing to the likes of you. We—"

"Go!" Claire ordered, as her frozen fingers began to try to unbutton the front of her habit.

There was a knock on the door and the butler appeared, carrying a silver tray. On it was a tea cozy. Something warm to drink, Claire thought, but she didn't feel too enthusiastic because she knew that the kitchens were so far from the main rooms of the house that by the time the food reached the people it was usually cold. But tepid tea was better than nothing at all.

"Rogers," the butler said sternly, "you are wanted downstairs."

Claire was very happy to see that the odious little woman didn't argue with the butler, but left the room without any argument. When she was alone with the butler, Claire stretched out a frozen, trembling hand to lift the cozy.

On the silver tray was not a pot of tea but a short, wide glass full of what she knew was whisky. She looked up at the butler in astonishment and he gave her the barest hint of a smile. "MacTarvit?" she asked.

"His finest. Twenty-five years old."

Claire's hand was shaking as she picked up the glass. As she raised it to her lips she looked up at the butler. "I love you," she whispered.

"Many young ladies have," he said and gave her a small smile.

Claire tried to sip the whisky, but as the welcome warmth hit her stomach she was greedy for more. She put the glass to her lips and drained it. Then she had to step backward and catch the post of the bed to steady herself. She looked up at the butler and he was staring at her in astonishment.

"I had heard you were a Scot," he said, and there was admiration in his voice. "You are indeed."

At that moment, the door opened and an angry Miss Rogers walked in. "No one wanted me downstairs," she said.

Calmly, the butler covered the empty glass on his tray with the cozy and turned to the woman. "Then perhaps I was in error. Ring for a bath for your mistress." There was command in the last order and Miss Rogers went obediently to the bellpull and gave a tug.

Claire, still standing by the bedpost, smiled at the butler when he reached the door. She wasn't sure, but she thought he gave her a wink before he left.

An hour and a half later she was bathed and dressed for dinner in a warm wool dress. Harry was waiting for her outside her room and he offered her his arm as they went down the stairs to dinner. She knew she had pleased him today, pleased him as she never had before. For the first time since she'd met him, he talked to her. Usually he didn't have much to say, but tonight he had a great deal to say—and every word of it was about hunting.

He talked to her of killing birds and ducks and deer. He spoke of going to India to hunt tigers and to Africa to kill elephants. "And you, darling, shall be right there with me."

At dinner, he gave her Leatrice's seat on his right-hand side, and all through the long meal, he talked to her of their future life together. He told her he'd teach her to shoot. He told her he'd teach her to ride to the hounds, chasing after a pack of excited dogs who were trying to kill a fox. He spoke of blooding her, which Claire came to understand was having the blood of a poor dead fox smeared on her forehead. "It all sounds marvelously exciting," she murmured and didn't finish her fish course.

After dinner, after the men and women had separated, women to the drawing room for coffee and men to the library for port and cigars, Harry walked Claire to her room.

He put his hands on her shoulders and looked into her eyes. "I like you better than I thought I would," he whispered. "You were good company today."

"But I didn't say a word all day. I just sat there in the rain and sneezed."

"You'll get used to it. Once you have your own shotguns you'll enjoy yourself even more than you did today. There's nothing like bringing down an animal. It's the thrill of it, you against them." He kissed her again. "As for not talking, I like a quiet woman. Women who are too clever can be a bore. Thank heaven you're not like that."

"True," she said softly. "I don't think I'm clever at all."

Harry heard no sarcasm in her voice. "Good," he said, then kissed her forehead. "Now I want you to get your rest. Remember that tomorrow it's partridge."

Claire nodded at him, then went inside her room. As Miss Rogers helped her dress for bed, Claire didn't listen to the woman's complaints. Instead, Claire's mind seemed to be numb. Shotguns, she thought. Dead birds. Dead tigers. Dead elephants. Captain Baker had written about elephants in his two books about his travels in India. They had seemed like rather nice animals and quite useful.

When Miss Rogers was gone, Claire sat at the dressing table and began to cream her face. Her skin was chapped from the wind and the cold. Slowly, she rubbed cream into her face and looked at herself in the mirror.

Duchess, she thought. She was going to marry Harry and become the duchess.

She wouldn't allow herself to think anymore as she got up from the dressing table and walked to the bed. Thanks to her exhaustion and the cold of the day she fell asleep quickly.

She was awakened before dawn by an angry Miss Rogers, who informed her that she had to get dressed because the men were leaving early to go hunting.

Claire dressed in her habit, which was still damp from the day before, without saying a word and made her way downstairs. The men were already mounted and waiting for her. Harry looked radiant with happiness and slapped her on the back when she was atop her horse.

She spent a second day crouched in a wet butt with rain pouring down on her. Every hour or so Harry would smile at her and tell her more about the wonderful shotguns he was going to give her for a wedding gift.

When she got back to the house, there was a hot bath waiting for her and a teapot set on a tray with a cup and saucer. When Miss Rogers entered the room, Claire was sedately sipping whisky from her cup.

On the third day she was again up before dawn. When she was downstairs Harry informed her that today they were going after rabbits and quail. That meant Claire got to walk across marshy land in the cold drizzle and watch the men slaughter a couple of hundred rabbits. Harry promised to buy her her own bird dog as an additional wedding present.

By the time Claire returned to the house, she was so cold she wasn't feeling anything. But more important, she wasn't allowing herself to think anything either. Harry had talked about shooting deer the next day. Claire was afraid that the sight of the death of one of those soft-eyed deer she sometimes saw wandering about might make her cry.

She creamed her face, then climbed into bed and tried to go to sleep, but a noise made her jump. In the dim light of the room she saw the big portrait on the wall move and knew that the door to the tunnel was opening.

She forgot her exhaustion as she leaped out of bed and ran toward the door. "Trevelyan!" she gasped.

The door opened but, instead of Trevelyan, there stood her bratty little sister holding a candle.

Claire turned away. "You should be in bed," she said tiredly and went back to her own bed.

Brat shut the tunnel door, put the candle on the bedside table, and climbed up on the big four-poster bed. "I hear you've become a hunter."

"A regular Diana," Claire murmured, then grimaced at Brat's puzzled look. "If you'd ever bothered to open a book, you'd know that Diana is the goddess of the hunt."

Brat smiled at her sister. "I'll bet Harry knows all about gods and goddesses. Is that what the two of you talk about all day? Or do you practice your Italian and French on each other? Maybe you discuss politics or religion, or maybe you talk about the history of the Scots. Maybe you talk about all the things you plan to do around this place when you're the duchess."

Claire's lips tightened. "Would you *please* go to bed?"

"What *do* you and Harry talk about?"

"That happens to be none of your business."

Brat stretched out across the foot of the bed. "Have you seen Captain Baker?"

"No, I have not. Nor do I plan to see him. To tell you the truth, I've been so busy I've not even thought about him."

Brat turned on her back, her hands behind her head and looked up at the canopy overhead. "I thought Trevelyan was the most unusual man I have ever met in my life. Did you see all the things he has in his room? He must have been a lot of places."

"If you spent some of your time doing something besides eavesdropping and such, and read any of Captain Baker's books, you'd know just how many places he's been and all that he's seen. He is a great man."

"So why did you get so mad at him when he married Harry's sister?"

Claire opened her mouth twice to speak, but closed it. "You wouldn't understand," she said at last.

"It was because of what you said about his being a hero, wasn't it? He's been a hero of yours but he's just ordinary, isn't he?"

"He is far from ordinary. He's . . ." She looked up sharply. "You have to go to bed."

"Do you have as much fun with Harry as you do with Captain Baker?"

"Of course I do. What a ridiculous question. Harry is the man I love. I want to spend as much time with him as I can. Captain Baker is nothing to me. Except that he's Harry's relative and I have to be nice to him."

"You were just being nice to him when you spent those three days nursing him, weren't you?" Brat gave her a sly look. "Did you take all his clothes off?"

"Out!" Claire said. "Get out of here at once."

Brat didn't move. "Be careful or you'll wake the old dragon," she said, meaning Miss Rogers. "Did you hear what happened after Leatrice got married?"

Claire wanted to tell her precocious sister that she wasn't interested, but she couldn't. "No," she said softly, "I didn't hear."

"The old hag, the old duchess, nearly died of apoplexy. She had a fit of some sort. Rumor has it she was foaming at the mouth."

"That's difficult to believe." Claire wasn't going to encourage her sister, but she wanted to hear all of it. "Harry said—"

"Harry doesn't know. He was out hunting." Brat gave Claire a look that showed she was laughing at her sister. "By the time Harry returned the old woman was cooing again. Of course that's all she does when Harry's around. But I heard she was threatening to kill whoever was responsible for Leatrice getting married. I think she was trying to punish her daughter for something and she didn't think the punishment was finished yet."

"I'm sure the gossip you heard was wrong."

"Mmmmm" was all Brat would say. "If Harry had to choose between you and his mother, who do you think he'd choose?"

"I'm not going to answer that question." Claire didn't want to think what the answer might be.

Brat was silent for a moment. "Do you miss Trevelyan?"

"Of course not. I have plenty to keep me busy."

Brat laughed. "They're saying in the kitchen that your habit is never going to get dry. It smells so awful they have to hang it in a room by itself."

"Then I shall have to buy another."

"And another and another and another. You're going to need lots of them if you marry Harry. Do you think you'll spend your life with him doing nothing but hunting?"

"No, of course not. I'll . . ." Claire trailed off, trying to think what she'd do after she was married.

"Do you think Captain Baker will ever get married?"

"Absolutely not! His kind *never* marries. Or if they do, they leave their wives crying somewhere while they go off to explore other places and . . . and other women."

"Are you sure?"

"I know him very well. I've read everything he's ever written and everything that's been written about him. I know him very, very well."

"It was nice of him to help Leatrice that way. He was risking a lot. If he'd been caught, I'd hate to think what the old hag would have done to him."

"It wasn't kindness, it was—" She grimaced. "I don't know why he did it. I'm sure he plans to write about it."

"I thought you said he writes about everything. Did you see the cartoons he made of you?"

"Yes, I saw them." Claire's head came up. "When did *you* see them?"

"Yesterday morning. I went to see him and—"

"You *what?* Have you been seeing him?" Claire grabbed her sister's arm. "After the vulgar things he said to you? I don't trust him alone with you. He—"

"He's a very nice man and he never touches me, if that's what worries you."

Claire released her sister's arm and leaned back against the pillows. "No, I don't think he would. He is an honorable man—in his own odd way." She paused. "How is he?"

Brat was thoughtful for a moment. "I believe he misses you."

Claire sat up straight. "He does? Has he said so? I mean, not that it makes any difference to me, but what makes you think he misses me?" Claire thought that if she were put on a medieval torture rack, she wouldn't admit to how much she had missed Trevelyan. He was impossible of course, grumpy, cynical, morose at times, always asking questions, often making her feel stupid and childish, but, heaven, how he made her feel alive. When she was with Trevelyan every nerve in her body was alive. He made her use her mind; he made her think about things that she hadn't even known were in her thoughts. He'd made her put her thoughts about the Scots into words. He'd made her think that she could do something with her life, that what she thought and felt could make a difference.

"He hasn't said that he misses you," Brat said, "but I can tell that he does."

"Oh," Claire said and leaned back against the pillows. "I haven't missed him at all. I have been quite happy with Harry. He's going to buy me a pair of shotguns. They have silver barrels, or silver on them somewhere. And maybe a dog, too."

Brat laughed at that in a way that made Claire blush. "You should see yourself when you come in from hunting. You look like a drowned rat and about the unhappiest person on earth. Everyone can see it except your precious Harry. He's so dumb—"

Brat rolled off the bed as Claire went for her throat. Laughing, Brat stepped away from the bed. "You're so funny that I almost forgot why I came here. Do you remember that man Jack Powell?"

"The man who says he went into Pesha when it was actually Trevelyan?"

"The very one. There was an article in the paper today. It said this man Powell was going to speak in Edinburgh and he was going to bring proof that he—not Captain Baker—had been into Pesha. The paper called it irr . . . irr . . ."

"Irrefutable."

"That's it. Nobody can question it." Brat yawned. "It looks like your Captain Baker isn't going to be remembered as the man who went to Pesha."

"But he *did* go to Pesha. Only he went. Not the man Powell. They can't—"

Brat yawned again. "I thought it didn't matter to you. You're going hunting with Harry. I guess I'd better go to bed. Vellie said he might come and read me a story tonight."

"You have no right to call him that. And what kind of story is he reading you?"

"Did I say reading? He *tells* me stories. Wonderful stories, all about Pesha. You should get him to tell you. Oh, I forgot, you aren't seeing him anymore. Well, good night. See you tomorrow." Brat grinned. "But if you're wearing your wet wool, I hope you don't mind if I don't get too near you." With that, Brat took her candle, opened the portrait, and disappeared into the tunnels.

Claire sat where she was for a moment, then turned and banged her fist into her pillow. Trevelyan was an odious man. Really, truly odious. Brat had asked if she thought he'd ever marry. Him? The woman who loved Trevelyan enough to want to marry him would be condemned to a life of misery and loneliness. She'd be lonely because he'd leave her and go off traveling on his own. And while his wife was sitting home alone worried sick about him, he'd be . . . be doing all the things with women that he'd written about.

She punched the pillow a couple of more times, then tried to settle down to sleep, but she couldn't close her eyes.

Heroes, she thought. It was one thing to adore a man from afar, but quite another to meet him in life. She remembered reading Trevelyan's books as a girl and thinking how divinely interesting a man he was when he wrote that he always tried to wear native garb wherever he was. She used to imagine him in his exotic costumes and think how romantic he must look.

But it didn't seem romantic when the reality was that each time she saw him he was wearing something different. One time he'd have on a long silk robe with brightly colored birds embroidered on the back, and the next time she saw him he'd be wearing the clothing of an eighteenth-century English gentleman.

No, spending time with a man like that was not what one should do. She was much better off staying with Harry and his family and her own family. Of course, she only saw her father in passing when she went out to hunt with Harry, and she saw her mother even less. Right now her mother was planning her wardrobe for Claire's wedding. It was hoped that the Prince and Princess of Wales would attend, and Arva had to think about how she looked.

Claire punched her pillow again and tried to sleep.

The next day, wearing her riding habit, which didn't seem as though it was ever going to dry completely, Claire again went hunting with Harry. She had tramped across marshlands, up a steep, heather-covered hill with him and his loader, until they finally came to a pretty little wooded area. She had not said a word to Harry throughout the long walk because he'd warned her of the need for absolute silence.

As they entered the wood, Harry whispered something to his loader and Claire looked about her. Standing not very far away was a magnificent buck and his three females. Claire smiled at the loveliness of the scene. She watched the lovely creatures, so sleek, so calm, so unworried.

The next minute Harry's rifle went off beside her and the great buck fell to the ground. The does ran away.

Harry and his loader were jubilant, talking excitedly about having brought the animal down in one shot. Claire watched them walking toward the big animal, then she saw the buck lift its head slightly. It was still alive.

She started running toward the deer, passing Harry and the other man as she ran. But before she reached the buck, Harry's rifle rang out again and the buck's head fell to the ground.

It was too much for Claire. She was too tired from days of hunting, too sick with all the hundreds of dead birds and animals she had seen in the last few days. She stood where she was, looking at the enormous deer that a mere few minutes ago had been alive and beautiful and now was lying dead. And for what? Harry didn't need the animal for food. He had killed it for *sport.* He had killed the animal because it gave him pleasure to do so.

"Great shot, wasn't it?" Harry said from behind her.

Claire turned toward him, her eyes blazing. "How could you?"

"How could I what?" He was genuinely confused.

At his lack of understanding, something within Claire broke. She doubled up her fists and began pounding on his chest. "You had no right to kill that animal. No right at all. It was beautiful and there was no reason. You—"

Harry caught her hands in his. "Darling, you have a case of wedding nerves. Everything will be all right. I know that when I took my first buck I was a little upset too."

She pulled away from him and saw he had no idea what was wrong with her. "Don't you do anything *useful?"* she shouted. "Don't you do anything besides kill things?"

Harry stiffened at that and dropped his arms from around her. "I am not an American, if that's what you mean."

Claire took a step backward and put her hand to her mouth to keep from saying another word. Her eyes filled with tears. How could she have said such a thing to the man she loved? She turned away and began to run.

She ran out of the woods, down the hill, across the fields, and when she reached her horse, she mounted as quickly as possible, wrapping her leg firmly about the sidesaddle. She kicked the horse forward and raced back to the house.

At the house she entered the main door and was greeted by her mother standing in the midst of what looked to be a hundred boxes of clothing, all the boxes bearing London labels.

"Come and look at the lovely things I've bought, dear," her mother said. "Look, here's a fan with diamonds on it."

Claire's eyes were so full of tears she couldn't see a thing. She merely shook her head and ran up the stairs to her room. Once inside she bolted both the bedroom door and the door leading into the dressing room where horrid Miss Rogers usually stayed.

Once she was alone and safe, Claire flung herself on the bed and dissolved into a flood of tears. She wasn't sure why she was crying; she told herself it was because of seeing the deer killed. Some part of her knew there was a deeper reason for her tears, but at all costs she didn't want to look at what was making her cry.

At times during the day people knocked on the doors but Claire didn't open them. She just cried.

Sarah Ann was in the stables when Harry returned. She tried to look as though she "happened" to be there, but the truth was Cammy had seen Claire return in a blaze of hooves and tears. Brat had run to the stables to see what was going on. Sarah was becoming annoyed with her older sister. For all of Claire's brains, she wasn't very good at figuring out what she *wanted* to do; Claire was ruled by shoulds. She *should* love Harry, therefore she did.

Harry came into the stable and Brat could see that he was enraged. He flung himself off the horse. Brat watched him silently. What she had never told anyone was how beautiful she thought Harry was. She liked the look of Trevelyan, but Trevelyan was not a man a woman—for that's what Brat considered herself—could live with. Harry, on the other hand, was a man one could spend a life with. Poor Claire was just too dumb to know how to handle a man like Harry.

"Leave you again, did she?" Brat said, making Harry start as he turned to her. Brat smiled at him as she bit into a fat red apple.

"What are you doing here?"

"Waiting for you," Brat said in a seductive voice.

Harry looked at her and gave a snort of laughter. "You'd better go back to the nursery."

Brat gave a chuckle and walked past him. She swayed her hips as she'd seen women do, swayed them in a way that Claire never did. Claire thought that the way to get a man was to talk to him. Brat stopped about ten feet in front of Harry and looked back at him over her shoulder. He was watching her, as she knew he would be. "Will you come and visit me?" she practically purred, then tossed her apple away and ran back to the house.

Harry stood for a moment looking after the young woman whom he'd thought of as a child, then he hit his riding crop against the stable wall. "Damn the lot of them," he said and went to the house.

The tunnel door opened and Brat entered. She stood by the bed and stared down at Claire for a while. "You and Harry have a fight?"

Claire sniffed. She was lying on her back. There weren't many tears left in her. "I don't know."

"Harry thinks you did. He went to Edinburgh. Didn't even pack. Just talked to his mother, then got on his horse and left. Only took five servants with him. The others are to bring his trunks and come later."

There seemed to be more tears in Claire, because they started flowing again. "He shot a buck. I was upset."

Brat played with the hangings at the end of the bed. "I don't think Harry's visit with his mother was very pleasant."

"I wouldn't doubt if he wanted to break the engagement," Claire said. "I was awful today."

"Maybe Harry wanted out, but I don't think our mother will allow you to break up with Harry. Do you know how much she's already charged to your name? To the new duchess of MacArran?"

"I don't want to know," Claire said.

Brat walked toward the portrait door. "I have to go now. I hope you feel better." She paused. "And I hope you make up your mind."

"Make up my mind about what?"

Brat didn't answer, just gave her sister a little smile and disappeared behind the portrait.

Claire turned onto her stomach and started crying again. Now she had angered Harry as well as his mother, and everyone in the house knew they'd had a quarrel. But then lovers always had quarrels, didn't they? Except that Claire knew her quarrel with Harry was no ordinary one.

So, he had gone to Edinburgh and now she was left alone in that house. She would have no company, nothing to occupy her mind, no one to talk to until he returned. She'd have to wait until he returned before she had someone to talk to, to—

She started crying harder, for she knew that she and Harry didn't talk. When Harry returned she was going to have to make up their argument. She'd have to tell him how very, very sorry she was, then she'd have to . . . What? Spend her days hunting and seeing more animals killed? Would she come to own a hundred riding habits and six dozen shotguns? Ten years from now would she still be attending tea with her mother-in-law, a tea where she was never so much as allowed to sit down?

Each thought made her cry harder.

Chapter Eighteen

Claire was awakened from a deep sleep by someone shaking her shoulder. She could barely open her eyes, since they were swollen from having cried for the better part of a day. The room was dark except for the candle the man standing over her held. Her head was pounding.

She managed to get her eyes open enough to see the glare of the white clothing Oman wore. For a second she was too groggy to respond, but then she became alarmed.

"What is it?" she asked, trying to sit up, but her muscles seemed to be weak. She was still wearing her damp habit.

"He has been shot," Oman said in his accented voice. "Someone has made attempt to kill him."

Claire's eyes widened. "Trevelyan?" she whispered, and Oman nodded. Claire was out of the bed in a second, but the moment her feet touched the floor, she swayed and put her hand to her head. It had been a long while since she had eaten. She looked at the clock on the mantel and saw that it was a few minutes after midnight.

"Did he send for me?" she asked. "How badly is he hurt? I doubt he'll have a doctor, will he? Is he going to be all right?"

To all of these questions, Oman merely said, "Come," and started toward the portrait door.

Claire followed him through the tunnel passages, and out onto the roof. She didn't think of what she was doing, but followed Oman, her heart pounding with every step.

When they reached Trevelyan's writing room, the first words she heard were a bellow of rage. "Where the hell have you been? I could have bled to death waiting for you."

Immediately, Claire smiled in relief. Any man who could yell like that wasn't yet on his deathbed.

She walked into his bedroom. "I can see that loss of blood hasn't sweetened your temper. Now let me see what's been done to you."

He was staring at her when she reached the side of the bed. The shoulder of his linen shirt was soaked with blood but his color was good and he looked healthy enough.

"What are you doing here?" There was hostility in his voice.

That answered the question of whether he had asked for her or not. "I heard you needed help and I came to give it." She reached out to touch his shoulder, but he pulled away and in doing so he grunted with pain.

"I don't need you."

"Then I shall call for a doctor." She started to leave the room.

"No!" he said sharply.

She turned back to look at him. "It's either me or a doctor. Those are your only choices."

He didn't answer, but he lay back against the pillows as though in surrender.

Claire went to him. Next to the bed Oman had put out surgical instruments, hot water, and rolls of cotton cloth for bandages. Very carefully, she cut away Trevelyan's shirt and looked at the wound. It was clean except for the blood around it, no gunpowder, no dirt or gravel in it, and, thank heaven, the bullet had gone through. The wound was in his upper arm, through the muscle but missing the bone.

Carefully, she began to clean the blood from the wound and from his chest. "Who shot you?" she asked softly.

"Could have been any number of people. I have angered a few people in my life."

"You? That's difficult to believe."

He opened his eyes and looked at her. There was a faint smile about his lips. "You've been crying," he said.

"When I heard you were injured I was in torrents. I cried all the way here."

He leaned back against the pillows as she began to bandage his arm.

"I heard that it was Harry who was making you cry. I heard that he shot a buck and you got very angry." He looked at her and his voice lowered. "I heard that he told his mother he couldn't marry you."

Claire's hands stilled. "Did he?" She tried to keep her voice from trembling but she couldn't. "You shouldn't listen to gossip. Who shot you? One of the hunters? Some of them are very bad shots. In the last few days I have seen many animals that were only wounded: birds missing legs or wings, rabbits without feet hopping away, a buck that wasn't dead, a—" She broke off, sure that she was going to start crying again.

Trevelyan was looking at her intently, watching her as she bandaged his arm. "What have you been doing in the two and a half weeks since I've seen you?"

"Has it been that long? It seems like only yesterday that I was sitting in this room drinking whisky and talking to you. Surely it's only been a few hours since I was dancing with the crofters and . . . and . . . Angus MacTarvit."

Just the sound of that name was too much for her. She sat down hard on a chair and began to weep again, her hands covering her face.

Trevelyan leaned against the pillows and watched her, his face betraying little emotion, but he knew what was wrong with her. He knew it because he had lived it. He knew very well what this house could do to a person's spirit. You either conformed or your spirit was killed.

In the long, long two and a half weeks since he had seen her, he had been kept informed of what she was doing by her beautiful little sister. Sarah Ann had daily come to his rooms and told him all the gossip of everyone in the house. He'd heard how Claire was trying to be what Harry wanted in a wife, but, more important, he'd heard how Claire's greedy mother was already spending the fortune that Claire was to inherit upon her marriage—marriage to the right person.

"I'm starving," he said loudly, over her crying. "I think Oman cooked a kettleful of something. Maybe you'd get me something to eat."

Claire began to sniff and looked about for a handkerchief. Finding none, she blew her nose on a piece of bandage. Feeling listless and miserable she left the bedroom and went to the outside room. Oman was waiting for her, and in his hand was a big tray bearing two plates heaped with food and two large glasses of whisky. Claire started to take the tray but he waved her aside and followed her back into the bedroom, where he placed the tray on the foot of the bed, then left.

Claire reached for a piece of chicken, but Trevelyan's voice stopped her. "I can't eat with you wearing that thing. You smell worse than a goat. Open that door and take out a robe, then get that dress off. Don't look at me like that! I'm not trying to molest you, I'm trying to eat my dinner without the perfume of that garment."

Claire didn't have the spirit to disobey him. She opened the left door of the wardrobe and saw inside a variety of loose robes. There was a blue one that was especially lovely and she took it out of the closet. Holding it, she looked about for some place to change, then Trevelyan motioned toward a tapestry. She walked over to it and found the door to what had to be the ancient medieval garderobe, the outdoor toilet that was indoors. She stepped inside the little room.

"And take off that corset," Trevelyan yelled from the bedroom. "I can't bear to hear you gasping for breath."

Claire thought she should protest, but she didn't, and in the next second she was tearing at her clothes, anxious to rid herself of the hated habit. And she took off her corset too. Then, when she realized that her undergarments were damp, she removed them too. She felt downright decadent and definitely sinful as she slipped the soft silken garment over bare skin. She unpinned her hair and tried to comb it with her fingers.

She ran her hands over the silk gown embroidered with little green butterflies and felt as though for the first time in days she could breathe again. In the house and with Harry she had to behave herself, but not with Trevelyan. Nothing she did or said ever shocked him.

She walked out from behind the tapestry and had the satisfaction of seeing Trevelyan pause with food on the way to his mouth. His eyes widened as he looked from her face down to her bare feet then, very slowly, back up to her face.

Claire felt herself blushing as she looked down at her hands.

"Come over here and sit by me," Trevelyan said in the sweetest voice imaginable. "Sit on my lap if you want."

Claire looked back at him and laughed, and the embarrassment was gone. She sat on the end of the bed, took a deep drink of her whisky, then began to eat. The food that Oman had made was so different from what she had been eating for the last two weeks. Some of the food was hot—spicy hot—some cold, some soft, some crunchy.

"Tell me what you've been writing," she said eagerly, her mouth full. "Tell me every word. Tell me everything you've been thinking and doing. And I want to know who shot you. Oman said that someone tried to kill you."

"He exaggerates. I'm sure it was just as you said: a hunter with a bad aim."

She ate a piece of chicken flavored with almonds. "But I thought you walked only in the early morning and after dark."

"I do."

It took Claire a moment to understand him. "Are you saying that someone shot you after dark?"

"I like this chicken, don't you?"

"Trevelyan, I want an answer!"

"Why is it that you're so docile with Harry and so abrasive with me? You'd think that, wounded as I am, you'd be kind to me."

She laughed at him. "I'm not in love with you. I don't have to pretend with you." As soon as she said it, her eyes widened. "I didn't mean that as it sounded."

Trevelyan took a sip of his whisky and looked at her. "What would you say if *I* asked you to go hunting?"

"Sit in the rain and watch you slaughter animals? You have lost your reason."

"Yet you do it with Harry."

"Could we change the subject? Who do you think was out shooting in the dark? Did you see the person?"

"I neither saw nor heard anyone." He kept eating and didn't say anything else.

"You don't think someone actually did try to kill you, do you?"

He took so long to answer that when he did Claire knew his answer was a lie. "I'm sure it was an accident."

Claire felt chills down her spine, for she knew without a doubt that someone had tried to kill Trevelyan. "Jack Powell," she said softly.

"Ridiculous. Jack has no reason to hate me. As far as I know he still thinks I'm dead."

"Brat said there was an article in the paper that said Powell was in Edinburgh and he was going to present irrefutable proof that he and he alone had gone into Pesha."

That news seemed to startle Trevelyan a great deal. "Did the paper say what the proof was?"

"No," she said slowly. "What do you think it is?"

Trevelyan took his time drinking his whisky. "Something that I thought was lost."

"Something that you brought back from Pesha?"

"Yes." He continued eating and said nothing for a while.

"We shall go to Edinburgh and get this thing. We'll steal it from this man Powell. What is it, anyway?"

"The Pearl of the Moon."

She leaned back against the post of the bed—Bonnie Prince Charlie's bed—and sighed. "The Pearl of the Moon. It sounds exotic and valuable. In the morning we'll—"

"*We* will do no such thing. You're going back to your room so I can get some sleep. If you can't sleep, why don't you write a long letter to the man you love and beg his forgiveness? I hear your mother's already charging clothes to the new duchess of MacArran. You've got to do your duty and marry a man who does little but kill animals so you can pay her dress bills."

Claire put her plate down. "I had forgotten how very rude you can be." She got off the bed. "I guess I'd better go now and let you sleep. If someone else shoots at you, why don't you call a doctor?"

"I shall."

Claire looked down at the silk robe she wore. "I'll change and—"

"Keep it. Just get out of here. I forgot what a humorless little prig you can be."

At that Claire, with her head held high, walked out of the room. But once she was in the writing room, she saw Oman sitting on the window seat, his head nodding in sleep. She put her finger to her lips to tell him to be quiet, then motioned for him to follow her.

She went down the stairs and outside into the moonlight. Oman was soon beside her. She looked up at the tall man. "Was it a murder attempt? Not an accident?"

"It was murder."

Claire sighed and she was amazed at how much fear she felt—and anger. How could anyone think to take such a great man as Captain Baker from the world? He was so young and he had so much yet to do.

She looked back at Oman. "Trevelyan said that Powell has something from Pesha called the Pearl of the Moon. Do you know what that is?"

Oman nodded.

"I'm assuming that this thing is very valuable. Would Trevelyan try to take it from Powell?"

"If the man Powell has the Pearl, then Captain will take it from him."

Claire took a deep breath. She had thought so. From the way the news that Powell had this thing had shocked Trevelyan she'd guessed he might try to take it back. "When will he leave?"

"Now," Oman said and moved past her to reenter the west wing.

Claire stood where she was for a few moments and looked up at the stars. There was no doubt in her mind that she shouldn't consider going with Trevelyan. She was a woman engaged to another man. She was a woman who knew exactly what she wanted and had gone after it. She was in love with Harry; she was going to spend her life being the duchess of MacArran.

On the other hand, she did owe Trevelyan something. He *had* been the one to help her in her scheme to marry Leatrice to James Kincaid. Never mind that the union hadn't seemed to change anything in the house, but Trevelyan had helped. He hadn't done it correctly, but that was neither here nor there.

And, also, Trevelyan *was* Harry's cousin. Wouldn't Harry want her to help any of his family who needed help? Wasn't part of being a duchess taking care of all her husband's family? She couldn't do things for her own family and neglect Harry's. If Harry were here, he'd no doubt help Trevelyan. He'd probably ride out on his big horse and go into Edinburgh and demand that this man Powell give him the Pearl of the Moon. Yes, of course Harry would do that.

She looked back at Oman. "Make him travel in a carriage and make him wait for me. I'll be in the stables as soon as possible."

With that she turned back toward the house, only to realize that she didn't know how to get into the house secretly. She couldn't go through the front door, as she was sure people would see her, and the only entrance to the tunnels that she knew was through Trevelyan's tower.

Oman seemed to know what her problem was. He started walking around the house, all the way to the east wing, and there, behind concealing shrubbery, was a small door. When Oman opened it, it creaked loudly. She started to say that she had no candle but Oman pointed to a niche in the wall where candles and matches lay. She lit a candle, then looked back to thank Oman, but he was gone.

Claire had no idea where she was or how to get to her room in the tunnels. She looked at the dust on the floor to see if there were tracks. She wasn't surprised to see that there were many tracks and all of them were made by a foot that looked to be exactly the size of her sister's.

Claire started down the tunnel, looking at the tracks and trying to figure out where she was. She came to a door and saw that the area in front of the door had been used so often that it was bare of dust. Cautiously she opened the door. It moved silently.

A stream of light so bright it could have been sunlight poured into the dark tunnel, and she heard a voice that could only have been her sister's.

"I will *not!"* Brat said.

Claire stepped into the room to see a small, gaudy stage encrusted with gilding. Standing in the middle of the stage was her sister, dressed in a skimpy costume of colored silks, and a tall, very thin man wearing rags. They both turned when they saw Claire.

"What are you doing up at this time of night?" Claire asked. "And what disgusting thing are you wearing?"

"I'm Salome and I'm supposed to get to dance but he says we don't have time."

The skinny man made an elaborate bow to Claire. "Camelot J. Montgomery at your service, ma'am."

Claire looked about the room, with its stage and its red plush chairs in front and its oddly dressed occupants, and opened her mouth to ask questions. But she didn't have time. She looked at her sister. "I need you."

"Can't find your way back?" Brat asked, smiling. "I charge for guiding. And speaking of garments, what are *you* wearing?"

Claire ignored the last question. "I need you for more than guiding, and I'll pay whatever you charge."

At that Brat's eyes opened wide and she smiled happily. "I'll see you later, Cammy," she called over her shoulder and led Claire into the tunnels.

Claire had no idea how Brat found her way around the tunnels, for they looped and turned every which way, but they were soon at the door that led into Claire's room.

"You've seen him, haven't you?" Brat said as soon as they entered the room. There was no need to say who "he" was.

"Help me dress. I'm going to Edinburgh with him."

Brat's eyes widened at that. "You're running away from Harry?"

"Of course not. Trevelyan is in trouble. Someone shot at him tonight and I think it's that man Powell. Trevelyan is going into Edinburgh to get the Pearl of the Moon."

Brat gave her sister a sly look. "Do you know what the Pearl of the Moon is?"

Claire paused in taking a wool traveling dress from the wardrobe. "Do you?"

"Maybe. How long will you be gone?"

"I don't know. A few days, no more."

"You're going to spend the night with Vellie?"

"I told you not to call him that."

Brat grinned. "Because it's *your* name for him?"

Claire was busy pulling on underwear. "Help me fasten this corset and don't talk so much."

Brat helped her sister dress as hurriedly as possible. "What are you going to do about Harry?" Brat asked.

"What do you mean, what am I going to do about Harry? I'm not going to do anything. We had a lovers' quarrel, that's all."

"And now you're running off with another man."

Claire paused in dressing. "I am most certainly not running off with another man, as you put it. Trevelyan helped me with Leatrice. You know that, you were there. Now Trevelyan needs help and I plan to help him. Besides, Trevelyan isn't really a *man,* he's . . . he's an institution. He's a scholar. He belongs to the world, and it's my duty as a citizen of the world to help him."

"Balderdash," Brat said. "You *like* him. You adore him. When he walks into a room your whole face lights up."

Claire finished buttoning her dress. "I think you have him mixed up with Harry. I love Harry. I adore Harry and my face, if it does light up, lights for Harry. Trevelyan and I are friends, or maybe we aren't friends, since he tends to study me, but—"

"Are you talking about those pictures he draws? He draws pictures of everybody. You should see what he drew of me. He made my face very old but my body is . . ." Brat grinned. "You never saw such a figure as he gave me! And he drew Cammy and me, and he drew me with Aunt May, and he drew me with the thieving aunts. You should see his pictures of Harry and his mother."

Claire paused as she put clothes in a leather bag. "Everybody?"

"And he writes about everybody too. Oman says he's had to add two tables to the room for Vellie's writings about our family. Oman says Vellie is now fascinated with Americans."

Claire put her hairbrush and bottles of creams in the case, and, as an afterthought, she slipped a large bottle of MacTarvit whisky into the case. Since her first hunting expedition, the butler had kept her supplied with the whisky. "I think you talk to too many people. I think this house is a bad influence on you."

"This house and these people are perfect for me." Brat smiled at her sister. "Can you say the same thing? Do you fit in here? Or do you fit in better with those people living in those nasty little white cottages? Do you fit with Harry or with Trevelyan?"

Claire snapped the case shut. She had no intention of answering her sister. "I think you know what to do while I'm gone. Lie to the best of your ability, which I must say is stupendous in its magnitude. Perhaps you should take up writing fiction. Lying comes so easily to you. Now come and give me a kiss. I won't see you for a while."

Brat quickly kissed her sister's cheek, then, on impulse, she hugged her fiercely. "Be careful. I wouldn't like for you to be shot. There are bad things in this house as well as good."

"If you mean Harry's mother, I'm sure I'm safe from her. After all, she wants my money."

"A lot of people want your money."

Claire was at the door. "Including you. Now behave yourself and don't wear all of my jewels at once."

Brat stood and looked at the closed door once her sister was gone. "I don't want your money," she whispered. "I want you to stop crying." She turned away, went to the box that held Claire's jewels, and withdrew a ruby necklace. "And maybe I'd like to stop being the poor one," she whispered, holding the jewels up to the light.

"No," Trevelyan said from inside the carriage, then banged on the roof with his cane.

The carriage didn't move and Claire climbed inside. "I'm going with you and that's final. You can't stop me without raising a great fuss and waking people up and letting them know you're here."

"Half of the household knows where I am. Thanks to all the people who troop in and out of my rooms there's no possibility of keeping my presence a secret."

Claire settled herself on the seat across from him, noting that for once he was dressed, rather surprisingly, in perfectly cut, fashionable attire. "Then that's more of a reason for me to go with you. I can protect you."

At that Trevelyan gave a derisive laugh. "You protect me? You can't even protect yourself from one crippled old woman."

His barb hurt, and Claire looked away from him.

Trevelyan was silent for a moment. "All right, maybe *no* one can protect himself from her. But you won't need to protect me from Jack Powell. He wasn't the one who tried to kill me."

"Then who was?" As she said this Claire stuck her head out the carriage window and told Oman to drive. When the carriage started, Claire leaned back in the seat and smiled at Trevelyan.

Trevelyan watched her for a moment. It was quite dark in the carriage, the only light coming from the lanterns on the outside. "You're not going for me, you're going because you're bored."

"I am not bored. Well, maybe just a little. With Harry gone I—"

"With Harry gone you're free. You can slip out of the house and no one else will notice. Actually, even if Harry were here he probably wouldn't notice where you were. I hear you're getting shotguns for a wedding present."

"I'd prefer not to talk about me and I'd definitely rather we didn't talk about Harry and me. Why don't you tell me about finding the Pearl of the Moon? Is it a very large pearl?"

"The Pearl of the Moon isn't a thing, it's a person. To be specific, it's a she. She's the head of the Peshan religion."

"You mean a sort of priestess?"

Trevelyan gave a one-sided grin. "Rather more like a princess. Or possibly a goddess, from the way she's treated."

Claire blinked at him.

Trevelyan smiled. "You want me to get Oman to stop the coach? Let you out? You don't look as though you like the idea of rescuing a woman. Would you rather it was the largest pearl in the world? I wouldn't risk my neck for a pearl of any size."

Claire was trying to absorb what he was saying. It certainly made no difference to her that they were going to rescue a woman rather than a rare jewel. "She must be very venerable. Did you bring her out of Pesha to prove to the world you had been there?"

"No. Nyssa came of her own accord. She left the city with me because she wanted to. Nyssa does whatever she wants."

"I see. I guess she's earned that right. She must have been a priestess for a long time."

Trevelyan didn't answer.

"Why is she called the Pearl of the Moon? Pearly hair, maybe?"

Trevelyan smiled at her in the darkness. "She's called that because it's believed she's the most beautiful woman in the world."

"Oh" was all Claire could say. "Oh." She looked out at the dark scenery they were passing. "Has she been a priestess for long?"

When Trevelyan didn't answer she looked back at him. He was smiling at her in a knowing way. "All right," Claire said, disgust in her voice. "You can stop laughing at me. I want to know all of it. I want to know the whole story from the beginning. How did you get this perfect beauty and why are we traveling in the middle of the night to go get her?"

"You can get out at any time." He laughed when she gave him a look of obstinacy. "All right, I'll tell you. It's a Peshan ritual and it's been going on for centuries. Every fifty years the Peshan priests leave their walled city and go out into the surrounding countryside and search for the most beautiful young woman in the world. They try to find girls who're about fourteen or fifteen, then they take them all back to Pesha and the people choose the prettiest to become the priestess."

"Oh, I see. And she's the priestess for her lifetime, then they choose someone else."

"Not exactly. They allow her to be the priestess for five years, then they kill her. Forty-five years later they begin looking for someone else."

"They what?"

Trevelyan shrugged. "It's their religion. Religions around the world are different. They have different rules."

"But this rule is hideous. It's awful. I hope you made a protest."

Trevelyan laughed. "I was one infidel alone in a sacred city. I wasn't in any position to stand in the town square and preach Buddhism."

"Christianity."

"What? Oh, right. The true religion. Did you know that all people believe their own religion to be the true one?"

She smiled at him. "Play the cynic all you want, but you did save her. When was she to die?"

"This year."

Claire let out a sigh. "But you took her away from that dreadful place and saved her life."

"Not actually. Nyssa and her maidens were walking through the streets and just as she passed, I fell down at her feet. Malaria. But Nyssa thought that I'd fainted at the sight of her beauty. She had me carried to her chambers, and when she found out that I wasn't dark skinned all over, she hid me."

"And she left the city when you did. Did no one try to stop her?"

"For the five years the girls are priestesses, they're allowed to do anything they want. They're given anything they want. Nyssa wanted to leave with me, so she did."

Claire leaned toward him. "*Why* did she want to leave with you?"

Trevelyan gave a crooked grin. "Did I tell you about the time we made camp on a village of stinging ants? They came out at night and were all over us before someone woke up and gave the alarm. Six men came down with fever after that and—"

"How did this woman find out you weren't dark skinned all over?"

"She looked," he said simply. "Jealous?"

"Don't be absurd. I was merely curious. You should understand that concept, as curiosity seems to be the ruling force of your life."

"Nyssa was curious too."

She looked out the window. "Did she fall in love with you? Is that why she left with you?"

"I think she wanted to see the world. She grew up in a farm village, very poor, and she wanted to see something besides Pesha."

"Not to mention the fact that they planned to kill her within the year."

"I'm sure that had something to do with it."

She looked back at him. "So she left Pesha with you and traveled across the country. But then you died, or Powell thought you were going to die, and he took all your papers and your Pearl of the Moon. Is that right?"

"More or less."

When she spoke her voice was barely more than a whisper. "Are you going to rescue her now because you love her? Is that why you were so upset when you thought Powell had her?"

"I was upset because I thought Powell might be holding her against her will. On the journey back from Pesha Jack had a tendency to look on Nyssa as something we had caught, something in the vein of a museum specimen. I wouldn't like for Nyssa to be held prisoner in a stuffy drawing room somewhere." He gave her a piercing look. "Some women can stand that, but others can't."

She ignored his last remark. "How did *you* view her?"

"As often as possible," he said, grinning, then frowned. "What is wrong with you? If anyone should hear this conversation they'd think you and I were the lovers and that you were eaten with jealousy over something I did months ago."

"That's ridiculous. Of course I'm not jealous. I am . . . I'm a scholar of Captain Baker, that's all. Maybe I'll still write that biography even though you aren't actually dead, so I need to learn all that I can about you. It would interest my readers to know if you took a beautiful young woman from a sacred city because you were in love with her. Readers would like that story, of the handsome young explorer with the beautiful maiden."

"When I first met you, you said I was old and ugly. Besides, Nyssa is far from being a maiden."

"Oh? Promiscuous, is she?"

"You can stop looking down your nose at her. You might behave differently if you thought you had only five years to live."

"I'm sure that I'd do just what I am doing. I'd marry the man I love and live happily ever after."

"At a silent breakfast table. In a house where you aren't allowed into the library and where you're supposed to supervise everything that a horse like Harry eats."

"Stop it! I'm sick of hearing you say terrible things about the man I love. Did you love this Nyssa?" She shouted the last.

"When you tell me the truth, I'll tell you the truth."

Claire looked away from him. He was such an infuriating man. He could drive a person insane. No wonder someone shot at him, tried to kill him. She looked back at him. "Is your arm all right?"

"I've had worse."

She smiled at him and suddenly all her anger evaporated. Sometimes when she was with him she forgot that he was Captain Baker. She almost forgot all the things that he had done and written, all that he knew. "Tell me about your journey into Pesha."

"So you can put it in your biography of me?" he asked angrily.

"Because I want to hear. Brat said that you'd told her stories of Pesha. What really happened? Did Powell enter the city with you?"

"No. I went alone." She smiled because she had been correct about Powell's lack of participation.

She turned to watch him as closely as she could. He was becoming so familiar to her that she could sometimes read his expressions. Those dark, almost black, eyes of his didn't seem to change but she knew that he was pleased by her questions. Then, quite suddenly, the atmosphere became charged. He was a man and she was a woman and they were alone together.

Claire wasn't sure why, but her heart began to flutter within her breast. She looked out the window of the carriage. "Tell me a story," she whispered.

She didn't look at Trevelyan when he gave a deep sigh.

"Where do you want me to start?"

"Three days before you entered Pesha." She took a breath and looked back at him. She *had* to make him talk. "What were you wearing? How did you disguise yourself? How did you learn to speak Peshan? What do the other women in Pesha look like—besides this Nilla, that is?"

"Nyssa," he said with a smile, then began to tell her of his journey.

Trevelyan was a good storyteller, having an actor's sense of timing, of where to leave the listener wanting more. He told of finding a man who had once been a slave in Pesha and taking the man with him on the long journey in search of the sacred city. He told of talking with the man and studying the Peshan language.

When Trevelyan started to tell of entering the city, Claire held her breath. Even though she knew the ending of the story, the way Trevelyan told it made her fear for his life. She could tell from what he said that the city was not made of gold, as fable had it, but was just a small, enclosed city, ancient beyond words, filled with old stone houses and, from Trevelyan's description, even older men.

"And what of the women?" she asked.

"The only women in the city are Nyssa and her eight maidens. The maidens serve the Pearl of the Moon for her five years as priestesses, then, after her death, they're sent back to their families. While they're in Pesha the maidens aren't allowed to consort with any of the men."

"Consort?"

"Sleep with them. Make love with any of them. Cohabit," he said.

"But Nialla is?" Claire asked quickly. "Allowed to consort, that is?"

"Nyssa may do anything that she wants. Do you want to hear more about the city or are you only fascinated with Nyssa's love life? Perhaps your fascination is caused by the barrenness of your own love life."

"Ha!" Claire said. "Go on with your story."

He told of Nyssa's having rescued him, having saved his life, for if he had been discovered he would have been killed. He told of staying with her in her private apartments. He described the apartments, telling how they were filled with the stolen treasure of hundreds of years. He described swords taken from medieval Spaniards, jewels taken from around the necks of Crusaders. He described silks and furniture and paintings. "Only the best is good enough for their priestess."

"Until they kill her," Claire said. "Do they kill her with a very sharp ax? I do so hope they are thoughtful in their method of killing the woman they have worshiped for five whole years. I'd hate to think of her being tortured."

"You shouldn't talk about what you know nothing of." He clenched his teeth together for a moment before continuing to tell her of his journey.

At dawn they stopped at an inn and had an enormous breakfast. Claire yawned.

"Why don't you stay here and sleep, and I'll go into the city and get Nyssa?" Trevelyan said.

Claire merely smiled at him, but smiled in such a way that she left no doubt that she didn't plan to let him out of her sight.

Trevelyan sighed. "All right then, hurry up and finish. We still have a long way to go."

Chapter Nineteen

They traveled until three in the afternoon, with Trevelyan telling her stories throughout the journey. He told of Africa and China and talked of the places he wanted to go. Only once did she feel any anger. He told how he'd gone into an African village where the chief had a great desire to see what kind of child would result from a union of black and white. So the chief had assembled twenty-five young women from his village and asked Captain Baker to impregnate them.

"What did you do?"

"I did the only thing I could under the circumstances."

Claire smiled. "You told him no."

Trevelyan's eyes twinkled. "We were an hour late getting away the next morning."

It took Claire several minutes before she understood what he was saying. She started to ask him lots of questions, but she forced herself to keep her mouth closed.

At three they stopped at an inn and Trevelyan hired two rooms for them. "We are near the city and Powell's house. We'll sleep until midnight."

Claire refused to go to bed until he'd sworn that he'd wake her and not leave her behind when he went to Powell's house. After she had Trevelyan's promise, she went to her room, so tired she could hardly remove her clothing. She dragged her nightgown over her head, then fell across the bed, too tired to even pull the cover up.

When she awoke, she realized that it was dark outside but there was a bright lamp lit within the room. She rubbed her eyes and looked about her. Sitting on a chair at the end of the room was Trevelyan, a sketchbook in his hand, and hanging from a hook in the ceiling was her bustle frame.

Claire rubbed her eyes again. Trevelyan was making a drawing of her bustle frame.

"Sleep well?" he asked without looking up.

"What do you think you're doing?" She flung the covers back, got out of bed, and jerked the frame from the ceiling.

"Interesting thing, that. There are some tribes in Africa that wear something similar, but theirs are made of grass. More of a basket than wire. Of course, in a pinch, the grass ones can be used to carry water. For the life of me, I can't see a practical use for that."

"I am *not* one of your tribes to be studied." She was standing near him, her eyes blazing.

He looked down at her in her nightgown and smiled. "I'd like to study more of you than just your undergarments." He glanced toward the bed. "We could postpone our visit to Powell's for hours. Hours and hours and hours."

Claire stepped away from him. "You shouldn't come into my room in the middle of the night. You should have knocked. You should have—"

He cut her off because he didn't want to listen to her. "How soon can you be ready? And don't wear that thing." He nodded toward the bustle frame. "We'll probably have to go in through a window and it'll never fit."

"I *have* to wear the frame. My dress is cut to go over it. Without the frame the dress wouldn't fit properly and it would drag in the back."

Trevelyan gave her a cold look, his black eyes sparkling. "Don't wear it." He turned on his heel and left the room.

Thirty minutes later Claire appeared downstairs wearing her dark green wool walking costume, with her bustle frame holding out the back of it. She also wore a look of defiance, one that told Trevelyan that she was ready for a fight that she meant to win.

He started to say something but then shoved a pasty into her hand. "If you can't get into the house it'll serve you right. Let's go."

Claire made him wait for her while she arranged with the landlord's eldest son to deliver a package for her. Trevelyan didn't ask her what she was doing and she didn't volunteer to tell him.

It didn't take long to reach Powell's pretty little Edinburgh town house with its bright red door.

"Are we really going to break in?" Claire whispered.

"Yes." Trevelyan looked down at her. "You can stop now if you want."

Claire shook her head no, then took a deep breath and followed Trevelyan to the back of the house. "Well?" she said once they were at the back of the house. "What do we do now?"

"We wait for Oman's signal."

Claire sat down on the side of a little porch and didn't say anything else. Within minutes came a noise that made her nearly jump out of her skin. It seemed that cannons were going off in the street in front of the house.

"Now!" Trevelyan yelled above the noise and threw a rock at the nearest window. Before Claire could think what was going on, Trevelyan picked her up and shoved her at the window.

Claire wiggled through the opening but then her bustle caught on the crossbar of the window. Without daring to look at Trevelyan she moved backward a bit, reached back to the frame and pulled it upward so it collapsed against her back. Still holding it flat, she finished moving through the window.

Once she was inside the house, it was only seconds before Trevelyan was beside her. They were in a service room at the back of the kitchen and they could hear the noise in the street outside. Near them they could hear people, servants she assumed, moving about.

Trevelyan took Claire's hand and confidently moved through the dark house toward a narrow staircase. It was obvious that he had been in the house before and knew it well. Once they were upstairs, twice they had to flatten themselves in doorways to keep from being seen. Claire saw Powell hurry down the stairs as he pulled a dressing gown on over his nightclothes. She recognized him from the several photographs she'd seen of him.

As the noise in the street continued, Trevelyan led Claire down a corridor of the upstairs until he came to a door at the end of the hall. It was locked. Trevelyan lost no time in raising his foot and kicking the heavy door in.

The minute the two of them stepped inside the room, it was as though they'd entered another country. The large room was hung with gauzy silks of a hundred pastels. One color seemed to blend into another. There was a smell of sandalwood and jasmine in the air. Trevelyan didn't seem to notice the surroundings, but Claire stood by the door and gaped. The floor was covered with expensive hand-tied silk carpets, one on top of the other, and through the draperies that hung from the ceiling she could see piles of silk-covered pillows.

Trevelyan pushed the gauze curtains aside and made his way through the room, Claire close behind him. He stopped in front of her so abruptly that Claire ran into the back of him. She peeped around him to see what had made him stop.

In front of him, kneeling on a fat cushion before what looked to be an altar, her hands clasped together in prayer, her head slightly bowed, was what was surely the most exquisite creature on earth. Claire saw only her profile, but the small features and the perfection of them was astonishing. Long, sooty lashes rested on a honey-colored cheek. Her lovely little nose made a perfect line down to her sculptured mouth.

Claire stepped from behind Trevelyan and stared at the woman. She was small, smaller than Claire, but the sheer silk robe she wore did little to hide the delicate, womanly curves of her body. She was so still that Claire wasn't sure she was alive.

There was a loud boom from the street outside, followed by shouts, and the noise brought Claire back to the present. "We have to go," she whispered urgently to Trevelyan, who was just standing there and staring at this woman. When he made no move to speak to the woman, Claire took a step toward her, but Trevelyan put out a hand and stopped her.

"She is praying," he said.

Claire waited a few more seconds, seconds that turned into minutes. If they were found in Jack Powell's house, would they be thrown into jail? Or would Powell merely shoot them?

At long, long last, the woman raised her head, then turned and looked up at Trevelyan. Claire had only a second to see the woman and she gasped at the beauty of her. A perfect oval face, perfect almond-shaped eyes, perfect nose, perfect lips. Claire hated her immediately.

Her hatred increased in the next second as the woman, in a voice that sounded as though someone had melted honey and poured it over vocal cords, said, "Frank!" and launched herself into Trevelyan's arms.

He was supporting her full weight, her tiny feet, shod in jeweled silk slippers, not touching the floor. She kissed him, kissed his chin, his neck, kissed all of him she could reach, all the while whispering to him in a soft, oozing language that sounded like a spoken love song.

"We have to go," Claire said. Claire didn't seem to be aware that Trevelyan was holding his head away from the woman's kisses. She didn't notice that Trevelyan was much more interested in Claire's reactions than in the beautiful woman's kisses. When the two of them didn't seem to hear her, Claire thought she'd nudge Trevelyan and make him hear. That's what she meant to do. What she *did* do was kick Trevelyan in the side of his calf at the same time that she hit him in the rib cage.

He grunted. "Why did you do that?" he asked as the woman kissed his neck.

"We have to go," Claire said through clenched teeth.

Trevelyan nodded, said something in the soft language to the woman, and she nodded but continued kissing the soft bit of skin just above his collar.

"Trevelyan!" Claire snapped. "We must go."

Trevelyan, smiling at Claire as though something she'd said pleased him very much, set Nyssa from him. It was only then that the woman noticed that Claire was in the room. Nyssa stepped back and looked at Claire's face. No, she didn't just look at Claire, she studied her. Then Nyssa looked down at Claire's feet and very slowly looked from her feet back up to her head.

Claire stood where she was, her eyes filled with anger.

Nyssa began to walk around Claire, pausing at the back of her. She said something to Trevelyan and he answered.

"What did she say?" Claire asked.

"Nyssa said that you have a behind like the hump of a camel. I told her you wore wire to make yourself stick out at the back, but that I assumed your purpose was not to make yourself look like a camel."

Claire glared at him.

Nyssa walked to the front of Claire then moved beside Trevelyan and began to talk to him.

"What is she saying now?" Claire asked.

"Let me see if I can translate it properly. She says that you have hips as wide as a cow's, skin the color of the underbelly of a frog—or she might have said a lizard, Peshan is sometimes difficult for me—and that you have a bosom like a mountain. Although she says that your bosom is probably as real as the protrusion on your behind is. She says that your eyes are too round and too trusting and that—"

"Tell her that every bit of my bosom is mine and that she has a bosom like a boy."

"Oh?" Trevelyan said with interest. "No padding at all?"

She looked at him. "Could we get out of here and take . . . her with us?"

"Then do what with her?" Trevelyan asked, obviously highly amused by all of this. "Toss her from the carriage as we go around a curve?"

Claire smiled at him. "I was thinking of tying her to a wheel. Someone as shapeless as she is would hardly make a lump."

Trevelyan laughed, then Nyssa said something to him. "She wants you to pack for her. She says that Powell has allowed her no maids so you may become her maid."

"Does she? Tell her her offer is too generous for me to accept; that I, a mere mortal, am not worthy to touch the luggage of the Pearl of the Moon."

Trevelyan laughed then spoke softly to Nyssa. She answered him in Peshan, and Claire saw Trevelyan frown and shake his head. He began to talk to her, then Nyssa answered. Trevelyan talked more; Nyssa stamped her foot.

"What's going on?"

Trevelyan kept talking to Nyssa and for a moment he didn't answer Claire. "She wants her cup," he said at last. "And I bloody well don't want to get it for her."

"What cup?"

Trevelyan started to speak, but Nyssa put her hand on his arm and looked up at him with pleading eyes. Claire was disgusted to see Trevelyan's face soften. She'd never seen that look on his face before. He looked back at Claire. "It's a gold cup. Jeweled. She brought it with her from Pesha and she says she won't go with me unless she has it."

"Where is it?"

Trevelyan shrugged. "Downstairs in a cabinet."

It was on the tip of Claire's tongue to say, "That's that." If this woman who called herself the Pearl of the Moon wouldn't go without her cup and Trevelyan didn't want to get her cup, then they'd just have to leave her where she was. Too bad. Claire had already started to look forward to the long carriage ride with this woman—that is, if one could look forward to insults and abuse.

Trevelyan read the look on Claire's face. "Jack has been holding Nyssa prisoner in this room. He won't allow her to leave it, even to walk in the park. She hasn't seen sunlight in weeks. I think Jack plans to exhibit her like an animal."

Claire looked at Nyssa. They were about the same height and probably about the same age, but they were very different in appearance. Claire had robust, healthy American good looks, with her pink skin and hourglass figure, while Nyssa was exotic looking, with her dark skin and small, delicate body. Nyssa was standing close to Trevelyan, leaning toward him, as though he could protect her.

"All right," Claire said. "We'll take her."

Trevelyan turned and smiled down at Nyssa and said something to her. Nyssa's dark eyes turned angry and she sat down on the cushion in front of the altar, her arms crossed over her chest. Trevelyan said something to her, then bent and picked her up. Nyssa started screaming. Trevelyan put his hand over her mouth but she bit his palm so that he half dropped her back onto the cushion.

"*I* will get her cup," Claire said and started for the door.

Trevelyan caught her arm. "I know where it is," he said heavily. "You stay with her. Pack some things for her. When I get back we'll go."

Trevelyan left Claire alone with Nyssa in the silk-draped room. Claire looked down at Nyssa, still sitting on her cushion, and Nyssa smiled at her. Perfect teeth. Of course, Claire thought, it was too much to hope that her teeth were black and rotten. Claire didn't return the smile. "If you want to take anything with you, you'd better pack it. I'm sure that whatever I have won't fit you. You'd never be able to fill out the top," she said, looking pointedly at Nyssa's small bosom.

Nyssa smiled again, and as though she understood, she got up and went to a carved and gilded chest against one wall of the room and began to remove garments. She put them in a large bag that was beautifully embroidered. When that was done, she took a little statue from her altar, dropped it into the bag, and went to sit on the cushion. She motioned to Claire to take a seat on another cushion but Claire walked away. It was difficult to feel comfortable with someone who had said your skin was the color of a frog's belly.

Claire walked about the room and looked at the silks. She pushed them aside and looked out the window, trying to see the street. But there were bars on the window and all she could see was the side of the house next door.

It seemed a long time before Trevelyan returned and from under his coat withdrew a gold cup set all over with rubies. It wasn't a very pretty cup, probably more valuable for its historic significance than for its artistic merit. Claire took the cup and held it up to the candlelight. Some of the rubies were of modern cut, some were mere lumps. All the edgings holding the stones to the cup were crude and misshapen. "Not exactly beautiful, is it?" she said.

Nyssa came to her feet and snatched the cup from Claire's hand and gave the American an angry look.

"Could we get out of here?" Trevelyan said. "Before the two of you get into a fistfight? Oman can't distract the people in the street much longer."

Claire started to follow Trevelyan out of the door, but Nyssa pushed past her and plastered herself against the back of Trevelyan so that Claire brought up the rear. When Claire started to say something, Trevelyan put his finger to his lips to tell her to be quiet.

The two women followed Trevelyan down the stairs, twice having to hide to keep from being seen by the people who were now returning to the house. Outside, the street was quiet. In the back of the house, Trevelyan unlocked the door and held it open for the two women. As Claire passed him, he whispered, "I wouldn't want you to get your camel hump caught again."

Claire didn't bother to answer him.

The three of them made it through several twisting streets and back to Oman, calmly sitting atop the carriage as though nothing had happened. Yet Oman's usually pristine white clothes were torn and blackened from gunpowder from fireworks, and there was a cut across his cheek. Nyssa greeted Oman with great pleasure and said things to him that made the tall man smile.

The second the three of them were inside the coach, Oman cracked the whip over the horses and they were off. Nyssa sat beside Trevelyan while Claire sat opposite them.

Claire wasn't sure what was wrong with her but she knew that she was angry, very, very angry. She leaned back against the wall of the coach and closed her eyes. She told herself that she wasn't in the least interested in what Trevelyan did with this woman, but she was aware of every word that they spoke to each other. She couldn't understand any of it, but she imagined that they were whispering love words to each other. And why not? Why shouldn't this woman be in love with a man who had saved her from death?

"Do you want to stop and sleep or drive on?" Trevelyan asked.

Claire knew whom he had spoken to but she acted surprised. "Were you speaking to me? I thought perhaps I had disappeared, that I had become invisible, that maybe I'd faded into the upholstery."

"Nyssa is asleep."

"That explains it," Claire said nastily. "You have no one else to talk to. But then I guess you've told her all your stories. After all, you did have a great deal of time together on the long journey back from Pesha."

"Nyssa is not a good listener," Trevelyan said softly. "Not many women are interested in what I have done. Not as you are."

A little of the hurt that Claire was feeling left her. "That's surprising. She seems to be *very* interested in you."

"In bed perhaps, but nowhere else. In my life I've found that for the most part people do not like to learn. They like to know and they like to tell others what they know, but they do not like the process of learning as you do."

"In bed?" Claire whispered.

"Good God, woman, I've just given you the compliment of a lifetime and you give me back jealousy?"

"Compliment?" Claire spat at him. "What compliment? She's the one you love."

Even in the darkness she could see his eyes. They were glittering. "You're wrong about that."

Claire looked away, then leaned back and closed her eyes. "It's none of my business what you do. We've done what we set out to do and I'm glad of it. Jack Powell won't be able to offer proof that he went to Pesha. Perhaps you can teach your . . . your paramour to speak English and she can tell the Royal Geographic Society how you rescued her, both from Pesha and from Powell. Now, if you don't mind, I think I'll try to sleep."

Claire couldn't sleep. She kept her eyes closed but she was too aware of Trevelyan and the woman snuggled together on the seat across from her. She was puzzled by the depth of her anger, but she told herself that it was because their conduct was unseemly. They weren't married, or even planning to be married, yet they were obviously lovers.

The sun rose, they stopped to eat and change horses, then they were off again. Nyssa woke up, and like a child, she was refreshed and restless. She and Trevelyan started playing a hand game to occupy themselves. Trevelyan asked if Claire would like to learn the rules and play too, but Claire said she'd rather not. She sat and watched them, watched the way they laughed with each other. She saw how easy they were in each other's company.

At one point Nyssa looked at Claire, then said something to Trevelyan. Trevelyan turned to Claire. "Nyssa says that you look old and sour when you frown like that. She says it'll give you lines in your face before your time."

"I'm not frowning. I merely . . ." Claire couldn't think of an explanation.

Nyssa spoke to Trevelyan again. "She says that you're very jealous of her."

"That's ridiculous. Did you tell her that I was the one who insisted on coming with you? That you didn't want me to go with you?"

"I've told her a good deal. I've told her all about Harry and your pending marriage to him, and I've told her about your family and about your dear little sister."

"I wonder exactly *what* you told her? Did you tell her that my sister is more beautiful than she is?"

Trevelyan smiled. "No, I didn't tell her that. I don't think she'd believe me."

"She's vain, isn't she? Vain and not awfully smart, judging from the silliness of your game. Can she read?"

"I doubt it."

Claire sniffed in satisfaction and looked away. She was determined not to look at them again.

* * *

When they arrived at Bramley it was one o'clock in the morning and Claire knew that she should go straight to bed. She hoped that Brat hadn't had any trouble covering for her. But as Oman helped her from the carriage, she looked at Trevelyan and Nyssa standing in the darkness, standing close together, and she didn't want to leave them alone. She kept thinking of them in Bonnie Prince Charlie's big bed.

"I'm starving," Claire announced. "Absolutely famished. Oman, I know it's late, but do you think there's any food in the tower? I absolutely *must* have something to eat." She could feel Trevelyan looking at her but she wouldn't meet his eyes. She didn't want to see that he knew what she was thinking.

When Oman nodded that he did have food, Claire put her head up and followed him into the tower, Nyssa and Trevelyan behind her.

Once in Trevelyan's writing room, Claire walked to the window seat and looked out. She still didn't want to look at Trevelyan and see what he knew. She should go back to her own room, back to where she belonged, but she kept seeing that woman kiss Trevelyan.

Oman served a cold supper in the bedroom. Claire took a seat across from Nyssa, then, to her surprise, Trevelyan pulled his chair up so that he sat next to Claire. So he can see *her* while she eats, Claire thought and bent her head over the food.

Nyssa spoke to Trevelyan in Peshan.

"She wants to know if you're a virgin," Trevelyan said.

Claire's head came up. "Tell her it's none of her business. Tell her that in my country it's impolite to ask such a question."

Nyssa spoke.

"She says that it's impolite in her country also but that she's the Pearl of the Moon so she can do whatever she likes. She asks if—" Trevelyan broke off and spoke to Nyssa. The two spoke for a few minutes. Oman was serving food and as Claire glanced at him, she saw that he was shocked.

"What's she saying about me?" Claire asked.

"Nothing much," Trevelyan answered.

"I want the truth. I want you to tell me what she's saying."

Trevelyan looked at Nyssa then at Claire. "She says that you have the look of a virgin. She says it's a shame that you haven't . . ."

"Haven't what?"

"Nothing," Trevelyan muttered and filled his mouth with food.

"I want to know!" Claire felt near tears. For hours now she'd watched the two of them together and she'd been angry every second of those hours. She was tired and she wasn't thinking clearly. "Tell me what she's saying. I'm not a child who has to have secrets kept from her."

Trevelyan looked at Claire, his eyes intense. His voice was quiet when he spoke. "Nyssa said that it's too bad you believe in keeping your virginity because, according to her, Captain Baker is a great lover."

Claire looked at Nyssa, sitting there in her diaphanous robe, her exquisite little face with its slight smile, and Claire was furious, furious that so much was assumed about her. Why did this semi-harlot assume that she, Claire Willoughby, knew nothing?

"Tell her I'm not a virgin, and that I've had many lovers."

"I'll tell her no such thing." Trevelyan sounded shocked.

Claire glared at him. *"You* are going to pretend to have scruples? *You?* You with your twenty-five women in one night? You are balking at one lie? Tell her I've had as many as a dozen lovers in one night."

Trevelyan's eyes started twinkling. "That's too many."

"Oh, is it?" Claire frowned. "How many's an impressive number?"

"One man who kept you awake all night."

"Just one?"

Trevelyan laughed at that. "One good one."

"All right, tell her that then. Tell her I've had the world's best."

"And who would that be? Harry?"

"You leave Harry out of this." Claire was losing her resolve to tell Nyssa anything. She looked back at her plate of food.

"I'll tell her you and I have spent nights of ecstasy together," Trevelyan said softly. "I'll tell her that of all the women I've had, you have given me the most pleasure."

Claire looked up at him, and the way he was looking at her made chills go up her spine. "You would do that for me?"

He gave her the softest, sweetest smile imaginable, and Claire smiled back at him. "Thank you," she said, then on impulse, she leaned forward to kiss his cheek. She meant to kiss the scar on his right cheek, to kiss that place that had once caused him such pain, but he moved his head, or perhaps Claire moved hers, and instead she lightly kissed his lips.

When her lips touched his, it was as though an electric shock went through her. She drew away instantly and put her hand to her mouth, looking at Trevelyan in horror.

There wasn't horror on Trevelyan's face; he looked surprised. For one split second, that guarded look of his was gone, and she saw that he was as shocked by the brief kiss as she was.

Claire forgot all about lies to impress Nyssa. She got to her feet instantly. "I have to go," she said, her voice sounding almost frantic. "Oman, will you guide me through the tunnels to my room?" Claire was busily fiddling with her skirt. Anything to keep from looking at Trevelyan.

"You don't have to go through the tunnels," Trevelyan said from behind her. "I'll take you to the servants' entrance." He spoke as though his jaws were clenched, as though he couldn't bear to give away words.

Claire started to protest, but she couldn't seem to get the words out. Silently, she followed him down the stairs. She had walked with him, behind him, before him, many times, but this time was different. This time it was as though the very air around her were charged. The air felt as it did before an electrical storm.

At the bottom of the tower, he held the door open for her and they stepped into the cool, moonlit night. Claire shivered once and began to rub her arms, then looked up to see Trevelyan staring down at her. His eyes were like two coals, burning as they looked at her. She looked away from him and he started walking again.

She followed him along the side of the house and as they walked, she looked at him. She looked at the tall leanness of him, at the breadth of his shoulders, at the way his hips moved when he walked. She'd once thought him too thin, too old, too sickly, too different from Harry to be considered a handsome man. But now she could see that there was nothing, absolutely nothing wrong with him. At this moment he looked to her to be the most handsome man on earth.

At the back of the house he stopped abruptly and turned to her. "Go in this door, through the first doorway on your right. There's a narrow staircase there and it'll take you to the second floor. I assume you can find your way from there to your bedroom."

She looked up at him and nodded, then he turned away. "Trevelyan," she called after him.

He stopped and turned back to her but took no step in her

direction. There was about three feet of space between them, but to Claire it might have been nothing. She could feel his nearness, feel the warmth from his body. The palms of her hands were beginning to itch.

"About what happened in there. I mean with Nyssa. I shouldn't have done what I did."

"What did you do?"

She'd never noticed his voice before. It was low and husky. It seemed to send tremors through her body. She tried to smile; she wanted to make light of what had happened and what she was feeling now. "The . . . kiss. It didn't mean anything. It was just that Nyssa annoyed me and I didn't like her implication that I was a woman who knew nothing."

He stood there silently, just looking at her, not saying a word.

"You have no comment to make?" she asked, somewhat irritably.

He didn't answer.

"I guess I'd better go in now," she said.

Still he said nothing.

"Then I wish you good night," she said.

He gave a curt nod, turned on his heel, and started walking away.

Although she knew it was wrong, although she told herself she shouldn't—couldn't—say another word, she heard herself whisper, "Vellie." It was the smallest whisper in the world, so quiet, so soft that the breeze in the trees overhead completely covered it.

But Trevelyan heard it. One second he was what seemed to be miles away from her and the next he was in her arms and his lips were on hers.

Lust, she thought. She'd heard it was one of the seven deadly sins but she'd never experienced it before. Now, his lips on hers, she knew she wanted to bury herself in him, lose herself. She wanted to drown in him. She turned her head, not knowing how she knew what to do, but she did, and she felt the sweetness of his tongue touch hers.

Her body arched as she pressed against him, her breasts hurting inside her clothes, hurting as they pushed against his hard chest. He moved one leg so his thigh was between hers, and Claire moaned as she clinched that heavy thigh of his with her own. Her fingertips felt swollen, aching with wanting to touch him.

Some part of her knew that this was the only time she could ever touch him, that this was the last night. After this she could never, ever again feel him next to her. She could forgive herself one lapse but not two. She wanted all she could get from this moment. She wanted to feel as much of him as possible.

Her hands moved over his back. How could she ever have thought him thin or old? She ran her palms up to his arms, felt the muscles there, then back down to his ribs and waist. Her hands moved lower and she knew she shouldn't, Lord help her but she knew she shouldn't, she ran her hands over his buttocks.

The next moment she turned her head away from him. "Stop," she whispered. "Please stop. I can bear no more."

Immediately, Trevelyan moved away from her and for a moment they stood apart, not touching, but looking into each other's eyes. Claire knew he was waiting for an invitation from her. She knew that all she had to do was hold her hand out to him and he'd come to her. And she knew that if she touched him again she wouldn't be able to stop. Her heart was thundering in her ears and her breath was coming in jerks, but she had enough self-control to keep her hands at her sides.

After a long moment he turned and walked away. This time she didn't call him back, but slowly, on weak legs, made her way up the stairs.

Inside her room Brat was sleeping in her bed. Claire reached out to wake the child, but then pulled her hand back. Her sister's livelihood depended upon her, Claire.

Claire sat down on the stool by her dressing table and looked about the big room. This was a room in the house of a duke, the house of a man she was to marry, yet she had just been kissing someone else. Kissing him, wanting him.

And what would happen if she gave in to her baser lusts? She would lose Harry; her parents would never approve of a man like Trevelyan and so Claire would lose the money her grandfather had left her. Then what? Her parents would no doubt spend her nearly ten million dollars within a couple of years.

Claire put her face in her hands, feeling disloyal. Her parents had been good to her and she owed them a great deal. But she wasn't a fool. If she married Harry, then the money would come to her and she'd be able to control it. She could invest it, watch it grow, and she could parcel it out to her parents, who had no idea how to control their own impulses. She could plan a dowry for her sister, see that

Sarah Ann married a good, stable man, a man like Harry. A man who bought pictures and horses, Claire thought and began to cry. Now she was betraying the man she loved and all because she'd kissed a man and felt lust for him.

"What's wrong?"

Claire jumped when Brat put her hand on her sister's shoulder. "Nothing," Claire said, drying her eyes. "I'm just tired, I guess. You'd better go to your own bed now."

Sarah Ann didn't move. "It's Trevelyan, isn't it?"

"No, of course not. Why should I cry over Trevelyan? I'm just tired. I would really rather be alone." Claire went on dabbing at her eyes and didn't look up until after Sarah Ann had left. She began to undress for bed.

Nyssa greeted Trevelyan at the door to the sitting room with open arms, but he pushed her away. He went to the bottle of whisky on a side table, poured himself a full glass, and drank it like water.

"What has happened?" Nyssa asked in English.

"Nothing has happened," he snapped at her.

She watched him as he refilled his glass and drank again. "It is around you."

"What is?"

"Desire."

He gave her a cold look.

"I can feel it; I can almost see it. All around you is desire. But it is not for me."

"Nonsense. You've listened to too many romantic stories." He went to the table where once his notes on Claire had been. Now there was a chessboard set up. He moved a white piece, a black piece.

"This woman means a great deal to you."

"You're crazy. I told you that she's to marry Harry." He looked at her, his eyes hot. "I desire a great many women. Perhaps she's one of them. She's no more than that."

"This desire you feel for this woman, how does it compare to what you've felt for other women?"

Trevelyan picked up the white queen. "Were all the women I have had and all the women I have wanted rolled into one, they would not equal my desire for her."

Nyssa was silent for a while. "Then you must go to her."

With that Trevelyan swept his forearm across the chessboard, knocking pieces to the floor. "And become her lover? Shall I love her, then stand back and watch while she marries Harry? Shall I remain here and wait until Harry leaves, then go to her?"

"Being the lover of a married woman has never bothered you before. I have heard you brag that you could climb in any window. I have heard you say that married women are your pleasure because they give to you their joy and to their husbands they give their misery."

"I want her misery too," he said softly.

"What?"

"I want her bloody misery too," he shouted. "I want *all* of the bitch. She—" He calmed.

"She what?"

"She takes away the loneliness. When I'm with her I'm not lonely." He stared at Nyssa awhile, then gave a half-hearted smile. "There are other women. There are women who don't believe that being a duchess is everything in life."

Nyssa snorted. "You give up easily. She is not married to this man Harry yet, but you act as though she is. You wait until she comes to you. I have never seen you like this. I have never seen you as the pursued one. You have always been the pursuer. Remember that pretty little woman in that village on the way back from Pesha? You wanted her and you went after her. Why is this one so different?"

"It is enough that this one is different."

"*How* is she different?"

Nyssa stood still and waited for him to answer. She had spent a great deal of time with this man and she knew him quite well, but the Captain Baker she knew and the man she had seen since he had come for her in Powell's house were not the same man. The Captain Baker she knew was an observer, a man who did not get involved, who allowed no one and nothing to affect him. But this American woman affected him. She affected him very much. He couldn't take his eyes from her. In the carriage, no matter what Nyssa had done to distract him, Frank's attention had always been on Claire—as hers was on him.

"You love her," Nyssa whispered, and there was wonder in her voice. She had tried to make Captain Baker love her but she'd had no success. "You are in love with her."

"Yes" was all that Trevelyan could say. "Yes, I love her. I love her mind, her body. I love her sense of humor. I love her thoughts. I love the way she thinks and what she says." He gave a sound that was a cross between hopelessness and despair. "I love her to the smell of her breath." He turned to Nyssa and for the first time she saw what few people had: she saw that little boy who used to climb into bed with Leatrice and cry. "I love her as I've never loved anyone or anything. Were she to love me in return, I'd give her whatever she wanted."

Nyssa had to sit down, and she looked away from Trevelyan's eyes. She didn't think she was supposed to see what he had just shown her. "You would tell her that you are Harry's older brother?"

"Yes," he said simply, then looked back at her. His guarded expression was back. He gave Nyssa a smile—a smile that she'd seen a thousand times, a smile that said he cared about no one and that he was an entity unto himself, that he needed no one. "Ah, well, such is life. No one can win every time. Would you like to play cards or would you like to go to bed with me?"

Nyssa didn't smile. "You should go to her," she said softly. "You should show her that you love her." Nyssa gave him a smile of great radiance. "You should make her miserable. Make her have to decide between you and this brother of yours."

Trevelyan started to protest that, but then he set his whisky glass down. "Yes," he said softly. "I will make her choose."

Nyssa said something else, but Trevelyan didn't hear her. He was already on his way out the door, on his way to Claire.

Chapter Twenty

As soon as Brat had gone into the tunnels, Claire angrily began to pull the pins from her hair, allowing it to hang down her back. She began to brush her hair as though her hair were her enemy; she attacked it.

It wasn't any of her business, of course. It wasn't any of her concern that Trevelyan was going to spend the night with another woman. It didn't matter to her. Trevelyan was Captain Baker, and Captain Baker was a renowned rake. A man known the world over for his exploits with women.

She tugged at the fastenings of her dress, unhooked her bustle frame, then untied her petticoats. Standing in her corset and underwear, she looked at herself in the mirror. She turned and pivoted for a moment, then put her hands over her face. It didn't matter, she told herself. It didn't matter what a man like Captain Baker did. It wasn't any of her concern.

She pulled off her underwear with what was almost violence, let the soft cotton garments fall to the floor, then slipped a pristine white cotton nightgown over her head. She went to bed, turned out the lamp, and closed her eyes.

She was afraid she might start crying but instead the moment she closed her eyes she was asleep. She was asleep and she was dreaming. She seemed to be in a hot country, a place of green plants and wildly colored birds. There was danger there and she was afraid. She stopped when she heard something moving in the jungle. She knew she should run but she couldn't. She stood where she was and stared in horrified fascination at the movement of the plants. The movement came closer and when she thought she might scream, the plants parted and there was Trevelyan. In the dream, Claire didn't know whether to be relieved or even more terrified.

Claire opened her eyes with a start. Standing over her, holding a candle, was Trevelyan. His eyes were alight with life and fire, and he was staring at her as though asking her a question.

Claire didn't so much as hesitate. It was as though he were a continuation of her dream. She put up her arms to him.

Trevelyan set the candle aside and went into her arms with all the ferocity of a beast from the jungle. He smothered her face with kisses, ran his hands down her arms, then lifted them above her head to hold them there.

Claire was still half asleep, and this man's touching of her was of another world.

"I want to see you," he said, and the way he said it made chills on her body. With practiced ease, he removed her nightgown, slipping it over her head.

When she was nude, Trevelyan leaned back from her. He picked up the candle and held it aloft so that he could see her, see the way her breasts rose and fell with her deep, quick breaths. He looked at her waist, tiny from years of being confined in a corset. He ran his hand along her hip, down her thigh.

He looked back up at her face.

Claire's breath was coming in short gasps and she felt hot. Trevelyan kissed her. She closed her eyes and let the sensation flow through her body. She could feel his kiss all the way to her toes.

When he drew back, she opened her eyes and looked at him. He was smiling at her. It was a smile she'd not seen before. It was a smile sweet and soft, and it made him look like a boy. There was none of the cynicism that she usually saw, none of the hardness that was usually about him. His eyes were gentle and kind. If she hadn't known him better, she'd have thought his eyes were full of love.

"Trevelyan," she whispered.

He put his fingertips over her lips, then withdrew them and kissed her. Claire stopped thinking. When he looked at her like that, she couldn't seem to form a thought.

He began kissing her body. Slowly, languorously, as though he had all the time in the world. No rush. He moved from her neck down to her breast, taking the peak in his mouth.

Claire arched her back and put her hands in his hair. His hair was soft and thick and full; she could feel the darkness of it.

Trevelyan moved downward, kissing her waist, his tongue making little circles about her navel.

All the time he was kissing her, his hands were touching her. Claire had never been touched before. She had grown up in a house where there was little physical touching, and until she'd met Harry she had not so much as been kissed. But now Trevelyan was touching her as though he meant to memorize her body, as though he had wanted to touch her for a long time and planned to enjoy it. His hands ran over her breasts, down her thighs.

He kept kissing her, kissing her thighs, then her calves, and at last her feet. His big hands caressed the arches of her feet.

Claire sat up on her elbows and looked at him. He was fully dressed and she felt rather like one of those women in a Renaissance painting who was nude while all around her were people in clothes. It was not a bad feeling. Perhaps she was Leda and he was Zeus come to mate with her and give her a child.

Trevelyan smiled at her as though he knew what she was thinking, then he put his hands on her knees and slowly slid them up her body, over her breasts, up to her neck, and at last to hold her face. He looked in her eyes then. No, he didn't just look, he studied her, as though he were looking for something, as though he were trying to find something within her eyes. He turned her face toward the light of the candle and continued to look at her.

"Not yet," he whispered at last, then, before Claire could ask what he meant, he kissed her again.

Claire thought she might die from one of Trevelyan's kisses. They made her forget everything. They seemed to make her entire body become involved. He lowered his body onto hers and Claire gasped. She had never heard of the gloriousness of the weight of a man on top of one's body. He was so large and she was so small, yet his weight felt heavenly. In the past, when she'd been told what men and women did in bed together, she had worried that the man might crush the woman.

She rubbed her bare thigh against his clothed one as he kissed her.

She knew he was teaching her about kissing, that he was taking his time and showing her what could be done with two mouths. He showed her kissing with his tongue and without it. He softly bit her lips, ran his tongue over them. He turned her head one way, then the other. He showed her deep kisses, soft kisses, hard kisses.

As she always had been in everything else, Claire was a quick learner when it came to kisses. At first she lay under him, passive, allowing him to be the teacher, then she began to push at him. He seemed to know what she wanted to do. He rolled off of her, but pulled her with him so she lay on top of him as she began to kiss him. She experimented. She tried this way and that way. She began to kiss his eyes, his temple; she bit his earlobe.

Trevelyan gave a little yelp when she bit too hard, then rolled her to her back. "Want to play, do you?" He put his face in her neck and growled. Claire giggled and pushed at him.

Trevelyan, in mock anger, began nipping at her shoulders, then lower, until he was at her breast. In moments, he seemed to go from being a calm man with supreme patience to a wild man.

Claire reacted to his passion. She tugged at his shirt, wanting to feel his skin next to her own. Trevelyan was out of his clothes in seconds, his mouth never leaving some part of her body while he undressed. She heard fabric rip once and she felt the way he moved his knee against her body while he undressed.

He began to kiss her mouth again, but there was a new urgency in his kisses—as there was in hers. Inside, she felt as though she were running, running toward something or someone, but she didn't know what.

When he was nude and she felt his bare skin against her own for the first time, she gasped, then she began clawing at him, running her nails against the warm skin of his back. She moved her thighs against his, feeling how hairy and rough they were; the contrast made her even more excited.

She was shocked when Trevelyan entered her. Shocked and in pain. She pushed away from him but he kissed her to keep her from crying out, then entered her fully.

"Lie still," he commanded. "The pain will stop in a moment."

She did as he said, but not because she believed him. She was sure she was going to be torn in half.

He began to kiss her again, kiss her neck. His hand moved to her breast, his thumb on the peak. From somewhere deep within her, Claire began to respond to this ancient ritual.

"Vellie," she whispered.

"Yes, my love, I'm here."

She moved her hips just a bit, clumsily. Trevelyan put his hand on her hip to guide her next movement. It didn't hurt. In fact she rather liked it.

Trevelyan put his hands on her thighs, holding her to him as he began to move himself out of her.

"No!" she cried and clutched at him. "Don't leave."

Trevelyan made the oddest sound. It was half chuckle, half groan, but it told her that he'd as soon die as leave her.

Claire couldn't help but smile as her arms tightened about him. Then, suddenly, her eyes opened wide as he slid back into her. "Oh," she said, surprised at the sensation. "My goodness."

Trevelyan lifted his head to look at her, saw her face and smiled at her. "I think you're going to take to this with the ease you took to whisky."

After that neither of them spoke again, for Trevelyan started his long, slow thrusts. Claire lay almost still, feeling this utterly new sensation and thinking that she might have died and gone to heaven.

Somewhere within his movements, she began to move also. Trevelyan held her hips and began to guide her, so that she matched her movements with his. She was amazed at how well they fit together. Their bodies fit, her head fitting neatly into his shoulder, his hips into her hips, his—

Her eyes opened wider as she began to feel something building within her. She clutched at him and raised her hips to a higher position.

"Trevelyan," she said, and there was a bit of fear in her voice. She looked at him and saw that strain showed on his face, as though he were trying to prevent something from happening. Inside of her, excitement kept building and building until she thought she might explode.

When she did explode, she knew it was the most wonderful experience of her life. She clutched at Trevelyan, her fingers burying themselves into the flesh of his back. His face was hidden in her neck; she could feel damp tendrils of his hair against her skin.

They lay together for a long while, holding each other tightly, until

Claire pulled away. She wanted to look at him. Once, many years ago, she had been in her house in New York and she'd been walking into the small dining room where her mother was having tea with some of her women friends when she'd heard her mother say to the other women, "But, dear, you never know a man until you've spent the night with him." At the time, Claire had been so embarrassed that she'd turned and gone back to her room, but now she had an idea of what her mother meant.

She moved so she could look at Trevelyan. His eyes were closed and he looked very young, like a boy. "How old are you?" she asked.

He smiled softly, his eyes still closed. "Thirty-three."

She caressed the hair at his temples, smoothing it back from his face. "I don't think we should have done this," she said softly.

His eyes opened immediately; they were fierce and angry. "If you're going to say that we've betrayed Harry, I think you ought to know that right now Harry is in Edinburgh with his mistress."

Claire was taken aback by the anger in Trevelyan's voice. "Are you jealous of Harry?"

"Of that damned mistress of his? She's forty-five, married, and has two children, one of whom looks remarkably like Harry."

At the moment Claire couldn't think about this news. Right now Harry seemed very far away. She kissed Trevelyan's eyelids. "I don't want to think about that now. I don't want to think about anything at this moment." Part of her knew that being in bed with one man when she was engaged to someone else was wrong, but another part knew that this man was Captain Baker. This was a man she had worshiped as a hero for many years.

She ran her fingertips down the scars on his cheeks, remembering every word he'd written about how he had received those scars. Gently, she pushed him to his back and began to touch the other scars on his body, thinking about how he'd received them. She kissed the new wound on his arm. On his shins were long scars from where he had lanced his own legs when malaria had swollen them so badly. He'd had to cut his legs to allow the blood out.

She sat beside him, touching him, looking at him. She was curious as to what a nude man looked like, and especially as to what *this* man looked like.

When she looked back at his face she saw that he was frowning.

"Do you look at me? Or are you planning what you will tell the world about Captain Baker?"

She stretched out beside him and smoothed his heavy mustache. "I don't know," she said honestly. "You've been so many people to me. When I met you I thought you were an old man, a weak, sick old man. Then I thought you were a cynic, one of those people who's decided the world is a bad place and has chosen to be miserable. Then I discovered that you're the famous Captain Baker. And now . . ."

"And now?"

"Now I don't know who you are."

"Let me show you," he said, and his eyes were bright with a flaming intensity. "Let me show you who I am. Give me the time until Harry returns. That's all I ask. Harry will probably return in four or five days, then you can go back to him. But before he returns, spend time with me. Every minute of every day."

Claire pulled the sheet up to cover her bare breasts. "I . . . I don't know. There's Miss Rogers and the duchess. I think Harry's mother already knows too much of what I do, and there's my own family to consider. My mother—"

"I will take care of Rogers as well as the duchess. As for your parents, they don't seem to bother themselves about the whereabouts of their daughters."

As Claire looked at him, she knew that more than anything else in the world she wanted to stay with him. At this moment she thought it possible that she might walk away and leave behind everything that was important to her. Her jaw tightened. "What about your perfect little Emerald of the Nile?"

He smiled at her. "Pearl of the Moon."

"It's difficult for me to remember," she said stiffly. "I'm afraid that I haven't had your . . . experience with her. Shall the world read about her in your next book?"

"Of course. It's what my readers like. Let me see if I remember what I wrote, for of course I wrote about Nyssa first, long before I wrote those boring parts about the measurements of the wagon wheels and such. I think I wrote something like, 'Nyssa was all woman, all fire, all passion. She was wonderful to make love to. When you went to bed with her, it was like testing your manhood.' "

Claire started to get out of bed, but he caught her arm and pulled her back. She wouldn't look at him or speak to him, but folded her arms across her breasts and stared at the underside of the bed canopy.

"Jealous?" he asked, his voice full of amusement.

"You may leave my room now. And you needn't bother to return."

He kissed her neck and her unresponsive lips. "It couldn't possibly matter to you what I did—or do—with Nyssa. You're in love with Harry, remember?"

"You're laughing at me again!" she spat at him. "At least Harry treats me as an adult. You laugh at me as though I were a child."

"You are a child," he said softly. "You are the most beautiful grown-up child in the world."

She wasn't sure whether to be pleased by his description or not. "I'm not as pretty as your moon pearl or as pretty as my little sister."

He kissed the corner of her lip. "You don't even know what I mean by beauty." He leaned back and smiled at her. "Have you ever done a truly selfish act in your life?"

She didn't know why this question should bother her so but it did. He made her sound like a do-gooder who was always suffering for a cause. "I've done many selfish things. At home in America I was quite indulgent with myself."

"You receive an allowance from your grandfather's trust. Tell me, have you ever lent your parents money?"

"Only a few times," she snapped, and when he smiled in a know-it-all way, she started to get out of bed. "I didn't like you when I first met you and I *still* don't like you."

He pulled her back to the bed then moved so that he was half on top of her. "What don't you like? That I see you as you are? That I don't just see you as a beautiful little American heiress whose money is the most important thing in the world? Or does it bother you that I see your parents as they are? Or maybe it's that I'm a realist and you're a romantic? Maybe you think you like Harry because he's as romantic as you are. Harry sees only what he wants to see. He thinks his mother is good because he wants to think the woman is good. He thinks he's in love with you because he wants to be."

"Leave Harry out of this! Harry is a good, kind person."

"Yes, he is. Harry hasn't a bad-tempered bone in his body. He's incapable of hurting anyone."

"Unlike you! You hurt everyone. You hurt everyone who tries to get close to you."

At that Trevelyan's eyes changed and he rolled off of her. "Yes," he said. "That's true."

She lay beside him, not touching him, angry at what he'd said about her, angry at herself for what they had said to each other and for what they had done together. She should not have allowed him into her bed. She should have told him to leave when he walked into her room and stood over her, but instead she'd welcomed him.

She felt him move as though to get out of the bed and immediately she turned and threw her arms around him. "Don't leave, Vellie," she said. "I am so very tired of being alone."

He held her to him very tightly, and in ways his holding of her was more intimate than their lovemaking. "You feel it too, don't you?"

"Feel what?" She pressed her cheek against his chest.

"The isolation. The loneliness."

She started to say that someone as famous as Captain Baker could never be lonely, that he had friends all over the world, but right now the man in her arms didn't feel like Captain Baker. This man felt like Trevelyan, the man who had fainted when she'd first met him, the man who had introduced her to whisky and had given her books to read.

Claire put her face up to his to be kissed, and after that they didn't say any more as he began to make love to her again.

When Claire awoke her little sister was sitting on a chair beside the bed. "You sleep like you were dead," Brat said.

Claire turned to look at the other side of the bed but it was empty.

"He's gone."

Claire sat up in bed, keeping the sheet about her nude body. "I know. Harry left yesterday. He went to Edinburgh on . . . on business."

Brat gave a little laugh. "Rogers broke her leg."

Claire gasped. "She what?" Trevelyan had said that he'd take care of Miss Rogers. He couldn't have broken her leg, could he?

"Last night she went to sleep in her own bed in her little room and this morning she woke up in a bed in the butler's room and she had a plaster cast on her leg. The cast reaches all the way from her hip to her toes. She also had a terrible headache and she remembers nothing whatever of what happened during the night. The butler told her that she was sleepwalking and fell down the stairs and broke her leg. The doctor came and set it for her while she was still asleep. The butler said that the doctor gave Rogers some awful medicine that made her forget everything that had happened to her."

Claire grimaced. "And where did the doctor get such a medicine?"

Brat smiled. "I think it came from Pesha."

Claire laughed. "I can imagine that it did."

Brat gave her sister an intense look. "Who's the woman with Vellie? I couldn't see her very well this morning, it was still dark, but she looked to be rather pretty. She was walking so close to him, had his arm tucked into her side and—"

Brat looked at her sister in astonishment as she leaped out of bed. She'd never seen her sister naked before and she was surprised that Claire would so forget herself as to appear so before another person.

"Help me get dressed," Claire commanded. "I have to . . . to . . ."

"Save Trevelyan?" Brat asked slyly.

"Something of that nature," Claire answered, drawing on her corset.

It was a mere twenty minutes later that Claire was storming up the stairs of Trevelyan's tower. She didn't know what she expected to find, but she'd had enough time to imagine some dreadful things. She rather expected to find that horrid Nyssa sitting on Trevelyan's lap. Instead, he was sitting quietly at one of his tables and writing with his usual concentration. He didn't look up when she came in, but held out his empty whisky glass in her direction. She guessed that he thought it was Oman who had entered the room.

Claire went to the cabinet where the bottle was, took it out, then went to refill his glass. As she poured, he looked up at her.

"I thought you'd be asleep," he said softly.

Claire's hand trembled as she set the bottle down on the table. One second they were looking at each other, Trevelyan's eyes black with intensity, Claire's eyes questioning and shy as she remembered all they had done to each other's bodies during the night. The next second she was in his arms and they were kissing with passion, kissing in a frantic way, as though they had been separated for years rather than hours. Trevelyan lifted her skirts, then pulled her into his lap as he began to untie the drawstring of the trousers he wore under his silk robe.

Claire was aghast when she realized what he meant to do. She started to protest, but he put his mouth over hers and she forgot all about protesting. She put her arms around his neck and kissed him hungrily.

At first she didn't hear the woman's voice to her left. If Trevelyan heard it he made no sign. He kept kissing Claire and tossing aside three of her petticoats.

Claire pushed at Trevelyan, trying to pull away from him. The woman spoke again. "Trevelyan!" Claire said sharply, pushing at him. She was trying to get off his lap.

Trevelyan said something under his breath. Claire couldn't understand it but she recognized it as Peshan. She heard the woman laugh and say something else.

Claire gave a mighty push at Trevelyan. He released her and she landed with a loud thunk on the stone floor. Claire looked up to see Nyssa standing two tables away from them. The woman looked to be even more beautiful in the early morning light than she had the night before. She wore a robe of yellow silk that made her brown eyes look almost golden. Claire remembered every word of what Trevelyan had told her about making love to Nyssa. Had he left her, Claire, in the middle of the night and gone to this pearl of beauty? If he'd made love to twenty-five women in one night, surely he could handle a mere two.

Claire got up and started for the door. "I have to go," she said.

Trevelyan caught her skirt before she could take a step. "You don't have to go anywhere."

Nyssa said something and Trevelyan replied in Peshan.

"What did she say?" Claire asked stiffly.

"Nothing of interest."

"What did she say?" Claire demanded.

Trevelyan gave a great sigh of weariness. "She said that the color of your dress was wrong for you, that it made you look pale and lifeless."

Nyssa said something else and Claire turned to glare at her. "Translate."

"Claire, love—" Trevelyan started, but then sighed. "She said that you're too heavy for your height and that men don't like fat women."

Claire clenched her teeth. "Tell her that men don't like flat-chested, scrawny women such as she. Tell her that in my country of America, where people are civilized, women are supposed to have some meat on them."

"Claire . . ." Trevelyan said in a pleading voice.

Claire turned to look at him, her eyes blazing. "You don't want to tell her, do you? Did you spend the night with her? Did you go to her after you left me?"

"After I left you I took care of that maid of yours. I haven't had *time* for any other women."

"And time was the only restraint on you, wasn't it? If you'd had time you would have made love to her."

"Actually, no," Trevelyan said quite honestly. "Nyssa's too demanding for me. Tires me out."

At that Claire could only gasp in horror. "I guess I'm an old maid compared to her. A gelding compared to a stallion."

"That didn't come out as I meant it to. I meant that—"

Quite suddenly it was all too much for Claire. She put her hands over her face and burst into tears. "I don't blame you. She's the most beautiful woman I've ever seen in my life, and I have no right to tell you what to do. You have every right to do what you want."

The hands that reached out to her weren't Trevelyan's. They were small hands of great comfort and they pulled Claire to a small shoulder. "I would give anything to have a bosom like yours," Nyssa said in English that had a lovely, soft accent. "And I think my skin is too dark. How do you keep yours so white?"

"I stay out of the sun," Claire said, sniffing, then pulled away and looked at Nyssa. She looked at Trevelyan. "You've been laughing at me again."

Trevelyan looked a bit like a man trapped. He opened his mouth to speak but Nyssa interrupted him.

"I asked him not to tell. He taught me English on the trip back from Pesha." Nyssa took Claire's hands in her own. "Frank says that I have you to thank for saving me. I don't like Jack Powell. He wanted to make a prisoner of me. He wanted to take me around the world and show me to people. There was no one to help me, as I thought Frank was dead." Nyssa smiled at Claire. "Will you forgive my little joke? I so liked to see you fight for Frank. I have never seen anyone or anything that could take his mind from his writing."

Claire looked at Trevelyan in question. "I have taken your mind from your work?"

Trevelyan shrugged. "Now and then. When I have to play the vicar and rescue people, or sit and watch you learn to dance, or take you to the houses of old men and watch you flirt with them. I also have to entertain your little sister and—"

Claire smiled at him and he looked away. "Why don't you two children run off and play together?" Trevelyan muttered.

Both Claire and Nyssa laughed at that.

"What shall we make him do?" Nyssa asked. "Shall we make him tell us stories or take us outside into the sunshine?"

"We're in Scotland," Trevelyan growled. "There is no sunshine. And in case you've forgotten, my presence here is supposed to be a secret."

Claire looked from one to the other of them and realized how well the two of them knew each other. It made her more jealous than thinking that Trevelyan had slept with the woman. "I have to go back to the house," Claire said. "They will miss me." She turned away and started down the stairs.

Trevelyan followed her but didn't say a word until they reached the floor below, the floor where Claire had fallen through the rotten boards. Trevelyan caught her arm and turned her toward him. "There's no reason to be jealous of Nyssa. She's nothing to me."

"But she's so beautiful and you've spent the night with her." She couldn't look at him because she didn't want him to see the tears in her eyes.

"Yes, I have." He paused and when he spoke again, there was anger in his voice. "Damn you! I may have made love to her but I've never said that I love her."

She didn't know what he meant and it took her a moment to realize that he was referring to the way that she said she loved Harry. *Did* she love Harry? How could she love Harry and want to be with Trevelyan? How she love one man and spend the night with another? But Trevelyan had said that he'd spent the night with a hundred women, a thousand, yet he seemed to distinguish sex from love.

Trevelyan saw the confusion on her face and pulled her into his arms, where she hid her face against his chest. "Shall we do what Nyssa suggested and spend the day outside?"

"The three of us?"

"Yes, the three of us," he said. "No, the four of us. We'll invite your little sister."

Claire sniffed. "My *beautiful* little sister. I'll be the ugly one."

Trevelyan chuckled, then put his hand under her chin and lifted her face to his. "You will be far and away the prettiest one to me. Do you know that I'm beginning to think that you're the most beautiful creature I've ever seen?"

"Really?" She looked up at him, tears sparkling in her eyes.

"Yes, truly." He kissed her softly, then his kiss became more passionate, more demanding. He put his hand on her thigh and began to pull her skirts up. "Why do you wear so damn many clothes?"

"Trevelyan, we can't do anything here. There are people and—"

He cut her off with his lips. "Damn the others."

"But there's no bed," she murmured.

Trevelyan gave a little laugh that was so full of innuendo that Claire could feel her scalp tightening. She didn't think much after that as he pulled her skirt up, lifted her leg so that it was about his hip, then took two steps, stopping when her back was against the wall. Her big underpants that reached to her knees were not sewn in the center seam. He parted them easily.

In the next minute his own robe was open and his trousers were about his knees. He entered her quickly and Claire gasped, startled. She had already forgotten what this new experience was like.

She put her head back and Trevelyan ran hot kisses down her throat as he held her hips in his hands and guided her in their quick, stolen lovemaking.

Claire's passion built and built as he slammed into her. Her weight was supported by him and she felt his body move against hers, in and out, building until she wanted to cry out. But his lips on hers kept her quiet until at last they exploded together.

She clutched at him, weak and spent, feeling helpless and powerful at the same time. "Trevelyan," she whispered against his neck.

"Yes," he said. "Tell me."

Claire shook her head. She wasn't going to say anything. Nothing at all, in fear of what she would say.

He held her there, against the wall, both of them fully clothed, yet joined so very intimately. "Give me my days," he said. "Give me these few days, that's all I ask. No promises. No regrets. Live for the moment and the moment alone. Don't think about tomorrow or about what anyone else wants of you. Can you do that?"

She nodded her head against his neck. What an extraordinary idea to think about living for the moment, to think of no one but herself. For an unknown number of days, she could stay with Trevelyan and not think about what her parents wanted her to do, about what she must do in the future. She could stop worrying about her sister's future. She could stop worrying about her own future under the rule of Harry's odious mother. She could laugh and talk to someone about things that interested her rather than pretend to like shooting and horses and dogs. For a few days she could stop trying to understand Trevelyan, stop trying to figure out who he was and what he was.

"You don't touch Nyssa," she said. When he didn't say anything, she looked at him.

"Not one touch? Not even kisses?"

For once she realized he was teasing her. "It's enough that I'm allowing you to look at her. And no comments to my sister about sitting on your lap, either."

"Only if you sit on my lap," he said huskily.

"I think I'd rather like sitting on you." She kissed him, then he disconnected them and stood her in front of him. Gently, he tucked a stray strand of hair behind her ear.

"Vellie?" she said. "Are there lots of ways to do . . . this?"

His eyes were bright when he looked at her. "Lots."

"I guess you've tried them all," she said bitterly and looked away.

"I have merely practiced for the real game."

She looked up at him and smiled. "I will give you your days. No, I will give myself the days. For the next few days, for as long as we have, I will think only of the present, not of the future or the past. Not your past or mine."

He caressed her cheek. "My past need not concern you—ever." He took her by the hand and led her toward the stairs.

"It's your future that concerns me now. What do you *plan* to do with Nyssa?"

"My only plan for the future is to show you every position, every nuance of lovemaking that I have ever learned."

Claire blinked at him. "I have always loved school."

He laughed and led her up the stairs.

Chapter Twenty-one

They had four days before Harry returned. The four most heavenly days Claire had ever experienced in her life. More than that, they were days such as she'd never dreamed could have existed.

As far as she could tell, Trevelyan didn't sleep. At least not enough to count. She thought that perhaps he made do with three or four hours of sleep a night, but that was all. He spent hours in bed with her, making love to her, keeping his promise to show her what he knew. He showed her positions. He touched parts of her body that she hadn't even known she had.

But their actual coupling was the least of their lovemaking. It was the things he did before he touched her that nearly drove her mad. He used words to make her ready. He told her erotic stories. The stories weren't vulgar; they always had funny little morals to them. They were just incredibly sexy.

Once Trevelyan told her one of these stories while she lay in Bonnie Prince Charlie's bed and watched him undress. He took forever to take off his clothes, all the while telling her the story of the love affair between a beautiful princess and her father the king's adviser. Had either of them been caught the king would have put them to death. But through the cleverness of the adviser, he managed to make the king allow him to marry the princess.

Trevelyan told the story slowly, telling in detail what the princess and her lover did in bed. By the time Trevelyan was undressed and ready to come to bed to her, Claire wanted to tear at him with her teeth. A naked, a magnificently naked Trevelyan walked toward the bed and Claire eagerly opened her arms to him. He stopped beside the bed and yawned.

"I think I'll write for a while," he said, then picked up a silk robe, slipped into it, and walked out of the bedroom.

Claire was astonished. How could he tell a story like that, then just leave her? She had every intention of telling him of his rudeness as she angrily got out of bed, pulled on one of his robes, and went into his writing room. He was calmly writing away, utterly unaffected by the passion that Claire was feeling.

She opened her mouth to tell him what she thought of him, but then she saw that his hand was shaking as he held his pen. She knew then that he was as affected as she was.

She walked very close to him and whispered, "Teach me how to sit on your lap." He dropped the pen instantly, his strong hands reaching for her, pulling her toward him. He taught her how to make love while sitting on his lap. He held her, caressed her, supported her weight as they made love.

If their nights were full of the pleasure of lovemaking, their days were full of other kinds of pleasure. Trevelyan had seen so much in his life, remembered all of it, and was willing not only to talk about it but to reproduce what he had seen. He showed her dances from Africa, games from India. He tried to sing folk songs from some of the countries he had visited, but he couldn't carry a tune. Claire was able to piece some of the words and tunes together enough to re-create some of the songs.

They walked together and talked and laughed. He drew her into bushes and kissed her. He had a way of kissing the back of her neck that made her quiver with desire.

When they weren't touching each other, he allowed her to read what he was writing. Once when Claire dared to make a comment, something to the effect that perhaps all his readers wouldn't be interested in the measurements of the rocks of the walls surrounding Pesha, they had a fight. Or at least it became a fight when Claire forced Trevelyan into speaking to her again. After her comment, he merely walked away, saying nothing to her. He said nothing when she asked him a question. He said nothing when she kissed him. He said nothing when she whispered an invitation in his ear.

She told him he was being childish and he turned on her with a gaze that made her take a step backward. He told her that she was the child, that he had boots older than she was. Her first instinct was to run away and hide, but she forced herself to stand her ground. She told him that his age was one of the main things wrong with him, that he was of an old-fashioned generation and that he had no modern ideas. She also made comments about his being a backward Scot.

He told her what he thought of America; she told him what she thought of pigheaded men who wouldn't listen to reason.

It was Nyssa and Brat who managed to stop the fight. Claire and Trevelyan had been yelling so loudly they could be heard outside. Nyssa and Brat came running up the stairs and stood against the wall, listening for a while, then Nyssa began to applaud. She told Brat to keep score and see who the winner of the argument was. The person who made the most vicious remarks won. She and Brat awarded Trevelyan four points when he made a derogatory remark about Claire's parents. Claire countered with a statement that Trevelyan had no parents, that he probably hadn't been wanted by his parents. Nyssa loudly declared that a deathblow when Trevelyan stomped out of the room.

Claire sat down on the yellow sofa, stunned at what had just passed between her and Trevelyan. She'd had no intention of saying the things she had. She knew nothing about his parents. How could she have said such things, and all because of his books? She'd had no right to criticize his books. What did she know anyway? It was just her opinion. For all she knew, his measurements were what his many readers liked the most.

Nyssa sat beside Claire and put her arm around her. "You had better go after him. He is like a wounded animal when he's hurt. He will not get over this easily."

Claire didn't like it that Nyssa knew so much about Trevelyan, knew things that she, Claire, didn't. But Claire didn't have time to think about that now. "Where do you think he went?"

"To the old summerhouse," Brat said. "He goes there often."

Claire nodded. Here was someone else who knew what she did not.

Claire left the tower and started the long walk to the summerhouse. It was two miles at least, and she knew that Trevelyan would be walking very fast. Since he'd recovered his strength, his pace had increased until she couldn't keep up with him.

He was sitting on a bench on the front porch of the little house, looking out toward the hills of Scotland. "What do you want?" he said to her, anger in his voice.

She sat beside him but didn't touch him. "We said some awful things to each other."

He didn't bother to answer.

Claire knew that she had hurt him in some deep, deep way but she wasn't sure how she'd done it. Was he so very sensitive about his writing? "I like your books," she began. "I've always liked them. I like *all* of them. Every part."

He looked at her as though he didn't know what she was talking about.

"Your books, remember? That's what we fought about."

He looked back toward the hills. "Was it? Maybe I should leave out some of the measurements. Maybe I should write two books, one for people who want to know everything and one for the masses. For the masses I'll tell all about Nyssa and the other beautiful women."

"I think the world can do without that book," Claire said stiffly.

"Maybe so," Trevelyan said without much interest.

Claire sat by him in silence for a while. She'd already learned that Trevelyan could talk for hours, but he could also be silent for hours at a time. "If what I said about your books didn't upset you, why are you angry at me?"

He looked at her in puzzlement. "I'm not angry at you. You have your opinion and I have mine."

"But you *are* angry at me. You stomped out of the tower and came here. You were furious with me."

Trevelyan looked at her as though she'd lost her mind, and Claire had her first experience of men rewriting history. "I did no such thing. I merely wanted some air."

Claire wanted to shout at him but she knew it would do no good. The next moment she realized that he was keeping something from her. There was something that he didn't want her to know. "What aren't you telling me?" she asked softly.

Trevelyan stood up and walked to the edge of the porch. "I have no idea what you mean. I've told you more about my life than I've ever told anyone."

"That may be true, but you've told me only about Captain Baker. You've never told me about your life before he was born. Where did you grow up? How are you related to Harry?"

"I'm getting cold. I think we should go back." He turned to look at her, lowering his lashes and giving her a lascivious look. "Or perhaps you'd rather stay here? We could go into the summerhouse and—"

"You'll give me your body but not your secrets. You know all there is to know about me but you tell me nothing about yourself. You share nothing private with me."

"I share all that I can with you."

"You share all that you *want* to with me." She turned on her heel and walked away from him.

He caught her when she was just a few feet away from the summerhouse. "Stay with me," he said. "Don't leave."

She looked into those eyes, those unreadable eyes, and wondered what was behind them. She wanted to pull away from him but she felt that he needed her. She leaned against him and he held her close. "All right, I'll stay."

He kissed the top of her head and continued holding her for a very long while. "So, you think I should leave out some of the measurements in my books, do you?"

"Why don't you let me take a pencil to them?"

"Allow *you* to edit them? You? A mere child?"

They argued all the way back to the tower. Claire argued with Trevelyan but she saw that half of what he was saying was to tease her. Yet when they had argued before, something she'd said had seriously upset him.

In their precious four days together, that was the only argument they had. The rest of the time they spent making love and dealing with Brat and Nyssa. On the first morning after Claire had agreed to spend the days with Trevelyan, she had not wanted to spend any time with the beautiful young woman. After all, what woman would want to spend hours beside a woman who was so beautiful that she was called the Pearl of the Moon and was worshiped by an entire city of men? It could make one decidedly uncomfortable. But besides Nyssa's beauty, Claire still remembered the dreadful things that Nyssa had said about her, that she was the color of the underbelly of a frog. There was also what Trevelyan had said about Nyssa being more woman than he could handle. Claire would have wagered there was nothing in life that could make her like Nyssa.

But Claire had not counted on Nyssa herself. Nyssa's aim in life seemed to be to do whatever she wanted whenever she wanted to do it. Trevelyan said that as the priestess of the Peshans, her only responsibility was to enjoy herself—and that Nyssa did. She laughed; she sang; she danced. She teased Trevelyan and made him smile, then, just when Claire was ready to walk out of the room, Nyssa started teasing Claire. Nyssa asked if she didn't find Trevelyan's moods most annoying, then she admired Claire's hair and asked if she could brush it for her. It was difficult to be angry at someone who was brushing your hair. Nyssa arranged Claire's thick hair into braids, then inserted three jeweled combs in them. After that she led Claire into Trevelyan's bedroom and soon had her dressed in one of his embroidered robes.

"Now for the face," Nyssa said.

Claire started to protest but she was too curious to want to stop. She watched in fascination as Nyssa opened her trunk and rummaged inside until she found a lump of black stuff that looked like charcoal. Nyssa had Oman bring her a brazier, then she lit the lump. As the black stuff burned Nyssa held an overturned bowl over the smoke. After a few minutes, there was a black residue on the underside of the bowl. Nyssa took a small brush from her trunk. Claire had to bite down a protest when Nyssa spit in the residue in the bowl and used the brush to make a paste. In the next minute, Nyssa quickly and expertly applied the black paste to Claire's lids and eyelashes. After this Nyssa applied powder and rouge to Claire's face, using more of the rouge on Claire's lips. When she was done, she handed Claire a small mirror.

Claire was sure that she'd look like a clown in a circus, but she didn't. Nyssa was an expert at applying cosmetics. Claire knew that she had never looked so good. She glanced toward the writing room.

"Go to him," Nyssa said. "He will like it."

Shyly, Claire went to Trevelyan's writing room, where he was at table number five. Whenever he was not actively engaged elsewhere, he was at one of his tables writing.

Claire stood by him for some minutes and had to clear her throat three times before he looked at her. When he did look at her, he studied her, then took her chin in his hand and turned her face this way and that. He said something to Nyssa in Peshan, then he kissed Claire and went back to his writing.

Claire felt somewhat disappointed as she walked back to Nyssa. "What did he say?" she whispered.

"He said that you were already perfect and that I might need enhancement, but you did not."

Claire smiled in delight, then went back to Trevelyan and kissed him soundly. Trevelyan was puzzled by this, as what he had actually said to Nyssa was that her application of the cosmetics needed work, that she used too heavy a hand.

After Nyssa had dressed Claire, she asked if she might put on Claire's American clothes. Nyssa's small breasts did nothing to fill out the top of the dress, so Claire wadded up several pairs of Trevelyan's socks and padded the bosom of the dress.

Happily, Nyssa paraded herself before Trevelyan and Oman, who admired both of the women outrageously.

It was during this fashion show that Brat entered the room. It was her first close-hand sight of Nyssa. From the moment Brat entered the room, the air was charged with tension.

Nyssa's lovely face changed from one of delight over the odd gown she was wearing. She stopped admiring her false bosom and stared at Brat. Claire knew immediately that Nyssa had never before seen another female who was competition for her when it came to beauty. But Brat was certainly competition. Whereas Nyssa's looks were dark, with dark eyes and hair, Brat's beauty was of the palest. Brat had light brown hair, blue eyes, pink lips, and skin the color of ivory.

Claire glanced at Trevelyan and saw that he was leaning back in his chair and watching the two young women with great interest. He had on his I'm-going-to-write-about-this face.

Brat was the first to move. She walked toward Nyssa, looked her in the eye, for Nyssa was small and Brat, at fourteen, had not gained her full adult height, then Brat doubled her fist and hit Nyssa smack in the face. Nyssa went sprawling to the floor.

"Brat!" Claire yelled at her sister, who was looking down at Nyssa as though she were her sworn enemy. Claire went to Nyssa to help her up and as she did so, she looked up at Trevelyan. "Help me," she ordered him, but Trevelyan just sat there smiling, obviously fascinated by the scene.

"I am so very sorry," Claire began as she helped Nyssa to stand. "Sarah Ann, I demand that you apologize this instant."

Brat stood where she was, her face hard and unmoving.

When Nyssa was standing, Claire went to her sister. "Either you apologize—and explain yourself—or I'll give you something to be sorry about."

Behind them Nyssa's laughter spilled out, and Claire turned to look at her.

"She has never been in a room with a woman prettier than she is," Nyssa said.

Brat didn't say a word, just kept glaring at Nyssa.

Claire looked at Trevelyan as though asking him for help.

Trevelyan shrugged. "You have your money and your sister has her beauty. Have you ever met an heiress richer than you?"

Claire looked at him as though he were insane. "What has this to do with money? My sister just hit someone and—"

She didn't say any more because Nyssa walked past her and put out her hand to Brat. "I will do your face as I have done your sister's," Nyssa said softly. "I have a blue robe the color of your eyes and I have silk shoes with little mirrors sewn on them."

Brat stood where she was for a few minutes, then, with her jaw still set, she followed Nyssa into the bedroom.

After that first episode, Nyssa and Brat became inseparable. Not that they liked each other, not that they ever said a kind word to each other. It was as though each didn't dare allow the other out of her sight. Claire thought that Nyssa was amused by this game, but that Brat was deadly serious.

At first the animosity Brat showed toward Nyssa bothered Claire, but Trevelyan shrugged it off. "It entertains Nyssa, so it's all right." She didn't understand his answer any more than she understood what was going on between Nyssa and Brat. Nyssa was nineteen, the same age as Claire, but the young Peshan woman acted much younger. She acted as though the very thought of responsibility might kill her. She told Claire that she meant to enjoy herself and that was all she planned to do in life.

Once Claire tried to talk to Trevelyan about Nyssa's future, but Trevelyan wouldn't discuss the subject. In fact the whole concept seemed to make him angry. "She's not like you," he half yelled at her. "Can't you understand that other countries have different ways? You complain that America is different from England and England is different from Scotland. But you have no idea how different the rest of the world is."

Claire didn't know what she'd said to cause such anger in him, but this particular anger was the least of what she didn't understand about him. Sometimes he looked at her with love and sometimes he looked at her as though he had no idea who she was. When he was writing he had an ability to concentrate that was almost frightening. Brat and Nyssa yelled at each other but Trevelyan would sit in the midst of them and seem as though he heard nothing. Once, when Brat and Nyssa began to fight over a particularly lovely red robe, Claire had to shake Trevelyan to get him to stop writing so he could negotiate between the two women. Trevelyan frowned, didn't look up, and said, "When they tear it in half, they'll be sorry. They'll learn more from that than I can teach them." He was, unfortunately, right.

On the morning of the fourth day, Oman handed Claire a letter. He said that a man on a lathered horse had brought it for her. Trevelyan turned away from his writing to look at her with great interest. As Claire reached out for the letter, she found that her heart was pounding. Had Harry heard what she was doing with Trevelyan? Was the letter from him?

"It's from the Prince of Wales," she said. Nyssa and Brat came out of the bedroom to watch her open the letter. Claire read it quickly, then looked up at Trevelyan. "The Prince of Wales has issued a royal warrant for MacTarvit whisky."

"He wants to *arrest* whisky?" Brat asked.

Claire smiled. "No, the prince says that it's the best whisky he's ever had and he wants the world to know it." Claire locked eyes with Trevelyan. "She won't be able to throw him off the land now. Not if the prince wants the whisky."

Trevelyan looked at Claire for a long moment. She couldn't tell what he was thinking. "She won't like that," he said at last. "You're interfering too much in her life."

Claire turned away from him, for something in what he said and the way he said it frightened her. "Shall we go and tell Angus MacTarvit?"

"Yes, please," Nyssa said. "We shall go now and you shall explain everything that you've done."

Trevelyan gave a nod to Oman, and thirty minutes later the group was piled into one of the MacArran carriages. They were an odd assortment of people. Trevelyan was wearing the plaid, which she now knew was the laird's plaid and which she again told him he shouldn't wear. He replied that Harry's kilts would be too short on him, the snideness of which was not lost on Claire. Nyssa was radiant in a golden brown robe that was heavily embroidered with a diamond pattern. Brat, not to be outdone by her enemy/friend, wore a blue robe and had flowers in her hair. Oman, of course, couldn't have looked more strange. Only Claire was "normal" in her plain red wool dress.

She didn't realize that she was looking at the group in the carriage as she feared the crofters were going to see them—as people from another planet.

Nyssa said something in Peshan to Trevelyan and he smiled.

Claire looked at Nyssa. "Translate please."

Trevelyan answered because Nyssa had turned and looked out the window. "She said that of all of us, the contraption on your behind made you the strangest looking."

"My bustle!" Claire said with indignation. "I'll have you know that—" She stopped because everyone in the carriage was smiling, and Claire began to laugh too. She grinned at Trevelyan. "At least you aren't dressed like George Washington today."

Trevelyan smiled back at her.

When they were still a mile from Angus's house, the carriage road ran out and they had to walk. Angus met them at the top of the hill, his gun nowhere to be seen. Behind him were about a dozen crofters. It looked as though they had seen the carriage from a long way off and had come to greet the passengers. The crofters were speechless as they watched the glittering, silk-clad group walk up the hill.

Angus, who had never before been at a loss for words, looked from Brat to Nyssa, then back again. His eyes grew wider with each look.

Trevelyan looked at Claire, saw that her feelings were on the verge of being hurt, then he grabbed Angus's thick arm and pushed him toward the cottage. "Come in here, old man. Claire has something to tell you."

The three of them went into the cottage. Claire sat on the only chair, Trevelyan took a stool and they waited patiently while Angus poured each of them a glass of his whisky. When they were served and Angus was seated, he spoke. "What brings the lot of you here?"

"This," Claire said and handed the letter to Angus.

He took it, looked at it, but didn't seem to comprehend the letter. Claire realized that he couldn't read.

"The Prince of Wales has issued a royal warrant for your whisky," Claire said.

Angus turned to Trevelyan as though for explanation.

"We went to Edinburgh recently, and the prince was visiting the queen at Balmoral. Claire sent him a bottle of your whisky and he liked it."

Angus frowned and looked back at Claire. She could tell that he still didn't understand. "You're protected by a prince now, a man who'll someday be king. He won't allow anyone to stop you from making your whisky, not even a duchess. People all over the world will want to buy your whisky. Especially Americans. Americans love anything Scottish. You'll have rich Americans coming here to bargain with you over the price. You can charge them thousands if you like. Americans love to overpay so they can brag to their friends about how much what they have costs."

Angus looked at Trevelyan.

"Unfortunately, everything she says is true."

Claire made a face at Trevelyan.

Claire could see that Angus was upset by what they were saying to him. Angus stood and turned his back to them for a moment. When he did speak his voice was not quite steady. "I have always loved the old ways. My family has always abided by the old ways."

Claire drew in her breath. "You don't have to accept the warrant. I don't know if there's ever been anyone who's declined it before but I'm sure it can be done. You can stay just the way you are if you want."

Angus turned a furious face to her. "Decline? Do I look daft to you? Stupid? Do you think I want to spend my old age freezing in this house? My children left because there was no work for them. I tried to sell my whisky in town but she—" He nodded his head in the general direction of Bramley. "She set upon my wagons and broke the bottles."

He grinned at Claire. "Some of the old ways are fine. You'll not get me out of my kilt, but I could do without a diet of stolen beef. I should like to buy . . ." His head came up. "I should like oranges in the winter."

He sat down on his stool and for a moment he stared at the floor. "If there's work, maybe my family can come home. I have four boys, all fine, strappin' lads. They're in America now and two of them have wives." Angus looked up at Claire and she could see there were tears in his eyes. "One of my sons has a child. I've never seen it and never thought I would."

Claire looked at Angus, feeling rather like crying herself, then she looked at Trevelyan. He was watching her with great intensity and he didn't look away when she stared back at him. After a while Trevelyan stood, held out his hand to Claire and moved toward the door. Angus didn't seem to notice when they left.

Still holding Trevelyan's hand, Claire followed him outside. To the side of the cottage they could hear the sound of bagpipes and Claire started in that direction, but Trevelyan pulled her toward the woods. "Where are we going?" she asked, but he didn't answer.

When they were hidden in the woods, he turned to her, took her face in his hands, and kissed her in a way that he'd never kissed her before. It wasn't a kiss of passion, it was a kiss of . . . of love, she thought.

Still holding her face in his hands, he moved back from her and just looked at her, as though he were memorizing her features.

"That was a very kind thing you did for him," Trevelyan whispered.

For some reason Claire was embarrassed by his compliment. "It's no more than anyone else would have done. I thought perhaps the prince would try the whisky if I sent it to him. I thought he liked me when I met him in London."

Trevelyan was still looking at her in his odd way, but then he smiled. "I think Nyssa has arranged a party. Shall we go and watch her dance?"

Claire knew that as long as she lived she would never experience a day such as the one when she told Angus about the royal warrant. Angus opened great kegs of whisky and passed it out to everyone—without charging a penny.

"The world is near its end," Trevelyan said under his breath to Claire.

The first time Claire had visited Angus she had tried to learn the dances, but today it was Nyssa and Brat who were dancing. When

Claire saw how good the two beautiful young women were, she stepped away and watched. Their feet skipped lightly over the swords laid on the ground.

When Brat tripped over her robe, Nyssa said that they wanted clothes like the Scots. One of the women offered her a long, homespun skirt, but Nyssa pointed to one of the boys and said that was what she wanted to wear. Some people told her that women did not wear the short kilt, but Trevelyan stepped in and said that Nyssa was to have whatever she wanted. Angus brought out two kilts of the dark MacTarvit plaid. The kilts looked as though they had been laid away for years, as though they meant a great deal to the old man. Nyssa took one of the kilts, then kissed Angus's weathered cheek. Brat, not to be outdone, kissed his other cheek.

Angus beamed, showing off a couple of missing teeth.

When the pretty young women reappeared from inside Angus's house wearing the kilts, their legs bare, there were some disapproving looks from the women and some leers from the men. Trevelyan went to Brat and Nyssa, offered each an arm, and escorted them to the pipers. All disapproving looks stopped, as did the leers. When the music was playing again, he walked back to Claire.

"It's as though your word is law," she said, looking up at him. "They didn't think the girls should wear the kilts until you said it was all right. And when you escorted the girls, the crofters gave their approval."

Trevelyan shrugged and looked away. "They're fine dancers, aren't they?"

Claire knew she was going to get no answers out of him. She stood to one side and watched as he moved among the people, talking to them. He seemed to know most of them by name and he asked after their relatives and their homes.

At noon Claire saw Trevelyan talking to two young boys, then she saw the boys hurry off down the hills toward Bramley.

"Where are they going?" she asked Trevelyan, but he chucked her under the chin and told her it was a surprise.

It wasn't until sundown that she found out what the surprise was. Trevelyan had arranged for all of the crofters, over a hundred of them, to be fed at Bramley, and they were invited to see a play in the theater of Brat's friend Cammy.

Trevelyan mounted a horse that a stable boy from Bramley had brought him and put his hand down to Claire to lift her up in the saddle before him.

When she was seated in front of him, she leaned back, feeling the strength of him. It was difficult to believe that this was the man who she'd thought was old when he'd fainted after catching her horse.

Trevelyan rode with her through the woods, away from the many people who were walking toward Bramley.

"I don't think your presence here is going to continue to be a secret," Claire said.

"No."

She had expected him to say more, but he didn't and she didn't press him. He was not going to tell her more than he wanted to.

"Do you sometimes feel that there are moments of perfect happiness?" she asked. "That there are times that you do not want to end?"

"No," he answered. "I always want to see what's going to happen."

She smiled in the darkness and was quiet as she rested against him. Right now she didn't want to think about the future.

They rode so slowly through the dark Scottish countryside that they reached the door to the east wing of the house at the same time as the crofters did. Inside they found tables in a sitting room Claire had never seen before being filled with food, and Camelot J. Montgomery was beside himself with excitement. He was going to have an audience for his plays.

Claire stood in the doorway and watched the people tentatively approach the tables and the food.

"Isn't this what you wanted?" Trevelyan asked her. "Isn't this the sort of thing you plan to do when you're the duchess? Isn't this equality something like what you Americans believe?"

"I guess so." She looked up at him, worry showing on her face. "What will Harry's mother do when she hears of this?"

Trevelyan shrugged. "She'll do nothing she hasn't done before. Now stop worrying and come and eat."

Claire allowed him to lead her into the room. She made an attempt to keep her worries to herself, but she couldn't help thinking of that woman and what she might do.

After the people had eaten, they went into Cammy's tiny theater. There were seats for only half of the people, but the others stood along the walls and looked in awe at the gilded surroundings. When the curtain rose, Claire thought she'd see an odd version of a play, but instead she saw Nyssa alone on the stage.

Nyssa was beautifully dressed in a heavy red robe that flashed with jewels. Behind the curtain a flute began to play an eerie tune.

Standing beside him, Claire could feel Trevelyan stiffen. When she looked at him, his eyes were wide and he looked almost angry. "What is it?" Claire whispered.

Trevelyan looked away from her, hiding his face so she couldn't see it, but she had the distinct impression that something was causing him great distress. "Tell me what's wrong?" she whispered. "Who is playing the flute?"

Slowly, Trevelyan turned back toward her, then he pulled her to him, her back to his front. "Watch," he said and his voice was husky. "She is going to dance. It's an ancient dance of great meaning."

"*What* does it mean?" Claire asked, trying to turn so she could see his face, but he wouldn't allow her to turn.

He put his lips close to her ear. "It is a sacred dance of death. All the young priestesses are taught this dance."

Claire looked at Nyssa on the stage. Nyssa removed her heavy robe and under it she was wearing thin, gauzy garments that barely concealed her lithe, golden-skinned body. Even though Nyssa's garments were provocative and even indecent, there wasn't a murmur from the audience. Everyone seemed to realize that he was seeing something that was far removed from a comedy.

Nyssa's dance, if it could be called that, consisted of slow, beautiful movements, movements that had no spontaneity to them, but were studied and perfect. She moved to the long, slow flute music with precision, her exquisite little face utterly solemn.

"I don't like this," Claire said and tried to move away from Trevelyan, but he held her fast.

"Nyssa believes in her religion with all her heart and soul," he whispered.

Claire continued watching the dance, but it gave her goose bumps, and when Nyssa at last slowly and gracefully fell to the ground in a deathlike pose, no one in the audience moved. Nyssa lay where she was for the longest time, and the audience mirrored her stillness. Then Brat ran from behind the curtains and grabbed Nyssa, pulling her up into her arms.

Nyssa opened her eyes and her laughter rang out through the audience. At that people began clapping.

Claire tried to turn to Trevelyan but he held her fast. "Watch," he said, and within moments the flute began again, only this time the tune was fast and exciting. Nyssa, smiling, pushed Brat away and began to dance again, only this time the dance was obviously not about death.

"And what is this dance a celebration of?" Claire said with sarcasm in her voice.

"Procreation," Trevelyan answered over the noise of the audience, which was beginning to clap and cheer at the sight of Nyssa's undulations.

Claire twisted to look at Trevelyan, saw that he was watching Nyssa with as much delight as all the other men were. "I need some air," she said, then had to repeat it two times before he heard her. He smiled down at her knowingly, then took her hand and led her outside into the cool night air.

He pulled her to the side of the house and in the darkness he began kissing her.

"Is this for me or for Nyssa?" she asked when she could catch her breath.

"Do you care?"

She laughed. "Not really." She put her hands in his hair and returned his kisses.

At one point she opened her eyes to see Oman standing behind them. He was standing quietly, his heavy-lidded eyes half lowered, as though he didn't mean to watch but had to. Claire pulled Trevelyan's hair. He didn't stop kissing her, but Trevelyan said something low in another language to Oman.

Oman answered, then disappeared into the darkness.

"What did he say?" Claire asked. Trevelyan was kissing her neck now and she couldn't think very clearly. Trevelyan kept kissing.

"What did Oman say?" she asked again.

Trevelyan moved away from her enough to answer. "Harry has returned," he said, then began kissing her throat again.

It was as though someone had splashed her with cold water. She pushed away from Trevelyan and looked at him. "Have you nothing to say?"

"I'd rather not talk now," he murmured and leaned forward to kiss her again. When she didn't respond, he said, "Let's go into the garden." He took her hand and started pulling her into the privacy of the trees.

Claire followed him, thinking that he was leading them into privacy so they could talk, but the moment they were alone, he grabbed her to him and began to kiss her.

"Stop it!" she practically shouted as she pushed at him. When she had at last broken away, he stood there in the bright moonlight with a puzzled look on his face. "You can't act as though nothing has happened. Didn't you hear what Oman said?"

Trevelyan's face changed and Claire realized that she hadn't seen his closed expression for days. It was as though a curtain had come down and he wasn't going to allow her or anyone else to see into him. "I heard him."

Claire took a step toward him, but he backed away. Claire's hands dropped to her side. "What are we going to do?" she whispered.

"People are free to do what they want in life."

"What does that mean? Is that something you read—or did you write it?"

"It is fact." His face was closing more, showing her less of him.

She put her hands over her face. "Trevelyan, please don't do this. Please don't shut me out. What am I going to do? What are *we* going to do?"

When he didn't answer, she looked at him. He was standing there, staring at her. He was so tall, so dark, so far away from her. He wasn't the Trevelyan who laughed with her. Now he was the Captain Baker of her childhood fantasies, a man as remote from her as a mythical figure.

She put her hands to her side. "I was just one of them, wasn't I? These last four days have been everything to me. Never in my life have I been so happy. I've shared so much with you. No, I *thought* I was sharing with you. I've never had anyone to talk to, not as I can talk to you. I can talk to you about what I read, what I think, what I hope. I can do anything I want with you, yet I was nothing to you."

She turned and started to walk away, but he caught her arm. "Why do you think you are nothing to me?" he asked softly.

She turned on him, furious. "Oman tells you that Harry has returned and you say nothing. You don't care that I have to go back to him, that I have to leave you and what we've had these last few days.

You got what you wanted from me and now I'm just a chapter in your book. Or do American heiresses get whole chapters? Maybe only women like your Pearl of the Moon deserve entire chapters."

"What do you want from me?"

She shook her head. "If you don't know, I can't tell you." She started to walk away but again he caught her.

He moved so that he was in front of her. "Tell me what you expect of me. Would you like for me to beg you to live with me instead of Harry? Is that what you want? Would you like for me to ask you to give up your dream of being a duchess and go live in a hut on the edge of a jungle with me?"

Claire's head was spinning. There was a part of her that wanted to go with Trevelyan, wanted to spend all of her life with him, but there was another part that told her that the last few days she'd spent with him weren't real. There was so much she didn't know about him. He asked questions but he didn't answer them.

"I don't know you," she said and there was agony in her voice.

"You know me as well as anyone ever has."

She raised furious eyes to his. "Don't you understand that I'm not talking about what we've done in bed together? I'm talking about love."

"So am I."

Claire turned away. She didn't want to cry now.

Trevelyan put his hands on her shoulders and she rubbed her cheek against his hand. "I don't know what to do," she said. "Tell me what to do."

He turned her around to face him and stared into her eyes. "You have to make your own decision. I can't make it for you. No one can live another person's life."

It wasn't what she wanted to hear. Why couldn't he be like other men and tell her that he loved her, that he wanted her? Why couldn't he say that he'd kill her or Harry or both of them if they so much as looked at each other again?

"Is that what you want?" he said, as though she'd spoken aloud. "Would you like for me to throw you over my horse and take you away from here? Would you like me to kidnap you and take you on my next trip? And if I did that, how long would it be before you began to hate me? Would you start hating me two years from now when you received a letter from your sister saying that your parents had spent every penny of your grandfather's money and they were now destitute? Or would you begin to hate me before that, when I went away on an expedition and left you behind to imagine what I was doing when you weren't there?"

"I don't know," she said honestly.

His fingers bit into her shoulders. "Do you love me?" he asked. "Me? Not Captain Baker, not some man you think you know because you've read his books, but me, Trevelyan?"

She hesitated, and in her hesitation, he moved away from her. "Of course I love you. I couldn't have done the things I did with you if I didn't love you. I've never done those things with anyone else. How could I have gone to bed with you when I was engaged to someone else if I didn't love you? If my parents had found out, if Harry knew, it would have hurt them very much. I couldn't have—"

When he looked at her his eyes were black with rage. He bent so his nose was nearly touching hers. "I have been to bed with hundreds of women. I have done things with them that you could never imagine, but I have not loved any of them, not as I have come to love you."

Claire took a step away from him. The intensity of him frightened her, and she knew that it was time for the truth. "You ask me if I love you. How do I know if I love you? I don't know you at all. You keep yourself from me. I know more about Captain Baker than I do about Trevelyan. Where were you born? How are you related to Harry? Why do the crofters treat you with such respect? I never know what you're thinking, what you're feeling. You say that you love me. For how long have you known that you love me? Days? Weeks?"

She looked at him, saw that he wasn't planning to answer her. "You say that I have to make my own decision. Am I to decide that you want me, that you want me to go with you, spend my life with you? *How* am I to know that you want that? You haven't told me that you want me. You haven't told me anything. Nothing! If I weren't such a snoop I doubt that I'd even know that you're Captain Baker. I don't think *you* would have told me."

When he spoke neither his look nor his voice had softened. "Do words mean so much to you? If the words are what you want, then I'll give them to you. I love you. I love you as I have never loved another woman. I think that perhaps I have loved you for nearly as long as I've known you. I would like for you to go with me. Now. Tonight. Ride away from here and never look back. I don't know what will happen in the future. I'm sure that I'll make the worst husband in the world. I'll leave you alone for years at a time while I travel. I'm cursed with bad moods. I'm a selfish bastard and I'm sure that I'll make you cry a great deal. I don't know what to say to you about other women. I think that monogamy will be difficult if not impossible for me, but I'll try it."

Claire knew that if she had any sense she would now throw her arms about him and leave with him. She wanted to do just what he suggested: get on his horse with him and ride away. She would never look back at the MacArran lands. She'd never look back at her present life. How many women had the fortune to have a man like the great, the famous, the world renowned Captain Frank Baker fall in love with them?

But Claire didn't throw her arms around him. If she left with him it would mean turning her back on her family. She knew that Trevelyan ridiculed her parents, thought they were a worthless pair, but they were her family. Perhaps he could get along with just himself, but could she? Could she walk away, knowing, as he had pointed out, that she would be condemning her sister to a life of poverty?

Trevelyan, watching her, started to walk away.

"Wait!" she called and went to stand in front of him. "I . . . I don't know what to do. I want to go with you but—"

"If you wanted to go, you would do so." His face suddenly softened and he smiled at her. "Your young duke is probably waiting for you. "You'd better go to him."

She took a step backward. "You don't care that I go to Harry?"

"I don't try to live other people's lives for them. If you make up your mind, I will be here for . . ." He looked toward the house. "I will remain here for another few days. Good night, Miss Willoughby."

Chapter Twenty-two

Claire cried herself to sleep that night, not falling into a deep sleep until early morning. She probably would have slept the morning away if Harry hadn't come into her room. What with Miss Rogers confined downstairs with her uninjured leg still in a cast and no one inclined to tell her that her leg wasn't broken, Claire was left alone. Even Brat, who often came to her room, didn't. She was probably with Nyssa and Trevelyan and Oman, Claire thought with bitterness. Claire put the pillow over her head and tried to go back to sleep.

At ten, a furious knocking at her door brought her out of her half sleep, but she didn't bother to answer the door. She didn't care who was there or who wanted to see her.

When she didn't get out of bed to answer the door, it was opened. Listlessly, Claire watched Harry enter her room. His arms were full of flowers and a large leather portfolio.

The sight of the handsome young man did nothing to cheer Claire. She lay in the bed, blinking up at him, not smiling, feeling no happiness at seeing the man she was supposed to be in love with.

Harry looked down at her for a moment then put his armload on the foot of the bed and went to open the curtains. Claire blinked at the bright light coming into the room and sat up, not bothering to pull the sheet about her.

Harry took a seat by the bed and looked at her. It wasn't difficult to see that she'd been crying. She looked much older than her nineteen years.

"I owe you an apology," he said.

Claire waved her hand in dismissal. She opened her mouth to speak but as her eyes filled with tears again, she closed it.

Harry started to hand her a handkerchief, but the one on the table by the bed was wet so he went to a tall chest of drawers and began frantically opening drawers until he found a clean stack of handkerchiefs. He handed her a wad of them and Claire blew her nose loudly.

"I came to apologize," Harry repeated, then put up his hand when Claire again tried to speak.

Harry put his hands behind his back and began to pace the room. "I don't think I appreciated you until I had some time away from you. Claire, my love, I'm going to be honest with you. When I first met you, my mother had sent me to London to get you. She'd heard that an American heiress was to be had and, well, there was the roof and all the people in my family who had to be supported and, to be honest, we need the money."

He stopped pacing and looked at her. "It was rather easy to win you."

Claire started crying at that. She was indeed easy to win. It seemed that she fell in love with every man she met.

Harry went to sit on the side of the bed and took her hand in his. "I started this because of your money but somewhere along the way I fell in love with you."

This made Claire cry harder and Harry kissed her palm.

"I was so angry when I left here last week. I realized that you hadn't enjoyed hunting with me, that you'd only gone with me to . . . I couldn't figure out why you'd gone with me. And I guess I'd known that you hated it. You always looked so unhappy and so . . . wet when we returned."

Harry smiled at her. "Do you know where I've been these last few days?"

Claire shook her head and blew her nose again. Of course Trevelyan had told her where Harry had been but she didn't know if she believed him.

Harry grinned. "I've been saying good-bye to my mistress."

At that Claire's head came up and she looked at him.

"Yes," Harry said. "I was so angry at you that I thought I'd spend some time with a woman who was honest and true, one who didn't lie to me and say that she liked something when she didn't. I was furious with you. When I got to Edinburgh, I went to Olivia and told her everything."

Harry gave a little chuckle. "I thought Livie would hug me and tell me what a dreadful woman you were, but you know what she did?"

Claire shook her head.

"She started laughing. I don't think I've ever seen anyone laugh as hard as Livie did. I thought she was going to burst her dress. At first she made me so angry I nearly left, but then Livie said, 'She must love you very much.' "

Claire's eyes widened as she looked at Harry.

"Yes, that's what she said. Livie said that any woman who would spend days sitting in the rain in a butt with me had to be in love with me." He gave a sigh. "Livie has never gone hunting with me. Anyway, Livie said that if she had your money and could buy herself any man she wanted she wouldn't sit in the rain for the Prince of Wales."

"She sounds nice," Claire managed to say.

"She is. You'd like her. I mean, that is, if you could meet her, but I guess you can't." He paused and looked at her. "Claire, why have you been crying?"

Claire started to answer him, but her tears started again.

Harry got up from his chair and went to stand before the big portrait that was the doorway to the tunnels. "It's Trevelyan, isn't it?"

Claire didn't answer him and Harry looked back at her. For the first time, Claire saw anger on that handsome face. "I don't need an answer. *All* the women fall for him. Every woman on the face of the earth. Wherever he goes, all the women love him. They all want to go away with him."

He looked down at the floor. "Will you go away with him?"

"I . . . I don't think so."

Harry gave her a hard look. "You want to though, don't you?"

Claire couldn't answer him. *Did* she want to go with Trevelyan? Did she want to put herself in the hands of a man who was as cynical as Trevelyan was? Did she want to live with a man who had seen and done as much as he had? Did she want a man who was as self-contained and cold as he was?

Harry saw her hesitation and he went to her, took her hands in both of his, and began kissing them. "Claire, tell me that I have a chance with you. Please tell me that I'm not out of the running yet. I won't ask you to go hunting with me. I won't ask you to do anything that you don't want to do. I know that I'm not exciting like Trevelyan is, but I can offer you some things that he can't."

He picked up the portfolio from the bed. "Look at this. While I was in Edinburgh, I paid off all your mother's debts. She's ordered a great many clothes. I had to sell a Gainsborough to get the money. The painting had been in my family for years, but it was worth it to do something for you. And here, I had my solicitors draw up papers putting money in trust for your little sister. It's a way to prevent anyone from spending her money. I also had a new will drawn up. It says that after we're married and should I die before your sister is married, she's to have an estate of mine in the Cotswolds. She gets the estate and all the income from it."

Claire picked up the papers, but her eyes were too blurry to read them.

"And look at this. It's a paper that puts a limit on your parents' spending. It's an allowance for them. They'll always be taken care of as long as I'm your husband, but they can't touch your principal."

He took a breath, then handed her another paper. "And this one limits *my* spending. After we're married, you shall have control of your money. You shall have a say in how it's spent. You can do what you like with the crofters' houses. I know they mean something to you. You can turn Bramley and my other estates into an American commercial venture if you want."

He placed the last of the papers on her lap. "Claire, I do love you. I know that I'm not like Trevelyan. I know that I could never offer you the excitement he does, but I can offer you and your family a secure future. I can offer them a home. All of you will be taken care of for all your lives. And Claire, I'll be good to you. I'll be as good as I can be."

Claire sat there in the big bed surrounded by the many papers and looked at them. This is what she wanted. She had wanted love and security for herself and her family and here it was in abundance.

She looked back up at him and he smiled at her, then picked up the flowers and handed them to her. They were yellow roses, her favorite.

He leaned forward and kissed her damp cheek. "Claire, I might not be as electrifying as Trevelyan, or as well read, or as heroic. I haven't done much in my life and I've seen only the ordinary things, but I think I can say that I'll make you a better husband than he will. I don't have his temper." Harry smiled. "I think I can say for certain that I'll be easier to live with than he would be."

He kissed her hand again. "Won't you please give me another chance? I won't be such a fool this time."

Claire gave him a weak smile and she knew that, the truth was, she really had no choice in the matter. She couldn't abandon her family. She couldn't run off with Trevelyan and give her parents every right to say that they didn't approve of her marriage to a penniless adventurer. And if they didn't approve, then Claire's grandfather's millions would go to her parents and they'd spend everything in a few years. Trevelyan had said that she'd come to hate him when she received a letter from her sister saying that she and their parents were destitute. What would her parents do when the money was gone? Neither of them knew how to work. Well, maybe her mother did, but it had been too long ago for her to remember.

"Of course I'll marry you," she whispered to Harry. "But I have to tell you—"

Harry put a finger to her lips to stop her from speaking. "I don't want to hear anything about you and Trevelyan. Maybe we should forget that these last few days happened. I shouldn't have left you alone. I shouldn't have become so angry. It was all my fault. I take full responsibility."

His words made Claire cry more. She didn't deserve anyone as nice as Harry. He had done everything he could to try to please her and all she was doing was bawling at the prospect of marrying him.

"I'll leave you alone now and you can get dressed. I've arranged for us to have lunch in the library. From now on the library is yours. You can come and go as you please."

He kissed her cheek again. "Please have luncheon with me."

She put the handkerchief to her eyes and nodded at him.

He rose from the bed and went to the door. "I shall be looking forward to our time together."

Harry closed the door behind him and went straight to his mother's room. When he reached the room there was no softness on his face.

"Well?" Eugenia demanded.

"I did everything you wanted."

"You showed her all of the papers?"

"All of them."

Eugenia looked up at her youngest child. "Don't look at me like that, Harry. I've done all of this for you." For the first time in her life, Eugenia saw coldness in her youngest son's eyes. She was used to seeing that expression on the faces of her other children, but Harry had never looked at her with anything but love.

"And you'll keep your part of the bargain?" he said, his mouth in a firm line.

"Of course. And now, my darling, stay and have luncheon with me. I have salmon, just as you like it."

Harry took a while to answer her. "No," he said at last. "I don't think I want to eat with you. I'm going to have my meal with Claire." He turned on his heel and left her alone in the room.

Claire spent the day with Harry. She wasn't very good company. She kept looking out the window, hoping for a glimpse of Trevelyan. She listened to Harry talk of his trip to Edinburgh, but she had to pretend interest in what he was saying. How very different his conversation was from Trevelyan's!

She forced herself to stop thinking like that. Harry was the man she was going to marry. Maybe he wasn't as interesting as Trevelyan, but then there wasn't but one Captain Baker on earth. It wasn't fair to compare an ordinary man like Harry to someone as world renowned as Captain Baker.

"I'm sorry, I didn't hear what you were saying," she said to Harry.

He reached across the tea table to take her hand. "If you're waiting for Trevelyan to come to you, he won't. He's not a man who can be owned."

"But he said that he loved me," Claire cried in despair.

Harry leaned away from her and she was sure she had offended him deeply. "Did he?" Harry asked softly. "I don't remember hearing that he's done that before."

Claire looked away and tried to blink away her tears. At one time the library had been her prime interest in life, but now all she could think about was Trevelyan. If he did love her, why didn't he come for her? How could he allow her to spend time with another man? Was he with Nyssa? Had he already replaced her with another woman?

Harry very kindly arranged for the two of them to have a private supper in the library, but Claire couldn't eat much. She picked at her food, pushing it around on her plate. Harry made a few attempts at conversation but became silent after he met with Claire's monosyllabic replies.

After supper Claire was so tired that she could hardly drag herself up to her bedroom and undress herself. Yet, when she was in bed, she couldn't sleep. She lay still and looked at the underside of the canopy.

When the portrait on the wall moved, she leaped out of the bed and ran to it. "Vellie!" she said, hope in her voice. He *had* come for her.

But it wasn't Trevelyan at the door but her sister, Brat. Claire turned away and listlessly went back to bed.

"You shouldn't be up," Claire said, but more from habit than because she meant it.

To Claire's consternation, Brat climbed in bed with her and hugged her sister tightly.

"What's going on?" Brat whispered. "I don't understand anything."

Claire hadn't thought her little sister was capable of being a child. Sarah Ann seemed to have been born old and knowledgeable. Yet this was a child who was hugging her now.

"I'm going to marry Harry," Claire said. She wasn't going to lie to the child.

"But you love Trevelyan and he loves you."

Claire took a deep breath. "Sometimes there's more to marriage than just love. Sometimes other things have to be considered."

"You mean me, don't you? You're going to marry Harry so you can get the money and keep me from being poor."

"What an absurd idea. I'm not doing any such thing. Harry is a lovely man. I agreed to marry him because I loved him, not for money. I'm sure Harry and I will have a very nice life together. I shall do something with this place and the other ones Harry owns. I'll bring them into the nineteenth century. We'll put bathrooms all over this monster house. You'll like that, won't you? You'll like living here, won't you? You said that you loved this house and all the people in it."

Sarah Ann took a deep breath. "I love you too. And I love Trevelyan and I love Nyssa." And I love Harry, she thought, but she didn't say that. Since Harry had returned he looked to be as sad as Claire. Sarah Ann knew the two of them were forcing themselves to marry. But why? That was what she didn't understand.

"When did this happen? I thought you hated Nyssa. She can say some cruel things at times."

"She doesn't mean them. She's . . . I don't know, I think I love her because she's happy. I don't know many happy people."

"I'm happy," Claire said.

"No, you're not. You aren't happy and Trevelyan isn't happy, Harry is unhappy and everybody's sad. I don't like it here anymore. I want to go home to New York."

Claire stroked her sister's hair. "We don't have a home in New York anymore," she said softly. "We don't have Father's yacht or the house in the country either. All we have is millions of dollars that we can't touch unless I get married. And I must marry a man who'll help me take care of the money."

"I don't think I like money. I think you should marry Trevelyan."

Claire managed to smile. "And go away and live in a hut somewhere? Should I take you with me? Would you like living on coconuts and never having pretty clothes to wear?"

"Is Trevelyan very poor?"

"I don't know," Claire said with some bitterness. "He has never told me anything about himself. I know practically nothing about him."

"But you know all there is to know about Harry, don't you?"

Claire sighed. "I'm afraid that I do. I don't think Harry is a very complicated man."

"I don't understand anything," Brat said. "I used to think that I understood everything, but I don't anymore."

"I think it's called growing up. Now, why don't you close your eyes and sleep a little?"

Sarah Ann, snuggled close to her sister, did close her eyes, but she didn't sleep, nor did Claire.

Chapter Twenty-three

"Wear the emeralds," Brat said as she rummaged through Claire's jewel box.

Claire gave her sister a weak smile. Claire was trying her best to conduct herself normally and to put on a face of happiness for her sister, but she wasn't very good at acting. "The emeralds would be lovely." Claire had allowed Sarah Ann to choose her clothes for dinner and Brat had chosen Claire's most lavish lace ballgown. Claire knew she was going to look a bit ridiculous at dinner, but she didn't care. For the two days since she'd seen Trevelyan, she didn't seem to care about anything. She walked about the estate with Harry, spent all her time with him, and tried to tell herself that she had made the right decision to marry Harry. But every time a branch twitched or someone walked into a room, Claire jumped.

Trevelyan's probably writing and doesn't realize I'm not there, she thought with a great deal of bitterness. So much for his "love" of me.

She looked in the mirror of her dressing table and smiled at her sister. Poor Brat, she thought. For the last few days Claire's depression had upset her greatly. Claire had never before realized how important she was to her little sister. But then, with a father who was usually away killing animals or sailing on his yacht and a mother who did little but plan one party after another, Claire was all the family Brat had.

"Nyssa was singing this morning," Brat said.

Claire's hands stopped on the heavy emerald necklace at her throat. "When did you see Nyssa?" she whispered.

"All the time. I don't think she sleeps. She says she doesn't want to miss anything and sleeping is like a little death."

Claire arranged the necklace. There was a chain of emeralds set in gold, each emerald about the size of a thumbnail. Hanging from the chain was a fat tear-drop-shaped emerald about an inch and a half long. The large emerald was called the Moment of Truth and was famous for bringing good luck to people. The necklace was the first thing her mother had bought when she had received her money from her father-in-law. Claire was sure the necklace would have to be sold soon after her marriage and the money used for a new lead roof for Bramley. Emeralds into lead.

"Was Nyssa alone?" Claire asked, trying to act as though she didn't care.

Brat was quiet for a moment. "Trevelyan is always with her."

"He isn't writing?"

"No. I haven't seen him write a word since . . . since the night Nyssa danced. Since the night Harry came back."

Claire nodded and tried to look busy as she straightened her jewelry box. Trevelyan had not taken long to go from loving Claire to being in love with his beautiful little Pearl of the Moon.

Claire stood up and turned to her sister. "How do I look?"

Brat smiled. "Beautiful. I think you're much prettier than Nyssa."

Claire laughed at that and held out her arms to her sister. "What a lovely liar you are. Now go and find Cammy or someone. I must see Harry."

"I bet Vellie would like to see you in that dress. And your hair looks so nice. Has he seen your emeralds? Maybe he'd like to draw them and put them in his books. Maybe you should show him—"

"No" was all Claire could say, but she kissed Brat on the forehead and slowly walked out of the room.

Harry was waiting for her at the bottom of the stairs. Since he'd returned from Edinburgh two days ago, it was as though he was afraid to allow her out of his sight. As far as she could tell he wasn't jealous of the time she'd spent with Trevelyan, and she often felt as though he'd rather be outside with her father and the other men, but still he stayed with her. Claire thought that if she had been feeling less miserable, she would have asked some questions. But as it was, she didn't feel much like bothering about anything in the world.

"You look beautiful," Harry said softly, looking her up and down.

Claire smiled a bit and thought that Harry was a bit too short, a bit too fair, that his eyes were too light, his hair wasn't the right length, and why didn't he grow a mustache? In other words, why wasn't he Trevelyan?

Harry held out his arm for her. "I want to show you something," he said, then led her back through the house, past the gold drawing room, past the dining room. He led her to the first-floor ballroom, a room that Claire had seen only once before. She had been appalled at the condition of the room, which had obviously been unused for years. The chairs placed along the walls were dirty and torn. There were cobwebs hanging from the ceiling.

But now, in the early evening, she couldn't see the dirt or the worn chairs, for the room was lit by hundreds of candles and everything glowed golden. In the corner of the room sat six men with violins.

As Harry led her into the room, he nodded to the men and they began to play a waltz. They weren't a very good orchestra, in fact they were actually rather awful, which made Claire smile at Harry as he opened his arms to her to lead her in a dance.

As one of the men hit a particularly discordant note, Claire smiled, a genuine smile, the first in days, and Harry leaned forward and softly kissed her cheek. "They were the best I could do on short notice."

Harry was a good dancer, and he whirled her about the ballroom until she was breathless.

"I will try to be a good husband to you," Harry said as he waltzed her by the windows.

Claire could hear another man saying that he would no doubt be the worst husband on earth.

Harry whirled her round and round until Claire was nearly dizzy, but she was smiling and Harry was laughing.

It was nearly sundown and the setting sun was glistening on the windows of the ballroom when Claire looked up from Harry's arms to see Trevelyan standing in the doorway. At once her heart leaped with joy. He *had* come for her!

But she took one look at his face and knew that the emotion on it wasn't jealousy at seeing her with another man, nor did he look as though he planned to demand that she leave with him, no matter what her protests. She knew what she did not see on his face, but she couldn't read what was there.

"Come with me," Trevelyan said.

"I don't think I can," Claire answered, moving back toward Harry. She didn't like the way he was speaking to her.

Trevelyan gave Harry a look that made Harry push Claire toward Trevelyan. "Go with him."

"Why do people feel that they must obey him?" she demanded of Harry. She was hurt. She hadn't seen Trevelyan since their argument in the garden. He had made no attempt to see her; he'd known that she was hourly in the company of another man, yet he hadn't seemed to care.

Trevelyan was across the ballroom in two strides and he clasped her upper arm.

"You're hurting me. I don't want to go with you."

"Nyssa wants you," he said.

At that Claire dug in her heels and tried to keep from being pulled. "You ignore me for days, even after what we did, and now you want me to go with you because of your little harlot? I will *not* go with you."

Trevelyan picked Claire up and carried her from the room. Claire looked back at Harry, as though for help, but Harry remained where he was. Claire crossed her arms over her chest.

"If you think you can use these tactics on me and get me to change my mind, they won't work. I'm going to marry Harry and give my family a home. I'm not leaving with you no matter what you say or do to me. If you carry me away from here, I'll find a way to return. You can't—"

"Shut up," he said.

"You cannot talk to me like—"

He stopped walking and looked down at her. He turned the full force of his dark eyes on her, and, involuntarily, Claire's hands went to her throat. "What is it?" she whispered. "What has happened?"

He didn't answer, but started walking again.

Claire began to become alarmed. His look had told her there was something more wrong than a lovers' quarrel. She turned her head and looked at the garden. On a little hill not far away, in what was the very prettiest part of the garden, was a low, three-sided shelter draped in Nyssa's bright colored scarves. Inside were many pillows, and Nyssa was lounging on them, wearing her embroidered red robe.

Claire would have said something to Trevelyan, but beside the shelter were two tall men, both with very dark skin, both wearing only loincloths. The men's bodies were painted with blue stripes and there were feathers in their long hair. One of the men was playing a flute. He was playing that awful tune that Trevelyan had said was a celebration of death.

"What is she doing?" Claire asked. "Who are those men?"

If Claire's body had not been against Trevelyan's she would not have known that he reacted to her question, for his face didn't change. His expression was still hard and unreadable, but she could feel an odd little catch in his chest.

"Nyssa is about to die," he said softly.

Claire wasn't sure she heard him correctly. She twisted in his arms. "She's what?"

"Nyssa is about to die. It is her time."

Claire could only blink at him in shock. It was a moment before she understood what he was saying. Did he mean that her five years as priestess of the Peshan religion were up and now she was to die? "Let me down," she said. "I can run faster than you can walk. We'll be able to stop them."

Trevelyan looked ahead at Nyssa as he held onto Claire. "We will not stop it."

Again it took Claire some time to understand him. She stiffened in his arms. "Not stop it? Are you mad? This is Scotland, not one of your heathen countries."

He stopped walking and glared down at her. "You are not to tell Nyssa that you do not believe her religion to be the true one. She has asked you to come because she cares for you. She wants to say good-bye to you."

Claire thought perhaps she was asleep and dreaming. Or had Trevelyan gone mad? "This is ridiculous. Put me down!"

They were close enough to Nyssa that Trevelyan could see her face now. Nyssa nodded at him, so he set Claire to the ground.

Claire wanted to run to Nyssa, but she didn't. She smoothed her gown, straightened the emeralds at her throat, put her shoulders back, and walked forward. She smiled down at Nyssa. "What is this I hear about death?" she asked, smiling. "It's a lovely day and tomorrow promises to be even lovelier."

Nyssa smiled up at her. "I wanted to say farewell."

"Good-bye? How absurd. Tomorrow, why don't we go to London? I can get Harry to take us. Have you met Harry?"

Nyssa's laugh rang out. "There will be no more tomorrow for me."

Claire looked at the two men flanking the enclosure. They were formidable-looking creatures. Claire sat down on a pillow and leaned toward Nyssa and began to whisper. "Scotland is a free country. You're safe here, but if you don't feel safe from those two, I'll see that you get to America. I'll take care of you as long as I live."

Nyssa, smiling, bent forward and kissed Claire's cheek. "You have been kind to me. I will say a word in your favor when I get to the land past death. I will be in great favor there, you know. I will remain beautiful forever."

Claire took Nyssa's hand in her own. "You will always be beautiful in this land, too, no matter how old you get. Beauty is in a person's bone structure. Nyssa, this whole charade is really absurd. You must get up from here and come back to the house with me."

"No," Nyssa said. "I mean to die here. This is a beautiful spot, is it not?"

Claire looked at Nyssa, then at the two men by the enclosure, then at Trevelyan who was a mere two feet away. "Would you please reason with her?"

Trevelyan, with great sadness in his eyes, looked at Nyssa and shook his head.

It was then that Claire began to think that this death threat of Nyssa's was *real.* She clutched Nyssa's hand tightly. "Nyssa, listen to me. You aren't in Pesha now. This is a different land and there are laws here. We can call the authorities and these men can be put away. They can be stopped from threatening you."

"But no one is threatening me," Nyssa said softly, still smiling. "This is my choice. I made it long ago."

"Yes, yes," Claire said impatiently. "But that was when you were in another country. Now you're in Scotland and—"

"It is all the same, wherever I am. I am still the Pearl of the Moon, and I swore that I would die at the end of five years."

Claire began to feel hot. She took Nyssa's other hand. "But you're not in Pesha now. You no longer have to abide by their hideous, cruel laws. You're free now to—"

Nyssa removed her hand from Claire's and stroked her cheek. "You do not know what my country is like. I laughed when Frank told me that you thought these Scots crofters were poor. You do not know what poverty is like. Not real poverty. You have never seen anyone starve to death."

"Of course not, and in America you'd never have to see such poverty again."

Nyssa put her fingers to Claire's lips. "I grew up in such poverty. My mother bore two children and died when she was seventeen. I have already lived two years longer than she did."

"In America the life span is—" Claire stopped at a look from Trevelyan as he knelt by Nyssa's head.

"In my country it is a great honor to be chosen as the Pearl of the Moon. There is no other way a girl of my class can hope to escape the daily struggle of trying to find enough to eat. And when a girl is chosen, she may select eight other young women to be her maids. In all, nine young women get relief from their agony, I forever and my chosen friends have enough to eat for five full years. It is the greatest honor a girl can hope for. I was most fortunate to have been chosen."

Claire gave Nyssa a patronizing look. "Yes, I am sure it was a high honor, but you escaped. You have been able to get free of that dreadful place and now you can do what you want."

Nyssa tipped her head back to look at Trevelyan. "She will not understand, will she?"

Trevelyan gave a brief shake of his head.

"It's you two who don't understand. You act as though this pagan religion has some merit. I can't imagine such a thing as this! Young, beautiful women being killed to honor some idol. I can't—"

She stopped because Trevelyan had reached out to her, his face angry, but Nyssa put her hand on his arm. "No," she said softly, then she lifted her head to look at the two men by her tent. "Leave us," she said, then nodeed toward Trevelyan, too.

When the men had walked to the bottom of the hill and the flute music had stopped, Claire took a deep breath. "Now you're out of danger," she said. "If we run—"

"No!" Nyssa said sharply. "Can you see nothing but what you already know? No one is forcing me to do this. I do this because I believe it in."

Claire could feel her own anger rising. "You want to die so you will be beautiful forever? I hardly think that a rotting corpse is a beautiful sight."

"I do this because it is what I *believe.*"

"But it's *wrong!*" Claire half shouted, and Trevelyan started toward them, but Nyssa waved him away.

"It is different, that is all, and I am ashamed for you that you think I would give up my life for physical beauty. The death of the Pearl of the Moon has happened every fifty years for centuries and it has kept my city safe. If the tradition is broken then Pesha will be broken."

Claire gave a sigh of relief. "It's not the death of women that has kept Pesha hidden, but lack of communication, lack of transportation. Someday there will be trains into Pesha. And it will happen in your lifetime."

"Not in my lifetime, for I die today."

Claire's apprehension returned. "Pesha has already been found," she said quickly. "So your death will be useless. Captain Baker found it. If he can get in, many others can. Queen Victoria will send hundreds of soldiers to Pesha. It has already happened. You can't stop it. And certainly your death can't stop it." Claire's face brightened. "You could go around the world telling people of your religion. You speak English so very well. You can educate the world. You can—"

Claire stopped because Nyssa had motioned to Trevelyan to come forward. Trevelyan walked to Claire, then picked her up by the waist and held her to him.

"Stop it!" Claire said to Trevelyan, trying to kick him. "Release me and go get help. I think she means to stand by and allow those savages to kill her. You have to stop this."

"No," Trevelyan said into her ear. "This is what Nyssa wants to do."

Claire stopped struggling and twisted to look at Trevelyan. "This is what you've meant these last days, isn't it? You kept saying that Nyssa is to be allowed to do whatever she wants." She pulled back from him. "You've know about this all along, haven't you? You've always known that she meant to die."

"I knew in Edinburgh when she wanted her cup."

"Cup? What cup?" Claire's voice was rising in pitch. "What cup?"

Trevelyan nodded toward Nyssa. One of the dark men was pouring a liquid into the crude cup that Nyssa had made Trevelyan get from Jack Powell's house in Edinburgh. For a moment Claire was absolutely still, Trevelyan's arm about her waist. She couldn't believe what she was seeing, what she had just heard.

As Nyssa put the cup to her lips, Claire screamed and began to fight Trevelyan. Claire kicked and clawed at his hands, she twisted and turned and tried with all her strength to force him to release her, but he held her strongly and firmly.

Only when Nyssa had drunk all that was in the cup did Trevelyan release her. Claire practically fell on Nyssa, grabbing her, sticking her fingers down Nyssa's throat, trying to force her to vomit. All the while, Claire was screaming, "Help me! Help me!" but not one of the three men moved. They just stood there watching.

Nyssa didn't vomit and the poison stayed in her.

Claire was by now holding Nyssa, and she could feel her small body growing limp. "Take care of him," Nyssa whispered. "He loves you." Nyssa took a deep breath, opened her eyes, and looked toward the setting sun. "Be sure that my cup is returned to the next Pearl of the Moon."

With that, Nyssa's body went limp in Claire's arms. "Nyssa," she said, then louder, "Nyssa!" Claire began to shake her.

Trevelyan pulled Claire away from the body. "They will take care of her now." To the side the man began playing the flute again in that hideous, mournful tune.

Claire was dazed. She had just witnessed the suicide of a woman she had come to love. She looked up at Trevelyan. "You could have stopped this," she said. "You knew she was going to do this. You heard that man play the flute at the theater."

"Yes," Trevelyan said softly. "I knew it was time. The Pearl of the Moon performs her dance of death no more than three days before she dies."

Claire turned away from him to look at Nyssa. If possible, she was more beautiful in death than she had been in life. Claire turned back to Trevelyan. "How could you have allowed this?" she whispered. "How could you have stood here and allowed this to happen?" Her voice was growing louder. "You could have stopped this. You could have done something."

"I do not decide other people's lives for them," he said, his eyes sparkling.

Claire knew he was referring to the two of them as well as to Nyssa. "You don't care, do you? You don't care enough about me or about

Nyssa. You let her die because you don't care about anyone or anything except your precious books."

Behind her the flute had stopped playing and the two men were beginning to move. Claire turned and when she saw the men, with their hideous blue stripes painted on their dark bodies, she couldn't bear to see them touch Nyssa. It was these men and their primitive religion that had persuaded a simple girl like Nyssa that she had to die for their beliefs.

"Get away," Claire screamed at the men. "Don't you touch her. Do you hear me, don't touch her!"

The two men stepped back, not understanding Claire's words but understanding her tone. One of the men reached for the cup, but Claire grabbed it first. She held it and looked at it, set with its crude rubies, and she hated the cup. She saw a rock nearby and she thought she would smash the cup.

Like a sleepwalker, she stood up and walked toward the rock, the cup held in her outstretched hand. She raised her arm to bring it down against the rock but Trevelyan caught her wrist and held it.

"You cannot," he said quietly. "It was Nyssa's wish that the cup be taken back to her people."

"So someone else can die from it?" Claire half yelled at him.

Trevelyan still held her wrist and locked eyes with her. "Yes. The cup is older than we can imagine." He looked at the cup, his eyes sad. "They put a ruby on it for every Pearl of the Moon who has drunk from it and died."

With horror on her face, Claire looked at the cup she held, at all the many, many rubies on it. She opened her hand to let the disgusting object fall. Trevelyan caught it before it hit the rock.

Claire took a step away from him, looking from him to the cup then back to Trevelyan's face. "You knew all of this and yet you allowed it to happen," she whispered.

Behind her the two men were again moving toward Nyssa's body. "Get your filthy hands off of her!" she shouted then moved between Nyssa and the men.

Trevelyan walked to Claire. "They will take her now and care for her."

Claire looked up at him. There was no disguising the anger, the hatred she felt for him.

Trevelyan's dark eyes did not change. He looked down at Nyssa.

"There is a ceremony they must perform, then the body will be cremated and her ashes taken back to Pesha. It is a long journey for the men and—"

Claire could bear no more of his coolness. She stood up abruptly, then turned on Trevelyan and began to beat his chest with her fists. "I hate you, do you hear me? I hate you. You killed her. You may as well have shot her. You killed her!"

Trevelyan made no attempt to stop her from hitting him. He just deflected her fists when she started to hit his face. He stood where he was, allowing her to vent her rage. And when Claire's strength left her and she began to cry, she turned away from him, but he made no attempt to touch her.

When she looked up she saw the two dark men walking away. One of them was carrying Nyssa's limp body and the other was holding the horrid cup.

Claire lifted her skirts and ran to the men. "You can't put another ruby on there for Nyssa," she said to the man.

He neither stopped walking nor looked at Claire.

"Rubies are for blood. Nyssa wasn't just one of the women you've killed; Nyssa was special." Claire grabbed at the necklace at her throat and tried to wrench off the emerald that hung down from it, but she was too weak to tear it off and her eyes were too full of tears to be able to see clearly. She started becoming frantic. The men were walking away with Nyssa.

Trevelyan was beside her. "What do you want to do?" he asked softly.

"Get away!" she said, tearing at the emerald and scratching her skin at the same time. "Nyssa will have an emerald for her life. *This* emerald. It's called the Moment of Truth. She can't have a ruby. I don't like rubies. I have never liked rubies." She started crying again.

Trevelyan brushed her hands away from her necklace, then with a quick, hard twist, he broke the tear-drop-shaped emerald away, then strode ahead to the two men. Claire followed him and listened while he talked to the men. They shook their heads.

"They *have* to take the emerald," Claire said. "They have to."

Trevelyan began to argue with the men and she could hear the growing anger in his voice. The men, for the most part, were silent, just standing there, Nyssa draped across the arms of one of them, and shaking their heads no.

Trevelyan's voice grew more urgent; he began motioning toward Claire. Still the men shook their heads no. Trevelyan's voice lowered into a tone that could only be a threat. After a few more words, one of the men held out his hand and took the emerald, then they started walking again.

Trevelyan turned back to Claire. "They will put the jewel on the cup. They have agreed that this Pearl of the Moon was special." For a moment he was silent, looking at her, then he held out his hand to her.

But Claire couldn't take it. She could not forget and certainly could never forgive that he had just allowed a woman to die. She turned her back on him and started down the hill.

"I think she'll sleep now," Claire said to Harry as she looked down at Brat. Sarah Ann had been so upset at hearing of Nyssa's death that a doctor had been called and laudanum given to the child to make her stop screaming.

"You look as though you could use some sleep too," Harry said, glancing down at Sarah Ann. He had stayed with her and Claire every moment until the doctor had come. At one point he'd hugged Sarah Ann to him, rocking her, soothing her while she cried.

Claire tried to smile, but she couldn't. The last few days, and especially the last few hours, had been more than she could take.

Harry took her arm, led her to a chair, then handed her a glass of MacTarvit whisky.

"He's gone, you know," Harry said softly.

Claire looked at him. "Who?" she asked but knew very well whom he was talking about.

"Trevelyan left a few hours ago. Right after you returned. He and that man of his."

Claire nodded. No doubt he had remained at Bramley because of Nyssa. He had been waiting for her to die so he would be free to go to his next conquest, his next adventure, to find his next subject for his books. "Good," Claire said. "I'm glad he's gone."

"I think you judge Trevelyan too hard."

Claire looked at Harry with anger. "He killed her. He stood there and watched her die. You should have seen him. He made no effort to stop her. He couldn't have cared less about her death. I'm sure he was planning how to write about it in one of his damned books."

"I'm not so sure Vellie—"

"Don't call him that! He's Captain Baker, the man who has seen everything, done everything, and has felt none of it. It's what I thought before I met him and it's what I'm sure of now. I never want to hear of him again."

Harry frowned and looked down at his whisky glass. "All right," he said softly.

Chapter Twenty-four

When Claire heard the knock on her door, she thought it was the footmen come to take her trunks downstairs. It had been four days since Nyssa's death and she had decided it was time to leave Harry's house. Harry had tried to talk to her of wedding dates, but Claire had been too despondent to speak of a wedding. Much to their parents' chagrin, both Claire and Sarah Ann were dressed in full mourning. But then, in the last few days her parents had complained a great deal about many things. Neither her mother nor her father wanted to leave Bramley.

"I don't see why you can't be married from here," Arva said. "I like this place and I want to stay here."

Claire had said that they had to leave, that she could no longer remain in the house. Arva had complained that her two daughters looked like nuns in their black and it was a wonder the duke still wanted to marry Claire.

"There are hundreds of leaky roofs in Great Britain," Claire had said. "*Everyone* wants to marry me." Arva had wanted that remark explained but Claire hadn't bothered.

But now, when Claire turned toward the door, it wasn't a footman but Leatrice standing there. Claire couldn't help smiling, for Leatrice looked wonderful. Instead of the drawn, frightened expression she used to wear, her cheeks now blossomed with color and she wore a very pretty, very plain blue dress, not an adolescent ruffle in sight.

Leatrice smiled and went forward to kiss Claire's cheek.

"You look very good," Claire said. "Marriage agrees with you."

"It does. I had no idea how much it would agree with me. James and I have so much in common, and after living here I find him very easy to please."

Claire smiled. "I'm so very glad for you." She could think of nothing else to say so she turned back to her packing. "I'm glad I was able to see you before I leave."

Leatrice walked to Claire and put her hand on her arm. "I came back to see you. Harry wrote to me."

"How kind of him."

Leatrice put her hands on Claire's shoulders and turned her around. "Harry is very worried about you. He says that a great wrong is being done."

"I can't imagine what that could be."

Leatrice gave Claire a hard look and her eyes reminded her of Trevelyan's. Claire looked away.

"I really must finish packing. I have so much to do. My family has imposed on your hospitality for so long. Much, much too long."

"I want to tell you about Trevelyan and my mother," Leatrice said.

Claire's hands paused for a moment then she began again. "I really don't have time. The footmen will be here at any moment and I must be ready."

"No one is coming. I've told them to wait."

"But I *must* leave," Claire said. "I can no longer stay here. I have to go. I have to . . ." She trailed off because she knew it was useless to argue. She wanted to hear what Leatrice had to say and at the same time she didn't want to hear. At the moment all she wanted in the world was to get out of that house that held so many good, as well as so many horrible, memories for her.

Slowly, Claire walked to a chair, seated herself, then looked up at Leatrice expectantly.

Leatrice took a deep breath. "I never wanted to live here with my mother. I never wanted to become the cowardly spinster who you first met. But what I don't think most people understand is that hate is as strong as love. Maybe stronger. Hate can keep people together just as much as love can. My mother and I hated each other."

"I don't think you should say that about your mother," Claire said.

"I merely say the truth. You see, I knew something about my

mother that no one else did and she hated me for it. More than hated me."

Claire didn't say anything.

"You've done something for me that I'll never be able to repay. You've given me something that can replace the hatred that has ruled my life."

"Love." There was cynicism in Claire's voice.

"Yes." Leatrice smiled. "It does sound melodramatic, doesn't it? I think that since you helped me, I should help you. I want to tell you about my mother."

"You don't have to." Claire was somewhat afraid of what she was going to hear about the formidable Eugenia. She thought she might believe anything she heard about the woman.

"I *want* to tell this story. I'm tired of carrying the burden of it." Leatrice took a deep breath. "When my mother was a young woman, she was very beautiful and full of passion." She smiled at the look of disbelief on Claire's face. "Yes, it is difficult to believe, isn't it? But she was. She fell madly in love with a handsome young man who was an officer in the navy. She loved him more than she loved anyone or anything on earth. She worshiped him."

Leatrice sighed. "Unfortunately the young man was no one. He was from a middle-class background and had no money at all. But Mother didn't care about any of that. All she wanted was the young man.

"But then something happened to change her life. Mother went to a ball, and since her young officer was there, she was happy and lively and beautiful and the young duke of MacArran—my father—fell in love with her. The duke was an impetuous man and the next day he went to my mother's father and offered for the hand of Miss Eugenia Richmond."

Leatrice paused. "You'd have to know my grandfather to appreciate what an odious man he was. I don't think he had a bone of kindness or softness in him. He thought there was only one way to do anything: his way. He told his daughter of the offer and told her the date he'd set for the wedding. He didn't so much as ask his daughter's opinion of the match. Mother, who had some stubbornness of her own, told her father she planned to marry her young officer. My grandfather didn't even get angry. He merely told his daughter that if she did not accept the duke's offer and act as though she were in love with the man, he'd see that her young officer was killed."

Leatrice smiled at Claire's expression. "The old man didn't want to risk allowing my mother to spend time with the duke. He allowed them to see each other seldom and never alone. It whet my father's appetite. He thought the woman he was marrying was modest and sweet tempered."

Leatrice's mouth turned into a straight line. "She married my father, but at the wedding she decided that since she couldn't take her anger out on her father, she would take it out on the man she'd married. On her wedding night she told my father she hated him, and would always hate him."

Leatrice paused and took a breath. "I think that at first my father thought he could win her love, that he could make his wife love him, but he soon found out that in stubbornness she was just like her father. She hated her husband as much as she loved her officer."

Leatrice's face began to show anger. "She bore my father three children. I think that I, the youngest of the three, was unplanned. I think there was an argument, and afterward, my father went to my mother's room in a rage. Nine months later I was born. After that night I don't think my parents had much to do with each other. I think they lived separate lives."

Leatrice paused and looked as though she were thinking. Her voice calmed. "But then, when I was about three years old, my mother's officer came back into her life. I think they met by accident the first time, but she found that she loved him just as much as she always had. He had never married. He told her he had loved her and her alone and always would.

"My mother felt she'd done her duty to her husband and had given him his required two sons, and so she planned to leave him."

Leatrice took a breath. "And us. She planned to leave her husband and her children because she hated us as much as she hated her husband. We were dark like all the Montgomerys, and the man she loved was blond."

The anger came back into Leatrice's voice. "My mother schemed with her lover and planned for the day they would leave. She secretly removed treasures from the house, things that could be sold, for she knew that when she divorced my father she would get nothing, and if anything her officer was poorer than he had been.

"The day arrived and everything went all right. My mother escaped the house easily enough and met her lover some ten miles away where he had a coach waiting. They hadn't gone very far when a dog or something ran across the road, the coachman lost control of the horses, and the wagon overturned. My mother's lover was killed instantly, as was the driver. But my mother was pinned under the wagon and lay there for several hours before she was found. Her leg was crushed."

Leatrice paused. "Six months later Harry was born. My father knew the child couldn't have been his, and by then he knew all about the family treasures she'd taken from the house.

"When Harry was about a week old, my father went to see his wife and her blond son. He looked into the crib, then went back to the bed and tossed a packet of bills onto her bed and left the room. The bills were charges made by my mother's lover for horses and gambling debts and clothes. The security for the debts was that he was marrying the duchess of MacArran."

Leatrice turned to look at Claire, saw the way Claire's eyes were wide. "I think my mother's mind was affected by all that had happened. Between losing her lover and her mobility, then learning that the man she'd loved all those years might have been the scoundrel her father said he was, her mind was unhinged. She divided her hate and her love into two parts: she hated anything and anyone that had to do with the MacArran name, and she gave all her love to her pretty blond son."

Leatrice stopped there while Claire absorbed what she had been told. "If Harry isn't your father's son, then he has no right to the title," Claire said softly.

"None." Leatrice's eyes were so intense that they again reminded Claire of Trevelyan's.

"Did your father disown Harry in his will?"

"My father was a good man and he would never have done that. He liked Harry. He liked all of us children, but his favorite was his eldest son, Alex. I think he made an error in spending so much time with Alex, because his second son and I were left too much alone. Alex had Father, and Harry had Mother, while—" She paused and stared at Claire. "Vellie and I had each other."

Claire gave Leatrice a look of astonishment, started to speak, then stopped. Suddenly everything made sense. She understood all of it.

She understood Trevelyan's hostility toward the duchess, the woman who was his mother. She understood the crofters' attitude toward Trevelyan. "Do all the people in this house know that Trevelyan is the duke?"

"Most of them. When he was a child he was sent away to live with my mother's father." Leatrice swallowed. "Vellie was not treated well as a child."

There were too many thoughts running through Claire's head. She knew that he had told her very little about himself, but she had not realized the depth of his deception. He had said that he loved her, but he hadn't loved her enough to tell her anything about himself. If he had told her he was the duke then her parents would have approved their marriage. Claire would have been given control of her grandfather's money and all their problems would have been solved.

But he hadn't done that. He had shared nothing of himself with her.

Claire stood up and went back to her packing.

"You have nothing to say?" Leatrice said. "I've just told you that the man you love is the duke and that the man you plan to marry isn't related to the Montgomery family, but you say nothing."

"What is his name? What is Trevelyan's name?"

"John Richmond Montgomery. His childhood title was the Earl of Trevelyan and Trevelyan seemed to fit him. I was the one who started calling him Vellie, since I couldn't pronounce Trevelyan."

Claire continued packing.

Leatrice clutched Claire's arm. "Is that all?"

When Claire looked at Leatrice, her eyes were blazing. "He didn't even tell me his name. Such a simple thing. He asked that I love him, that I spend my life with him, yet he couldn't so much as tell me his name." She looked back at the trunk.

"You don't understand. Vellie is—"

"A cold man," Claire said, and when she looked at Leatrice, there was rage on her face. "I loved him. I fell in love with him in spite of his bad temper, in spite of his pessimistic outlook on life. I forgave him for not telling me he was Captain Baker. I forgave him for laughing at me, for using me as one of his subjects. I forgave him and I loved him, but he doesn't know how to give love in return."

Leatrice opened her mouth but Claire continued. "He stood by and watched Nyssa die without even attempting to stop her. He always stands on the outside of the world and watches it. He said he loved me, but he doesn't. He confuses sexual pleasure with love. They aren't the same thing. He has 'loved' thousands of women all over the world, and I was fool enough to think that I was different."

"You *are* different," Leatrice said. "Vellie has never told a woman he loved her."

"Would you stop calling him that absurd name? He's a grown man. No, he's not a man, he's a . . . a machine. He's an observing machine. A machine that goes around the world watching and writing about it. I doubt if he's ever really felt anything in his life."

Leatrice was silent for a moment. "I want you to read his letters," she said softly.

"No," Claire answered. "I must leave. Quite suddenly I can't bear the sight of this house."

Leatrice put her hand on Claire's arm. "I know we haven't been fair to you. Mother sent Harry to London to get you. You were brought here because of your money, but Claire, you've given all of us more than money can buy. Because of you I have James and at last Harry has seen what his mother is like."

Leatrice's voice lowered. "It was Mother who had Vellie shot at."

Claire's hands stopped their movement.

"I told you her mind was affected. She wanted the dukedom for her precious Harry, and when she heard that her second son had come back from the dead, she assumed he was going to take the title. She hired someone to try to kill him."

Claire looked at Leatrice with a mixture of horror and disbelief.

"My family is not like yours. My mother's hatred has distorted us all. But I think her hold on us is broken now. Someone wrote to Harry in Edinburgh and told him what Mother was trying to do to Trevelyan. Mother knew that you were spending a great deal of time with Vellie and she was afraid that you and your money would marry Trevelyan. She was afraid that Vellie would have second thoughts about claiming the title. Harry returned to try to persuade you to marry him because he was afraid for his brother's life."

Leatrice smiled. "Harry has always adored his older brother. Harry was always much too lazy to do anything himself so he's lived vicariously through Vellie's exploits. I think Harry might lay down his life for his older brother."

"He might even marry a woman he doesn't love to save his brother."

"He was going to do that until he returned and saw that Vellie loved you."

Claire snorted at that.

Leatrice looked sad. "I wish I could make you believe me. I wish I could make you see Trevelyan as he really is."

"I wish you could have seen him stand by and let a young woman drink poison. No, I don't wish that on anyone. If Trevelyan had trusted me . . . If he'd loved me enough to share some of himself with me . . ." Claire sighed. "It's too late now, and it doesn't matter anyway. I'm assuming there's a reason why Trevelyan isn't claiming the title of duke. My guess would be that he doesn't want the title, and he plans to allow Harry to continue being the duke."

"Yes," Leatrice said. "Trevelyan wants only to be Captain Baker. I doubt if he'll ever return to us after what has happened this time."

"No, I don't think he will. I don't—"

Claire didn't finish her sentence because the door to her room opened and in walked Harry. Behind him were four footmen bearing trunks. "Put them there," Harry ordered.

When the footmen were gone, and the bedroom door closed, both Harry and Leatrice turned to look at Claire. It was then that she realized what the trunks contained. She knew without a doubt that they were the letters from Trevelyan. At one time her dearest wish in the world had been to read the private letters of Captain Baker. But now she looked at the trunks as though they were filled with cobras.

She took a step backward and shook her head. "I have to leave."

Harry leaned against the door. "You're not leaving here until you read them. *All* of them."

Claire looked at the two people. Harry's handsome face was set, unmoving, while Leatrice's eyes were pleading. "It won't do any good. Reading a bunch of letters isn't going to change anything. Trevelyan's not going to claim to be the duke, therefore my parents won't approve the marriage and I'll lose my grandfather's money. And I'm not going to leave my sister to the mercy of the fates."

"You're not leaving," Harry said.

Leatrice went to the first trunk and opened it. Inside were neatly bundled letters, hundreds of them. "He started writing me when he was first taken away, when he was nine years old. Shall I tell you about that day?"

"No," Claire said firmly. "I don't want to hear a word about it."

But Leatrice told her anyway, and when she finished, Claire began to read the letters.

Chapter Twenty-five

The duke of MacArran requests the company of Miss Claire Willoughby, the handwritten card read.

Claire read the card, then dropped it back onto the silver tray that the butler held. "Tell Harry I'm busy packing," she said and turned away.

The butler didn't move.

"Well?" Claire said, looking at him. Her temper was short and she was anxious to leave Bramley.

"It is the true duke who asks you," the butler said.

It took Claire a moment to understand what the man was saying. "Trevelyan?"

The butler gave a small nod.

Claire walked back to him, picked up the card again, looked at it, then tossed it back to the tray. "Tell him that we've said all there is to say to each other. Tell him that I have things I must do. Tell him I am sick of the entire Montgomery family. Tell him that I never want to see him or any of his relatives again."

"Perhaps madam would enjoy telling him herself."

Claire started to say that she wouldn't enjoy anything about Trevelyan, but then she thought of several things she could tell him. "Where is he?"

"In the blue bedroom. It was his father's room."

Claire nodded, then motioned that she'd follow him. I'll tell him what I think of him, then I'll leave here forever, she thought. I shall never have to see any of this family again, and, most of all, I won't have to see or hear of Captain Baker again.

The butler opened a door to a large bed chamber that must have once been beautiful, but now the silk on the walls was faded and torn. The deep-blue silk bed hangings were dirty.

Trevelyan was standing with his back to her, looking out the window, and for once he was dressed properly. No embroidered silk robe, no velvet boots. He wore a perfectly cut morning coat. His hair had been trimmed neatly to a decent length. If she hadn't known better, she would have thought he was a handsome young gentleman.

"I am here," she said to the back of him. "What do you want of me?"

He turned and she saw that he looked tired, as though he'd slept less than he usually did. It had been nearly a week since Nyssa had died, and nothing that had been said had changed Claire's anger. Every minute of every day she could see Nyssa's laughing face. She could hear Brat's cries of horror after she'd been told that Nyssa was dead. Claire remembered seeing the smoke from the fire that she was sure was the burning of Nyssa's body.

Trevelyan walked toward her. Claire held her ground, but when he reached out to touch her cheek, she turned her face away. His hand dropped to his side, then he turned away and went back to the window.

"Leatrice said she told you of our mother."

"Yes," Claire said coldly. "I was told the great family secret."

"And you have read my letters to my sister."

"Those too."

"And what did you think?"

Claire took a moment before answering. She had spent days reading those letters and in them she had seen a man who was capable of great love. She had read how he had seen death all over the world. Were she indeed Captain Baker's biographer, the letters would allow her to write a story of great power. But she knew now that she would never write that biography. "I found the letters extremely interesting."

"But neither the letters nor the tale of my mother have made you forgive me?"

"No. I cannot forget Nyssa." Her voice lowered. "I cannot forget that you gave me so little of yourself."

He looked at her for a moment then turned back to the window.

"When I was a child, my grandfather thought it was a good discipline for me to never have anything I wanted or liked. If I said I liked a certain type of bread, then he saw to it that I never had that bread again. If I said that I hated carrots, then I was served carrots three meals a day. Since then it has been difficult for me to ask for what I want most."

"Yes," Claire said angrily, "I have heard more than I want to know about your childhood. I am sure it was dreadful. I am sure you had a mother who hated you, a father who didn't know you were alive, and a grandfather who was cruel to you. You have more than enough reason to brood and sulk. You have every excuse in the world to feel a great deal of self-pity."

Trevelyan turned and looked at her, his eyes wide.

She grimaced. "Did you expect sympathy from me? Isn't your own self-sympathy enough? You have the pity of your brother and sister and, as far as I can tell, the pity of nearly everyone in this house. Poor Johnny. Poor little earl who no one ever loved. Of course it never seems to have occurred to anyone that if you had behaved yourself and thought of anyone besides yourself you might not have been punished as often as you were. I can imagine that you delighted in telling your grandfather that you hated carrots. Did you learn to lie to him and tell him that you loved what you hated?"

Trevelyan stared at her, blinking, looking as though he were shocked by her words, then he began to smile. The smile broke into a laugh. "As a matter of fact, I did. The cook once made some almond cakes that were heaven. At the first bite, I spit it out and said they were the nastiest things I'd ever eaten and that I would never eat another one. My grandfather served them to me every meal for months until I reluctantly admitted that I was beginning to enjoy them. To this day I like to celebrate any victory with almond cakes."

Claire did not smile. "Is that supposed to amuse me? It sounds to me as though you and your grandfather were well matched. I imagine he knew that. Of course, in the end, it was you who won, wasn't it? You left him when you wanted to and you did what you wanted. But then you have always done exactly what you wanted to do, haven't you? No one has ever hindered you, or even influenced you, in any way."

"My mother—"

"Ha!" Claire said. "You cannot lie to me now. I know too much about you. I think that if I'd spent more time with that woman I would have realized she was your mother. You two have a sameness of temper about you. You are both the personification of selfishness. She uses her lost love as her excuse and you use . . ."

"Yes," he said softly, "what do I use?"

"Whatever is available. May I go now? You have tried to win my pity and you have failed. All of you have failed in your attempt to make me feel sorry for the poor, unwanted duke."

Trevelyan walked to a high-backed chair and sat down. "Did I fail in my attempt to make you love me?"

"No. I loved you for a while, but that was before I knew you."

Trevelyan sighed. "So now you will marry Harry and breed blond brats."

She took a deep breath. "No, I don't intend to marry Harry. I think I'm too much of a romantic. I want to marry a man I love. I know that will be difficult, especially since I have—"

"Have what?"

She looked at him in defiance. "Loved you. Loved someone like you," she said softly. "You will be a difficult memory to supersede."

He gave a smile of irony. "I am thankful for any praise from you."

They were silent a moment.

"Have you said what you wanted to say to me?" Claire asked. "I have things to do."

"Claire," Trevelyan said softly. "I love you. I have loved you for a long time. I . . . I believe that I need you."

Claire's lips tightened. "Yes, you need me. I am the only person on earth you cannot intimidate. I'm not afraid of you. I don't cower when you look at me or shout at me. How refreshing—and infuriating—that must be for you. The great Captain Baker, the man who can make men tremble merely by looking at them, cannot put fear into a mere nineteen-year-old American."

Trevelyan smiled at her. "How right you are. From the moment I met you you were ordering me about. The first thing you said to me was that I was to fetch your horse for you. You have told me I was wrong on every count. You have criticized my books, my clothes, what I say and how I say it. Do you know how well matched we are?"

Claire turned away so he wouldn't see the tears that sprang to her eyes. She knew how well matched they were. She knew very, very well. Trevelyan was the only person in the world who was as curious as she was, who wanted to learn, who wanted to know about the world and what was in it.

When she looked back he had risen and was standing behind her, close enough to touch, but he didn't touch her. "Is your love for me completely dead?"

"No," she said honestly. "I think I will go to my grave loving you, but I will not live with you. I will not live with a man who can stand outside of life and not participate in it."

"I participate enough to—"

She turned on him, furious. "No, you don't! You make excuses. You say that you love me but that you can't interfere in my marrying someone else. You make excuses as to why you can't take your rightful place as the duke, but the truth is, if you were the duke, you'd have to involve yourself with other people, like the crofters and your mother. It's much easier for you to stand back from the world and watch it."

She took a deep breath. "You know what I think? I think you asked me to marry you, but you didn't really want me to. You told me how I'd hate you in a few years so I *wouldn't* marry you."

He didn't say anything for a moment, just stood there looking at her. "What would make you know that I love you? What would make you believe that I want you with me forever?"

Claire gave a nasty laugh. "Show me that you're not a man who can stand by and watch a young woman die. Show me that you're human. *Show* me that you're the man who wrote those letters. I haven't seen that man."

Trevelyan didn't say anything for a moment, then he walked to a tapestry along one wall and pulled it aside. She heard a door open.

Claire heard Nyssa's voice before she saw her.

"You have left me in there too long," Nyssa complained. "I am blue with cold. You—" Nyssa broke off as she looked at Claire's face, her eyes wide in astonishment. "You have not told her," Nyssa said to Trevelyan. "You could not have left her untold."

"I did," Trevelyan said, smiling down at Nyssa. "She would not allow me to tell her, so you are my gift to her."

Claire turned on her heel and started toward the door, but Trevelyan caught her arm.

"I thought you'd be pleased."

"Pleased that you tricked me? How you must have laughed when I begged the men to put the emerald on the cup for a woman who wasn't dead."

Trevelyan's face hardened. "Do you always believe the worst of me?"

Claire jerked from him and started toward the door.

Nyssa blocked her way. "I am most tired of this," she said to Claire. "The man is insane with love for you. You must forgive him whatever you think he has done."

Claire glared at Nyssa. "I believed you were actually committing suicide. I didn't know it was a joke, but then I have never been told anything about him."

Nyssa's laugh trilled out. "But I did die. The Pearl of the Moon died as she was to have died. Frank decided to wake me and ask if I did not have second thoughts."

Claire frowned and Nyssa pulled her toward a chair. "Come, and I will tell you all of it."

Claire allowed herself to be pulled to the chair and began to listen to Nyssa's story. She did not look at Trevelyan, who stood with his back to them, looking out the window.

Nyssa told how she had meant to die when she had taken the poison—at least she thought it was poison, but Trevelyan had suspected that it was merely something to make her sleep. When the men from Pesha had been so anxious to burn Nyssa's body, he thought that perhaps the burning was what killed her. Trevelyan knew that the two Peshans were merely messengers and that they might not know that the drink was not poison. Trevelyan gave the two men enough gold coins to persuade them to part with Nyssa's lifeless body. He gave them ashes from MacTarvit's fireplace to take back with them to Pesha.

After Trevelyan had possession of Nyssa's body, he and Angus spent three days waking her from her drugged stupor. Nyssa told of the bad-tasting drinks they had given her, how she had wanted to sleep but Trevelyan had made her walk. She told how Trevelyan had not slept for three whole days because he was afraid that if he slept, then Nyssa would, and she might not awake.

Nyssa told how Trevelyan had said that if Claire wanted Nyssa alive, then he was going to bring her back from the dead.

"I have died, as the Pearl of the Moon was to die," Nyssa said. "And now I may live as I want. Frank says that I may stay here with his family for as long as I want." She turned to look at the back of him. "I may go now?"

Trevelyan nodded and Nyssa left the room.

Claire stayed in her chair for a moment, then rose and went to him. "Why did you do it? Why did you save her?"

"Because I wanted you." He turned to her and his eyes were burning. "I wanted to go away. I wanted to leave that day of Nyssa's death. I wanted to be able to shrug and say that it was the will of Allah if we were not to be together."

Suddenly, he grabbed her shoulders. "Claire, if you marry my brother, I will kill both of you. If you want a woman who wants to die to live then I will do all in my power to make it happen. If you want to be a duchess, then I will be a duke. Claire, don't leave me."

It took her a long while before she smiled at him. And as she smiled at him, she slid into his arms, and she knew that it was the right place for her to be.

"No, I won't leave you," she whispered. "I will never leave you again."

Epilogue

Claire confronted her parents with the news that she was marrying a man other than Harry and they, predictably, said they would not approve her marriage to an explorer. Trevelyan closeted himself with her parents for fifteen minutes and when he opened the door, her parents, white-faced, said they would agree to the marriage. None of the three of them would tell what Trevelyan had said to make them change their minds, and Claire didn't like to think about what he must have said—or threatened.

Claire married Trevelyan in a quiet ceremony, and as soon as he was well enough, they went to Africa, where Trevelyan, still as Captain Baker, could make more of his journeys into the interior. Claire stayed on the coast and waited for him. She wrote a book about their life in Africa, which, to Trevelyan's disbelief, became a best-seller. Encouraged by her success, Claire wrote several more books about their travels, and when she had a few gray hairs, she wrote the book that was the achievement of her life: a biography of Captain Frank Baker. But with the exception of the biography, Claire's books did not withstand the test of time as Trevelyan's did. His books were irreplaceable studies of people as they were before the influence of Westerners; a hundred years later the books are still read and enjoyed by generations of scholars and adventure seekers.

Claire and Trevelyan were temperamentally well matched. They traveled all over the world together and were inseparable companions for all of their very long lives.

Claire's parents and her sister stayed with the Montgomery family, and eventually Brat married Harry—who kept the title of duke. They were well suited to each other. They loved each other in the physical sense but led completely separate lives. Brat became a renowned hostess and Harry was the greatest huntsman in England. The extraordinary beauty of the two of them produced a few exceptionally beautiful children.

Because Brat was very conscious of the possibility of poverty, she became an excellent money manager and greatly increased the Montgomery fortunes (Claire helped her with this).

Eugenia, the dowager duchess, retired to the dower house when Brat married Harry and was little seen after that.

Angus MacTarvit's sons came back from America and began producing MacTarvit whisky on a larger scale, and they were very successful.

Nyssa stayed with the Montgomery family and lived to be ninety-five years old. She never married, and to the day she died she believed herself to be the most beautiful woman in the world—and she always had many young men around her who believed this as well.